LIKE A BURNING FIRE

LIKE A BURNING FIRE

IRENE BRAND

kregel
PUBLICATIONS

Grand Rapids, MI 49501

Like a Burning Fire

Published in 1996 by Kregel Publications, a division of Kregel, Inc., P.O. Box 2607, Grand Rapids, MI 49501. Kregel Publications provides trusted, biblical publications for Christian growth and service. Your comments and suggestions are valued.

Cover illustration: Ron Mazellan
Cover design: Alan G. Hartman
Book design: Nicholas G. Richardson

Library of Congress Cataloging-in-Publication Data
Brand, Irene.
   Like a burning fire / by Irene Brand.
      p.   cm.   (Legacies of faith series)
     1. Church History—Middle Ages, 600–1500—Fiction.
2. Europe—History—392–814—Fiction. 3. France—
History—To 987—Fiction. I. Title. II. Series: Brand,
Irene B., 1929– Legacies of faith series.
PS3552.R2917L54   1996   813'.54—dc20 96-10341
                                    CIP

ISBN 0-8254-2145-4

Printed in the United States of America
1 2 3 4 5 / 00 99 98 97 96

Have the Franks for your friends, but not for your neighbors.
—Eighth-century Greek proverb

And when the tooth of Lombardy had bitten
The Holy Church, then underneath its wings
Did Charlemagne victorious succor her.
—Dante, *Paradiso* XX:57–60

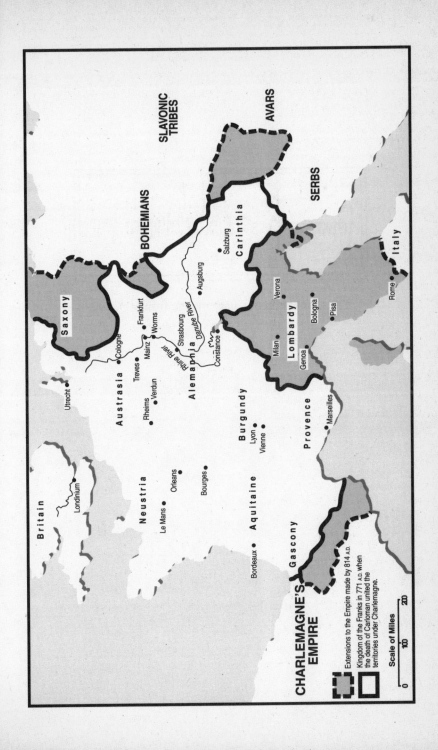

CHARLEMAGNE'S EMPIRE

Extensions to the Empire made by 814 A.D.

Kingdom of the Franks in 771 A.D. when the death of Carloman united the territories under Charlemagne.

Scale of Miles

0   100   200

SLAVONIC TRIBES

AVARS

BOHEMIANS

SERBS

Carinthia

Salzburg

Augsburg

Saxony

Italy

Verona

Rome

Lombardy

Bologna

Pisa

Milan

Genoa

Frankfurt

Cologne

Worms

Mainz

Strasbourg

Danube River

Constance

Alemaphia

Rhine River

Treves

Rheims

Verdun

Utrecht

Austrasia

Burgundy

Lyon

Vienne

Provence

Marseilles

Britain

Londinium

Neustria

Le Mans

Orleans

Bourges

Aquitaine

Bordeaux

Gascony

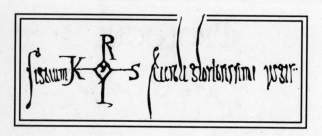

The monogram of Charlemagne from A.D. 790

PROLOGUE

Famine raged throughout Frankish Gaul. Priests prayed for abundant crops and required penance from their parishioners to sway the Almighty from His punishment on them. But the Christian Franks had not forgotten the old gods, and when the drought continued, they turned again to ancient practices. Weather wizards exacted fees from the populace to pray for a good growing season. Sacrifices were performed in honor of the spirits of trees, stones, and springs. Enchanters baptized bells to make them capable of scaring away the demons who troubled the people. Still the devastation persisted. Animals died for lack of grazing and water. Bodies of peasants littered the fields. Infanticide was common. Rather than see their children slowly starve to death, churls and noblewomen alike killed their newborns. Most infants were born weak and listless because their mothers had lacked proper food to nourish them in the womb.

Alone in her hut, one widow gave birth. Her hands closed around the neck of the baby, but a lusty bellow halted her. *No sickly child this one, but a robust boy fighting for life.* She washed her son, wrapped his body in a soft pelt, and placed him in a basket. With trembling knees, she walked the half-a-day trek to the monastery, stopping on the way to have a parish priest draw up a document for her. She hid in the trees until darkness was complete; then she crept toward the building. Placing the basket tenderly on the stone step, she reached into her garments and withdrew a small box. Opening the lid, she ran her hands over the carved vase it contained. If sold, this item would provide enough food to sustain her a few more days. Hunger gnawed at her innards, and the temptation was strong, but her love for the child was greater. The vase was his heritage, and she laid it beside him. The mother knelt to kiss her son one last time before she vanished into the darkness.

1

The stone walls of the monastery presented a formidable barrier to the stoop-shouldered man who hobbled from the carriage. Signaling his driver to tie the horse to a nearby tree, he stood indecisively for a few moments gazing at the austere building. Absolute silence marked his surroundings, almost as if the monastery were deserted, but Basil knew it housed more than fifty monks, one of them the young son of his recently departed master.

The certainty that his mission would not be welcomed by the young man nor his abbot did not deter Basil, and he moved toward the imposing wooden doors. As he lifted his hand to knock, he heard the muted chanting of the 119th Psalm, "The word is a candle to my feet, and a brilliance to my walk." The monks were observing the divine office of sext, and he would not be admitted until their prayers concluded.

Basil eased his gnarled frame to the wooden bench beside the door. Rabbits played on the lawn of the monastery, and a calm breeze wafted the scent of the sea toward him. As he reveled in the quietness, Basil wondered why this monastery hadn't been destroyed as so many others had been during the reign of Constantine V, the present emperor. The monks were Constantine's greatest opponents in his effort to rid the empire of image worship. The emperor had made war upon the clergy who clung to their icons.

When shuffling feet indicated that the prayers had ended, Basil knocked on the door. No one answered his summons, so he knocked again, more brusquely this time. Soon the door squeaked open, and a black-robed monk stood before him.

"I am Basil, servant to the recently departed Avidius of the house of Trento. Matthew, the son of Avidius, lives here. I have a message for him."

"What is the message?" the man asked quietly.

Basil shook his head. "I will see Master Matthew myself."

The monk hesitated momentarily, then motioned Basil into a large musty-smelling foyer. The door swung shut and plunged the room into darkness. The only light was provided by one small window above the door. Groping as he walked, Basil followed the silent man up a stone stairway to a small receiving room.

"I will tell the abbot you're here."

The bare feet of the monk made no sound on the stone floor as he disappeared through a curtained doorway. The walls were bare, without any statues or drawings. Outwardly, at least, this monastery had obeyed the emperor's restriction on images. Squinting his eyes, however, Basil made out a large representation of the Christ beneath a thick coat of gray plaster. The abbot had obeyed the emperor's order, but if any monk were so inclined, he could still kneel in veneration of this icon.

Basil settled down on a stone bench, expecting a long wait, but he had hardly closed his eyes for a quick snooze when the curtain opened. *The abbot!* There was quite a contrast between his appearance and that of the lowly monk who had admitted Basil. Swathed in a full-length, long-sleeved, white linen alb and with a jeweled cross around his neck, the abbot's presence immediately brightened the drab room, but the stern lines of the man's face and the coldness of his eyes did not encourage Basil on his mission. Visitors obviously weren't welcome, and Basil could understand that, given the government pressure upon the monasteries in the past few years.

"Did you wish to see me?" the abbot demanded in a cold voice.

"No, I did not," Basil replied. "I asked to see Brother Matthew, a member of the Trento family."

"He is no longer a member of that family. When our brothers enter the cloister, it is their desire to leave the world behind. Brother Matthew would not thank you for disturbing his sanctuary."

Basil suspected that was true, but he had no choice. Convinced that Matthew would not be summoned unless he revealed his mission, Basil said, "Brother Matthew's father has died, and it is about the disposition of his considerable estate that I must speak to him." The look of avarice on the abbot's face and the speculative gleam in his eye disgusted Basil. It wasn't difficult to follow the abbot's thoughts: Matthew had taken a poverty vow—thus any wealth he inherited would go to the monastery.

"Come into my office," the abbot said, "and I'll send for Brother Matthew."

Basil suppressed the laugh that bubbled to his lips as he followed the abbot into a large room, well lighted from an oval window that overlooked a garden. A cozy fire burned on the small grate. As he waited, Basil shook his head in dismay that the brilliant son of his master had denounced the world and buried himself behind these stone walls. Basil considered himself as religious as the next man, but he viewed Matthew's entrance into holy orders as a great waste of talent.

The abbot returned alone, but soon a man in his mid twenties, tall and erect in bearing, entered the room. Keen, piercing eyes reminded Basil of the monk's father. Matthew's appearance would stand out in any crowd. His dark eyes flashed in recognition.

"Basil!" Matthew said in a halting voice that croaked from disuse. Obviously, Matthew had not talked much since he became a monk. Basil blinked away threatening tears.

"It's been a long time, Matthew," he said as they clasped hands.

14

The abbot cleared his throat, perhaps to remind Matthew that he had renounced earthly friendships. Matthew stepped backward and bowed his head. Basil winced when he saw that shaved crown.

"You said you have a message for Brother Matthew?" the abbot prompted. "We must not keep him from his service in the hospital." The abbot seated himself behind a massive desk, indicating that Matthew and Basil would not be left alone. Basil eased his painful knees by sitting again on the bench, while Matthew continued to stand.

"Your father is dead, Matthew," Basil said gently.

"I feared as much when I saw you. May God rest his soul. You have grown old in his service, Basil, and I hope that he has rewarded you sufficiently."

"More than sufficiently, Matthew, but it is about the rest of his estate that I have come. Since you took a vow of poverty when you entered holy orders, your father made other disposition of his wealth." Basil couldn't suppress a glance toward the abbot, whose face wore a surprised scowl.

"If I may, I will read a portion of his last will and testament." Basil pulled a rolled parchment from his garments and read, "Because of his entrance into the service of the church, my only child, Matthew, will not be able to inherit my property. Therefore, I convey the bulk of my estate to the guardian of the Trento Alabaster. My final request is that my son, Matthew, be released from holy orders for the time it takes to find the person who now holds the Alabaster."

Matthew lifted his head quickly and glanced toward the abbot before he exclaimed, "But that is impossible. I've dedicated my life to the service of our Lord. It might take years to find the guardian of the Alabaster."

"And what is the Alabaster?" the abbot demanded.

"A religious relic, Father, that has been in the Trento family since the first century. The alabaster vase filled with spikenard was taken to the tomb to anoint the body of our Lord Jesus, but the tomb was empty and the spikenard was never used. Our ancestor Suetonius Trento bought the vase, and it's been in the family since that time."

"And who has this Alabaster now? Where is it?"

Matthew looked to Basil for an answer.

"We do not know," Basil responded. "It has never belonged to a member of the Constantinople Trento family; thus my master's desire to bring the present owner to our city."

"The Alabaster sounds like a treasure that we should preserve in our monastery," the abbot stated. "Now that we're forbidden to display icons and images, this relic would draw pilgrims to worship here and perhaps keep the emperor looking with favor upon our institution. I'm sure no other cloister could boast an item like the one you've mentioned."

"But you don't understand," Basil insisted. "The vase *must* stay in the Trento family. I've heard that Constantine the Great once cast covetous eyes upon the Alabaster and placed it in one of his temples. That night the walls of the temple collapsed, and the emperor wanted nothing further to do with the vase."

"It's *you* who do not understand," the abbot said with a sneer. "If this Alabaster has the history you say it has, then it should be under the guardianship of the church rather than being carried around the world by anyone who receives it as an accident of birth. And if this monastery is the holder of the Alabaster, then it seems to me that the estate of Marcus Trento would come to us."

"But, Father—," Matthew started, dismay clouding his features.

The abbot held up his hand for silence. "How long has it been since this Alabaster has been seen?"

"Not in the time of my father nor his father," Matthew answered.

"Then it may already be lost—as has been the chalice and other items connected with the earthly ministry of Jesus."

"I do not know, Father."

"Then it's your duty to find out. You must follow your father's instructions to learn if the Alabaster still exists. That service may well be as important to the church as your work here in the hospital. Since we do not know the circumstances you will find yourself in to complete this assignment, I will request the bishop to absolve you from all your vows to the monastic rule until you return the Alabaster to me."

Matthew bowed his head in submission. "May I have a week for prayer and fasting to prepare myself? It will not be easy to enter the world after five years behind these walls."

"Your wish is granted." The abbot turned to Basil. "You may expect Brother Matthew seven days hence."

A smile spread across Basil's face as he left the monastery and limped toward his carriage. The abbot might think he already had the Trento wealth in his clutches, but in Basil's opinion, as soon as Matthew was discharged from his vow of obedience, he would owe no obligation to his abbot until he again entered the walls of the cloister. By that time, if Basil had anything to do with it, the holder of the Alabaster would be securely entrenched in the house of Trento.

❊   ❊   ❊

Matthew returned to his work in the hospital. Though his touch was tender and his manner loving as he knelt to minister to the sick and dying, his thoughts were troubled. This small ward had been his salvation, for it had given him the opportunity to do in divine service what he had hoped to do in secular life. The hospital, established to make their final days on earth dignified and peaceful for the aged and the blind, had prevented the destruction of this monastery when the emperor had leveled so many others.

"I cannot do it!" Matthew mumbled aloud more than once, drawing questioning looks from his fellow monks. *I have no choice—if the bishop releases me,* Matthew's thoughts countered. *But how can the bishop release me from my covenant? I made my vows to God, not to the bishop. How can I go back into the world and stir up the longings of a past it has taken five years to obliterate from my mind and heart?* No, he couldn't do it. If the abbot didn't like it, he could invoke a heavy penance. Nothing the abbot could impose would be as stressful as the burden he had brought with him to the monastery.

A bell sounded in the courtyard, and with relief, Matthew left the infirmary to file with the brothers silently into the dining area, where he received a pottery plate containing a loaf of brown bread and a portion of lamb stew. He stood beside a long table until the abbot blessed the food. Visiting with his fellows was not allowed, so Matthew ate swiftly, trying to concentrate on the voice of the monk who was reading a passage about the life of the saints. When a bell sounded, the reading ceased, and Matthew joined the others as they paced out of the cold room.

As Matthew reached the sanctuary of his unheated cell, he sank to his knees beside the crude cot. This had become his home, and he delighted in the solitude. How could he leave it for the clamor of the world—the chariots in the hippodrome, the hawking of peddlers beside the huge equestrian statue of Justinian in the main square of Constantinople, and the constant traffic of merchants, manufacturers, craftsmen, common citizens, and slaves as they provided commerce for Byzantium, the Roman Empire of the East?

Burying his face on the rough bed covering, Matthew composed himself for prayer and voiced the thought uppermost in his mind, "Lead me not into temptation." But communication with God eluded him. While Matthew longed to envision the face of the Savior to succor him through this trial, the face of another insinuated itself into his consciousness.

"Oh, God, no," he whimpered. "Do not test my faith again."

Despite his pleadings, a vision of Sophia infiltrated his soul. How foolish of him to believe he could forget that mass of dark, curly hair, those intelligent gray eyes gleaming from a smooth olive complexion, and that profile resembling a Greek goddess. He had thought God had rewarded his years of service by clearing

18

his mind and heart of his beloved, but that was not so. He could hear her silky-soft voice as if she spoke to him now. Matthew sobbed. He couldn't bear a renewal of his sorrow.

During four hours of solitary prayer, Matthew begged for direction. Before the bell called him to vespers, the decision had been made for him and he was at peace. In the midst of Matthew's deepest suffering, Jesus seemed to speak to him, and the message was clear: *Go! It is my will that you do your father's bidding, just as I followed my Father's will. Go, and I will go with you.*

❄   ❄   ❄

Seven days had passed since Basil's visit to the monastery. A wintry blast swept over Matthew as he closed the cloister door behind him and stepped out into the bright light of a sunny December day. He blinked at the unaccustomed brightness and pulled forward the hood of his cloak to shield his eyes. He breathed deeply of the crisp air. In spite of his reluctance to undertake this mission, his steps quickened as he anticipated seeing his home again, and he wondered what his life would have been like if he hadn't entered the monastery.

Although the Trentos had always been wealthy, his grandfather had added to the family's holdings by engaging in the silk industry that Emperor Justinian had introduced into the empire. Trento silks and brocades were famous throughout the world. Matthew had been expected to take over the business, but the loss of the woman he loved had ruined his life. In the monastery, he had finally blotted from his memory the scene when he had told his father his plans, but now the angry words they had exchanged surged into his mind. *I have forgiven my father's actions,* Matthew thought, *but did my father ever pardon me?* He feared he would never know.

Unaccustomed to so much walking, Matthew was weary at the end of the four-mile journey, but his steps quickened when he neared the street leading to his father's house. Across the fronts of dwellings grapevines grew profusely, some extending to the branches of the black cypress trees that lined the street.

The wooden Trento house sat roomily on the grounds, rising to two stories. The beauty of the simple structure was its symmetry and proportion. The front door of the house furnished the only ostentation; the two leaves of the door opened broad and square and were decorated by perforated copper knockers in the form of harps. An oval pane above the door was filled with a wooden fan. Numerous latticed windows spread across the front of the house, and above the lattices, small round panes were set in broad, white-mullioned plaster. The second story of the house, supported by oak timbers curved like a ship's bow, overhung the street. The roof was constructed of imported red tiles.

Matthew passed beyond the main entrance to the small door at the rear of the house that opened into a spacious garden where a hodgepodge of stone-pine, cypress, and chestnut trees provided the family with shade and privacy. He leaned against a decorative fig tree and observed the dripping fountain set against the wall. The grayish marble had been carved in a low relief of flowering branches and small basins. At the top, water spewed from the mouth of a sculptured lion and trickled into the first basin, then overflowed into two basins below, alternating back and forth in a series of basins until it splashed into a semicircular pool set into the ground, where dozens of colorful fish flashed through the clear water. Matthew eased down on the marble bench facing the fountain. Most of his pleasant childhood experiences had occurred in this spot.

Knowing he couldn't postpone his homecoming any longer, Matthew turned toward the house. Basil opened the door and bowed to Matthew. "Welcome home," he said, and Matthew felt as if Avidius Trento himself had voiced the greeting.

"Tell me, Basil," he said eagerly. "Did my father ever forgive me?"

"He left a sealed letter for you if you ever returned home. It's waiting for you in your father's office. I will bring you refreshment in that room."

Matthew hurried down the broad, marble-paved hall that ran from street to garden. He paused on the office threshold, overcome with emotion as he looked at the room. A series of niches decorated with painted flowers and gilded molding covered the wall behind his father's desk. They were empty now of the icons that had been there in his grandfather's day, for Avidius had been quick to obey the emperor's orders. A long, low couch furnished with colorful rugs and embroidered cushions ran the length of the wall under the street windows. An oval woven rug covered the middle of the floor. Matthew crossed the room and held out his cold hands to the fireplace, which was vented by a tall, pointed hood. The warmth of the room comforted him almost as if he had been received into his father's arms.

A parchment lay conspicuously on the top of his father's desk. Matthew broke the seal with trembling fingers, and his tears began to flow when he read the first words.

My Dear son,

I pray that you will forgive my harsh words at our parting. God forbid that I should stand between you and what you believe your duty to be. Since you will read this after my death, I beg you to pray that my journey to heaven will be a smooth one. I hope that you have forgiven me for my actions that caused you so much grief. I have prayed often that my heavenly Father will also forgive me. Because I respect the vows you've taken, I have legally omitted you from my last will and testament, but I beg that you will lay aside your duty long enough to fulfill my last wish. It has always been a burden to the Constantinople Trentos that none of our family has ever possessed the Alabaster. The considerable estate that I leave behind should be an inducement to the present holder of the family heirloom to make his abode in our city, but that person has to be found.

I may be assigning you an impossible task, for even my grandfather had no knowledge of where the Alabaster was last seen, but I suggest that you begin your search in Rome.

After dining alone, with servants at attention to serve him, Matthew climbed the double stairway to the upper story, where another large hall lined with niches opened into several small sleeping rooms. The upstairs windows were of stained glass, the only decoration in the otherwise sparsely furnished bedrooms. The rooms had changed little since his grandfather's day; they contained only chests and low beds covered with blankets.

Matthew discarded his clerical garments and bathed in the warm water flowing through the tub that his father had installed in the house. Though this reprieve from his vows had not been his idea, his conscience rebelled as he luxuriated in the comforts he had once enjoyed. Finally, he reasoned that if he had to become a citizen of the world to accomplish his father's bidding, he couldn't do it by keeping one foot in the monastery.

He awakened the next morning to the jingle of horses bringing produce into the city. He thought of the vegetable and fish markets where these products would be sold, almost smelling the pungent odor of fresh fish and the harsh scent of onions and garlics. He must take time to visit the markets before he left Constantinople.

Hearing the murmur of Trento servants preparing the day's food, Matthew left his bed and reluctantly donned the elegant robes that had been laid out for him. They hung loosely on him now. He wondered why his father had not disposed of his clothing. *Had he held on to the hope that I would return?* The smooth, ornamented brocade felt foreign to his skin after five years of wearing the rough woolen habits of the monastery. When his shaved hair grew again, there would be little left to suggest that Matthew Trento was on leave of absence from holy orders except, perhaps, the hint of eternity that had come into his eyes when he'd made his peace with God in the monastery.

As Matthew ate a breakfast of figs and brown bread, Basil approached him. "A great event will occur in the city today, and perhaps you will want to witness it."

Matthew glanced up questioningly.

"The Byzantine Empire will welcome its future empress today. I have been promised entrance into the sacred palace to view the festivities. You will be permitted to accompany me."

"I must confess my ignorance, for I've been cut off from secular life for five years. Who is emperor now?"

"Constantine V is still emperor, and his son Leo is wedding Irene, an Athenian. She is an orphan without any royal background, but she was chosen for her great beauty."

"I will go with you, although I find it difficult to plunge so soon into worldly activities."

"A friend of mine, Elisha, is a eunuch assigned to the court of the new empress, and he will meet us at one of the gates of the palace."

An hour later, Basil and Matthew joined throngs of other Byzantines moving through the Golden Gate and along the Mese, an arcaded, shop-lined avenue that led toward the sacred palace. Basil's age didn't permit a rapid journey, and Matthew took advantage of their slow progress to study his surroundings. "I'm enjoying this more than I anticipated," he admitted to Basil as he delighted in the glittering roofs and towers of Constantinople's resplendent buildings.

"The Rome of the East!" Basil said with pride.

After his prolonged absence, Matthew looked at the city with the eyes of a stranger. He had always admired the Forum of Constantine, encircled by columns. In the center rose a porphyry column nearly a hundred feet tall, topped by a statue of the first Christian emperor, whose diadem was said to include a nail from the cross of Jesus. The palladium of ancient Rome rested beneath the column.

They continued along the main avenue, passing the Golden Milestone, from which all distances were measured. The site was protected by an elaborate cupola. To the northwest, Matthew caught a glimpse of the Church of the Apostles, the resting place of Constantine and many of his family members. He looked toward the domed Hagia Sophia, built and dedicated in 537 by Justinian, the emperor who believed that his cathedral rivaled Solomon's famed temple in Jerusalem. Matthew remembered being in the vast nave of this edifice when it was filled with worshipers, and in his mind he heard the priests chanting while incense swirled toward the gilded dome.

Matthew and Basil found a convenient spot to wait until the elaborately garbed and veiled future empress was carried on a gold-decked litter through the city to the sacred palace. Motioning to Matthew, Basil led the way to an arch leading to the palace grounds, where they were soon admitted by Basil's friend.

"Come this way," Elisha said quietly. The tall, dignified eunuch led them to a balcony where they had a commanding view of the throne room. Matthew eyed the splendor of bronze doors and ceilings overlaid with gold and silver. Golden lions guarded the throne where the emperor and his son, Leo, waited expectantly. In spite of the hundreds of gathered notables, a hush settled over the huge room when the double bronze doors were opened to admit the future empress. She was escorted by the two Byzantine ambassadors who had discovered her.

With downcast eyes, she approached the throne and bowed before the emperor and her future husband sitting on their golden thrones. In the presence of the assembled court, the two men lifted the veil that hid her face and dropped a silken mantle over her long golden robe. Emperor Constantine himself set the crown upon her head, and Leo fastened jeweled pendants in her ears.

The assemblage then proceeded to Saint Stephen's Church, where the new empress received the homage of the high officials of the monarchy. She appeared on a balcony to accept the acclaim of the people before the marriage was solemnified by the patriarch, Nicetas. Surrounded by a brilliant following of patricians, senators, and maids of honor, the nuptial crowns were placed upon the heads of the bride and groom.

Both Matthew and Basil were weary after this final ceremony, and they made their way slowly toward the Trento home. "This has been a noteworthy day," Matthew said to Basil as they did their best to elude the crowd swarming around them, "but is it a good day for Byzantium?"

"What makes you say that?"

"A premonition, perhaps. Somehow I doubt that when Irene becomes empress she will always be concerned for the good of the empire. I mistrust the look of ambition on her face."

Basil smiled wryly. "You may be right. Although it isn't widely known, Elisha tells me that the new empress is sympathetic to image worshipers. If she should rise to power, she might add to the serious religious conflict that has disturbed the Byzantine Empire for more than forty years. But she is a devout, pious woman, so perhaps her dedication will outweigh any controversy she might foster."

"It would be interesting to watch her progress, but I suppose I will not be here. I expect that this search for the Alabaster will not be a short one. Do you have any suggestions to help me?"

"Your father and I talked about it often. He knew that he was asking a lot of you, but he felt that you owed that much to the perpetuation of the house of Trento. Incidentally, he did set aside a portion of his estate for you should you ever leave the cloister. In the event that you do not find the Alabaster, you may have the privilege of claiming the larger estate yourself. If you do not, and the owner of the Alabaster doesn't claim it, upon your death it will go to the church."

"That is generous of my father, but I do not like it when the church continues to accumulate so much wealth. If we must take the vow of poverty, then what need has the church of money?"

"I do not have the answer to your question, nor can I give you much advice on this search. You will be provided with unlimited funds, and you should start your search in Rome. Your father believed Trento family members still live there."

"Very well. I will make preparations and book passage to Rome as soon as possible."

Matthew spent the next day searching along the waterfront for transportation to the West. It was an all-day job, and dusk was falling when he returned to his home. "I've found a captain whose ship will be leaving port in two weeks," he reported to Basil. "He's an Italian, and his home port is Ostia, the harbor that services Rome. Now comes the hard part—what shall I take with me?"

"We must provide for your finances," Basil directed. "Since it isn't wise nor practical for you to carry excessive funds on your person, we can make arrangements for a letter of credit to one of the banking institutions in Rome. You shouldn't travel alone. Why don't you take a servant with you—someone who could see to your needs and serve as a companion?"

"Do you have anyone in mind?"

"The household servants are too old to undertake such a journey, but we have several strong workers in the silk factory who might welcome a chance to travel. I'll find out from the manager who would be the most trustworthy."

"I will not take a slave," Matthew said, and with an understanding look of compassion, Basil nodded.

Believing it advisable to take local products for gift giving, Matthew spent several days shopping. He visited the workbenches of artisans to purchase gold boxes and jewelry. He bought copper and tin containers and costly bottles of perfume. Several silver cups were also added to his pack. He bought at a high price two decorated prayer books and some illuminated gospels. He visited the Trento silk factory and chose various bolts of highly prized brocades and plain silks. It was quite possible that such elaborate gifts from the East might gain him entrance into areas and households that would otherwise be closed to him. By the time the servants had packed his belongings, Basil had chosen a companion for him.

Gerona, five years older than Matthew, was not a tall man, but he had a burly physique, calloused hands, and a florid complexion sprinkled with freckles. Shaggy brown hair fell around his face. Gerona laughed easily, and his dark brown eyes were bright, alert, watchful. Matthew eyed dubiously the wicked-looking dagger encased in a sheath at Gerona's side, but he did believe that Basil had made a wise choice.

"He will be a perfect balance for my seriousness," Matthew said. "You can take the man from the monastery, but not the monastery from the man. He will make a pleasant companion."

"Yes, you will be safe in his hands. And you must guard yourself, Master. You're going to the barbarian nations."

With a slight smile, Matthew said, "Remembering our history, I can't believe the Romans will be worse than our own Byzantines."

"You will see," Basil said through tight lips.

❀ ❀ ❀

On the last night before his departure, Matthew went to the room where he had last seen Sophia. He had avoided this place, even though, for him, her presence still pervaded the whole house. Every waking hour since he had left the cloister had brought some remembrance of her. He thought he had made his final good-bye long ago, but his return home had brought forcefully to his mind that, alive or dead, Sophia still held a place in his heart.

2

Hildebeck, like most other villages in Saxony, was made up of dwellings constructed of woven wattles dabbed with mud and covered with thatched roofs of straw and reeds. Thirty of these single-roomed buildings used for sleeping, workshops, and storehouses faced a communal mead hall, which occupied a prominent place in the center of the village. Most cooking was done on a huge hearth in the central hall, but inside each house was a wooden floor with a small stone pit for heating. A few benches and beds served as furniture.

The village was full of activity as the residents prepared for winter. One man guided a plow pulled by four oxen, while his companion walked behind him sowing barley seed in the newly furrowed soil. Near the mead hall, women winnowed the year's grain crop. Each time the dried stalks were tossed into the air, the wind blew away the chaff. Children were piling wood on the porch of the mead hall, where two women sat and chatted as one spun fleece into yarn on a weighted spindle and the other wove the thread into fabric on a crude frame. Boys drove herds of pigs into the forest to forage on acorns and other nuts before the first snowfall. Two old men enjoyed the late afternoon sun as they walked slowly around the village.

All work stopped when a harsh horn blast pierced the calm of the village. Pig herders left their charges. Women deserted the loom. The plowman abandoned his oxen. The old men hobbled in the wake of their fellow villagers, who were disappearing into the forest at a rapid pace. The warriors were returning!

The trumpet continued to blast as the peasants rushed along the path, and they soon met the trumpeter. Anxious parents and wives strained their eyes as the clansmen came into sight. Their chieftain rode at the head of the procession, and behind him walked weary Saxons loaded down with booty. Following the warriors, a Saxon guard herded three prisoners—a priest and a woman holding the hand of a young child.

A victorious bellow resounded through the forestland, for much booty had been taken, and all of the men had returned safely. Another shout erupted as the villagers contemplated the victory celebration to their god Thor that would take place that night in the mead hall.

Redith, wife of Widukind, had not gone to welcome the returning warriors. Indeed, she was not eager to see her husband. *How can I tell him that I have failed him again,* she thought, *that our child was stillborn?* He would be expecting a son, but there would be none, nor could there ever be now. *Will he divorce me?* Widukind was ambitious to become chief of this village, and he wanted an heir.

Redith watched warily from the inside of her house as her excited neighbors gathered in front of the mead hall. She didn't want anyone to witness Widukind's sorrow when he learned of her mishap. She only hoped someone didn't tell her husband before she could. As she waited for him, she gazed at the prisoners, and her eyes fastened longingly on the small girl with flaxen hair and bright blue eyes. The child watched the commotion curiously and without fear, having no idea that her capture would make a change in her life. Fear marked the wild eyes of the child's mother, who kept a fierce hold on her daughter.

Redith saw Widukind look around for her. Redith's heart leaped at sight of him, as it always did after a long absence.

Physically, Widukind wasn't a man to stand out in a crowd. He was of medium height, slim and erect, and he had wide, deep brown eyes to match his hair and beard. Hundreds of Saxons could have been described in the same manner, but what set Widukind apart from the rest of his fellows was his crisp, authoritative voice and his cool, collected manner. Here, definitely, was a man who was master of himself. He was stern with other Saxons and ferocious in battle, yet with his wife he was of a different personality—gentle, kind, and good.

Finally, Widukind spotted his wife, and with a smile, he rushed into the house. He stopped at the threshold when he saw her leaning against the support post of the building. "And what news do you have for me?" he said softly, noting her slender body in a glance.

"News you will not want to hear, Widukind. The child was born dead. I have failed you again." Redith looked down sorrowfully.

He crossed the room and wrapped her in his arms. "You are still young. We will try again."

Stifling her tears, she shook her head, and his rough beard grazed her cheek. "No. This time there were other problems. They tell me I can never bear a child."

She paused to let that penetrate his mind, while admitting to herself that it was a relief to acknowledge the fact. The many months of waiting and hoping followed by the loss of the baby was an experience she didn't want to repeat. "I think it's time you put me away and took another wife," Redith stated softly.

Widukind pulled back and stared at his wife, then shook her roughly. "No more talk of that kind. You're more important to me than a household of children. It doesn't matter."

But she knew it did, and she said, "What about the Frankish child you've brought back? Would it be possible for us to take her?"

Widukind wouldn't meet her eyes. "The chieftain may have other plans for her. Enough of this talk. We must prepare for the feasting."

"I don't feel much like celebrating."

"You will feel better now that I'm home. Wait until you see the booty we've taken."

❀ ❀ ❀

A blazing fire along one wall of the room provided warmth and light for the huge banqueting hall. The carcass of a wild boar sizzled on a spit, and various dogs, tempted by the zesty aroma, hovered near the fire waiting for a handout. Colorful round shields decorated the rustic wooden walls of the room.

Almost all of the village's fifty residents were present when Redith and Widukind entered. They took two vacant places at the table near the chieftain. The Frankish female prisoner circulated among the Saxons, filling their drinking horns with mead. She wouldn't meet the eyes of any of her enemies, but she glanced often toward her child sleeping on the packed dirt floor. The priest, hands clasped in prayer, knelt beside the child.

To please Widukind, Redith had put on a new violet-colored robe she had made in his absence and draped a white scarf over her hair and shoulders. Her husband had wrapped his muscular legs in new brown bindings and donned a short green robe. Redith had washed his long hair and brushed it and his beard until the hairs bristled with vitality.

A minstrel strolled around the hall playing a lute and singing of the glories of the Saxons and the greatness of Thor, their chosen god.

Thor, eldest son of Odin,
  The king of the gods and goddesses, is a powerful fighter.
His great strength is known to all.
  By his chief weapon, the hammer Mjollnir, many enemies
    will fall.
The hammer never misses its mark and flies back to Thor.
  Thor creates lightning when he throws Mjollnir,

And thunder rumbles when his chariot races across the sky.
    Thor has a great appetite.
He once ate an ox, eight salmon, and drank three barrels of
    mead.
    He created the tides when he tried to drink the sea dry.
He battled Hrungnir, the giant, who tried to slay Thor with a
    huge stone.
    But Thor threw Mjollnir at the giant and Hrungnir fell dead.

The Saxons interrupted the minstrel often by lifting their horns of mead and shouting, "Praise to almighty Thor. He has given us victory over our enemies."

Interest in the minstrel and his songs vanished when packs of booty were spread out on the dirt floor. Men and women pushed and shoved to snatch pots, items of clothing, tools, and weapons. The Frankish woman stared with tears streaming down her face as two Saxons wrangled over a sword. *Had the sword belonged to her husband?* Redith wondered. She longed to comfort the woman, but she knew she must not. Widukind was considered one of the most valiant soldiers in Saxon forestland, and she would shame him by showing pity to their enemies. Not for the first time, Redith admitted that she was a poor wife for a Saxon warrior.

"Is there some item you want?" Widukind asked her.

"Nothing," she declared, though her wistful eyes strayed toward the sleeping child.

Widukind waved aside the prisoner when she offered him more mead, and he surveyed his drunken companions in disgust. His sobriety was one thing that destined her husband for greatness, and Redith looked upon him fondly.

"In a short time," he said to Redith, "they will be so drunk they wouldn't know an enemy if he walked into the hall. There's always a possibility that the Franks will follow us home."

"But don't you always confuse them in the thick forest?"

"Usually, but the Franks are crafty, and since we haven't had any snow to block the trails, we should be alert for an attack. We took this woman and child from the chief's home in the Frankish village we destroyed."

"What of the holy man?" Redith asked.

"His name is Sturm. We found him in the forest as we returned home. He is a Christian priest, supposedly come as a missionary to the Saxons."

The fighting and squabbling over the plunder was approaching violence when the chieftain cried, "Enough. Take what you now have and be satisfied." He laid aside the knife he had used for carving his meat, stood, and banged his drinking horn on the table. The noise of the revelers dwindled and they looked toward their leader.

"We have many reasons to be thankful," he said. "We have had a bountiful harvest, and the gods have given us a safe return from the lands of our greatest enemies, the Franks, who have forsaken the old gods for the one they call Christ Jesus."

Redith glanced toward the priest, wondering if he understood the Saxon tongue. She decided that he did, for at the chieftain's words, he fell to his knees and started chanting in a language foreign to her.

"We have brought much booty for ourselves from the Frankish lands, and also a sacrifice for the Saxon gods. Bring the child to me."

The priest threw his body across the sleeping child, who roused and cried out, but two burly Saxons easily cast the priest aside. One of them lifted the bawling girl and carried her to their leader. The mother screamed and ran toward her daughter, but she was caught from behind by a Saxon warrior.

"Do something," Redith cried to Widukind, but he shook his head and restrained her when she tried to rise.

The chief took the girl in his strong grasp and lifted the sword from his side. Talking and laughter ceased and the only sounds were the crackling of the fire, a dog gnawing on a bone, and the moans of the Frankish mother, who still struggled in the arms of her captor. The scent of the roasting meat, which had been pleasing to Redith before, now caused her to gag. Suddenly, the silence was rent by a violent rumble of thunder—so strong that the torchlights flickered, and the log walls vibrated. The Saxons looked around in amazement, their uppermost thought being, *Was not the sky clear when we entered the building?*

"Thor!" a Saxon called. "Thor is moving across the sky."

"He has hurled his hammer. Perhaps Thor is angry. Where will Mjollnir strike?"

During that momentary pause while the mystified Saxons cowered and awaited the judgment of Thor, the Frankish mother broke away from the one who held her, darted toward the banquet table, grabbed the carving knife, and plunged it deeply into the chieftain's throat.

A terrorized howl erupted from the chieftain's mouth, and blood spewed from his fatal wound. Lifeless fingers released their hold on the child, and the mighty Saxon fell forward across the table. Shouting fiendishly, enraged warriors grabbed the woman and hurled her from one to another, delivering ferocious blows to her body. While Widukind shouted in an effort to restore order, Redith took advantage of the bedlam to pull the child from beneath the dead leader. When she passed the priest, who stared stupefied at the commotion, she motioned for him to follow her. He seized a loaf of bread from the table before they exited the hall.

Crooning softly as she worked, Redith stirred up the coals in the middle of her hut to make enough light to bathe the frightened, blood-splattered child. The priest squatted nearby, chewing on the bread.

She motioned toward a jar. "There's water if you want to drink." He nodded his thanks and lifted the jug to take a long draft.

Holding the child close to her and patting its back, Redith said, "I would help you escape if I dared."

"I would soon be recaptured," the priest stated. "The Saxons know the forestland and I don't. Besides, perhaps I've been brought here for a reason. As a prisoner, I might be able to accomplish my mission more easily than if I were a free man."

"And what is your mission, holy man?"

"To turn the Saxons from their pagan ways toward Christianity."

"That will never happen. More than one missionary has been killed by the Saxons."

"I know that, and among them the great Boniface, who was martyred by pagans. Still, he made many converts in Saxony, and I will follow his example."

"Are you willing to die for such a hopeless cause?"

He nodded solemnly. A sound at the door alerted Redith, and she turned to face her husband, her arms tightening around the child.

He threw water on the coals and plunged the room into darkness. Laying his hand on her shoulder, Widukind said, "You did right to bring them here. Our villagers are wild."

"What about the woman?"

"She is dead, mercifully so. Her body has been hacked into pieces and thrown to the animals. I have no stomach for that sort of thing. In battle, I will slay as lustily as any other warrior, but I do not make war on women and babies."

"What can we do?"

"Nothing, for now. In the morning, our people will be calmer, and as we prepare for the burial of our chieftain, they may have mercy on these prisoners. Let us lie down. I, for one, am weary after our long expedition."

Widukind stretched in front of the door, and Redith covered him with wolf skins. She handed a pelt to the priest, and cradling the now-sleeping child in her arms, she lay beside her husband. Their chieftain was dead, but the woman's life had been taken, so surely the debt had been paid. *Will that satisfy my bloodthirsty neighbors? Or will they demand more satisfaction?* Her arms closed protectively around the girl.

Grunting hogs rooting outside the hut awakened Redith at dawn's first light, and the putrid odor of the animals penetrated the walls. The holy man breathed easily in his sleep, as if he didn't have a care in the world. Most people feared capture by the Saxons. *Why is this man different? Does his religion give him peace instead of the fear that the Saxons feel for Thor?* Redith wondered. She remembered the words he had muttered before he went to sleep last night, "I will lie down and sleep peacefully, for You, O God, make me dwell in security."

When Redith moved to relax her strained muscles, the child in her arms moaned pitifully, but slept on. Sensing that Widukind lay wakeful, she whispered, "What will happen now that our chieftain is dead? Will this bring the opportunity you wish?"

"Perhaps. I've been pondering our future since I awakened. Will the Saxons continue to war with the Franks until one of us is annihilated? Could it be possible for us to live in friendship?"

"We have much in common with the Franks. To look at this child, one can't tell if she is Frank or Saxon, and to be truthful, it doesn't matter to me. Widukind, I want a child. Why can't I have this one?"

Widukind talked on as if he hadn't heard her plea. "If the Saxons had a leader to unite us, we could keep the Franks at bay. I believe I can be that leader, and I'll need to start somewhere. Perhaps Hildebeck is the place." He threw aside the wolf skins and stretched to his feet, ready to start the day. "Don't become attached to that girl. I don't know what will happen to her."

❀   ❀   ❀

Located between the protective walls of the village and the dense forest, a clearing encircled by towering trees marked the Saxon place of worship. Prominently displayed in the center was a crudely sculpted stone tree, to which the villagers bowed and brought offerings.

Near the sculpture, the chieftain's body, wrapped in a gray woolen cloak, lay on the funeral pyre surrounded by stacks of wood. Villagers knelt beside the corpse, mourning one who had been a good leader for many years. Girls pranced around the framework waving branches of rosemary. The Saxons would mourn until sunset, when the body would be burned. They believed that as the body was consumed, the deceased's soul was carried away in the smoke. Everyone wanted to be on hand to share in this departure. Tomorrow the ashes would be sealed in an urn and stored in the house of the dead, which was attached to the village wall.

Rather than attend the death vigil, Redith stayed at the house with the two prisoners, hoping they might escape the notice of the mourners. By midday, however, their absence had been noted, and a village elder came for them. When Sturm saw the funeral pyre, he moaned and fell on his face, praying for the Saxons who had stooped so low in pagan ways.

Redith knelt beside him. "What is wrong?"

"The body must not be burned. There will be a resurrection of the body on judgment day."

"But it is the Saxon way, holy man."

"A way I hope to correct." Sturm lifted his head and prayed, "Father forgive these people. They're ignorant of the true faith. How can they be taught?"

Throughout the afternoon, Sturm continued his chanting in a language Redith didn't understand. She knelt by his side, covering the child with her cloak. The sun neared the western horizon and shadows of the giant evergreens fell across the clearing. A flock of crows gathered in the beeches at the edge of the forest, and their garrulous bickering added to Redith's anxiety. What had only been a gentle breeze when she had entered the clearing had increased to a strong north wind. Suddenly the wind ceased. The crows stirred among the tree branches, took wing, cawing loudly, and skittishly swept across the skies to disappear in the distance. A supernatural calm settled over the clearing, and the villagers looked around uneasily.

The elders gathered in consultation, often glancing toward

Redith and the prisoners. When one of them started in her direction, Widukind hurried to her side. "Remember you are a Saxon, Redith. A sacrifice needs to be offered for our leader."

"But why not an animal sacrifice?" Redith asked nervously.

Sturm rose from his knees when the elder neared and reached for the young girl. "Take my life instead of the child's," Sturm stated firmly.

The Saxon pushed the priest aside and snatched the girl from Redith's resisting arms. The frightened blue eyes of the child filled with tears, and her wailing resounded throughout the forest as a man bound her arms and legs and tossed her on the funeral pyre. Widukind was no longer Redith's kind husband, but a Saxon lusting for the defeat of his enemies. He locked Redith's arms in a numbing grip to keep her from interfering.

A Saxon warrior held up a lighted pine knot, emitted a lusty whoop, and leaned toward the pyre. A mighty blast of thunder rocked the earth. A streak of lightning bolted from the heavens, and the Saxon holding the torch was struck to the ground. Thunder rolled again, the earth trembled, and the child tumbled from the pyre. A boisterous wind buffeted sheets of rain through the clearing. A tree that formed a part of the Saxon religious ritual toppled to the ground, its branches crushing the funeral pyre.

"Thor! The god is angry!" Widukind shouted. "The child must be saved." The terrified Saxons fell to the ground beseeching Thor to have mercy on them and to protect them from his great fury. Widukind picked up the girl and thrust her into Redith's arms.

Redith dodged huge pellets of hail as she ran toward her hut. "Thank you, Thor, for saving this child," she cried, wondering at the magnificent display of the power of the gods. She had never seen anything to equal what had just happened. Then a thought stopped her midstride. *Is it Thor's power that stopped the burning? Or did the Christian God intervene to save the life of the child?*

3

For two months Father Sturm had been a prisoner of the Saxons. He had been treated well enough, but his efforts to turn the villagers from their pagan beliefs had been a failure— except for Redith. Somehow he thought the Saxon woman might be questioning the deity of Thor and Odin. Perhaps it was love for the Christian girl that had made her more receptive to hearing his message.

Will they ever release me? Sturm wondered as he hovered near the fire in the mead hall. The daylight hours lessened as winter swept Saxony, and the villagers spent more and more time in their hall. Widukind had become the leader of Hildebeck, and every week he entertained chieftains from other villages who pledged their allegiance to him. Before spring, he hoped to speak for the majority of the Saxons.

The door opened and a Saxon Sturm hadn't seen before entered the room. "Who is this?" Sturm asked the churl who tended the roasting stag on the fire.

"A Saxon spy who spends his time among the Franks," the churl answered. "He comes home when there is something to report."

"Do you have many spies among the Franks?" Sturm asked, amazed at this information.

"You should ask Widukind, if you dare."

Widukind welcomed the newcomer and shouted, "Bring some mead and roast meat for our messenger! He's come from afar."

Widukind stroked his beard and waited patiently while the spy wolfed down his food and drink. This was one attribute of leadership that Sturm had observed in the new leader; he didn't rush into any situation—he bided his time.

"Our chieftain is dead," Widukind informed the spy, "and I have been elected to take his place. I will hear what you have to say."

"Pepin, king of the Franks, is dead," the spy announced.

A mighty shout from the assembled Saxons rose so loud that it seemed the ceiling would lift. Sturm chanted a prayer for the departed soul of Pepin, whom he had called friend.

"The kingdom has been divided between his two sons, Carloman and Charles."

"Who rules the border with Saxony?"

"The elder son, Charles, sometimes called 'The Churl' because of his loutish ways. He will not be a good neighbor. He will exact every bit of tribute."

"Who remembers the origin of this tribute?" Widukind asked, and an elderly man at the table lifted his hand.

"The tribute was imposed in the days of Clovis, king of the Franks. It was to be an annual payment of five hundred cows, but our ancestors did not always pay it. After several other campaigns against the Saxons, Pepin restored the tribute in the form of three hundred horses."

Widukind sat down and lounged against the log wall of the building. "It is my opinion that the annual tribute to the Franks is no longer in force. That misguided oath was given to Pepin; if Pepin no longer lives, then the treaty is canceled. What say you?"

A lusty cheer showed the Saxons approved, and Widukind called, "Holy man, come here. Do you write the Frankish language?"

Sturm approached. "I do."

"Then write a message for me to Charles, king of Franks. In it you shall inform him that the Saxons will no longer pay the tribute levied on us by his father, Pepin the Short. You will write the message and deliver it."

Hearing the wind blowing through the rafters of the mead hall, Sturm shivered at the thought of journeying through the forest to the Frankish kingdom, but had he any choice? However long the journey, it would be good to return home. He took the parchment and stylus a Saxon handed him and started to write.

❈ ❈ ❈

Several months passed before Father Sturm finally found King Charles at Aix-la-Chapelle. Inclement weather had delayed his journey for days at a time, and since Charles's court was a roving one, the priest would arrive at one estate only to find that Charles had moved on. It was late March when Sturm stumbled into the Frankish king's council room.

Taking in the scene with a glance, Sturm noted how much it resembled the Saxon mead hall. Torches and candles mounted on iron crescents lighted the room. The tables were laden with succulent roast boar, stacks of rye bread, rounds of cheese, and pots of lentils, chick peas, and leeks. Sturm's stomach churned at the spicy aroma wafting from the tables. Several Franks hovered around a hogshead of ale on a table near the door, and casks of wine were abundant.

Men, accompanied by their women, lounged around long plank tables feasting and drinking. *When they are so similar, why can't the Saxons and Franks live in peace?* Sturm wondered. A minstrel strolled around the hall extolling the virtues of Beowulf, a legendary hero claimed by all northern Europeans.

> The wicked Grendel, hater of men
> Preyed upon the thanes of King Hrothgar, Danish king.

> No one could thwart the monster
> > Until brave Beowulf came from the land of the Geat.
> He battled the feared Grendel
> > And delivered the death knell.
> There was rejoicing in the land of the Danes
> > Until Grendel's mother avenged her son's death.
> Again the warrior Beowulf went out to battle.
> > He plunged into the depth of a gory lake
> And slew the monster-woman.
> > He used an ancient warrior's sword made by giants of old,
> A weapon so heavy no ordinary man could wield it.
> > He severed the woman's head and peace reigned again
> > > among the Danes.

Sturm edged toward the fire that crackled in the huge open fireplace. He didn't want to disturb the singer, but his hands were numb, and his face stung as he knelt before the blaze.

> For fifty years Beowulf ruled his people
> > Until a fiery dragon began to harass the Geats.
> The aged warrior went again to the fray.
> > In delivering the death blow to the fire dragon,
> He was fatally wounded, but in perishing
> > He brought peace and prosperity to his people.

The Franks applauded the minstrel and threw silver coins at his feet. Sturm knew that every king hoped to lead his people to victory over their enemies, and he was sure that King Charles envisioned himself as a potential Beowulf, but only time would prove that to be so. Already Sturm had heard the prophecy that Charles would move against his enemies like a burning fire, a refining flame to make Frankish Gaul superior among the countries of Europe.

The personality of Charles dominated the scene, even as Widukind's character held sway in Saxony. The Frank, possessing an imposing, well-built figure that measured several inches over six feet, was a head taller than most of his subjects. Large and lively eyes peered from a tanned face topped by cropped dark hair. After the minstrel completed his performance, Charles started relating a tale of his childhood in a high musical voice, but he broke off when Sturm removed his cloak and revealed his clerical clothing. Tossing his half-eaten chunk of meat to a dog, the king motioned for the priest to come forward.

Charles's mother, Bertrada, sat to his right, while his left arm encircled the shoulders of a blonde, buxom woman who was heavy with child. Charles fancied himself a defender of the church, and he bowed deferentially to the priest. "Welcome, Father Sturm. It's been a long time since we've enjoyed your presence."

Sturm approached the table, bowed to the king, then turned to Bertrada. "I have not seen you since the death of your husband, Pepin. I have offered prayers for his soul."

Bertrada was a chunky woman with a pale complexion. Her dark, restless eyes exhibited no remorse as she acknowledged Sturm's condolences with a nod.

To Charles he said, "Pepin the Short is not the only ruler to have died recently. One of the main Saxon leaders has died and Widukind has taken his place."

"Widukind?" Charles mused. "I've never heard of him." The name must have meant something to many of the assembled Franks, however, for Sturm sensed a heightening tension as a faint murmur stirred throughout the room.

"I daresay you will," Sturm said wryly, "for he's uniting the Saxons. I've been a prisoner of his countrymen for several weeks this winter, and I bring you a message from Widukind." Sturm pulled the parchment from the folds of his garments. "I was released for the purpose of delivering this message to you."

Charles quickly scanned the message that Sturm had written, then slowly read the words aloud. "Since Pepin the Short is dead, and since the oath of loyalty was given to Pepin rather than to the Frankish kingdom, upon his death, the Saxon responsibility ended. No more tribute will be paid."

A scowl spread across Charles's features. He threw the parchment to the floor and stamped it into bits. "We will see about that. I will assemble the host at Mayfield, and we will teach these Saxons a much-needed lesson. They have made several raids into Frankish lands this winter, and I will not tolerate that. What do you know about their defenses?" he hurled the question at Sturm.

"I saw no village except Hildebeck, so I do not know the general strength of the Saxons. It is my opinion that their greatest asset is the vast forestland. If they're routed in one place, they only have to disappear into trackless wastelands to elude their enemies. If I recall, your Merovingian ancestors made many unsuccessful campaigns against the Saxons."

"Regardless, I will not accept this rebellion."

The woman at Charles's left pulled on his robe. "Yes, what is it, Himiltrud?" Charles said impatiently.

Through teeth clenched tight in pain, the woman said, "Will someone assist me to our quarters? The pain is too intense for me to go alone."

Charles quickly assessed the situation and shouted for a servant to attend Himiltrud. "Mother, will you also go and help?"

As the three women left the hall and climbed the wooden steps to the floor above, Charles swept his arm. "The rest of you should go to your own houses. There can be no more merrymaking tonight. Tomorrow, we will rejoice over the coming of my firstborn."

Sturm walked to the central hearth and held out his hands to the warmth.

"Where do you abide, Father?" Charles asked, joining Sturm by the fire.

"With your permission, I will lie by this fire tonight and return to the monastery tomorrow."

"I intend to stay here and await the birth of the child. I will welcome your company." Charles signaled for a slave to bring some refreshment, and he lolled on the floor opposite the priest.

Sturm eased his lanky body onto a bench and sipped on the warm ale the servant brought him. "I have not congratulated you on your ascension to power."

"Although I always knew that someday I would be king, it came more quickly than I wanted. My father kept me at his side, and I learned administration and warfare from his example, yet I find it difficult to give up my carefree ways of riding the forest and hunting with my friends. My mother says it's time I settle down, but at twenty-six years, I'm not ready. I had not expected my father to die so soon."

"Have you married the woman who is now bearing your child?"

Charles waved a careless hand. "By Frankish customs, yes."

"For the child's sake, it would be well to have the blessing of the church, whose leaders frown on concubinage and the easy dissolution of marriage."

"I didn't think it was necessary," Charles said stubbornly, and Sturm wondered how far Charles's piety extended, especially when it disrupted his personal life. Sturm looked forward to the day when the church would make marriage an indissoluble sacrament. The present method of divorce was too easy; a husband, with little provocation, could send a woman back to her own family. This practice often led to open warfare between the clans. Now was no time to argue with Charles about the depth of his Christian faith, however.

Just as Pepin had taught his sons to rule, Bertrada had reared her sons to be devout, but Sturm knew that the spiritual knowledge of the average Franks had little impact upon their way of life. Charles had also been given an adequate academic education. His native tongue was Frankish, but he knew the other Germanic dialects, and he read and spoke classical Latin, the language of the church. He had the attributes of a great leader, but only time would tell if his better qualities would outweigh his undisciplined nature.

Sturm would have liked a time for rest, but as the night wore on, Charles's thoughts turned to the past as well as the future, and the priest wrapped his cloak around him, adjusted to a reclining position, and listened to the king's reflections.

"Does it seem to you, Sturm, that the Christian world is sinking into darkness? Learned men predict that the world has entered its last millennium and that it will end abruptly not many years hence, perhaps as few as two hundred years from now. When I contemplate these things, my mind wanders to the golden age when our ancestors moved into this region, a time when active trade resulted in great wealth."

"Yes, but that was before the final decay of the Roman Empire. Only the minstrels keep alive the glories of the ancient world. We are living in a time when the deepest darkness of the ages has overspread Europe, but we must not despair. The future is before us. Your father made an effort to bring western Europe out of the darkness. You should carry on his work."

Two canines nudged their way in beside the king—obviously unhappy at the two humans who had usurped the warmth of the fire that they usually had to themselves. Absentmindedly, Charles pushed them aside. "My goal is to bring light out of obscurity, and a burning fire out of the darkened embers of the past. My armies will march each spring to spread Frankish influence."

"But the answer is not in the sword," Sturm said quietly.

The cry of a child sounded from the second floor, and Charles leapt to his feet, his musings on the future forgotten. He kicked at the dogs, who howled at his sudden movement. "I'm a father!" he said joyfully and moved to the foot of the stairs, looking up expectantly.

It seemed a long time before Bertrada appeared on the steps, carrying a small form wrapped in a blanket. She walked slowly down the stairs, and Sturm moved to Charles's side.

"A boy?" Charles asked, his high voice screeching the question.

Bertrada nodded and Charles said, "Then he will be another Pepin. Will that make you happy, Mother?"

Bertrada did not look happy. She pulled back the coverlet. The baby's features seemed perfect, and Charles reached out a trembling hand to caress the tiny cheek. Bertrada slowly turned the baby over in her hands.

Charles gasped, and even Sturm was stunned when he saw the tiny, twisted body. *A tragedy!* Charles's firstborn was destined to live out his days as a hunchback, and since any kind of deformity was loathsome to the Franks, this son could never rule his countrymen.

❋ ❋ ❋

Despite the deformity, within six months of the birth of Pepin the Hunchback, Charles was carrying the boy with him as he rode around his domain. After the first shock of the child's imperfection, Charles had formed a warm attachment to his son. Except for the crooked back, the child was alert and intelligent.

Though Charles loved his son, he no longer felt any passion for Himiltrud. *Do I blame her for Pepin's imperfection?* he often wondered. Whatever the cause, his ardor for his wife had cooled. Since his mother was away visiting his brother, Carloman, Charles spent more and more time traveling to his other estates and hunting with his friends. He found comfort in the arms of more than one willing woman.

Bertrada's visit with his brother lengthened into months, causing Charles concern about her absence. He was overjoyed when he returned to his current headquarters in late summer to find his mother in residence again. "Your journey has been long. We've missed you," Charles said warmly.

"After a visit with Carloman, I traveled into Bavaria to assist Father Sturm in some negotiations. Then I went southward to Italy for a few months. It was a profitable journey."

Bertrada didn't divulge further details of her journey at first, but her keen eyes observed the strained relations between her son and Himiltrud during the evening meal. Though his wife attempted to beguile him with passionate glances and caresses, Charles was brusque and rude to her. And in spite of an absence of several weeks, the king made no move to follow Himiltrud up the stairs when she retired for the night.

Encouraged by what she had seen, Bertrada approached Charles with her news when they were finally alone. "Son, you'll be happy to know that I've arranged a marriage for your brother to the daughter of your cousin Tassilo, ruler of Bavaria." No one knew better than Bertrada of the ever-present friction between her two sons, but no one knew better how to sway Charles. He would not want Carloman to advance more than he.

"Why do you think that would bring me happiness? Tassilo has not stayed loyal to the pledge he made to our father. He desires to rule independently. I could never be in an alliance with him."

"And for that reason I didn't consider asking you to marry the girl. But do you have anything against the royal house of Lombardy?"

Charles glanced piercingly at his mother, as if he only now had discerned the import of her words. "I suppose not."

"I thought so, and that's why I started negotiations with Desiderius, ruler of that country, about uniting you to his family. He has a daughter, Desiderata, whom he will give you as wife."

"What advantage would such a union be to the Franks?"

Bertrada knew that she must be most astute if she was to succeed in wedding her churlish son to a cultured wife who would refine his uncouth ways and keep him from warring—especially against his brother. Bertrada's greatest fear was a civil war between her sons. Carloman would never initiate such strife, but she had no doubt that Charles wouldn't hesitate if his brother offered him sufficient provocation.

"As you know, Tassilo is married to a daughter of Desiderius, and if you marry Desiderata, you and Tassilo will be brothers-in-law, as well as cousins." She held up her hand when Charles started to protest. "With your brother Carloman married to Tassilo's daughter, a formidable four-way alliance would be presented to our enemies."

"It may also give the Bavarians and Lombards an excuse to meddle in Frankish affairs," Charles growled.

With a supercilious smile, his mother replied, "Don't you think you're strong enough to resist that?"

"Of course I am! And two can play the meddling game. If Tassilo and Desiderius try anything, they'll have the Frankish host to contend with. Go ahead with your negotiations, Mother. To wed a princess is a challenge I might welcome."

"Has it ever occurred to either of you," Himiltrud's voice sounded from the stairway, "that Charles already has a wife and son?"

The two conspirators started guiltily and looked quickly at the woman standing on the top step holding Pepin on her hip. *How much has she heard?* they wondered.

When they remained silent, Himiltrud spoke venomously, "Do you intend to have two wives? Why don't you move all of your women into the palace?"

"It will be easy to get rid of you," Bertrada said, while Charles failed to come to the defense of his wife. "Your marriage was never blessed by the church."

Walking slowly down the stairs, Himiltrud tossed her head. "Oh, yes, the church. Charles, the great defender of the church! You scoff at my pagan ways, yet you would abandon your wife and child. Is this what your religion teaches?"

"You could not even give the king a healthy son. He will be well rid of both of you," the queen mother said. "He needs strong sons to carry on his heritage. It's necessary for him to have a new wife."

"Who can say I couldn't produce a healthy child if I had the chance?" She stabbed an accusing finger at Charles. "He warms other women's beds—not mine."

Charles at last found his voice. Slamming his huge fist down on the table, he shouted, "I spread my favors where I will! Let this be understood—Pepin is *my* son. No matter what else happens, he stays with me."

Himiltrud gave her husband a glare that burned through him. "You take my child away from me, and you'll live to regret it." She flashed a look of hatred at Bertrada before she went back up the stairs.

4

FRANKISH GAUL, 769–770

Leaving the colorful tent, Matthew Trento huddled deeper into his cloak as the cold mountain wind penetrated his silk garments. A full moon hovered on the horizon, casting deep shadows over the snow-crested Alps surrounding the camp of the trader Drago. Tinkling bells of grazing horses and donkeys echoed around Matthew, and he breathed deeply of the mountain air scented with the perfume of pine and fir. His stomach growled when the aroma of baking bread wafted through the camp. It had been a hard journey since morning, when they'd last eaten. He flexed his muscles to ease the fatigue of his body. Gazing at the mountains and remembering the difficult journey they had experienced, it was a relief to know that he was nearing his destination. *Am I any closer to finding the Alabaster than when I left home?* He hoped so.

Seeing the trader approach, Matthew wondered, as he had often done since they had left Rome, about the nature of this man. In the year since they had departed Constantinople, Matthew and Gerona had encountered some unusual people, but none more so than Drago. They had occasion to observe Drago as he bought and sold his wares on the long journey from Rome to Frankish Gaul, but the man remained a mystery. He was as unpredictable as a chameleon. When he was dealing with church

51

leaders to buy or sell them religious relics, his voice was pious and humble. Upon reaching a toll booth, he donned the garb of a religious pilgrim so that he could avoid paying the fee. When he set up his tent in a marketplace, he wheedled and bargained like a Saracen. Out on the trail, his language was vulgar and harsh when herding his animals. As Drago's character changed, so did Matthew's opinion of him. First he liked the man, and then he didn't. Matthew had never trusted him enough to divulge the nature of his business in Gaul, although the trader may very well have been his greatest source of information. Drago had traveled all over Europe and might just know who had the Alabaster. After seeing the look of avarice on the trader's face when he bargained for precious objects, however, Matthew decided that even if Drago did know who owned the vase, he would not divulge the information without an exorbitant price.

"We are within a day's ride of Frankish Gaul," Drago said. "I have kept my word and delivered you safely."

"That you have, and you shall have the remainder of your fee on the morrow," Matthew stated.

"You don't want to travel northward with me then?" Drago inquired curiously.

"No, I will spend a few days in the vicinity of the Rhone River before I travel farther." The cook struck a gong to summon them to the cooking fire, and Drago turned on his heel without further comment. He had tried often enough on the journey from Rome to learn what had brought Matthew to Europe, but perhaps he had given up finding out.

With only a minimum of trouble, Matthew had found a branch of the Trento family in Rome. He'd had an enjoyable sojourn with his relatives, but had learned very little about the family relic. During the time of Constantine the Great, Lucius Trento had inherited the Alabaster, which he had taken with him to Gaul. As far as any of the Roman Trentos knew, the vase had never been returned to Italy. Matthew almost gave up hope then of ever finding the vase, for with a lapse of over four hundred years, how could he possibly pick up the trail? His Roman hosts tried to convince him that it was hopeless.

"My dear Matthew, surely you would not think that a relic almost eight hundred years old could still exist," Omar Trento argued. "And especially in Gaul, which is part of the Frankish kingdom now. That country has been beset with internal problems for years. Right now they may be on the verge of civil war, for Pepin the Short has died and his two sons, Charles and Carloman, do not get along well together. It is a situation that does not bode well for Gaul *or* Rome."

"How could a problem in the Frankish kingdom have any effect here?" Matthew inquired.

"Several years ago, Pope Stephen II sought aid from Pepin the Short against the Lombard kingdom of northern Italy," Omar explained. "Pepin supported the pope's claim that the papacy was the legitimate heir to the Roman Empire comprising the whole Italian peninsula and that as primate of the church, the pope had some authority over all Christian kings. In exchange for this support, the pope conferred on Pepin and his two sons the title Patrician of the Romans, which implied a duty to protect papal lands. The Lombards on our northern border have never recognized that Italy should be under the jurisdiction of the papacy. The pope fears that he will no longer have the might of the Franks at his disposal should the Lombards attack Rome."

"Will the sons uphold their father's pledge?"

"That's doubtful, for it seems the Franks are negotiating with the Lombards, who would like to take over the whole of Italy."

Confronted with this political situation, Matthew considered seriously the advisability of continuing his search. That night he recalled the message he had received from Christ in his monastery cell: *Go, and I will go with you.* Remembering these words, Matthew realized he had no choice but to go on.

"Though it doesn't sound like a good time to travel to the land of the Franks, I'm still compelled to do so," Matthew said to Omar the next morning. "Do you have any suggestions to ensure the success of my journey?"

"You'll need a guide, I should imagine, and one that speaks the Frankish dialect. I assume that you cannot speak it?" Omar questioned.

"I write and speak both Greek and Latin—none other," Matthew replied.

Searching for a guide had led Matthew to the trader Drago, who declared himself to be a world traveler in search of rare items. He claimed to be conversant in many languages. He was on his way back to Frankish Gaul, and he would be happy to have Matthew's company.

"Are you a Roman?" Matthew asked.

"If it pleases you," Drago responded.

"Are you a Frank?" Matthew persisted.

"If it pleases you."

Perhaps noting the hint of anger on Matthew's face, Drago had laughed and said, "I'm a citizen of every country. This has added to my success as a trader." Matthew had indeed found it difficult to ascertain Drago's nationality, for he easily assumed the identity of whatever people he visited. His physical characteristics differed little from hundreds of other men that Matthew knew. He was a slender man, and his brown eyes and hair were like many other Italians Matthew had met. Out on the trail, Drago allowed his beard to grow, but when he set up shop in a village, he was smooth-shaven.

During their long and arduous days together, Matthew had paid the man to teach him and Gerona the Frankish tongue, and he felt that they could manage on their own now. He was not reluctant to separate from Drago the next day. It surprised him that when they finally did part, the trader said, "We will meet again, my friend Matthew." Matthew wondered if the statement was a promise or a threat.

✺   ✺   ✺

When Matthew looked down on the Rhone Valley, he understood the lure it would have had to Lucius Trento in bygone centuries. After the ruggedness of the Alpine crossing, his eyes feasted upon the rolling hills covered with vineyards, the valley's broad grain fields, and the neat hamlet of Corneille nestling along a sharp curve in the Rhone.

Matthew had learned in Rome that Lucius Trento had married into a family by the name of Conrad that had lived near Corneille. He and Gerona arrived in the small village when the church bell was chiming the vesper hour. The main street was deserted, and judging from the scents of cooked cabbage and roast pork wafting from the dwellings, Matthew decided the natives must be at their supper.

With a laugh, Gerona patted his stomach. "Smells good."

Matthew agreed. "I'm famished, but we'll look for lodging first."

After walking the length of the main street without finding an inn, Matthew said, "I'll go into the church to see if we can pitch our tents on their property."

The rustic wooden edifice was situated near the center of the village, and Matthew walked through the open door. Burning candles around the carved wooden altar lighted Matthew's way as he moved forward through the room, which was devoid of furnishings except a bench along one wall. The familiar aroma of incense greeted him. A priest knelt before the altar chanting the vespers ritual, and Matthew knelt beside him and joined in the words: "My soul magnifies the Lord. My spirit rejoices in Christ my Savior."

The priest lifted his eyes at the sound of Matthew's voice, but he bowed his head again and completed the ritual, ending with a selection from the psalms. "You are my God, and I praise You. You are my God, and I will lift You up. Give thanks to God, for He is good. His loving kindness lasts forever. Amen."

The priest stood and surveyed Matthew with cynical eyes, taking in his costly clothing. "You speak the words of a priest, yet you do not dress the part."

"I entered holy orders six years ago, but I'm on special assignment for my abbot now. For the success of this mission, it was decided I should travel in lay clothing."

"And why have you come to Corneille?" the priest inquired as he motioned Matthew to the rustic bench. Altar boys crept in quietly to light additional candles, and Matthew waited until they exited before answering.

"I'm searching for a family that may have lived nearby several centuries ago. Do you recognize the name Trento or Conrad?"

"There's a family in this parish by the name of Conrad that has occupied a farm along the Rhone for generations, though I have never heard the name Trento," the priest answered. "You could question the head of that household. I invite you to lodge with me tonight and resume your journey in the morning. In fact, if you wish, I will travel along and introduce you to the Conrads."

"I have a servant with me, and we have tents for lodging, but I would like permission to set up our camp on the church property. Or perhaps you could direct me to another likely spot."

"There is a wide lawn beside my abode. You are welcome to settle there."

The next morning, Matthew left Gerona to guard their belongings as he joined the priest in the hour's walk to the Conrad farm. A steady rain drenched them before they reached their destination—a neat farmstead situated alongside the Rhone. At their approach, a sturdy farmer hailed them from the door of a stone house that resembled a fortress and looked as if it had been on this spot for centuries.

"Come in out of the elements, Father," the farmer called. "Why do you journey in such weather?"

"I have brought a visitor for you, Conrad." He turned to Matthew. "Is this business secret? If so, I shall wait outside until you're ready to return to the village."

"It is secretive, but I will trust you with it, for I may need you to help with translating, if you will. The Frankish tongue is new to me."

The priest nodded and followed Matthew into a room cluttered with farming implements, crude household items, and children. Madame Conrad placed bowls of cool wine before them, and Matthew sipped appreciatively. Then he said haltingly in his recently acquired language, "Do you know anyone by the name of Trento?"

Conrad hesitated. "No. Do you, wife?"

The woman shook her head.

"I'm looking for a relative of mine," Matthew explained. "I believe he may have married into your family years ago."

"How long ago?" Conrad asked.

"Around four hundred years."

The burly Conrad shook with laughter. "I do not remember what happened then." He tapped his head. "Sometimes I do not remember what happened yesterday." He laughed again. "I have many ancestors, but I do not recall their names."

"Allow me to tell you a story," Matthew began. "In the first century, one of my ancestors was traveling in Jerusalem during the week Jesus was crucified. He did not witness the resurrected Lord, but he heard many stories about Jesus' earthly appearances. This man collected items of antiquity, and before he returned to Italy, he visited the shop of Mary and Cleopas, followers of Jesus. They had an alabaster vase of spikenard that Mary had carried to the tomb on the first day of the week to anoint the body of Jesus. Of course, since the tomb was empty, there was no need for the ointment. My ancestor brought that vase home with him, and it passed from generation to generation as a sign that Christ had risen. The holder of the Alabaster is responsible for the perpetuation of the Trento faith. We believe that Jesus died for our sins and that by His sacrifice we obtain salvation as a free gift from God; it is not something we attain by our works. I'm looking for the person who has the Alabaster."

The priest smiled, and spoke in Latin, "If the man who holds the Alabaster is a Frank, I doubt he's carrying on that tradition. Very few of our people, the clergy included, believe in salvation by grace. My countrymen pay lip service to Christianity, but they still hold to the superstitious beliefs of the pagan gods. They do not comprehend a salvation that cannot be earned."

"And yet you are enlightened," Matthew replied also in Latin.

"I have not always lived in this small village. I asked to be transferred here from a large parish in Paris. Our bishop there taught us the true meaning of the Scriptures, but it isn't a commonly held belief."

"Regardless," Matthew said, reverting to the local tongue, "I am searching for that Alabaster and the person who holds it today. My search led me to the Trento family in Rome, and the only information they had was that the Alabaster had been brought to Gaul by Lucius Trento during the time of Constantine the Great."

The Conrad family had no trouble comprehending Matthew's halting narrative, for the priest had supplied the words that Matthew didn't know.

"That is an interesting tale," Conrad said, "and I wish I could help you." He motioned upward. "On the hill overlooking the valley are the ruins of a dwelling that according to my grandfather were ruins even in his time. I've heard that house belonged to a Roman who had married into our family, but I do not know his name."

Conrad's wife touched her husband's arm. "The book, Conrad?"

He looked at her vaguely for a moment, then his face brightened. "Oh yes! We have a book that has been in the family as long as any of us can remember, but nobody can read it. Not even my grandparents." He snapped his fingers at a boy who sat beside him. "Bring the book."

The boy scrambled up the open steps at the side of the room, and the sounds of his search reached them as he shoved objects over the floor in the loft above their heads. Madame Conrad refilled the wine cups and passed a plate of brown bread spread with butter. Several minutes elapsed before the boy returned with a package wrapped in a skin. He handed the package to Matthew. Vermin had been chewing at the skin, which was mildewed, dusty, and covered with cobwebs. A spider slithered down Matthew's robe, and the dust he inhaled brought on a fit of sneezing as he unrolled the skin. His heartbeat accelerated when he uncovered a voluminous book, bound with thin pieces of wood protected with leather, the text written on a good grade of parchment. He laid back the wooden cover and looked at the inscription page. *Little wonder that none of the Conrad family could read it,* thought Matthew. *The book is written in Greek!*

With a catch in his voice, Matthew read aloud, "I, Lucius Trento, take pen in hand on the seventeenth day of March in the year 340, to write this account of Constantine the Great, the first Christian Roman emperor. It has been ten years since I left the service of Constantine, after being in his company for over thirty years. Three years ago Constantine died, and since the empire is being divided at this time, I feel it is necessary to record an eyewitness account of the work of Constantine."

Matthew caressed the book, at once feeling a bond of kinship with that Trento of long ago. His throat was too tight for speech. He could only look around at the Conrads with misty eyes.

"It seems that your search has been rewarded," the priest said.

"In part, at least," Matthew agreed with difficulty. Looking at Conrad, he said, "Would you be willing to part with this book? I will pay you well for it."

"This is the first time I've laid eyes upon the book since I was a boy, and I see no need for me to keep it. I will sell the book for a price agreed upon by you and the Father. He will know the value of the book better than I."

Matthew was pleased with the price suggested by the priest, and he counted out the gold coins, which Conrad accepted eagerly. He also gave Madame Conrad a silver cup that he had brought from Constantinople. With a cry of delight, she placed it on the stone windowsill, where it shone brightly in contrast to the otherwise drab furnishings.

"We do not often see gold here—most of our coins are silver," Conrad said. He went to the door. "There is still a light rain falling. Will the two of you partake of some food with us and wait for the showers to cease?"

Matthew was eager to read his new purchase, but he could not refuse the invitation. By the time they had finished the frugal meal of cheese and pea soup, the sun was shining. The grass was still wet and slippery when they made their way back to the village.

"Will I impose upon you if I stay until I've read the book?" Matthew asked his companion. "It will take many days, I'm sure, for the ink has faded in spots, but I don't want to resume my journey until I read the text, which may give me additional clues about the Alabaster."

"You're welcome to stay," the priest encouraged. "It's lonely for me here. In spite of my desire for a slower way of life in my old age, I miss the company of other priests."

❋   ❋   ❋

For the next three days, Matthew pored over the book. Lucius was a graphic writer, and Matthew gained a new insight into the greatness of Constantine I. Thinking of the political intrigues in the Byzantine Empire now, he mourned that there was no one strong enough to take control as Constantine had done.

Throughout the book, Lucius had drawn illustrations, and a recurring one had been the image of an ornately carved vase. Matthew was sure that this must be the family Alabaster, for Lucius had intertwined in the narrative various sensational happenings about the relic, which had been willed to him by his grandfather. The vase had been hidden during the persecutions of Christians, it had been stolen by thieves and coveted by Constantine the Great, but through it all, Lucius had held on to the treasure. Over and over in the story, Lucius insisted that the Alabaster had no miraculous power; he said it was only a symbol of what Jesus had done.

After studying the drawings, Matthew had a good impression of the slender, delicately carved Alabaster. Streaks of black punctuated the golden background, bearing upon its smooth sides a carving of Abraham preparing to offer Isaac as a sacrifice. He deduced that the Trento vase must be one of a set, for the numeral three often appeared on the drawings.

With a sigh of relief, Matthew finally turned to the last page, where another picture of the Alabaster had been drawn. He read Lucius's last words:

> And what will happen to the family relic when I'm gone? Will my son regard it as highly as I have? Will he consider stewardship of the Alabaster to be a burden? And most of all, will he preserve the family teaching that salvation is the gift of God to all who will accept it?

Matthew turned the leaf wistfully, hoping that he would find further information, but there was no more. Although he spent the next two weeks wandering through villages up and down the Rhone searching for a clue to the Alabaster's location, Matthew found nothing except an old herdsman. The herdsman's words convinced Matthew that he must travel westward into Frankish Gaul.

"I've heard tell," the ancient herdsman said, "that a few centuries ago, a plague spread throughout Gaul. Hundreds of people died, and in some of the northern areas, the population was almost completely wiped out. About that same time, a famine hit the Rhone Valley, and many families migrated northward. You may do well to continue your search in other areas of Gaul. I would especially suggest that you visit the court of King Charles. You might have a long wait, but in time, you'll probably find someone at the court who will have the information you want."

"Where is the king's palace? What city should I seek?" Matthew inquired.

His informant smiled. "The king has no permanent abode. His palace is wherever the king chooses to spend the night. He is a man of the people. The rule of Charles has been like a burning fire—refining in some ways, but destructive in others. You would do well to be careful, my son."

Matthew thought this way of traveling could be time-consuming, but not having any better plan, the next week he and Gerona joined a caravan of merchants taking their fall crop of wine north into Alemanni. They parted company with the merchants at Chalon, and Matthew sent Gerona into the city to gather information. The servant's eyes brimmed with satisfaction when he returned a few hours later.

"We are in luck, master. Inside the city, I encountered a royal party from Lombardy conducting their princess, Desiderata, to Gaul to marry King Charles. If we attach ourselves to them, we can be assured of finding the king, for some of his men are accompanying the Lombards."

"It is a good idea, but I doubt a royal entourage will allow the addition of two foreigners to their group."

"But I have not finished," Gerona interrupted. "The royal princess is ill, and her attendants are very anxious because they cannot get the woman's fever to fall. I mentioned that my master was a doctor learned in the medical knowledge of the East."

"Gerona, that is stretching the truth considerably. My only skill is in the dispensing of herbs and potions."

"The Lombards are quite eager to have you call upon their mistress."

Leaving Gerona to watch their baggage, Matthew took his bag of herbs and followed Gerona's directions. He soon found the royal camp near a fast-flowing stream north of the city. Several crudely dressed armed men lounged on the ground at a distance from the royal tent, and Matthew deduced they were the Frankish bodyguard. He approached a thin man with a solemn expression, who watched warily as Matthew came near.

"I'm Matthew of Constantinople," Matthew said to the man. "My servant tells me that you have use for the limited medical skills I learned in Constantinople, a city that has provided medical attention to its poor and destitute for years."

"I, Angelo, will be in your debt if you will look at the princess," the thin man said. "She is sickly by nature, but the sickness has persisted longer than normal."

He quickly ushered Matthew into the tent where the princess lay languidly on a cot. The woman was heavily veiled, as were the two attendants flanking her. The eyes of the princess were feverish. In a listless voice, she gave permission for Matthew's examination, which she endured silently, except for one fit of coughing.

"It's my opinion that your fever has already broken, but I will administer some herbs I have in my pack that might ease your discomfort," Matthew explained to the princess.

"May I inquire what you will give her?" Angelo asked. "I will have to sample the medicines before she can take them. My master, the king of Lombard, has entrusted her to my care."

"Some very simple herbs that I have prescribed before." Matthew lifted some leaves from a pouch he carried. "These are from a shrub, *Ephedra sinica,* and have long been used to treat lung ailments. I will add a few leaves of belladonna to relieve her coughing spasms."

Matthew gave instructions about administering the drugs to the tallest of the women servants, who observed him with speculative gray eyes gleaming above her white veil. *Is the woman trying to convey a message to me?* Matthew wondered.

Angelo followed him from the tent. "Could you tarry with us for a few days? We have need of an educated man. We do not understand the language of these people along our route, and since you speak our Latin tongue as well as the local dialect, I would be obliged to you."

"Cannot the Frankish bodyguard interpret for you?" Matthew asked.

Angelo lowered his voice. "We do not trust them completely."

"What is your destination?"

"We are to meet the Frankish royal party at Mainz, where a wedding will take place between our princess and King Charles."

"I have been looking for an escort into Frankish lands. If I may have the privilege of traveling on to Mainz with you when you resume your journey, I will gladly attend your mistress and act as your interpreter."

The little Lombard could hardly contain his joy at having some added help for his mistress, and he encouraged Matthew to move his possessions to their camp. He was no happier than Matthew, who considered it beneficial to have a good reason for approaching Charles's court without an explanation of his mission. Because the princess Desiderata's recovery was more rapid than usual, Matthew was given much of the credit, and he was accepted into the inner circle of the Lombardy group by the time the journey resumed.

The young princess often requested Matthew's company, and either in the presence of Angelo or her two female assistants, Desiderata talked about her past and her future. Matthew soon deduced that she was uneasy in her mind. When he was certain that her distress wasn't caused by physical conditions, he asked one evening, "What is troubling you, Princess Desiderata? Are you homesick?"

"Perhaps a little, but it's the lot of members of royal families to be disrupted from their homes. There is more than that. I do not look forward to this marriage—I've been told that the king of the Franks is a crude, uncouth person. If that is so, I fear we will have little in common." She fluttered her neatly manicured hands.

"I wish that I could allay your fears, Princess, but I have no knowledge about the man, nor have I ever talked with one who knows him. It's said that he is a powerful ruler."

"Yes, of course—that's the reason my father was eager for this alliance. Under Pepin, the Franks were hostile toward us, and Father believes that if Charles is his son-in-law, he'll be rid of the Franks in his internal affairs."

"It seems to me that Charles will be more inclined to meddle when he's a member of the family," Matthew speculated.

"Well, I can't give an opinion on the situation, for Lombard women are not encouraged to think for themselves. I only know that when Pepin's wife, Queen Bertrada, made overtures to my father about a marriage with Charles, my father agreed immediately."

"I wish you well in your match," Matthew said sincerely.

❋　　❋　　❋

Each evening after he had dined, Matthew made it a habit to withdraw by himself so that he might engage in a moment of meditation at the vesper hour. One night when they were within a few day's travel of Charles's court, Matthew found a sanctuary along a fast-flowing stream tumbling through a rocky ravine surrounded with abundant shrubs and trees. He sat down, leaning his back against a tree. Except for the sound of the flowing water, the glade was quiet, and the solitude reminded Matthew of his life as a monk. As the months sped by, his peaceful sojourn at the monastery receded far into the past. Days often passed without any thought of the vows he had taken, and it disturbed him that he had so easily succumbed to the secular life. *If my mission is successful,* he thought, *and I find the owner of the Alabaster, will I be content to return to the cloister?*

Matthew's musings were disrupted by one of Desiderata's serving women, who quietly entered the glade and stood before him. Matthew hurried to his feet. "Am I needed? Is the princess ill?"

The woman shook her head, lifted a hand, and removed her veil. Matthew stared, mouth agape. "Sophia?"

"Yes, Matthew. I never thought to see you again," she said in the soft, silky tones that had haunted his dreams for years.

"Sophia!" he said again, and gathered the woman into his arms. "Nor did I think I would ever see you again. Where have you been? What has happened to you? Is it safe for us to talk now? Sit down."

"A slave does not sit in the presence of her betters."

"Are you a slave of Desiderata?"

She nodded, and Matthew said, "Then I will not cause you trouble. We'll both stand. Tell me what happened to you. I returned home one day, and you were gone. My father would never tell me what had occurred."

"He sold me to a Roman who lived in Ravenna, Italy, who in turn sold me to the king of Lombardy."

Matthew gasped. This was even worse than he had feared. "Have you been mistreated?" he whispered, searching her eyes to find an answer to his question.

"Not in the way you mean, but I loathe being a slave. Being born into a distinguished Greek family does not prepare one for servitude."

Memories flooded Matthew's mind—the day his father had brought home the beautiful Greek girl who had been enslaved by the Byzantines, and how her presence had graced their house as she served them. Within a matter of weeks, Sophia and Matthew knew they were in love. They had carried on secret meetings until one day Avidius Trento had caught them together. Bravely, Matthew told his father of his love and his wish to marry the servant girl. Avidius had taken the news calmly, but a few days later when Matthew returned from his studies with the city's chief medical men, Sophia was gone. His father would not tell Matthew of her whereabouts.

"I love you still, Sophia. I have never forgotten you," Matthew said warmly. He pulled Sophia into his arms, and his blood raced in anticipation as his lips descended to hers. Time stood still for both of them as their passions mounted, bridging those long years of separation. Matthew exulted that he had found her again—until reality seared his mind. He released Sophia and backed away from her, breathing deeply as though from physical exertion. His face turned a ghastly gray, and life seemed to ebb from his body.

I can't do this. I can't! He had forgotten one very important event of the past. Unable to cope with the loss of Sophia, he had renounced the world for the cloister. His vow of chastity now separated him from the woman he loved.

5

FRANKISH GAUL, 770–771

Sophia stared in disbelief as Matthew pushed her away. "I didn't think your feelings would ever change," she whispered.

"No, no. I have not ceased to love you," Matthew explained, "but after your disappearance, when I couldn't find out from anyone what had happened to you, I didn't care whether I lived or died. I became a monk."

Sophia spread her hands wide, pointing to his brocade robe, disbelief in her eyes.

"I left behind my monk's garb to come to the land of the Franks on a special mission. Once that is completed, I'm obligated to return to the monastery."

Sophia's shoulders slumped, and she turned aside. "The only thing that has sustained me during my servitude was the hope that I would see you again. I'm thankful that I have, even though the meeting has brought pain. In my dreams, I've even pictured us together at last, but there is no way now to bridge the gap between us."

Matthew took her hand and kissed it. The answer was in his tortured brown eyes. Sophia moved closer, put her hands on his shoulders and tantalizingly pressed her lips to his. The closeness of her body incited a flame that roared through Matthew like a fire, and his arms tightened around her in a grip that caused Sophia to gasp, but his lips crushing against hers stifled further protest. She squirmed in his arms, and he released her reluctantly.

"Forgive me, Matthew," she whispered, "but I had to have that much at least."

He watched her fade into the dusk before he fell prostrate on the damp ground. "Father in heaven, lead me not into temptation." Not since the day of his consecration as a monk had Matthew groveled before his Lord. In humiliation and pain, he enumerated his many sins and called upon God to forgive them. He remembered the time that Jesus, too, had suffered temptation, and how He had been victorious over the wiles of Satan. Though Matthew spent hours upon his knees in self-remorse and supplication, the next morning when he returned to the Lombard camp, he realized he had not won a victory. For him, the battle had only begun. In the excitement of the pending alliance, Sophia was busy, and she didn't approach him again.

Desiderata's agitation increased as they neared Mainz, and Matthew tried to calm her. "Do not pay attention to rumors, Princess. You may find the Frankish king more pleasant than you think."

"But how will I converse with him? I do not know the Frankish tongue," she protested.

"He speaks Latin, I believe."

Matthew found it difficult to concern himself with the problems of the princess, for with his discovery of Sophia, he had been plunged into a despondence more devastating than the despair that had first sent him to the monastery. The passions of the past haunted him day and night, as he dreamed of having Sophia in his arms again. *Would it be such a terrible thing to renounce my vows and take her as my wife? Who could stand in my way now that my father is gone?*

Gerona was quick to note Matthew's mood, and he said, "I saw you with the Lombard woman."

Matthew looked at him quickly. He knew that Gerona took

his guardianship role seriously and that he often stood watch when Matthew wandered off by himself. *How much had Gerona witnessed?*

"She's someone I knew in the past, Gerona, but I cannot talk about it."

"Strange that an aristocrat of the Trento family would be on friendly terms with a slave," Gerona said invitingly, but Matthew avoided an answer, for the Frankish city was in sight.

Matthew could tell that Desiderata's fears lessened somewhat when she and Charles met. Though the king's simple woolen robe, cut below his knees, appeared quite dowdy beside the gold-embroidered garments of his bride-to-be, his superior stature—a good head taller than the other Franks around him—was impressive. Adding to his splendor was the long sword with golden hilt and hangings swinging at his side.

King Charles and the queen mother, Bertrada, walked down the steps of the royal residence, a two-storied log and stone structure that rambled across the landscape and was surrounded with fruit trees. Barns, stables, and storage buildings were located to the rear of the king's residence, and the town of Mainz had built up around the royal quarters. Matthew found the setting pleasant to the eye, but he wondered how Desiderata would view it. Charles reached out a hand to his intended bride and drew aside her veil. Desiderata retained her composure without blinking when Charles's eyes quickly assessed her person. A smile spread across his face, indicating that he liked what he saw.

"Welcome to Frankish Gaul, Princess," he said in a high-pitched voice, which seemed out of place for such a large man. He took her hand to conduct her inside the royal residence. Angelo directed the serving women to follow the princess. Matthew could not take his eyes from Sophia as she passed into the house, but she avoided his gaze. The rest of the Lombards set up camp on the outskirts of the town, and Matthew and Gerona accepted their invitation to lodge with them.

The next day, a simple ceremony was conducted by the bishop

of Mainz to make Desiderata a wife—simple, indeed, when Matthew compared it to the wedding of the empress of Byzantium. Matthew did not attend the wedding, but everyone was invited to join in the feasting that followed the wedding vows. The celebration was held on the broad expanse in front of the palace.

Dressed in a white silk gown embroidered in gold threads and wearing a small jeweled diadem on her head, Desiderata looked like a queen. When Matthew presented his good wishes to her, he immediately discerned that the bride was distressed.

"I did not know that he already has a son nor that he had put away a wife to marry me. Do you suppose my father knew that and did not tell me?" She wrung her slender hands in agitation, the blue eyes took on a haunted look, and she shuddered. "The child is like an animal—he scampers around on his hands and knees, and his body is horribly twisted. This house is terrible— a dirt floor, animal odors all around, few windows. I don't know if I can bear it."

Although Matthew hadn't seen the court of Lombardy, he imagined that the young woman had grown up in luxurious living. He could understand that this log building with its dirt floor covered only by straw would seem a hovel to her.

"I wish I could help," he said as he squeezed her hand.

Matthew left the royal palace to wander among the throng. Not surprisingly, he encountered Drago the trader, who had set up a booth across from the palace.

"Friend Matthew," Drago called. "I didn't expect to see you here. By this time I thought you would be on your way home."

"The lure of a royal wedding enticed me," Matthew said. "How is business going today?"

"Poorly, poorly," Drago groaned, "but I hope that it will become better. I have some prized relics that the noblemen will long to have for their private collections. They will stop by when the feasting is over. The Franks are my best customers, for the cult of relics is viewed with horror by the pagans, who regard this Christian reverence for corpses as a pollution."

"What relics do you have for sale?"

"The bones of several saints. A bottle containing the blood of Saint Boniface. I even have the robe of Saint Soterius, who was beheaded at Rome for her faith during the reign of Diocletian. The king will probably pay dearly for that item."

"Why are relics prized so highly by these Franks?" Matthew inquired as he settled on a bench beside the trader.

"Oh, for many reasons. They believe the relics put them in contact with the wonder-working saints in heaven. Many think that the possession of relics protects them from natural, human, or demonic afflictions. The hopeful will travel many miles to touch relics that have reportedly bestowed health on a sickly body. King Charles has accumulated many relics, hoping they will perform a cure for his hunchbacked son."

"So the new queen is not his first wife?"

Drago guffawed lewdly. "Maybe so, maybe not. The first woman wasn't recognized by the church. Charles has always been popular with the ladies."

"What happened to the other wife? Did she die?" Matthew asked nonchalantly, for if Drago thought that Matthew greatly desired the information, he wouldn't reveal it without a fee.

"No, Charles kicked her out. She's gone back to her brother, who is a rogue of some reputation in the area. She vows vengeance on Charles for depriving her of the boy, Pepin."

"So it would seem that life may not be too pleasant for the new queen."

"One who has known the marble-floored palaces of Lombardy and the luxuries of the warm, well-favored climate of Italy will hardly feel at home in Gaul. This is another mistake of the Frankish king—he makes many of them."

When a customer approached, Matthew wandered out to the encampment of the Lombards and told Gerona to go enjoy the festivities while he stayed with their possessions. Matthew decided he would spend one more night there before moving on. He had lain awake most of the previous night praying for guidance, wondering where he should go from here. His meeting with Sophia had only compounded his problem, for the temptation was strong to renounce his vows, marry the woman, and return to take his place at the head of his father's house. If he did that, he would no longer need to search for the Alabaster.

The next morning as Matthew strolled around the area, he was approached by a servant of King Charles. "Are you Matthew, a resident of the city of Constantinople?"

Matthew inclined his head. "At your service."

"Charles, king of the Franks, has requested that you wait upon him sometime this morning."

"Very well. I have no other plans. As soon as I visit my tent, I will attend the king." Choosing three gifts from the items he had brought from home, Matthew hurried to the palace, only to be kept waiting most of the morning while the king dispensed justice among his subjects.

Charles had apparently not allowed time for a honeymoon, for he sat on a raised wooden platform in the assembly hall listening to the complaints of his subjects. The hall was a center of activity where domestic and governmental problems were aired and resolved. Clerics, bishops, and distinguished nobles fraternized with minstrels, court poets, herdsmen, and the keepers of the royal dogs and falcons.

When the hall emptied, Charles came down from the platform and motioned Matthew forward. "You are Matthew of Constantinople?"

Ordinarily, Matthew would have prostrated himself before a ruler, but he had noted that this habit of the East was omitted in the Frankish court.

Bowing, he said, "Yes, your excellency, and I would offer these gifts from my homeland. If it pleases you, a length of brocade for your new queen, an illuminated volume of the gospel of John, and a golden chalice for you."

Charles hardly looked at the piece of fabric, but his hands lovingly caressed the voluminous book, carefully lifting the cover and gazing at the pages of the book, which were decorated in the best Byzantine artwork available. "Ah, the workmanship!" He held aloft the gilded goblet depicting a scene of Christ and His disciples at the Last Supper. His big hands wonderingly smoothed out the crimson silk interlaced with golden threads, and then looked down at his woolen garment with a frown.

"Receive my thanks. This goblet will become a part of my treasure trove, the book will hold an honored place in my library, and I shall look forward to seeing my queen dressed in this fine silk. Do you plan to sojourn long in our land?"

Matthew had pondered how to explain his presence in Frankish Gaul without revealing his search for the holder of the Alabaster. *But if I don't mention the vase,* thought Matthew, *how will I ever find any clues?* For the present, he decided to avoid a direct answer. "There arises in all of us the desire to make a pilgrimage. I had often thought of visiting Rome, and while there, I heard of the Frankish lands and I moved on this way."

"I repeat my question, do you plan to stay in Gaul?"

"Not if it displeases the king."

"But that is the point, I wish you to stay. I desire to know more about the city of Constantinople and to learn how the artisans make objects like these. You're invited to become part of the court and stay as long as you like."

"In what capacity, sire?" Matthew questioned. "Surely not as a visitor."

"You could acquaint me with the history of the East and be my advisor on foreign relations. Also, our youth need some instruction in Greek and Latin, as does their king. You seem the right person to advise me on how to upgrade the culture of the Franks. You could be useful to me in many ways." He smiled wryly. "My new wife tells me that we're sadly lacking in the niceties of life."

"Does the court reside permanently at Mainz?"

"No, we headquarter at several places in a year's time. As soon as we observe Christmas, weather permitting, we'll leave here and make several visits before we come to Valenciennes. I trust that some of our stops will be more agreeable to my wife than Mainz."

"Then for the time being, at least, I will stay with you," Matthew agreed.

"You will be compensated for your services with food and board in the king's quarters, clothing from our storehouse, and a percentage of the harvest from my estate at Heristal. Does that please you?"

"More than agreeable, sire. I look forward to a sojourn in the land of the Franks."

Although Matthew spoke calmly, inside he was exhilarated. God had answered his prayers by providing an inconspicuous means of traveling in Frankish lands. Under the protection of the king, he could travel widely and have access to much information. And where the king went, his wife and her attendants would go. Not least of Matthew's joy was the fact that he would be in a position to see Sophia often.

❋ ❋ ❋

During the next two weeks, Matthew spent a few hours each day with Charles and enjoyed indulging the man's insatiable curiosity about the eastern empire. In the afternoons, he walked around the town learning on his own the differences between the barbarian West, as it was always called in Byzantium, and his own country. The town buzzed with activity because many peasants had come to town hoping to catch a glimpse of Charles and his new bride.

A few days before Christmas, Matthew passed by Drago's stall, where his servants were folding the tents in preparation for departure. "Ho, Drago, leaving us so soon? I would have thought the Christmas season would be an opportune time for you to make a profit."

The trader shook his head. "No, at Christmas the Franks are so busy feasting that they will not buy."

"It's a day of feasting, then—not worship?"

Drago eased down on a bench, where he could direct the packing, and motioned Matthew to join him. "They'll worship, too, in the cathedrals, and Charles will have services performed by one or more bishops at the palace. The Advent season starts on the fourth Sunday before Christmas Day and lasts until December 24, culminating in the midnight mass. Then the feasting starts and lasts for twelve days."

"Christmas celebrations in Byzantium are liturgical in nature, very solemn occasions observed in the churches."

Drago gave a short laugh, and his brown eyes snapped maliciously "The Franks are not so religious, although King Charles likes to parade his piety. Every manor—and this is true of Charles's estates—ceases work for several days at Christmas. The workers bring their offerings of grain to the count, or to the king, and he in turn gives them a feast. The peasants bring in logs for the yule fire and sticks to stoke the blaze. The poor must bring their own dish and mug, but the noblemen furnish food and drink."

"I'm surprised you're leaving when there will be so much free food," Matthew said jokingly.

"There are times when I cannot abide the Frankish court, and Christmas is one of them." Drago rose to give directions to his servants for the final packing of his wares, and as he climbed on his horse, the trader said, "Well, enjoy yourself, my friend Matthew. There will be plenty of bread and broth, two kinds of meat, and various savory messes. Remember me when you say your midnight mass," he added ironically.

In spite of Drago's words, Matthew looked forward to the Christmas celebration with anticipation. On Christmas Eve, he entered the crowded council hall and knelt beside Angelo, the queen's counselor from Lombardy. Charles, Desiderata, and Queen Mother Bertrada sat in their best garments at the front of the room. This was the first time Matthew had known Charles to lay aside his linen shirt, tunic, and breeches for a garment interwoven with gold, jewel-decorated shoes, and a golden crown.

The king held his dwarfling son on his knee. The queen's attendants knelt behind her chair, and Matthew was happy to note that Sophia was there. Though separated by a hundred Franks, to be in her presence made the worship more meaningful for him. For the time being, he disallowed his passion for her and considered her as a friend.

Two bishops, vested in elegant robes, stood before the assembly. A dozen monks chanted psalms from a small elevated platform behind the bishops. The chanting decreased to a whisper when a monk stepped forward to read Luke's account of the birth of Christ. The moral meaning of the feast was explained by a bishop, who referred to the epistle of Titus, where the apostle Paul had written that the incarnation of Christ enabled all people to live righteously. When the readers used selected passages from the psalms, Matthew recognized the bishops' purpose of using the Old and New Testaments to bear witness to the birth of Jesus, Son of God. The words from Psalm 110, "The Lord said to my Lord, sit on my right hand," were a prophecy of the lordship of Jesus Christ over the whole world.

Matthew left the hall assured that God, in spite of human frailties, would yet accomplish the work of His Son on earth, and that Matthew Trento would have a place in that ongoing mission.

After Christmas, Charles's court moved to Ingelheim, where the king promised Desiderata she would find a home more to her liking. Matthew personally preferred the royal residence at Mainz, for at Ingelheim only a wooden hall separated the house from the marketplace, which was banked with dung heaps where the swine rooted. The residence smelled constantly of the cow sheds next door. The only claim to culture was a hall containing some Roman paintings of fauns chasing nymphs. But Charles was proud of his accomplishments at Ingelheim. He had planted an orchard around the grain mill, where a water wheel turned

the huge stones. A brook flowed into the pond, which was popu-
lated by many waterfowl. Other birds—fine pheasants and
pigeons raised by the royal Seneschal—supplemented the supply of meat. Matthew found the orchard pleasant, for it reminded
him of the peace of the cloister. He walked there daily, where by
chance he sometimes met Sophia, who was free to take a walk
when her mistress slept.

Though Sophia often looked at him with passionate eyes, she
did not touch him again, and Matthew was careful to keep their
meetings on an impersonal level. Only to himself would he admit how much he looked forward to the few words he exchanged
with her about the affairs at the court.

"And how does your mistress like this palace?" he asked one
day.

"She hates it as she does everything else in this country—
especially the king, whom she barely tolerates. She says the
king lied to her about this place."

"Of course, King Charles has not seen anything better than
his own palaces, and he does not realize how inferior they are. I
would assume that the Lombard court was lavish."

"Not as lavish as the palace in Constantinople or the noble
houses of Greece, but the queen's home had marble baths, mosaic floors, and rooms made pleasant by tapestries. In all fairness,
this climate is not good for the queen. You are aware of the
weakness of her lungs."

"Let me know if there is any way I can help her."

"Oh, undoubtedly she will send for you. She seems to like
your conversation."

*Is it jealousy that I see gleaming in Sophia's eyes above her
veil?* Matthew groaned inwardly. He knew how she felt. He could
hardly suppress his impatience when he saw Gerona and Sophia
in conversation. It was perfectly admissible for two servants to
fellowship, but if Matthew were often in Sophia's company it
would be cause for gossip. He should go away—their own relationship was so hopeless. He needed to leave the court, complete

his search for the Alabaster, and return home, whether empty-handed or successful. *Dare I admit to myself that I don't have the courage to go away when I have only just met my beloved again?*

Matthew had grown fond of Charles, who had invited him to take the evening meal at his table, often requesting Matthew to read aloud some of the Roman classics or Greek writings. Matthew translated the works into Latin so that Charles could understand them. One evening, Charles seemed discomfited and obviously paid little attention to Matthew's reading. After a few attempts to interest him, Matthew returned the books to the bag he carried. When he rose to leave, Charles detained him. "Stay, I would talk to you after the others retire."

Charles dismissed the minstrel after only one song, and the others, taking this as their cue, also left the hall. "I have had a most disturbing letter from Pope Stephen," Charles said, immediately coming to the cause of his distress, "and I wanted to discuss it with someone. I fear that the bishops in residence will not be sympathetic to me."

"I heard in Rome that the pope was not agreeable to an alliance between the Franks and Lombards," Matthew commented.

"That is a mild assessment of his reaction. In this letter, he says that the Lombards are not fit to be counted among the inhabitants of the earth—that they're treacherous, odorous, and as tainted as lepers. Marriage to one of them would be equal to contaminating oneself with a savage. The pope evidently thought this letter would reach me before the marriage. He addressed this to my brother, too. Here, you read it!" He thrust the parchment toward Matthew.

The pope had heard that Desiderius, king of the Lombards, was trying to unite his daughter to one of the Frankish kings. Charles's father had promised firm friendship with Saint Peter's successors, and Pope Stephen reminded Charles that papal enemies were to be Frankish enemies, and papal friends, Frankish friends.

Charles interrupted Matthew's reading. "And I well remember that pledge, too. The pope journeyed across the Alps in the wintertime when I was a boy of twelve, and my father sent me to meet him. Stephen II, bedecked in sackcloth and ashes, prostrated himself before my father and begged for help against the Lombard king. The Frankish noblemen joined my father in promising protection of the papacy against that proud tyrant."

When Charles fell silent, Matthew read, "If either of you brothers marry the Lombard princess, you will have broken your promise to the papacy." Matthew laid the message aside. "Why have you shared this with me? I'm not in a position to advise you."

"I'm troubled, and I needed to talk to someone. The bishops are not in sympathy with my second marriage and now the pope is angry with me. Am I in danger of losing my immortal soul, Matthew? That troubles me."

"It does not lay in the power of the bishops nor the pope to determine the destiny of your soul. When Christ died on the cross, He paid the penalty for all your sins. If you accept that sacrifice and have faith in Him, your soul is safe with Him through eternity."

"I have never heard such words before. What about the penance for sins?"

"If you sin willfully, you will suffer the consequences for your sin, but that does not mean your soul is lost."

"Those words are hard for me to comprehend. I will think more upon them. My immediate problem is what answer shall I give to the pope?"

"What answer can you give him except that you have already married Princess Desiderata? And surely the king of Frankish Gaul is man enough to keep the promise to the pope regardless of whom his father-in-law might be."

"You're right," Charles said, obviously relieved. "I will tell the pope to notify me about the activities of the Lombards, and that I will continue to keep the faith of my father to the papacy."

He paused and a look of misery covered his face. "I understand from my wife that you are schooled in medicine."

"Somewhat."

Charles hesitated. "I wonder if there is anything you can do for my poor twisted boy. He's a bright little fellow and has great potential, it seems, but he's so misshapen that he can never lead a normal life. I've exhausted all possibility of cures in Gaul." His troubled eyes gleamed hopefully. "I would pay any amount to get a whole body for him."

"I'm sorry, your excellency. All I can do is dispense herbs and other medicines. Your son needs surgery that I do not know how to perform. As far as I know, no doctor has been able to surgically straighten a hunchback. I'm indeed sorry."

"Poor boy. He'll never have a chance to succeed me, for the king of the Franks must be a strong man. Would to God he were like Waldulf."

"Waldulf, sire?"

"A young man of my acquaintance with all of the qualities for greatness. You will see him when we resume our journey. He is the son of Count Willehad, and I always sojourn with them when I go out to survey my domains. In fact, I intend to be at the manor in two weeks for Waldulf's coming-of-age exercises. Perhaps you will join me."

"I would be honored, sire."

6

Frankish Gaul, 771

He had stood patiently in the same spot for more than an hour, his gloved hand held aloft as a perch for the trained falcon. A mixture of sleet and rain drenched his clothing, and the boisterous wind ruffled his long hair. Occasionally, he lifted his left hand and wiped moisture from his eyes, but he stayed in place on the high knoll.

He searched the horizon, but no birds appeared. The falcon's strong claws tightened around the boy's gloved hand, and his master envisioned the impatient dark eyes behind the blindfold. Waldulf murmured reassuringly to the bird, and patted the long, pointed wings curving backward into a sickle shape. The falcon excitedly opened its beak, showing the sawlike edges and notches.

Numbness moved slowly from the top of Waldulf's arm to the tip of his fingers, but his body tensed as he heard a sound from the river. The haze was too thick for him to see the ducks, but the eager twisting of the falcon on his hand indicated a flock rising from the water. He jerked off the blind, gave the command, and the hawk catapulted from his hand and in seconds was lost to view.

Waldulf wiggled his fingers and a tingling sensation chased away the numbness, but his hand was soon aloft again when the squawking falcon reappeared carrying a duck, neatly killed from a powerful bite to the neck. Twice more Waldulf gave the command and the hawk swooped away to return with its prey. The last fowl became dinner for the hawk, but the boy lifted the other two ducks, and with a smile headed down the hill toward the manor. This assignment from his tutor had a twofold purpose he was sure; it was an endurance test as well as a check on his fowling skill. Waldulf was happy—he had passed both tests.

The rain and mist had dissipated by the time Waldulf reached the manor. Leaving the ducks in the kitchen, he reported to his tutor and then turned into the main hall of the manor house. He had left this morning without eating, and he needed a repast. No one had any time for him, so he snatched a loaf of bread off the table when the cook wasn't looking and went to lounge before the fire. Steam soon rose from his wet clothing, and he dozed contentedly.

Waldulf was rudely awakened by his mother, Adela, who cried, "Waldulf! Go and make yourself presentable. The king is expected momentarily."

"It's only Charles," the boy said sleepily. "He comes here every year. You know he isn't concerned about clothing. He'll probably look worse than I do."

"I imagine you'll see a distinct difference in his appearance, especially now that he's married to the princess of Lombardy."

"What happened to Himiltrud?" Waldulf inquired.

"Don't ask tiresome questions, son. Go and change into clean clothing."

The royal entourage was approaching by the time Waldulf returned to the main hall, and he stood beside his father on the front steps of the manor house to receive the guests.

"Just as I predicted," Waldulf said quietly to his mother, as he observed that Charles was covered by a hooded headdress, a shirt of rude linen, with an outer vest of otter skin protecting his shoulders and chest. His legs were wrapped in narrow strips of cloth, and he wore heavy shoes normally used for hunting or fighting. Compared to Count Willehad, who had donned an embroidered silk tunic over woolen trousers, the king of Frankish Gaul looked dowdy.

Charles dismounted, and after a bowed greeting to Count Willehad, he moved to the enclosed carriage that had followed his armed escort. He handed down his bride, who wore a great mantle over a large-sleeved tunic, fastened at the waist with a jeweled belt. A gold bandeau and a gem-studded headdress held her veil, which had been thrown back to reveal a pallid face. Her lackluster blue eyes stared haughtily at the sodden landscape and the rambling log dwelling.

"Who would choose that insipid woman as a wife for the churlish Charles?" Waldulf whispered to his mother, who silenced him with a menacing glare as she moved forward with the count to greet the king and queen.

"Welcome to Willehad Manor," the count said.

With difficulty, it seemed, Charles timed his steps to those of his wife. He shook Willehad's hand, and then bowed low over Adela's outstretched fingers. "I have looked forward to this visit, especially to witness Waldulf's manhood ceremonies." He turned to Waldulf and his eyes lit with admiration. "Blast me, if you're not the finest specimen of manhood I've seen in many a day." He turned and called to one of the men who'd ridden with him. "Come here, Matthew."

Matthew dismounted wearily. He was not used to so many hours in the saddle.

"This is Waldulf, the lad I spoke to you about just a few days past. Is it any wonder that I covet a son like him?"

The boy, almost intimidatingly tall for one of his age, stepped forward to meet Matthew with a friendly, unspoiled manner. Waldulf possessed an open countenance, fair, wavy hair, and a sparkle of animation in his blue-green eyes.

"You must make Matthew's acquaintance, Waldulf," the king said. "He's a learned man recently come to us from Constantinople. You can benefit from time spent in his company."

Count Willehad beamed at his son. "Why don't you entertain Matthew during his stay here, Waldulf? Perhaps he can indulge that insatiable curiosity of yours."

"It will be my pleasure. Come, sir, I'll conduct you to a room. After you've refreshed yourself, I'll show you around the manor."

Waldulf guided Matthew to a log barracks behind the main house, explaining that the guest rooms in the manor were filled with the royal family and their servants.

"This will not be luxury lodging, sir, but it should suffice for your needs. The churls have provisioned it with the necessities. I'll wait here until you're finished," he said, indicating a bench beneath a nearby beech tree.

A short time later when Matthew emerged, he joined Waldulf on the bench. "Tell me about yourself, Waldulf."

"But I'm to learn from you," Waldulf countered.

"Which you will, but I'm interested to know more about you."

"Tomorrow will mark my fourteenth year, when among the Franks one is considered to have reached manhood. I will have to prove my skill in any way that my tutor asks me to."

"Are you uneasy about the performance?"

"No, sir, for I've had a good tutor, and he has worked with me relentlessly for more than two years. I should acquit myself well," Waldulf replied, without any hint of arrogance.

Waldulf proved to be a good guide, and he evidenced a love for his home as they sauntered around the manor grounds, which Matthew considered more imposing than the king's estates he had seen thus far. Willehad Manor consisted of a complex of buildings protected by a wooden stockade. The family residence, guest chambers, kitchen, and storerooms were built facing inward around an open courtyard. Outside the stockade were the stable, barns, grain storage, workshops, and quarters for the servants. A tall watchtower overlooked the encircling countryside dotted with cottages and cultivated fields. Cattle and horses grazed in another wooden enclosure. The fields were barren at the time, but they were plowed and smoothed down in readiness for the planting of grain in the spring. Waldulf pointed out a church in a quiet setting not far from the stockade.

"The priest spends most of his time at the manor, praying over our meals, often joining Father on hunts. He says a ritual in this building on Sundays for the workers."

The small church was surrounded by a cemetery, and as they approached, Waldulf said, "Many of our relatives are here—a brother and sister of mine. My parents were not fortunate in having a large family. I'm the only one to survive."

"How far back can your ancestry be traced in this region?" Matthew asked curiously.

"For centuries. My Germanic ancestors settled here long before the coming of the Romans."

So much for the hope that Waldulf's family might have emigrated from the Rhone Valley! Matthew thought.

The priest came to the door of the small church, and when Waldulf made the introductions, Matthew said, "Have you been here long, Father?"

"No, only a few years, but I was at a neighboring manor for several years."

"Then you would probably know many people hereabouts. Have you ever heard of anyone named Conrad or Trento? That would be a family name, not a given one."

"No, I do not believe so, but I will think about it and check back into the parish records."

As they moved on, Waldulf said, "My father travels widely, sometimes on missions for the king—he may know of these people you're seeking. Have you come to Gaul searching for them?"

Matthew evaded the question. "I'm interested in knowing if any of my relatives may have come here many years ago."

Count Willehad had declared the next day a holiday in honor of his son's coming-of-age ceremony, so nobility and laborers gathered in the large field outside the stockade. A small platform had been erected to seat the royal party and Waldulf's parents. Everyone else sat on the ground or stood.

Waldulf was dressed in a green silk tunic, which fell gracefully over woolen breeches. He wore a white mantle around his shoulders that clasped in front with a silver buckle. He stood to one side of the throng without showing any emotion except a gleam of eagerness and anticipation in his blue-green eyes.

Count Willehad opened the ceremonies. "This is a great day for my household. It is also a day of remembrance. This week I've been recalling scenes from my son's childhood—when he took his first step, the first time he mounted a horse. I was on a mission for King Pepin at the time of Waldulf's birth, but I came home when he was two months old and held him in my arms for the first time. I loved the boy dearly, which I still do until this day."

Willehad sat down, and Waldulf's tutor, a burly, squat man, stepped forward. "It has been my pleasure to work with young Waldulf for the past two years, and I present him to you today as a 'man' worthy of your family."

A mighty war horse was led into the area below the spectators. Waldulf ran toward the horse, and with one leap was astride the animal's back. Kicking the horse into a gallop, he unlooped the bow from his back, fitted arrows, and shot at targets situated around the area. In each instance, the arrow hit the center of the mark.

A hooded falcon was brought to him, and Waldulf placed a heavy glove on his right hand where the bird perched. Still astride the horse guiding it with his knees, Waldulf's eyes scanned the skies. When he saw a flock of pigeons lift from a nearby field, he jerked the blindfold from the falcon and gave the command for flight. Within a few minutes, the falcon returned with a pigeon in its claws.

The tutor turned to Willehad. "You have seen the expertise of your son in hunting. Is there anything else you would see him do?"

"Perhaps his skill in physical combat?" the count suggested.

Waldulf dismounted and disrobed until he stood naked to the waist. The spectators applauded the brawniness of the lad as the absence of clothing revealed his muscular torso. At a motion from the tutor, an older man, as well-built as Waldulf but with more weight, was brought forward. The tutor tossed a leather mat on the ground.

The two contestants approached from opposite sides of the mat, circling and maneuvering to gain an advantage. Waldulf's opponent made the first contact when he grabbed Waldulf's ankle and drove his body backward, but Waldulf broke from his grasp without losing his footing. Closing again, the two wrestlers came to grips in a standing position, but when neither of them could force the other down on the mat, the tutor broke their hold and commanded them to start over.

Once Waldulf forced his opponent down and grabbed his thigh in an effort to gain enough leverage to press him back on the mat, but the other wrestler broke Waldulf's hold and struggled away from him. The match continued until both wrestlers, the advantage often passing from one to the other, dripped with perspiration and panted loud enough for the spectators to hear. Finally, the tutor pronounced the combat a draw. The two combatants shook hands and flopped down on the mat side by side to regain their breath.

The crowd cheered and Count Willehad stated his satisfaction. Although he had not won a victory, Waldulf had held his own against a superior opponent.

The tutor mounted the steps and stood in front of Willehad. "I present your son—no longer a boy, but a man."

The tutor stepped aside, and Waldulf struggled into his tunic and mantle and approached his father, who beheld him with worshipful eyes.

"It is the destiny of Frankish noblemen to be at the disposal of their king, to be fit to follow him into battle. You have proven today that you have the capabilities of a true warrior. Therefore, I present your personal sword." The count reached behind his seat and brought forth a long sword with a jewel-embellished hilt protruding from a leather sheath.

Waldulf took the sword. "I declare the name of this sword to be Wildsong. It will become my constant companion until the day I die." He hooked the sword to his belt, knelt before his king, and took the oath of fidelity. "I swear to my lord, Charles the king, to keep faith with him all the rest of my life without deceit or ill will."

The king acknowledged Waldulf's oath with a solemn nod, and a great cheer arose from the crowd. After the ceremonies were over, a great feast was held in honor of Waldulf's achievements.

As the day came to a close, King Charles approached Matthew and said, "The time has come that we must move on. Tomorrow we will visit a monastery not far from here. Then we will continue our journey to the other royal estates."

"Yes, your excellency," Matthew replied. As the king stepped away to speak once again with young Waldulf, Matthew thought about visiting the monastery. *How will it feel to be back in that familiar world after all that has happened?*

❋   ❋   ❋

When they reached the monastery, a half-hour's ride from Willehad Manor, a lanky monk stood on the front step to greet Charles and his entourage. "It is my pleasure to welcome you to the monastery."

Charles peered intently at the face shadowed by the hood. "Why, it's Father Sturm. We have not seen you for many months."

"I am not often at the monastery. I have been on missionary journeys into Saxony and Bavaria."

Sturm conducted them to a receiving room to the right of the main hall. "In the absence of the abbot, how may I help you?"

"I simply wanted to pay my respects to the abbot, but since you're here, I will discuss the Saxon problem with you. You say you have been there recently?"

"I returned a month ago from Westfalia."

"I had hoped to take the field against those pagans last year,"

Charles said ferociously, "but conditions in the south of my kingdom prevented that."

"If you go to war against the Saxons, you will destroy the work we are trying to do. Warfare and the teachings of Jesus do not mix."

Charles looked at him in amazement. "But I thought it would be helpful to your efforts if the pagans were subdued."

Sturm shook his head. "Subdued, perhaps, but not scourged. Jesus said to love our enemies, not to destroy them with the sword."

"I know no other way, Father," Charles said, and his face was stony. "The Saxons have repudiated the treaty they made with my father—that is a slap in the face to the Carolingian line. I intend to see that they keep their pledge."

"There is nothing I can do about it if that is your choice, but I have warned you before that the Saxons will not be an easy conquest. They live in isolated villages in a trackless forest, a bewildering maze to the stranger, and Widukind is a wily leader. It will not be easy to wage war in Saxony."

"The Franks have faced difficult situations before, and we've prevailed."

Sturm smiled wanly. "It is your choice."

"I thought I might appease Pope Stephen if I warred against the Saxons. He is displeased because I have taken a new wife."

Sturm made no reply, and the silence lengthened in the room until Charles said belligerently, "Well, what do you think about it?"

"The church has not yet passed a mandate that a man cannot put away his wife, but it is becoming customary—one man for one wife. There are situations where divorcing one's wife might be justified, but if I understand the situation correctly, you had no such justification."

Charles rose to his feet angrily and seemed almost on the verge of striking the candid priest, but he controlled the impulse, instead saying heatedly, "It's sometimes expedient to make political marriages."

"I will not argue the case with you. You asked for my

opinion—you have it. A king should set an example for his people. Since you count yourself a defender of the church, be a worthy example."

"If I loved my enemies instead of fighting them, it wouldn't be long until the Franks were destroyed. I live a devout life in private, but it is not practical to carry piety onto the battlefield."

When Sturm gave no answer to this comment, Charles prepared to exit. "Even if we do not agree, I would like to call you 'friend' and consult with you from time to time," he said to the priest.

"You honor me, and we shall be friends. Now, if you'll follow me, I'll lead you to the dining area. The monks have prepared refreshment for the king and his party."

As Matthew walked about the small monastery, he felt as if he had come home, for he had missed the serenity and spiritual environment of the cloister. Every time he thought he was adjusting to the secular world, something would remind him of his vows and his commitment to the secluded life. It had been two years now since he had left Constantinople, and although he'd unearthed a few clues, he was still far from finding the Alabaster. More than once he had been tempted to go home and claim the estate himself, especially when he considered buying Sophia's freedom and taking her for his wife. This visit to the cloister put a damper on his dreams by reminding him of his vows.

When the royal party was preparing to leave the monastery and return to Willehad Manor, Matthew approached Sturm. "I would like a private audience, Father, and we leave the area tomorrow. May I talk with you today?"

"The hour before the evening vespers, if you like," Sturm suggested.

"I'll be here if at all possible," Matthew replied.

The sun was not far from the horizon when Matthew hurried toward the monastery. Sturm waited for him, and they huddled on a wooden bench beneath a widespread oak tree. The winter breeze was brisk, discouraging delay, so Matthew quickly explained his reason for being in Frankish Gaul.

"I'm becoming discouraged, Father Sturm. It's been two years now, and I have no idea what to do next."

"How may I help you?"

"As I understand, you have journeyed far and wide in this land. Have you ever encountered any family named Trento or Conrad?"

"I do not believe so. Of course, if that is a family name, I might not have heard. It isn't customary among us to use a surname."

"Then my task seems almost hopeless."

"I would not encourage you overmuch," Sturm said, "but I believe that with God all things are possible. If it is His good pleasure, you will be successful in your search."

"Thank you, Father. You've strengthened my resolve. It does seem to be important. My ancestor, Suetonius Trento, charged the holder of the Alabaster to perpetuate the message that Christ died for our sins and arose on the third day. Because of what He did, we do not have to work for our own salvation. Do you agree that this message is needed in our day?"

"Yes, but I doubt that our people can understand those words. Even our king believes that he has to earn religious favor by waging war. I had hoped he might subdue his neighbors through peaceful means, and I offered that option to him. Sad to say, I do not think he will heed my advice. But as for your problem, I would persevere."

Though Sturm had answered all his questions, Matthew left the conference with a feeling of disquiet. *Why do I feel the priest is not telling everything that he knows?*

❀   ❀   ❀

The king and his court left Willehad Manor the next day on a tour to show Charles's new bride the royal estates, none of which pleased the queen. The journey was delayed when Desiderata once again fell ill. Matthew was assigned to doctor her, a task that was to his liking because it gave him an excuse to spend some time in Sophia's company.

As Desiderata recovered, she often engaged him in conversation. "Matthew," she said plaintively one day, "you're the only one who seems to understand why I am not happy here. No one else realizes that this country is barbaric. My husband talks of his pagan neighbors, the Saxons. Surely, they can't be worse than the Franks. You're from Constantinople and you've seen Rome. You do understand my problem, don't you?"

"Yes, I do, but have you explained to the king why you're dissatisfied? He's really trying to please you."

Desiderata went on as if Matthew hadn't spoken. "And this endless traveling around the country! Why can't he stay in one place and build a worthy palace?"

"Instead of storing enough provisions at one estate to sustain his court through the year, it seems advisable for the king and his household to travel from one place to another. Also, each dwelling is cleaned after the king and his party leave."

"Clean! That's another thing—castaway food is littered all around the dining hall. I wouldn't think of eating there."

Her refusal to eat in the dining hall had caused the biggest rift between Charles and his queen. Lombard pages carried specially prepared food to Desiderata on silver platters, and she drank from glass goblets. Matthew felt sorry for her, but he could see Charles's point also. Matthew understood that it would not be pleasant for the robust Charles to have such a finicky wife, and Sophia had also confided to him that Desiderata rarely opened her chamber door to the king.

Despite Desiderata's displeasure at traveling, the royal court continued to journey throughout Charles's domain. Although Charles had indicated his intention to fight against the Saxons, he was not ready for the campaign during 771, for it was the king's habit to make maps and study in depth any area that he planned to invade. These usual preparations had been delayed while Charles courted his queen. Since their relationship was strained, the king had little to show for his efforts.

Matthew didn't share the queen's displeasure at seeing the

country. Though by the end of the summer he had made no progress toward finding the Alabaster, he had enjoyed observing the physical facets of Gaul. Deep bays indented the rugged coast of the channel between Gaul and the English kingdoms, giving way to low, rounded hills and rolling plains farther inland. The northernmost region consisted of a flat area that was broken by forest-covered hills and drained by several major rivers. The soil there was highly fertile, and grain fields contributed much to the kingdom's food supply. Farther west near the Saxon border, the wooded area was rugged, but on the Rhine Valley's steep slopes and flat bottomlands, livestock grazed contentedly and farmers raised a variety of grains and legumes.

In midsummer, the royal court had arrived at a village in Alemanni by invitation of Duke Gottfrid so that Charles might be present at the harvesting fair. The duke also wanted Charles's bishops to consecrate the relics that the king had secured for the parish church. As they approached the village, Duke Gottfrid and his family rode out to meet the royal guests.

"You honor us by this visit," the duke said to Charles as he bowed before him. A pretty girl came forward with a sheaf of flowers for Desiderata, and when she curtsied before the king, he lifted her hand and kissed it. The girl blushed crimson before she ran back to the duke's side.

"My niece, Your Excellency," the duke said.

Citizens lined the street waving and cheering at the royal party as they entered the village. "It seems that the king is quite popular here," Matthew said to Gerona, who rode beside him.

"Yes, King Charles bought the relics of Saint Soterius from the trader Drago, who brought them from Italy. The saint was beheaded during the reign of Diocletian when she would not sacrifice to pagan gods. I believe she was a woman of noble birth who dedicated herself to God."

Matthew looked at his servant in admiration. *Where did he learn all of these things?* But Gerona's easy manner and friendliness encouraged confidences, and Matthew didn't doubt his words. However, if Drago had furnished the relics, Matthew could only hope that the king had not been duped into buying the bones of some ordinary Roman. Matthew had watched too many of Drago's negotiations not to be suspicious of everything he did, and Drago made no secret of his loathing for Charles. He would like nothing better than to best the king of the Franks in a business deal.

"This village may very well become a pilgrimage for people hoping for physical and spiritual cures," Matthew said. "There isn't another shrine close by."

"I see there's a market ahead. One of the king's advisors told me that it's been set up for this special occasion, but it might become permanent now that they have these relics."

"Speaking of Drago, I see he's in business here." The colorful striped tent of the trader was easily spotted. "I don't believe he ever misses an opportunity to turn a profit. One never knows where he'll next be seen."

As they passed his tent, Drago acknowledged them by motioning toward his wares. "Special relics, icons from the East, Italian marbles for sale," he shouted.

"It always pays to watch your pockets when that one is around," Gerona said after they'd passed on.

They ceased their conversation when they heard fiddle music and observed several dancers swirling to the music in the middle of the street. "Look!" Gerona said. "There's the duke's niece again."

The dark-haired beauty bowed before the royal party and held out her hand to the king. Smiling, he dismounted, clasped the girl's hand, and swung into the dance with her. For one so large, Charles was surprisingly light on his feet.

"What is your name, damsel?" Charles asked.

"Hildegard," she answered in a shy, pleasing voice. "We welcome you to our feast day."

Charles found her hands firm and warm, and her friendliness

especially welcome after the coldness he had been experiencing from his wife. The music ended and Hildegard disappeared into the crowd. Charles stared after her longingly.

Gerona said softly, "The king always has eyes for a pretty face. It's a good thing the damsel left him."

Matthew looked down when he felt a tug on his boot. Sophia stood beside him. "Do you know who she is?" she asked, pointing in the direction where Hildegard had been.

"The duke introduced the girl as his niece. I assume that she comes from a noble Swabian family."

"The queen saw them dancing, and she is displeased. I will stay with her for awhile."

Matthew and Gerona exchanged glances as Sophia slipped away through the crowd to Desiderata's carriage.

The parish church was too small to accommodate even half the crowd, who watched excitedly as Charles presented a reliquary to Duke Gottfrid. The reliquary was about a foot high and the sides were covered with pearls and precious stones. Twelve red rubies formed a cross in the center of one side. According to Gerona's informant, the relics were encased in blood-soaked earth from the saint's grave.

Duke Gottfrid handed the reliquary to the parish priest, and a procession of priests and bishops preceded the relics into the church, followed by the duke and King Charles. Quietly, Matthew joined in their chanting as the relics were blessed, earning him a searching look from those around him.

Noontime was marked by feasting and singing in the village square, but the festivities halted when two pilgrims approached Charles, one man leaning heavily upon the other.

"Mercy! Mercy!" they called.

"Who are these men?" Charles demanded of the duke.

"Pilgrims from Rome, sire."

"Ask them to approach me."

When the two men came closer, it was obvious that one of them was blind.

"What has caused your misfortune, man?" the king inquired.

"We have been to Rome. Brothers, the two of us. We'd saved for years to finance this journey of a lifetime, but alas, it turned into agony. The Lombards are terrorizing the streets of Rome, and my brother was blinded by the mobs. The pope fears that the Lombards will soon take control of all the papal lands."

Charles swore and rose to his feet angrily. "How do they dare to perpetrate such actions?"

"Who's to stop them?" the pilgrim answered. "The Bavarians will not—the king of Bavaria is the son-in-law of Desiderius, the Lombard leader. And I met no Frankish army on its way to the Italian peninsula as I crossed the Alps. The pope has no army, so who is there to protect the papal lands?"

Charles raised his fist to strike the man for his impudence, but he controlled his anger and spoke to his chamberlain. "Give these men enough provisions to take them on their way."

Charles's anger still raged when his council gathered around him for the evening meal. "What a mistake when I agreed to marry a Lombard princess! Why did I allow my mother to influence my decision? Where do my loyalties lie—to my mother? to my wife? to my father's memory? to the church?"

"The Scriptures teach that one must forsake his family in order to do his duty to the church," one of the bishops who sat by his side rejoined.

Charles gave no reply to this comment, and Matthew had learned that when Charles thought most deeply he said the least. He waved everyone out of the room, and Matthew wondered what decision would come from this time of solitude. He knew that Charles normally wanted a group of people around him.

❀　❀　❀

The next day, the royal party moved on to Charles's residence at Frankfurt. On the day following their arrival, Charles sent for Matthew early in the morning, even before Matthew had dressed for the day. Without breakfasting, he hurriedly answered the king's summons.

"Friend Matthew," Charles said immediately when Matthew entered the bedchamber where the king was dressing. "I want to have an audience with the queen, and since she is friendly with you, I believe it would be well for you to be present. I have sent word that I must see her—will you go to her bedchamber and escort her into the council hall?"

At this hour, Matthew hardly expected Desiderata to be out of bed, let alone dressed, but when he knocked on the door, he was admitted by Sophia. He answered her questioning look with a shrug. Desiderata stood in the middle of the room, fully dressed.

"What is the meaning of this outrage?" she demanded of Matthew. "It isn't even dawn."

"I do not know. The king asked me to escort you to his presence. Did his messenger awaken you?"

"As it happens, I'm unwell this morning, and I was already awake."

Matthew decided she must be ill, for Desiderata leaned heavily on his arm as they descended the stairs. Matthew marveled at her courage, for he didn't detect any sign of fear when she stood before Charles. She bowed slightly in deference to her husband.

"I no longer want you for a wife," Charles said bluntly, and at those words, Desiderata lost her composure. If it had not been for Matthew's steady arm supporting her, she would have sunk to the floor. "You must pack your belongings and leave immediately," the king stated coldly.

"Why?" she whispered through lips that seemed too stiff to move.

"I do not have to give you a reason. It is my desire that you no longer be my queen. I will order a group of soldiers to escort you to Lombardy. Be ready to leave at midday. Matthew, I would like for you to be a part of the envoy to ensure her safe passage."

A flush of anger shaded Desiderata's face, and with an effort she lifted her head and turned her back on Charles. As they left the room, Queen Mother Bertrada entered, and she hurried to

Desiderata. "What is wrong?" she asked, but Desiderata shook her head.

Bertrada turned toward Charles. "What have you done?" she demanded.

"I'm divorcing Desiderata. I no longer want her for a wife."

"My son, think of the implications. You are making an enemy of the Lombard king."

"Mother, it is time that you realize *I* am the ruler of the Franks. If I had not followed your advice, I would not have married this woman who has brought me nothing but unhappiness. Though I revere you above all women, I will not tolerate your involvement in state affairs again. You may stay at this court as long as you wish, but you are forbidden to meddle ever again in either my political or personal affairs."

Matthew looked at Bertrada's slumped shoulders. He had never heard Charles use such harsh language to his mother, and he doubted that he had ever done so before. Sobbing, Bertrada brushed by Matthew and Desiderata.

The rejected queen dropped Matthew's arm and walked on tottering steps up the stairway.

"A word with you, Matthew," the king called. "I suppose you think I'm wrong?" he said belligerently when Matthew halted.

"Yes, I do," Matthew said evenly. *What do I have to lose in speaking my opinion?* "Even if you wanted to depose your wife, you could have done it in a more kindly manner."

"But the woman has caused me to break my father's commitment to the papal state," Charles protested.

"Put the blame where it belongs. Certainly Desiderata had nothing to do with this marriage. She was only a political pawn used by her father."

"She's barren. I need a wife to bear me strong sons."

Matthew didn't answer. Obviously the king's conscience had weighed on him and he was trying to outreason it with his arguments.

"If the king will excuse me, I must prepare for this journey you've requested me to take," Matthew stated quietly.

"Are you coming back?"

"I do not know."

"I would like you to return. I need people around me who will not always agree with me. You have been a steadying influence in my kingdom."

If Queen Desiderata leaves, Sophia will be gone from Gaul, too. Matthew wasn't sure he wanted to stay any longer.

7

A heavily veiled Desiderata descended the steps, surrounded by her Lombardy servants. Charles, at the doorway holding his son, made no gesture of farewell, nor did the deposed queen look in his direction. Though her head was bowed, she walked proudly, back erect. Before her servants lifted Desiderata into the curtained wagon that had brought her to the land of the Franks, Bertrada came from the house and embraced her. The queen mother said no word, but she faced her son defiantly as she reentered the house.

Angelo, the Lombardy royal representative who had come to Gaul with Desiderata, stood by the carriage and addressed Charles. "We will meet again, king of the Franks—without doubt on the battlefield. King Desiderius will not take kindly to his daughter's disgrace."

Charles made no response, refusing to credit the man's taunts. Since he had yielded to impulse and repudiated his wife, his thoughts had dwelt more and more on the attractive girl he had met at the celebration a few weeks ago. What he needed now was a hunting trip. *Perhaps if I hunt in the Swabian forests, I might come home with more than four-footed trophies.* The thought was not unpleasant to him.

Charles stolidly watched the Lombard caravan until it

disappeared from sight, then he entered the council hall, calling to his servants, "Make ready for a hunting expedition! We leave at daybreak tomorrow." He handed Pepin to the child's personal servant. "I'll be taking the boy along with me, so you prepare to go also." Charles would be sure that his next wife had a chance to see his handicapped boy before they wed. He wouldn't have another woman who deliberately spurned his firstborn.

Riding on the left flank of the former queen's caravan, Matthew wondered about the repercussions of this episode. *Can Charles afford to estrange a neighbor as powerful as the Lombards? Does he dare to offend the church by divorcing another wife? Can he do without the advice and affection of his mother? And what is to become of Desiderata?* Matthew admitted that she and Charles were ill-matched and that she would probably be happier in her father's palace, but he realized that as "used goods" she would be an unlikely candidate for another marriage.

Angelo had absolutely refused to permit any Franks to travel with them but had made no objection to the presence of Matthew and Gerona. As the Lombardy procession moved southward, Matthew silently contemplated Sophia's future. *Can I allow her to go out of my life again?* That was the reason he hadn't given King Charles a promise to return to Gaul. Surely Desiderata must feel some obligation toward him. *Would she be receptive to my desire to buy Sophia's freedom? And if she were free, what then?* Matthew's pulse quickened at the possibility, but every time he thought about wedding his beloved, his conscience drove him to his knees to ask for forgiveness. *My beloved or my God? What a choice to make.*

The caravan had all the appearance of a funeral procession, and Matthew compared the solemnity to the joy of twelve months ago, when he had accompanied the princess on her wedding journey. That had been a pleasant time when both Lombards and Franks exulted in their new friendship. There was no merrymaking this time. Matthew hadn't seen Desiderata speak to anyone. All day she sat in the secrecy of the carriage, usually with Sophia for company. When they stopped for noon, she secreted herself in a tent until it was time to move on. At night, her food was carried into the tent by her companions. Matthew had signaled to Sophia to join him on more than one occasion, but she always shook her head guardedly, making him wonder why the queen was keeping her servants with her all of the time.

On the sixth day, the procession didn't move out as usual, and Gerona brought the news, "The queen is ill. We won't be moving today."

"How do you know that?" Matthew asked.

"I saw Sophia for a few minutes, and she told me."

Matthew looked suspiciously at Gerona. *Why would Sophia meet with him?* Instantly ashamed of his reaction, Matthew said, "Then I'll probably be requested to attend her before long."

Angelo came with the summons before midmorning, and Matthew followed the Lombard to the queen's tent. Desiderata reclined on a bench with pillows bolstering her body. Matthew noted at a glance that she wasn't suffering from her chronic lung ailment. After she greeted him, Desiderata sat for several minutes in silence. Matthew risked a quick glance toward Sophia, who knelt by the queen holding her hand.

Speaking at last, she said, "What I say to you now will require your confidence."

"As you wish," Matthew said solemnly.

"I'm with child."

Matthew was speechless as he swept the woman's body with a quick glance. Beneath the light covering, it was easy to discern that Desiderata's pregnancy was far advanced.

"Does the king know?" he asked quietly.

She shook her head, and for several minutes, the only sound in the tent was the former queen's labored breathing.

As experienced as Charles was with women, he wondered how she had been able to keep this pregnancy from him. Perhaps this was the reason she had repeatedly denied the king his conjugal rights.

"Why didn't you tell him?" Matthew dared to remonstrate. "He wouldn't have sent you away if he'd known this. Your infertility was one reason he gave to me for your banishment."

Desiderata closed her eyes and made no answer.

"Perhaps the queen doesn't want any unsolicited advice," Matthew said, "but it's imperative that you return to Gaul."

She shook her head stubbornly. "No. I hate the thought of bearing his child. I don't want it. That's why I sent for you."

Matthew's eyes narrowed. "If you wish to end the pregnancy, I shall refuse to help you. Even should I agree to such an action, the queen's life would be endangered. How far into this pregnancy are you?"

"The child is due to arrive at any time. I am not thinking to destroy the child. I simply do not want a reminder of the miserable year I've spent with the Franks. As soon as the child is born, I want you to take it away—for the child's sake as well as my own. If my father and King Charles know of this child, they'll use it as a political pawn, one against the other. I would not want a child of mine to go through what I have endured." She looked pointedly at him. "Will you do it?"

Stunned by her request, Matthew couldn't speak at first, but he finally stammered out a reply. "Gerona and I are ill equipped to take care of a baby. This is a desolate area—what could I do with this child?"

"If you do not agree to this, I will not bear the child. I don't need your help—I have a Lombard midwife among my servants who is wise in the ways of ending pregnancies."

"But you are sure to die yourself!" Matthew protested.

"I do not care." The hopelessness in Desiderata's voice as well as the determination in her unhappy eyes convinced Matthew that she spoke the truth.

"Will not those in your entourage report this matter to your father?"

"They'll take a vow of secrecy or else they'll lose their tongues," she said venomously, and again Matthew didn't doubt she meant what she said. "Besides," she continued, "I'm expecting you to conceal this child so my father could never find it even if he looked." She struggled to a reclining position and held out a trembling hand to him. "Please, Matthew, if you have ever felt the least shred of friendship for me, hide my child."

"Allow me to think on it," Matthew said, and he left the tent. *Must I continually be involved in the affairs of Charles? I came here to find the heir of the Alabaster, and that possibility seems more and more remote as I'm drawn into the intrigues of these Westerners.* For several hours, Matthew walked through the mountain passes without appreciating the beauty of the snow-covered peaks and the noisy, swift-flowing water that tumbled down a rocky stream bed. A solution to the problem formed in his mind after a time. *The woman is desperate. But is she desperate enough to agree to my plan?*

When he returned to the camp, Sophia waited in front of the tent and told him the queen was resting but would see him later on in the day. He motioned for her to follow him out of earshot. "I have come up with a plan, but I must ask your permission before I approach the queen. I'll agree to take the child if she will grant your freedom so that you can go as its nursemaid."

Sophia gasped, and Matthew continued, "If she will not voluntarily free you, I will propose to buy your freedom. I cannot bear to see you enslaved any longer, especially by the hand of my own father."

"And then what?" Sophia asked pointedly.

"I do not understand."

"And then what?" Sophia repeated. "I'm no more equipped to care for a child than you are. It isn't a chore for a single woman. Besides, I'm not sure I want the responsibility of caring for a child of one king and the grandchild of another."

"I haven't had time to think farther than the moment. I will take care of you, Sophia—be assured of that. At times I can contemplate no greater happiness than to have you for my wife, but I do not know whether I can ever forsake the vows I've made to God."

"I told you years ago that the heir to the house of Trento should not marry a servant. I do not expect you to marry me."

"You're a high born person, and it wasn't your fault that your family was captured in warfare. Many empresses of Byzantium have come from lowlier origins than yours. That will not deter me if I can make the decision to marry. The question now—will you do as I ask?"

"It has been preying on my mind that I must leave you again, Matthew. And I would like to be free," she said slowly. After a moment, she said, "I will agree to your plan."

"Take Sophia with you!" Desiderata shrieked when Matthew presented his proposition. "She's one of my most trusted servants! I can't get along without her."

"But she would also be a trustworthy servant to care for your child. Don't you feel any responsibility for its welfare?"

"If you refuse to do my bidding, then you'll be responsible for the death of this unborn child."

"Only you, Your Eminence, will be responsible for that. Let that weigh on your mind. If I take the child, you lose Sophia. The decision is yours."

"What is she to you?" Desiderata asked suspiciously.

"A person in bondage and a worthy nursemaid for your child," he replied. He doubted the answer suited the queen, but in the end she agreed to his proposition.

While the Lombards tarried at the camp until Desiderata was able to move on, Matthew and Gerona made plans. "First, we must have some means of feeding the child until we can find a safe place for it," Matthew said. "Will you scout around and see if you can find some milk goats to take with us?"

Gerona nodded assent. "What kind of a story are we going to tell if we encounter any Franks before we put this child in a safe place? I would assume you mean to place him in a monastery?"

Another plan was forming in Matthew's mind, but he couldn't divulge it yet. "We must not forget that I have promised to provide for Sophia, too. We have quite a task on our hands."

By the third day, when Sophia brought the news that the queen was in labor, Gerona had found two goats and assured Matthew that he was trying to think of a story to ease their safe passage into Frankish lands with the child.

Matthew was not called upon to assist with the birth, but it must have been an easy labor, for in a few hours the lusty sounds of a crying child infiltrated the camp's quietness.

"The child is a boy," Angelo reported to Matthew and Gerona. "What a pity the queen will not take the child to his father. He could someday rule in his father's place. Is it fair that he not be given a chance?"

Shaking his head to Angelo's hopeful glance, Matthew said, "In return for Sophia's freedom, we have promised Desiderata that we will never reveal the child's identity. I won't tell Charles that she has borne him a son."

When Matthew saw the beautiful boy, he had to agree that it was a pity to deceive Charles. The boy had the rich, dark coloring of his mother, but he had his father's round head, large and lively eyes, and a thatch of dark hair.

In less than a week, Desiderata declared that she wanted to resume the journey, although Matthew, disliking the pallor of her face, urged her to rest a while longer. She refused to look at her child until the day of their departure. Although her face was emotionless, when she passed her hand over the child's smooth cheek, a tear slipped from her closed eyelids and made a rivulet down her face. Sophia held the child in her arms and stood beside Matthew as the Lombards disappeared from view.

"I doubt she'll live to reach Lombardy," Sophia said, with tears in her voice. "She's too weak from constant hemorrhaging for such a journey, but I think she wants to die at home." She looked down at the child she held. "Poor baby! What will happen to you?"

"Sophia, I've come up with an idea that will require sacrifice for both of us," Matthew said gravely. "Please think upon it. I don't believe we can ever keep the secret of this child's birth as long as he is in Gaul." He paused to let that thought penetrate her mind. "Although I do not want to be parted from you, would you be willing to take this child to Constantinople? I will take you to Ravenna and put you on a ship to Byzantium. I'll send a letter to my steward, Basil, so that you can return to the house of Trento. You will not be a servant there anymore, but will serve as the hostess. The care of the boy will be shared by that household. When I have exhausted all means to finish my mission, I'll join you."

"I fear the responsibility, but how can I refuse you?" Sophia answered.

"I will have Gerona sail with you and the child, since I could not rest easy if you had no protection."

When Matthew approached Gerona with his plan, he laughed merrily. "That's a much better plan than mine. I've had enough of the Franks and I want to go home. I'll be happy to watch over them on the journey."

Matthew's suspicions were aroused, for he had noticed that Gerona frequently sought Sophia's company. "You seem eager to leave me."

"Not you, master, but it has been a long time since I've seen my homeland. When we started out, I had assumed this would be a short journey, but you seem in no hurry to go home. If you doubt my loyalty, I will return as soon as I've delivered Sophia and the child to your household."

Ashamed of his suspicions, Matthew said, "Not until you've had time to visit with your family. I can send for you if my journey lengthens."

To make the journey to Ravenna as inconspicuous as possible, they avoided villages when they could, but it was slow travel with the goats, who wanted to graze along the trail. Sophia wearied of the rough ride, but surprisingly the child, whom they called Alex, thrived along the way, apparently having inherited the robust health of his father rather than the weaknesses of Desiderata.

The day before they reached Ravenna, Matthew sent Gerona forward to scout the city's waterfront to be sure it was safe for them to enter the city. When they made camp, Matthew was acutely aware that he and Sophia were alone. He sensed that she must share the tension that gripped him, for as they prepared and ate their meal, she was strangely silent.

"I will clean our utensils, if you want to put the child to bed," Matthew said. "No doubt you're tired."

"No, Matthew, I'm not tired," she said, but she picked up Alex and carried him into the tent. Matthew had elected to sleep under the stars, so he had not put up a second tent. The night was mild, and after he finished the camp chores and bedded down the animals, he banked the fire and moved into the shadows to lie down on his bedroll. He clasped his hands behind his back and contemplated the starry sky.

He intended to meditate on Scriptures he had learned about the heavens, but his mind wandered, crying out to him that this was a night made for love. He lay alert, wondering what the night might offer. He watched the blinking stars and the slight sliver of moon that made no impact upon the darkness. It must have been well after midnight when he sensed Sophia's presence. Groping slightly, she sat down beside him. He reached out a hand, and she caressed it with her warm fingers.

"And so we must part again?" she whispered in her soft, silky voice.

"I can go with you, if you'd rather, and then return to Gaul at another time."

"No, I would not suggest that. Your plan is a sound one. If the Lombards should be watching, they would not suspect Gerona and me. But I'm sad, for I have the feeling that we will never see one another again."

Matthew sat up abruptly. "I could not bear that, my dear. For this past year, I've been happy knowing that you were near and that I could see you often. Even when we couldn't speak, your presence meant so much to me."

"The very thought of separation is painful to me, too, but we must be practical, Matthew. I'm setting out on a long sea voyage. You will return to Gaul, and life is very uncertain there."

After a long silence, Matthew said haltingly, "So we have only tonight?"

Her fingers tightened around his hand, and Matthew knew her yearning matched his. She came willingly into his arms and they held each other through the night.

      ❋   ❋   ❋

Ravenna was the most Greek feeling of all Roman cities, and trade with Constantinople was brisk, so booking passage proved easy. Thus, Alex was less than a month old when Matthew stood on the dock and watched the departure of the ship carrying Sophia out of his life again. He would miss Gerona, too, for the man had become a friend as well as a devoted servant. Even before they were lost to view, he was sorry he hadn't accompanied them.

With a heavy heart, Matthew arranged for transportation back to Frankish lands in the company of a caravan of wheat merchants who had brought their grain for shipment to Byzantium. They were a rough lot, and Matthew found little in common with them. When they encountered the trader Drago near Chalon, Matthew was happy to part company with the farmers and travel instead with the trader. Matthew knew he would have to be careful in what he told the shrewd Drago about his activities the past month, but the peddler was too full of his own news to question Matthew a great deal.

"Have you heard what happened in the house of Lombard since the return of the deposed queen?" Drago asked eagerly.

Without replying, Matthew looked questioningly at the man.

"Desiderata died soon after returning to her home, and her father blames her death on King Charles."

"I didn't know, and I'm sorry to hear it. I had grown fond of her." *What change will this make in Alex's life?* Matthew wondered. *Now that Desiderata is dead, will I be free to tell Charles that he has a son? Am I being fair to suppress this knowledge?*

Drago continued to comment on the Lombards' wrath against Charles. "Desiderius decided to strike at Charles by humiliating Pope Stephen III. The Lombard was in Rome when representatives of Carloman, Charles's brother, supposedly conspired against the pope. Desiderius seized the conspirators and killed them. When Carloman heard of this, he believed that Stephen had arranged the deaths of his men, and he made plans to march into Rome to avenge them."

"King Charles will not like that," Matthew commented.

"Exactly the reason Desiderius intervened in the situation. He would like nothing better than to see a war break out between the two brothers." Drago paused briefly. Then, with a smile, he added, "The Saxons would be happy about that, too."

"Has Carloman's army marched yet?"

"Carloman won't be marching anywhere again. He's dying, and I'm on my way to take the news to King Charles. If he hasn't heard already, he might reward me richly for bringing the news."

"Don't you ever think of anything but financial gain?" Matthew smiled.

With a fiendish laugh, Drago drawled, "Many other things, friend Matthew, more than you will ever know."

"Why would such sad tidings deserve a reward?"

Drago looked smug. "Because King Charles is ambitious, and if his brother dies, what stands in his way to take control of all of the Frankish lands?"

"Does Carloman have children?"

"Yes."

"Then wouldn't they inherit their father's holdings?"

"Not if Charles claims them first."

As they sat around the fire waiting for its last embers to die,

Matthew wondered about Drago. *Where is the man's home? What is his nationality? Why is he so secretive?* Matthew had often considered questioning Drago about the Alabaster, for he'd found no other person who had a better knowledge of what was happening on the continent of Europe. He didn't really trust the man, but as he watched Drago carefully shine a silver buckle from his trading stock, he asked, "Have you found any rare trade items since we last met?"

With a foxy smile, Drago said, "You might be interested in my latest acquisitions since they came from your part of the world. I purchased three Byzantine icons from pilgrims who passed through Constantinople on their return from the Holy Land. The emperor has forbidden not only the worship, but also the ownership of these icons. There are many on the foreign market."

"Many people still worship in secrecy."

"So they say. I understand that Empress Irene is one of those, although her husband doesn't know it."

Matthew had learned as a child that it wasn't wise to comment on the lifestyle of Byzantine royalty, so he remained silent.

"How about you, friend Matthew? Could I interest you in some Byzantine artwork?" Drago said as he drew two golden chains hung with images from his pocket. One was a Byzantine cross of enamel, gold, and silver portraying the mother of Jesus with four saints around her. The other icon was made of delicately carved, painted wood showing the face of Jesus with a cross in the background.

"No, you do not tempt me," Matthew said with a smile. "I'm an iconoclast—I don't hold with veneration of any kind of image."

"You had best not tell that to King Charles," Drago said as he secreted the icons in his garments. "He has ordered many pictures painted in Frankish churches, although he has not gone so far as to suggest they should be worshiped."

"I've discussed the situation with the king. He believes that the pictures will serve as a means of instructing those who cannot read. King Charles is concerned about the ignorance of his countrymen."

"I agree they are an ignorant lot."

Matthew hesitated, but then throwing caution aside, he said, "Though icons do not appeal to me, I am interested in alabaster items. Do you ever come across any alabaster vases in your travels?"

The peddler's eyes probed Matthew's briefly, then he looked away. Matthew's pulse quickened.

Still without meeting Matthew's eyes, Drago asked, "Are you looking for a particular item or will any vase do?"

"I had ornately carved vases in mind."

Matthew watched breathlessly while Drago rummaged in his packs and drew out a wooden carving of a vase. Matthew had memorized each detail of the vase illustrated in Lucius Trento's book, and without question, this carving could easily have been copied from the alabaster vase Matthew sought. He drew in his breath sharply, trying to remain calm so that Drago wouldn't suspect his interest.

"Yes, that type of thing in the original is what I seek. Where did you find this item? Do you know where the vase is that the artist used for his model?"

"You have many questions, friend Matthew, but I have few answers. To your first one, I must say that I don't remember where and when I obtained it, and I do not know where the original vase is."

"Have you ever seen the vase?" Matthew persisted.

With a crafty look in his eye, Drago hesitated, saying at last, "I have a poor memory, friend." He stood up and started preparations for sleeping.

Matthew suspected that the trader knew something about the vase but wondered if Drago was only a good actor hoping to be paid if he pretended to have knowledge about Matthew's quest. He had observed Drago in too many transactions to believe that his memory was faulty. Matthew dwelt on this new aspect of his search after he rolled into his sleeping gear, but all hope of resting departed when a terrible thought entered his mind. *Could Drago be the man I seek? Does he have the Alabaster?* Matthew couldn't sleep after this frightening possibility occurred to him. *How could I turn the Trento fortune over to a man of such questionable qualities?* For the time being, he must continue to cultivate Drago, who might be the key to uncovering the mystery of the Trento relic.

❀ ❀ ❀

A week later, when Matthew and Drago arrived at the king's residence, they learned that Charles and his major advisors were gone, as was Queen Mother Bertrada.

"The queen mother went to be at the side of her son Carloman, who reportedly is dying. King Charles has gone to the vicinity to be nearby when his brother does die," a servant informed them.

Matthew had been wondering how he could avoid telling Charles of his activities during his absence from Frankish Gaul, but when the king finally returned, he was so full of his own advancement that he didn't question Matthew.

"Sole king of the Franks," he stated over and over as he roved around the council hall.

The minstrel strummed a harp and sang of Charles's rise to fame.

> King Carloman lay dying.
> Through the forest with his falconers and huntsmen
> Rides the great Charles.
> To onlookers it may seem that he searched for deer,
> But the king had mightier game in mind,
> For a strong escort of swordsmen raced at his side.

Poor king Carloman's death came quickly.
    His mother, his widow, his two sons mourned
While Charles met his brother's counselors at Corbeny.
    Some thought the kingdom should be held
For the sons of Carloman, but
    Charles demanded and received all of the rule.
The whole Frankish kingdom would be governed by a
        strong man,
    The mighty Charles, great ruler of the Franks.

Learning much from the man's words, Matthew pitied Carloman's widow and her children, who had taken refuge at Pavia, the capital of Lombardy. *Does Charles realize that he's placed a powerful weapon in the hands of Desiderius, who hates Charles because of his daughter's repudiation?* When Carloman's children grew up they might well challenge Charles's right to the whole of the Frankish kingdom, and if so, they could probably count on the support of Lombardy.

Deprived of the chance to tell Charles of his brother's demise, Drago quickly delivered the news that Desiderata had died soon after her return home. Matthew was appalled at Charles's lack of grief, and he wondered if he was the only one who mourned the young woman. He soon learned, however, that some of the king's major counselors had defected because of this second divorce. Although Charles ignored all opposition in his joy at being sole king of the Franks, Matthew doubted that Charles's future would be troublefree.

8

FRANKISH GAUL, SAXONY, 772

Waldulf's long hair fanned out behind him as he raced his horse recklessly along the uneven ground. Heedless of danger, he thought only of the message he carried for his father. Barnyard animals and fowl scattered before him as he rounded the corner of the stockade and pulled up in front of the manor house. Jumping from the horse's back, he bounded into the main hall.

"Father!"

Count Willehad turned from a table where his account books lay and smiled at his son.

"The king is taking the field this summer. He has called for the host to assemble at Worms in May."

"And that excites you, son?" the count inquired.

"Yes." Waldulf added hesitantly, "That is, if you allow me to march with our men."

"What foe does the king plan to engage this summer?"

"I received my information from a pilgrim who passed through the village this morning, and he said that the king plans an invasion of Saxony," Waldulf said impatiently. *What does it matter who the foe is?* thought Waldulf. *What advantage is reaching manhood if I can't march with the host?*

"Oh, yes, the king has wanted to march on the Saxons since he became king, but he has been otherwise occupied."

"He has enough provocation this time—they've burned a border church."

"About you riding with the army, Waldulf—I have no objections," the count began.

Waldulf shouted exultantly, but the count held up his hand. "But I must give you some idea of what you will encounter. All you've ever seen of war is our regiment marching out in new garments, singing songs of conquest. Their return is celebrated with feasting and thanksgiving, while we often forget those who died on the field of battle. Nor do we consider those who are injured and are never able to ride forth again. We forget the work that lies undone when our peasants are off fighting."

"But I thought you liked to fight, Father!" Waldulf exclaimed.

"Perhaps when I was young like you, but it isn't a matter of *liking* to fight. I have been loyal to my king, who has allowed me to continue on this land granted to my ancestors, and I have always answered the king's summons. However, I have learned that war settles nothing and often brings on more trouble. So I'm content to stay at home and let you ride in my stead—one of us needs to stay at the manor."

"But I don't want to keep you from going," Waldulf protested, realizing that the prospect of marching to war without his father had lessened his anticipation considerably.

"We shall decide definitely when we read the king's summons, but you should have your chance to command. You've been trained to do so, and you'll be more effective if I'm not with you. Your first task is to call up our men and plan their provisions. I will advise you, but the work shall be yours."

Adela entered the room, and she paled when she learned the nature of their conversation. "But he's too young to march alone," she said nervously. "I insist that you go with him if he must fight."

The count patted her hand. "We'll see, my dear. Don't fret about it as yet. The boy has sworn fidelity to the king, and it's his duty to answer the call."

"What preparations need to be made in advance, Father?"

"Each freeman in the empire is responsible for host service, and he must take enough provisions for three months. We do not pillage among our own people, but when we are in enemy territory, it is acceptable to plunder. Those who have fought before will know what to take along, but it's your duty to see that they have the proper provisions and equipment."

Adela watched them as they bent over the desk, and her courage ebbed. *How could I live without either of them?* she wondered. Willehad was right—perhaps only one of them should go.

"Each man should have flour, wine, and salt pork. He should provide an axe, adze, hatchet, pick, and shovel."

"What about carts for hauling provisions?"

"One cart for every three or four men will be sufficient."

❀   ❀   ❀

The next week as Waldulf moved among their tenants telling them to prepare for the upcoming expedition, he sensed hostility and unwillingness toward the king's plans.

"A man never gets ahead," one farmer complained. "We can't work our fields when we're off each summer fighting. And if we do have a free year without following the king into battle, then the stores we have reserved are used up during the war years. We can never gain."

"But don't you receive a share of the booty taken from the enemy?" Waldulf asked.

"Even when we take booty, by the time it filters down to the little man, there's not much left."

The wives stood in their doorways, lowering glances in his direction, and Waldulf went home much subdued. Already he was learning the truth of his father's words—there was more to war than seemed evident at first. And recalling the priest's teachings, it seemed that Christians were supposed to live in peace. He lay awake long into the night wondering about the future.

But his spirits lifted the next day when the king's messenger arrived at the manor with the request for the regiment, asking that someone should take a message to Charles about the number of soldiers he could expect.

"Would you like to be the messenger, Waldulf?" his father asked.

A few weeks earlier Waldulf would have jumped at the chance, but his days of recruitment had taught him many things, and he hesitated. "Do you think I'm capable of doing that?"

Pleasure lit Willehad's eyes, recognizing this hesitation as a sign of maturity. "I don't know, and neither do you. I believe you can do it, but the decision is yours."

Waldulf took his pet falcon, mounted his horse, and rode to a secluded part of the estate. He hadn't exercised the bird for a few days, and it seemed he could think better when he was alone. He'd been eager to be recognized as a man, but now he began to wonder. *Am I ready for the responsibilities manhood entails?*

"I'd better be," he mumbled. "Father is giving me an opportunity to prove myself. I must not fail him."

Waldulf knew his father would advise him if he asked, but he was determined to plan this journey himself. The king was presently at Lorsch, a four days' journey. *Should I travel alone,* he wondered, *or should I join myself to a caravan?* During this season there were plenty of travelers on the roads, but not all of them were honest.

Waldulf returned to the manor by midafternoon with three plump birds for the kitchen, then he set off for the village. At the monastery, he inquired if there were any pilgrims on the road. None had been seen, but the monk who came to the door directed him to the field behind the monastery where several peasant families were resting before they continued their southern journey. Seeing their sorry state, Waldulf thought that he would be more protection for them than they would be for him. Reasoning that highwaymen might forbear to attack such a ragtag assemblage, he made arrangements to leave with them three days later. The journey would take more time in the company of others, but he knew it wasn't prudent to travel alone. Willehad approved the arrangements when Waldulf returned home.

On the appointed day, Waldulf rolled a few belongings into a light pack, strapped on his sword, Wildsong, and left the manor. Willehad stood with an arm around the weeping Adela as Waldulf rode away. He was on his own.

The travelers were within one day's journey of Lorsch when they were attacked by masked highwaymen, and Waldulf was too stunned to do anything while the robbers shamelessly stripped the peasants of their animals and all items of worth. The leader of the group, a fat, balding man, surveyed Waldulf critically, apparently taking in his rich garments.

"What's royalty like you doing with this rabble?" He nodded in the direction of the peasants who huddled together in their misery. "And why are you wearing such a fancy sword? I didn't see you using it—must be for decoration." He guffawed and winked at his companions. Blood rushed to Waldulf's face, and his shame was almost unbearable. The man was right. He'd failed his first test. He stood tongue-tied while the man continued to mock him.

"Speak up, boy. I asked you what you're doing with these people."

"So that I wouldn't have to travel alone," Waldulf mumbled.

"If you chose them for protection, you made a poor choice. What's your name?"

Waldulf shook his head, and the man slapped his face. "Speak up. Who are you? Where are you going?"

Waldulf dropped his hand to his sword, but he answered, "Waldulf of Willehad Manor. I'm going to Lorsch."

"Ah! Come here, sister." Waldulf's eyes bulged when he noticed that one of the thieves was a woman.

"This young one is heading for Lorsch—going to offer his services to King Charles, no doubt. What should we do with him?"

The woman's dark eyes surveyed Waldulf boldly. "Let's take him along with us. We may send him on with a message for His Eminence, King Charles of the Franks."

"He's obviously afraid to use this sword, so I may as well take it," the thief said, but when he started to lift it from the scabbard, Waldulf kicked the man's shins and clawed at his face. Stunned at first, the man stared at Waldulf, and then he snarled, "You young idiot! I've killed men for less than that." He pulled back his arm, and his fist smashed into Waldulf's jaw. Waldulf's limp body flew through the air and landed in a clump of briers.

"Do you want the sword?" the woman said to her companion.

"No, let the boy keep it if he wants it that much. I admire courage, even if it is futile."

"Shall we take him with us, then?" the woman asked.

The man looked over at Waldulf, who was pulling himself out of the clump of briers and brushing himself off. After considering a moment, the thief said, "No. Give him your message for the king, but let's leave the poor fellow here." He laughed and signalled to his companions to ride away.

❋   ❋   ❋

Never was Waldulf more conscious of his youth than when he rode into Lorsch and started looking for the king's residence. A stone monastery dominated a hillside overlooking fields of vineyards, and Waldulf turned the donkey into the grounds hoping for some information. The donkey had been cantankerous, and Waldulf cursed the highwaymen who had taken his fine horse.

"Matthew!" he cried, his spirits lifting considerably at the sight of the man leaving the monastery. "Matthew," he called again.

Matthew had been deep in meditation, his head bowed, and he looked around at the unfamiliar voice. It took only an instant for him to recognize the boy, whom he had thought about often in the past few months. He waved his hand, and Waldulf urged his weary mount to more speed. Matthew's cheerful greeting turned into shock as he observed Waldulf's bedraggled state.

"Boy, what has happened to you?"

"I was on my way here to report to the king when thieves waylaid me. They roughed me up but finally released me. They stole my horse but at least allowed me to ride this dispirited nag. A woman seemed to be one of the leaders of the group, and she sent a message to the king."

"May I inquire what the message is?"

Waldulf hesitated. "She didn't say it was a secret, so I may as well tell you. It sounds like something out of the holy writings: 'Tell old Pharaoh let my boy go.'" He looked at Matthew expectantly. "Do you know what that means?"

"I can guess. You may have encountered the king's first wife, who is angry because he kept their son when he divorced her. Let me take you to the king."

Waldulf had expected a king's residence to be magnificent, and he looked around in disappointment as Matthew led the way into the rambling log building. The central room was not as showy and impressive as their own manor house, although the atmosphere in the room was pleasant. Charles sat at ease beside his young wife, Hildegard, who held the hunchbacked Pepin on her lap. Life for Charles had improved considerably since his marriage to this young and gentle girl. Well trained before she came to his home, she spent hours each day working at the loom, weaving items for the household as well as weaving her own neat garments. She tallied the king's possessions, including all the provisions and levies brought in from his many estates. Although Matthew had been fond of Desiderata and had mourned when he heard of her death, he conceded that Hildegard was more suitable as a wife for the Frankish king.

Charles recognized Waldulf at once, and the boy bowed deferentially. "I've come with a message from my father about the strength of manpower in our county. You can expect one hundred men to meet you at Worms in May. I will have the honor of riding with the king this year."

Hildegard, still carrying Pepin on her hip, brought a bowl of wine, which Waldulf sipped gratefully. He smiled his thanks at her as she stared at him.

"I would beg the king's pardon for my appearance," Waldulf said, "but I was captured by highwaymen several days ago. They took all of my possessions except my sword. My release was granted on the condition that I carry a message to you from a woman who resides with the robbers."

Waldulf handed a message to Charles, who hurriedly broke the seal. Anger covered the king's face as he read. "That woman will plague me to the grave," he muttered. "She doesn't want the boy—she simply doesn't want me to have him." He cast an angry glance toward his hunchback son. "One of these days I'm going to get even with her."

Matthew was of the opinion that Charles's love for his son had waned considerably since his marriage to Hildegard, and he wondered if Charles wasn't keeping the boy to spite his former wife.

"I will have you outfitted from my clothing storehouse, Waldulf," the king said. "After you have rested a few days, you may return to your father, but I will not have you go alone. Several of my private guards will go with you. Matthew, I'll ask your indulgence to accompany Waldulf and take my greetings to his father. You may ride with their levy of soldiers to the gathering at Worms."

Waldulf stood proudly beside the stockade with Wildsong strapped to his side and watched the contingent of soldiers ride by. One hundred infantrymen from their province marched behind a small group of horsemen, the foremost carrying a triangular banner bearing the image of a falcon, similar to one a Roman cohort might have displayed.

Each soldier carried a bow and a few arrows. Behind the men, a baggage train of two-wheeled carts transported the food, wine, clothing, and spare equipment. A herd of cattle brought up the rear. There were almost as many servants as soldiers—wagon drivers, herdsmen, cooks, and carpenters. Most of these men were armed, too—especially the drivers, who were expected to defend the baggage train and take their turns at guard duty.

When the last of the troops passed, Waldulf embraced his weeping mother, clasped hands with Willehad, and hurried toward his horse. Matthew, already in the saddle, waited for him. Only he was close enough to see the mist of tears in Waldulf's eyes.

Matthew remained silent until Waldulf regained his composure. Although the ceremony he had witnessed a year ago had supposedly marked Waldulf's entrance into adulthood, Matthew knew this expedition was really what would make the man. Waldulf set a slow pace and rode far behind the soldiers for perhaps an hour without speaking. Finally, he favored Matthew with a fleeting smile.

"If I'm the leader of this expedition, then I should be at its head."

He kicked his horse into a gallop, and smiling, Matthew rode by his side as they passed up the baggage train and the foot soldiers. By the time they reached the front of the company, Waldulf's shoulders were thrown back, and he no longer resembled the faltering youth of an hour ago.

"It means a great deal to have you riding beside me, friend Matthew," Waldulf said, "especially since my father would not come. I've been doubting for days that I'm capable of this command."

"The wisest of men are those who sometimes doubt their capabilities. You'll no doubt make mistakes, but how else can you learn?" Matthew pointed out.

When Waldulf's troops joined the rest of the Frankish army at Worms, his courage faltered again when he realized that he was the youngest commander there, although many of the soldiers were boys of his age.

"Looks as if we're going to a party," Matthew remarked as they rode into the camp. "I hadn't supposed that the king would bring his family along, but there are Hildegard and little Pepin beside him."

"Surely women won't go into Saxony?" Waldulf questioned.

"I believe Charles has an estate nearby where he will probably leave his family."

"There's Drago, the peddler. I believe the man must be triplets. You can't turn around without seeing him."

Matthew laughed. "Just a good businessman, Waldulf. That is if knavery and trickery can make you one."

Matthew lifted his hand in greeting to the peddler and thought about the copy of the Alabaster the man possessed. The possibility that Drago might be the man for whom he searched still persisted, and Matthew had been avoiding him. He wouldn't want the fortune his ancestors had accumulated to pass to one so unscrupulous, but if Drago were in truth the man, what could he do about it? The thought came unbidden as it had more than once: *Why not go home, say I was unable to find the Alabaster, renounce holy orders, accept the estate, and take Sophia as my wife?* He could still be a devout Christian and do much good with the money. He could endow the monastery and be of more use to it that way than with his presence. The face of Sophia flashed before his eyes, and he realized that this possibility had become much more attractive as the months passed. He had heard nothing from her except a brief message several months ago that she had arrived safely at Constantinople.

But you took a vow, his unrelenting conscience prodded. Matthew pushed the thoughts again from his mind and turned his attention to the preparations around him.

The assembled troops spent several weeks engaged in war games and exercises under Charles's experienced eyes. By the time set for marching, Matthew observed the host with more confidence than he had when they had arrived in camp. Perhaps they *could* wage an offensive war against the Saxons.

The horsemen wore short, high-necked leather jackets covered with iron plates and iron half-helms. Heavy, pointed iron shields protected their bodies, and they carried long swords, curved ripping knives, and light lances for their defense. The foot soldiers wore similar tunics of mail and iron caps. They held round wooden shields in front of them, painted in either blue or red, and had bows of yew wood strapped to their backs.

The army set out for the Rhine in early July, and on the march Matthew often rode by Charles's side.

"I'm surprised at the small number of men you have," Matthew said to Charles one day, "This is a small army compared to Byzantine standards."

"The Franks have no standing army, though every Frankish freeman is liable to serve unpaid in the army and furnish his own equipment. All those obliged to serve are rarely called out. We only summon soldiers from particular provinces when needed. Alternating troops gives the freemen time to work their fields and lay aside some foodstuffs for the year they are called to march. I didn't ask for a vast host this time for I don't expect this to be a full-scale war. I merely intend to teach the Saxons a lesson."

The night before they crossed the Rhine, Charles called his host together. His high-pitched voice did not carry well, and the commanders crowded close to Charles to hear his message, which they would then convey to their men. The forested hills looked foreboding, but Waldulf had left his fear behind, and his eyes gleamed in anticipation of the upcoming fray as he listened to Charles's instructions. By his side, Matthew observed the boy's excitement with fondness.

"As soon as we cross the river," the king instructed, "we must watch closely for ambushes. The Saxons are a crafty enemy and we must not underestimate them. Stay alert! In order to supplement our supplies, you may start gathering up any grain and swine that we find in forest clearings."

"May I ask our destination?" one of the commanders questioned.

"Eresburg on the Diemel River. The fortress there must be destroyed before we can conquer the rest of Saxony."

"You will not find that so easy," a count cautioned. "I understand that fortress was built to protect their sacred grove. They will not fade away into the forest and vacate this place as they often do their villages.

"We are prepared," Charles said gesturing toward the war machines, rams, catapults, and stone-throwers massed at the rear of the troops.

"Their methods of warfare haven't changed much since Roman times," Matthew remarked quietly to Waldulf.

"And from what my father says, this equipment will be useless in the Saxon forests. He was on an expedition with King Pepin a few years ago. The forests are vast and without the paths necessary to accommodate these war machines."

"Perhaps the king thinks he can clear the forest as he goes," Matthew suggested.

For several days, Charles led his horsemen and archers on foot along the rivers beyond the Rhine without encountering any Saxons. One evening, Frankish scouts reported that they were near the fortress. The advance guard, which included Waldulf's troops, moved forward quietly to avoid alerting the enemy. At nightfall, they inched forward into the trees lining the banks of the Diemel. On the heights above them was a bulwark of logs, not more than five feet high.

Matthew, thinking of the fortifications around Constantinople, whispered to Waldulf, "Highly overrated fortress, I'd say."

Waldulf's teeth flashed bright in the gathering dusk. "Yes, but our war machines will be difficult to maneuver up that hill, giving the Saxons an advantage."

"Not if God is on our side," Matthew said, motioning to Father Sturm, who was on his knees praying.

"I've often wondered if God loves the Franks more than the Saxons," Waldulf stated.

"Not if I read the Scriptures correctly, but don't try to convince King Charles of that fact," Matthew replied.

❋   ❋   ❋

Before nightfall the next day, Matthew questioned more than ever that God was party to the destruction that had taken place. An advance guard of the Frankish army had crossed the river in an early dawn fog and had pulled two of their battering rams up the hill before daylight. So complete was the surprise that the Franks had crumpled one section of the log wall before Saxons knew there was an army approaching.

Troops poured through the opening while the battering ram continued to do its destructive work. Charles always directed the fighting from the rear, but he gave orders to put the inhabitants to the sword. Although a few escaped into the forest, before the day was done, the mutilated bodies of nearly fifty Saxons lay in the midst of the ashes of the buildings that had been torched.

This was Matthew's first experience with battle, and he watched the carnage in shock. He had been sent in with the troops to take care of the wounded, and after he tended to the injured Franks, he moved among the Saxons, giving aid where he thought it would be useful. The Franks had been ruthless in their slaughter; there was little need for his ministrations. Father Sturm had the greatest task, as he was the one to administer last rites to the dying. Matthew assisted him when there was nothing else that could be done for the injured. He wearily washed the blood from his hands and looked around for Waldulf. The boy was no place to be seen, but a servant directed him toward a clearing in the forest where Waldulf sat against a tree, his chin lowered to his breast. His clothes were spattered with blood, and the stench of the carnage clung to the boy. Matthew eased his weary body beside him.

"My father tried to tell me what war was like, but I didn't believe him. I don't know if I'll ever fight again," Waldulf said wearily.

"This is my first experience with warfare too."

Waldulf looked at his hands. "Will I ever be able to feel clean again? Can I forget the look of horror on the faces of the Saxons I killed?"

A slithering sound behind them brought Waldulf to his feet in a rapid leap. He grasped the hilt of his sword while he pivoted quickly to survey the forest. The skin crawled on the back of Matthew's head, and he thought, *How careless we have been!*

Instead of arrows flying toward them, they heard a whimpering sound. Walking alertly forward, side by side, they found a white-faced child at the edge of the forest. At sight of them she jumped up to run, but her leg folded under her and she collapsed.

"It's a Saxon girl," Matthew said. "I believe her leg is broken." He knelt, and with tender fingers flexed the child's leg. She moaned and sat up, trying to crawl away. Large, frightened blue eyes stared at them.

Waldulf knelt beside her. "Don't be afraid, little girl. We won't hurt you. Let my friend tend to your leg."

She probably didn't understand his words, but his kindly tone must have assured her of his good intent, for she relaxed. Matthew's fingers moved swiftly over her leg.

"It isn't broken, but there's a sprain. She shouldn't walk."

"I can carry her, but what shall we do with her?"

"Take her back to camp, I assume. If her family lived here, they must be all dead, for the Franks spared neither women nor children."

Horror filled Waldulf's eyes. "What if I killed her parents? That would make me responsible for her."

On the way to Charles's camp, they met Sturm. When he

noticed their captive, he spoke to her in her native tongue. An amazed look spread over his face as he talked with the girl. Matthew beheld the scene impatiently until the priest said, "King Charles will rejoice over this capture. This is Printha, who was only visiting here. She says she's the daughter of Widukind."

"And who is Widukind?" Waldulf inquired.

"The most wily leader of the Saxons, who will not take kindly to the capture of his child."

9

SAXONY, 773–775

W hat have we here?" Charles said when Matthew and
Waldulf entered his tent with the Saxon child. When
Waldulf started to release her, the girl gripped him tightly around
the neck.

"We found the child near the village," Matthew explained.
"She has a sprained ankle."

King Charles motioned to Sturm who stood in the background.
"You can speak her language. Find out what you can about her."

Sturm moved forward and extended a comforting hand toward the girl, but she hid her face on Waldulf's shoulder. "I
have already questioned her," Sturm said. "She is Printha, the
daughter of Widukind."

Charles gave an exultant laugh and rose from his seat. "Does
that mean that Widukind was killed in the battle? If so, we have
won a greater victory than I imagined."

Sturm again queried the girl, and with a fiery spirit, she
straightened in Waldulf's arm and spat furious words in Charles's
direction.

Smiling, Sturm translated. "She says that her father was not
here, else the Franks would not have perpetrated such a slaughter."

"We will take the child with us when we return to Frankish
lands. Guard her well," King Charles ordered Waldulf.

"Will you explain that I must doctor her ankle?" Matthew said to Sturm. "I do not want the child to fear me."

Waldulf knelt on the ground, and Printha held tightly to his arm as she hesitantly extended her leg toward Matthew. He admired the courage of the child who didn't flinch as he examined her. She nodded her agreement when Sturm translated Matthew's instructions that she must not walk on the foot. The furtive eyes of the girl indicated her desire to escape, but she was wise enough to know she couldn't go far on an injured ankle. When Matthew cleansed her face, which showed the ravages of the fight at the fortress, he was struck by the beauty of the child. Intelligent blue eyes were surrounded by a heart-shaped, honey-toned face.

Waldulf hovered around the girl until the king recalled him to his duties. Now that the fortress had been taken, Charles gave orders to proceed the next morning but to do so carefully. He had learned from a male prisoner that in a hidden valley nearby was the central worship shrine of the Saxons.

Horses were left behind the next morning when the Frankish host moved cautiously into a forest to the right of the destroyed fortress. Matthew felt as small as a mouse as he followed them. Towering evergreens grew so thick that only a few rays of sun penetrated the heavy cover. The forest closed in around the Frankish soldiers, and Matthew could hardly see the men nearest him. *If this is an example of Saxony's forestland,* he thought, *it's no mystery why the Saxons have eluded the Franks for so many years.*

Waldulf appeared by Matthew's side, and the boy's eyes gleamed with excitement in the semidarkness. "I've never seen such lofty trees. Does the place give you a strange feeling— almost as if it *is* a holy center?"

Matthew nodded, and he rubbed his hand over the rough bark of a tree. "Any of God's creation is holy, and a grove like this always induces me to worship. There is something else, though— almost a mystical feeling here."

After a few more miles of stalking, they saw the forest lighten ahead, and the Franks soon broke out into a clearing where a cluster of huts surrounded a tremendous tree trunk that had been carved into a statue of a head without eyes.

Sturm came to Matthew's side. "That's Irminsul, the tree god of the Saxons. I've heard of it since I came to this area, but I could never visit it because the shrine has always been heavily guarded."

The troops circled the idol, some even daring to reach out a tentative hand to touch it, as they awaited the king's arrival.

When Charles arrived, he stared at the image for a moment, then shouted angrily, "An abomination to our God. Cut the thing down."

No one leaped forward to do his bidding, for the Franks still stared with awe at the strange statue. They were not far from paganism themselves, and they feared to trifle with this god.

"Cut the thing down," Charles roared, and the count of Metz ordered two of his men forward. They chopped until they were exhausted, inflicting only a few dents in the tree. Other men stepped forward and chopped and chopped and chopped, but more than an hour elapsed before the statue finally squeaked and toppled earthward. When the giant idol hit the ground, tremors shook the earth even after it crashed into the huts, where it rolled back and forth several times before it finally came to a halt.

"This reminds me of an earthquake I experienced in Byzantium," Matthew said to Sturm.

"Gold!" a Frank shouted, and those who had sought cover to escape the fall of the statue raced from their hiding places to the crushed huts, where a hoard of gold and silver was spread on the ground. Men fell to their knees among the treasure, scooping up coins by the handful and secreting them in their garments.

"Greed!" Sturm said, "It's the bane of every nation. Why must man live by stealing from his neighbor?"

"Whether right or wrong, plunder is their only pay for fighting. Full pockets here may mean the difference between starvation for their families in the months to come," Matthew replied.

"Granted that is true, but I do not like war."

Charles strode into the midst of his men. "Aha! A wonderful bounty. We have been rewarded for our campaign. I would like a memento for Hildegard, and you men can have the rest." He waved Sturm and Matthew forward. "Come, choose some plunder for your labor. All of this treasure will be taken to Gaul."

Sturm shook his head and turned his back upon the looters, but Matthew—more from curiosity than desire—walked by Charles's side among the debris. All of the huts had harbored only coins, but the ruins of one structure contained various vessels. Charles picked up a silver drinking bowl with a crude drawing of the statue chiseled on the side.

"This will be a good gift for Hildegard," the king said.

Most of the items were of gold and silver, but Matthew's eyes were drawn to a carved alabaster vase depicting the offering of Isaac by Abraham—exactly like the illustrations in Lucius Trento's book. In disbelief, he picked up the vase with trembling hands and turned it over. The numeral three was on the bottom, along with some Latin letters. He brushed away dust and made out the word "Trento."

I have found the Alabaster!

"Have you chosen something that interests you, Matthew?" the king asked.

"Yes, sire, I'll take this vase if it pleases you," he said, his voice shaking.

Charles looked at him strangely. "Alabaster, is it? Not as valuable as gold or silver, but if it suits you, take it."

Matthew picked up a wooden box lying near the Alabaster and placed the vase in it. He wanted to shout praises to the heavens that his mission had been successful, so he hurried away from the searching host. He entered the forest and bowed his head in thanksgiving to God, but in the midst of his exultation, Matthew paused.

I have the Alabaster, but I don't know the guardian, and my search won't be completed until that individual is found!

Matthew dropped to the ground and groaned. Sturm came to his side.

"What is it, Brother Matthew?"

"You will remember that I told you about my quest for a family heirloom. Among the damaged huts, I found it—this alabaster vase that I feared had been lost forever. At first I thought that was wonderful, but now I realize this only compounds my search."

"Yes, I can see that it would. No doubt the Saxons obtained this vase sometime when they raided Frankish lands. You will have to search longer to find the owner."

"But at least it's a blessing to have the Alabaster back in the family."

"As I understand the specifications of your father's will, the holder of the vase would be the heir. You're a Trento and the vase is now yours—don't you qualify?"

"Lead me not into temptation, Father Sturm. If I were to do that, I would have to renounce my vows to our Savior. I did not take those vows lightly, and I will not forsake my Lord now. God has led me to the Alabaster; surely He will yet lead me to its owner."

"I would still urge you to give up the search at this point. Further seeking might bring trouble," Sturm mumbled.

"For me, you mean?" Matthew sought to understand the priest's comment.

Sturm said, "I do not know the future, Matthew. My mortal mind alone says that this may be the time for you to return home."

Matthew regarded him thoughtfully as they returned to the Saxon shrine. They encountered Waldulf carrying a bag of coins, but concern marked his features. "The Saxon girl is ill, Matthew. Will you come to check her?"

Matthew found Printha rolling back and forth on her pallet, her face red and splotched. "If only we had some fresh water to bathe her, but this drought is cruel to both beasts and humans." Matthew mixed some dried herbs with a small amount of tepid water from the horn he carried, and Waldulf slowly spooned the brew into the girl's mouth. The two men sat beside her until the herbal potion calmed her.

"Poor little thing," Waldulf said. "To be separated from her mother and father is cruel. I wish that King Charles would return her to her people rather than take her as hostage. This is another part of war that I do not like. My father warned me it would be this way."

He looked at the box Matthew carried. "What took your fancy?"

Matthew opened the old box and lifted out the Alabaster. "A vase."

Waldulf reached for the vase. "Very unusual markings. We have some alabaster items at home, but they are much larger than this." He returned the vase to the box quickly. "Handling that vase gave me the same eerie feeling I had when we entered this forest. Am I becoming too superstitious?"

"This is a relic that needs to be handled with reverence, Waldulf. Someday I will tell you more about it."

Waldulf cast a surprised look in Matthew's direction, but before he could question further, Printha stirred, muttering in her native tongue. Waldulf lifted her hand. "I must learn to talk with her if she is to live among us. That is, if the king will allow it."

Charles met with the leaders of the host that night to discuss continuing the campaign. When Waldulf rejoined Matthew at Printha's side, he said, "We have decided to return to Gaul. The king believes the Saxons will have learned without further invasion that the Franks will not tolerate continued attacks to our nation. Besides, the commanders are greatly concerned about the lack of water for the host and their animals. We head toward home in the morning."

Waldulf went to Matthew early the next morning, shaking him rudely awake. He carried a bowl of water, the contents sloshing over the sides. It was not like the boy to be so careless of water in this drought-stricken land.

"A miracle, Matthew. The priests are calling it a miracle. A torrent of water is gushing from a nearby hill—enough to fill the bed of a dried-up stream. King Charles says it's a vindication of his destruction of Irminsul. I brought some fresh water for Printha."

The sound of rejoicing Franks resounded over the hills, for they believed the miracle indicated divine approval of their offensive actions against the Saxons.

"It's a miracle as great as when God provided water for His people in the wilderness. God is pleased because we destroyed the Saxon shrine," Charles asserted when he rode to the head of his assembled host and signaled their return to Gaul.

"The Saxons will look upon this deed as a desecration of their traditional gods," Sturm muttered to Matthew. "They will take their vengeance upon the Franks."

"And I doubt that Widukind will take kindly to the fact that Charles has abducted his daughter," Matthew said, motioning to the cart that was conveying the ailing Printha to Gaul.

❀   ❀   ❀

Once across the Rhine in Frankish territory, the host paused for a night of feasting before they dispersed to their homes. During the gaiety, Charles singled out Waldulf for special commendation.

"You have proven your manhood on this expedition, young Waldulf. You have pleased me well," Charles said.

Waldulf knelt in front of his king to swear allegiance. "You honor me, Your Excellency. My father will be gratified that I upheld the family honor."

"In fact, you have pleased me so much that I'm going to request your father to assign you to my court. You may attend the palace school and mature in my service. I will send that request to your father when you return home. I will expect you to wait upon me in a fortnight."

Waldulf bowed his head in obeisance and repeated, "You honor me, sire." He held his spear to his left forehead, his eyes shining. When the king dismissed Waldulf, Matthew rushed to the youth's side. "You are to be congratulated, young Waldulf. Since you aspire to follow in your father's footsteps, this will be good training for you."

"My father will feel honored, although he will not want me to leave home. Nor will my mother. Yet it is also a relief for me to join Charles's court, for I can keep my eye on the Saxon girl. For some reason I consider her my responsibility. Will you watch over her until I return?"

"I'd be happy to," Matthew stated.

❋   ❋   ❋

With her health regained, Printha proved a tolerant prisoner. She seemed to accept her circumstances and even tried to learn the Frankish tongue, which was quite similar to her native language. She took a fancy to the hunchback, Pepin, and could be often seen leading him around the courtyard of Charles's home. This endeared Printha to Charles, and he treated her more like a daughter than a prisoner. She also found pleasure in the company of Drago, the trader, who was one of the few people in Gaul who could converse with her. Drago often presented her with gifts from his stock. It amused Matthew to note Drago's kindness to Printha, but he realized nothing about Drago should surprise him since he had more coats than a chameleon.

Matthew was impressed by Printha's keenness as he instructed her in a new language and culture. He was especially moved by her interest as he introduced her to Christianity. She never wholly committed herself to the new religion, but Matthew felt that the truths of the Gospel had been planted deep in her heart and would, in time, bear fruit.

If the Saxon girl bemoaned her captivity, she didn't show it. Matthew credited her friendship with Waldulf for her adaptability. Within a month of her residency at the Frankish court, Waldulf and Printha were conversing well. Printha was a quick student in learning the Frankish dialect, and as Waldulf instructed her, she taught him the ways of the Saxons.

Each morning Waldulf and Printha, along with several other sons of nobles, came to Matthew for lessons in Greek and Latin. Matthew enjoyed watching the children mature both physically and intellectually, and a year passed by quickly. He often despaired that he had made no progress in finding the holder of the Alabaster and that each day kept him separated from Sophia.

Many problems continued to plague the king of the Franks, not least of which was the absence of the queen mother from his court. Bertrada had not returned to Charles's court after the death of Carloman, but had chosen to devote her time to work at the monastery at Purm. Though she visited Charles occasionally, the death of her youngest son had blighted her life, and she was happier in the peaceful surroundings of the cloister. She preferred not to be involved in the harrying incidents of the kingdom. Internal conflicts had heightened, with increased attacks by highwaymen upon peasants and pilgrims. Charles suspected these attacks were led by his former wife, Himiltrud.

Now that he thought the Saxons were sufficiently subdued, Charles turned his mind to the contention between the Lombards and the pope, which he had disregarded the year before because of his campaign into Saxony. In the spring of 774, Charles led his hosts across the mountains and defeated the Lombards. He forced the surrender of Desiderius and his wife and Carloman's widow and her children, all of whom were deported to Gaul and secluded in monasteries. During this journey, Charles made his first visit to Rome and was so impressed by the ancient culture of the Romans that he came away determined that his own people must improve their way of life.

During the many months of Charles's campaign to the Italian peninsula, he had moved his household to Geneva and had taken Printha with him. Since Count Willehad had not been obligated to furnish troops for the expedition, Waldulf returned to the manor to spend several months with his parents. Matthew, too, had requested leave from Charles's service during the Italian campaign, and he spent those months touring Frankish lands from the Pyrenees to the English Channel, eastward to the Rhine into the regions of Saxony controlled by the Franks, and throughout the heartland of Charles's kingdom. He found no one who had ever heard of a Trento or Conrad, and he concluded that the search was fruitless.

When the victorious Charles came back from Italy, Matthew returned to his court, intending to stay in Gaul through the winter and then return to Byzantium. He wrote Basil that he had exhausted every possibility of finding the Alabaster heir and intended to be at home the following year. He added his greetings to Sophia and asked the steward to advise her of his traveling plans. Then Matthew settled down for a few months of teaching in the palace school.

In the meantime, Waldulf was learning the art of administration. He sat with Charles when the king listened to the complaints of his subjects and dispensed justice. The rest of the day Waldulf was free, and after securing a horse for Printha, he roamed across the countryside with her.

"I do not think I like horseback riding," Printha said on their first journey. "Saxons walk most of the time. Forests are not practical for horse riders."

"Once your body becomes used to it, you will see the advantages. We can travel farther, and it will be less tiring. I would like to take you to my home someday, and it's a long journey on foot."

"Waldulf," Printha asked suddenly. "Will you help me run away to my own people? I am not happy here except when I am with you."

"I did not know you were unhappy!" Waldulf said with surprise.

"I miss the forest and my mother. The Franks have been kind, but it is not the same as being with my own people. I've been here for months—I thought I would be released long before this."

"I'm sorry to learn you are dissatisfied, but I cannot go against the command of my sovereign. I've sworn loyalty to King Charles, and I beg you not to ask me to break that pledge. Perhaps someday in a hostage exchange you will win your freedom. I will miss you when that day comes, however."

"And I you, Waldulf. Also little Pepin. He is a sweet child in spite of his twisted back."

When they stopped near an abandoned village, Waldulf helped Printha dismount. They walked back and forth until the stiffness left Printha's legs. Then they sat down and leaned their backs against a huge beech tree.

"I do understand how you feel, Printha, for I miss my home too. It's an honor to be singled out by the king to live in his household, but I often yearn for my parents and the carefree life of the manor."

"Why don't you go home then? You're not a prisoner."

"In a sense I am. The nobles are dependent upon the king for the continuance of their land grants. If I were to anger King Charles, he might take away my father's lands. So I must stay as long as he wants me to. Perhaps when his own children mature, he will release me. He seems fond of the three of them."

"Charles I like, as well as the baby Adelaide, but I do not care for Carloman. He is such a peevish child. Now the queen is with child again, and I think she is to deliver soon."

"Then perhaps both of us will soon be released—the school will be too full of Charles's family for us to stay there. Tell me what your home is like."

Printha smiled slightly. "Our homes are not as stable as yours. They are made of woven wattles dabbed with mud, and they are not intended to last very long. When the land around our village no longer produces well, we simply abandon the place and find a new site, and in a few years, the forest takes over the clearing. It's a hard life, but a carefree one. We soon learn the dangers of the forest and how to avoid them."

"Do you have any brothers or sisters?"

"No, I'm the only child of Widukind and Redith. Many of the villagers accuse me of being overly pampered, since Redith waited so long for a child. I love them both very much."

"Frankish children are taught to loathe the Saxons, so it surprises me that a delightful child like you is the offspring of those I've been taught are my enemies."

She touched his hand, and the look in her eyes was more passionate than her youthful years should warrant. "You could never be my enemy, Waldulf. Now tell me about your home, your childhood."

"I, too, am an only child and have also been accused of being pampered by my parents, especially by my mother. We live in a large manor house built of stone and logs, actually more commodious than the current residence of King Charles. A priest tutored me during my childhood so I learned to read and write in Latin as well as our Frankish tongue. From my tenth birthday on, I had a mentor who taught me riding, the use of weapons, and falconing. I miss my pet falcon, too. I trained him myself."

"That sounds wonderful," Printha said, smiling at Waldulf.

"I guess we should get going," he suggested. "We'll ride again in a few days." Waldulf helped Printha back into her saddle and the two rode off toward Charles's estate.

After her muscles got used to riding, Printha was able to travel greater distances from home with Waldulf. One day as they rode through a marshy area, Printha gazed around wonderingly.

"Waldulf, did we come this way when Charles brought me here as a prisoner?"

"No, this is farther west than the way we came then."

"And I haven't been this way with you before?"

"No, in fact, it's a new territory for me. Why do you ask?"

"It seems familiar to me." When they came to the ruins of a village, Printha reined in her horse. "What happened to these houses?"

"I don't know, but probably they were destroyed in a raid."

"Could it be that the Saxons raided here, and I might have been with them?"

"But surely they don't take children along when they fight the enemy."

"I've never known them to do so, but I have the strange feeling I've traveled this way before."

A moaning sound accompanied by a rattling of chains spread over the clearing, and Printha moved her horse close to Waldulf. He held out his hand to her.

"What is it?" she whispered as the sound came closer.

"I'm not sure, but we must flee."

Before they turned their horses around, however, a human figure encased in chains ambled into view. Waldulf moved back to Printha. "It must be the penitent, Folz," he explained. "I've heard about him, but hadn't seen him before. He won't harm us, but no one is supposed to talk to him."

"Pity! Pity!" the shackled man called weakly as he stumbled toward them. Waldulf had never seen such a derelict. Folz's long hair hung below his waist, his eyes were sunken in his head, and his body was caked with dirt.

"Why, the poor man!" Printha said as Waldulf urged their mounts away from the clearing. "What has happened to him? Shouldn't we help?"

"He's been sentenced to live in isolation as a penance for some sin he's committed."

"But who has sentenced him?"

"A bishop of the church."

"That seems a cruel thing to do in the name of religion. You Franks say that the Saxons are heathens, but we show more mercy than that. I think we should go back and help him."

"And take a chance that I might lose my own soul? Not only has he committed an unpardonable sin, but anyone who helps him is condemned, too."

They met Sturm before they returned to Charles's court. When they told him of their experience and Printha voiced her horror at such treatment, he gave the girl a strange look.

"Do you know what sin the man committed?" Waldulf asked.

"He was the chieftain of Nehouse, the village you saw," Sturm explained, "and he betrayed the trust of his people. He was lying out in the forest in a drunken stupor when the enemy attacked. They burned the village and its inhabitants. The bishop sentenced him to a life of wandering, wearing the chains, never bathing."

"But what does he eat?" Printha asked.

"Berries, beetles, wild game, I suppose," Sturm said.

"And how long does this penance last?" Waldulf inquired.

"A lifetime, perhaps, unless he is pardoned."

The fate of the man worried Printha, and she pestered Waldulf constantly about Folz's treatment, many times persuading him to ride to the site to leave food. They didn't see Folz again, but they always had the feeling he was watching them. When they went to Nehouse, Waldulf had a difficult time persuading Printha to leave, for she searched through the debris looking for clues to the village's inhabitants. More than once Waldulf lamented inwardly that they had ever encountered Folz. He knew if the priests learned of their efforts to befriend the outcast, they would both be in trouble.

10

I don't know why you are so persistent about going to that place," Waldulf said angrily. "Is it to see Folz again? I've told you the man is an outcast, and that Franks are forbidden to have anything to do with him."

"But I'm not a Frank, so the ban doesn't apply to me."

"I'm not going with you anymore. Father Sturm has found out about our continued trips there, and he's sent me word to desist. I'm not going again."

Printha herself didn't know what fascination the area held for her and why she was determined to aid the outcast. Perhaps it was pity for him, but she knew that without Waldulf's companionship she wouldn't be able to continue her visits to the abandoned Nehouse. Although Charles was kind and lenient to her, there was no doubt that she was a prisoner, forbidden to leave the confines of his estates unless she had a Frankish guide.

After Waldulf refused to go with her, she asked Drago to accompany her to the village site, but he turned on her angrily for the first time. "No, I will not take you there. It will only cause trouble if you insist on befriending Folz."

A few weeks after Waldulf and Printha had quarreled about her interest in Folz and the desolate village, Waldulf approached her in a contrite mood. "I'm sorry I spoke so sharply to you

149

about the penitent man. If you want to ride elsewhere, I'm at your service."

Printha was wise beyond her years, and she favored Waldulf with a forgiving smile. "Not today—maybe tomorrow."

"I won't be here tomorrow," he said, excitement in his voice. "The king has organized a hunting expedition, and I've been invited to go along. He hasn't asked me before."

"How nice for you, Waldulf."

"But what will you do while we're gone? The king plans to take little Pepin with him, so you won't even have him for companionship."

"Oh, I can help Hildegard with her weaving. She is teaching me how to operate the loom," Printha said offhandedly, an idea forming in her mind. "Or I can help with the children. I am particularly fond of baby Hrotrud."

When the men left the next day, Printha was pleased to note that even Matthew was among the hunting party. All morning long she worked with Hildegard, but by noon, the weary queen was ready to seek her bed.

Carrying a packet of food, Printha slipped out to the stables and led her unsaddled horse quietly into the forest without detection. By standing on a fallen log, she finally mounted the tall barebacked beast.

Printha had learned her forest directions at Widukind's side, and she had no trouble following the unmarked path to the site of Nehouse. Before dismounting, she looked around and listened intently to see if she could hear Folz's chains, but nothing except the trill of a wren broke the silence of the clearing.

Printha slid from the horse's back, walked to the spot where they'd been leaving the food, and laid down the loaves of bread and slab of meat she had pilfered from the palace kitchen. Even the birds had become silent, and no other sound could be heard except the slight crunch of her boots on the rocky path. Her eyes darted around the clearing. The silence was menacing, and she yelped when the bushes parted before her. Folz's demented eyes, screened by his bedraggled hair, peered at her. She backed away.

"Child. Child. Do not be afraid. Talk to me. I have a message that must be delivered to King Charles."

Printha paused, but she didn't move closer to the derelict, aware too late of her folly in coming here alone. Folz couldn't do her much harm since he was chained, but the forest held other dangers, such as the thieves who continued to terrorize the countryside.

"Who are you?" he croaked. "Where do you live? Why have you been feeding me all of these months?"

"I'm a Saxon prisoner in the house of King Charles," Printha said, trying to be brave. "I feel pity for your plight—the Franks call us pagans, but we do not treat our own people this way."

"Do not pity me, child. I brought this punishment upon myself. I deserve to be punished, but I do thank you for the sustenance you've provided." His voice cracked and squeaked as he talked and Printha had trouble discerning his words.

"How long have you been under this judgment?" she asked.

"I've lost track of the years. But this physical punishment is not as great as my own mental anguish, for I caused the deaths of my kinsmen. Ah, yes, I deserve to be punished."

"But forever? Is there no hope of forgiveness?"

He shook his head sadly.

"Did you say you had a message for the king?"

"Yes, and it's urgent. I was sleeping up in the hills two nights ago, and I overheard a plot to take the king's life."

"What Frank would do such a thing?" Printha asked, surprised.

"The king has many enemies. And the ones I heard plotting against him were his first wife, Himiltrud, and her brother. They rule over a band of renegades."

"Then you must come into the palace and tell the king yourself."

"I'm not allowed to associate with others. You will have to take the message."

To do so meant that Printha would have to reveal the source of her information and thereby make trouble for herself, but she had little other option. "How is this assassination to take place?"

"Spies have been set to watch the king, and when he goes off on a hunting trip, Himiltrud and her men will attack him. She knows that Charles takes Pepin along when he's hunting, and they will snatch the child after Charles is killed."

"But the king left just this morning to go hunting and took the boy with him!" Printha exclaimed. "Matthew and Waldulf went also. While I might not risk my life to save the king, the other two are my best friends."

"Then no time must be lost. You must ride to warn him—the Franks need King Charles. Take the loaves you brought me to sustain you on this journey."

"But I don't know where the hunt is to take place," Printha said anxiously.

"Go eastward. The king does not hurry when he's on an outing, nor does he proceed quietly. You will encounter his party."

Printha replaced the loaves in the sack she carried, and following Waldulf's example, she ran toward her horse and leaped astride his back in one quick movement.

She raced out of the clearing, but she slowed her mount once she was out of Folz's sight. *I am a Saxon,* she pondered. *Wouldn't Charles's death be to the advantage of my people?* She knew that as long as Charles lived, he would be a perpetual foe of the Saxons. *If he died I could return home. But what about the other members of Charles's party? Would they escape harm?* She revered Matthew and loved Waldulf. When she considered that the renegades might not spare the two best friends she had in Gaul, Printha kicked wildly at the sides of her mount. She must not waste any time. If she were only on speaking terms with the God of the Franks, Printha would have called on Him to help her.

Printha relied once again on the forest direction she had learned from Widukind, and while daylight lasted she made good time. When darkness fell, however, her progress slowed to a crawl. Even with the light of a waning moon, she had difficulty seeing the small trail she'd been following. Near midnight, she detected riders to the north. Fear immobilized her temporarily. She slipped off the back of the horse and held her hand over his mouth to keep him quiet. *It must be the renegades,* she thought. *Do they know of my presence?*

When her first wave of terror passed, Printha contemplated how she could use the presence of the thieves to her advantage. Leading her horse, she went forward deep in thought. *Of course! If I follow the raiders, they will lead me to Charles. All I have to do is keep them from detecting my presence.*

She remounted and walked the horse as quietly as possible, pausing periodically to determine the direction of the thieves. After several hours, they halted their horses, and except for the drone of insects, all was quiet. Printha tied her horse to a tree, and slithering along the forest floor, she moved toward the area where she had last heard the riders. A snort and the muffled stamping of horse's hooves alerted her to their presence, and she peered through the underbrush to see about twenty bodies sprawled on the ground. This must mean that they were near Charles's camp and were waiting until daylight to attack. Inching backward, she circled the watchful group of renegades and crawled forward until she saw the Franks' camp ahead of her. As far as she could tell, there was no guard. *How foolish!* she thought. *If King Charles only knew how often Saxons roamed these forests, he would not be so careless of his safety.*

Most of the Franks were wrapped in their blankets around a smoldering campfire that cast a hazy light over the clearing. Printha crawled warily among them looking for Waldulf. When she saw the sword, Wildsong, lying beside a sleeping form, she knew she'd found him. Waldulf was never far from that sword.

"Waldulf!" she whispered, tapping him on the shoulder.

He stirred, and she whispered again, "Quietly, Waldulf, do not make a sound."

He sat up. "Am I dreaming?" Then he saw her, and he said loudly, "Printha!"

She pushed him back to the ground. "Shhh!"

"I'm *not* dreaming. What are you doing here?"

"I've an urgent message for King Charles. I must see him at once. Thieves are lying in wait ready to attack at dawn."

"In the tent," he whispered. He wiggled out of his blankets and crawled on his belly beside her toward the tent.

Charles awakened easily at Waldulf's word, "A message for you, sire."

In the darkness, Charles could not see Printha, and he gasped when she started to speak. "Himiltrud and her band of renegades are poised at the edge of this camp. As soon as day breaks, they plan to kill you and take Pepin. You have only minutes to prepare."

Charles did not bother asking how she knew this. "What side of the camp?"

"To the east."

With his hunting knife, he slit the western side of the tent, and the moonlight filtered in. Without a sound, he strapped on his sword and gathered up the sleeping Pepin. "How many are there?" he asked quietly.

"I do not know, your excellency. Perhaps as many as twenty."

"Waldulf, move among the men and have them join me in the forest west of here where our horses are tethered. We will flee rather than fight since I do not know how powerful they are."

Before the Franks could mount and be off, the renegades' shouts filled the air. *They must have a lookout even if Charles doesn't,* Printha thought. Charles thrust Pepin into her arms, and soon the arrows they'd intended for hunting were hurtling through the air in an ambush on the attackers as they crossed the clearing.

The battle was swift, and the clearing was soon littered with the attackers' bodies. The woman, Himiltrud, was one of the first to fall, and Matthew and Waldulf exchanged quick glances.

The remaining raiders soon faded into the forest, and still on guard, the Franks eased out into the clearing. Charles stood for a moment over the woman who had once been his wife, but his face remained emotionless when he turned away.

"I would have had no peace as long as she lived, so it's good riddance, but God rest her soul."

In that moment Matthew came near to hating the man he served. *How can he be so callous?* Matthew wondered. *He repudiated Desiderata without a qualm of conscience. He calmly accepted the news of her death. And now he stands over this first wife and says, "good riddance."* Charles religiously attended services in his chapel morning and night, but the words of the Scriptures he listened to so eagerly had no effect in the man's life. *How greatly is the message of the Alabaster needed in this country!* Matthew thought.

"We must hurry away from here! The raiders may get reinforcements and return," Charles shouted to his men, who were collecting the renegades' weapons as booty.

Charles approached Printha and removed Pepin from her arms. She jumped on behind Waldulf as he mounted his horse, and the Franks kept a rapid pace until they had put many miles behind them.

When the king called a halt, he turned to Printha. "It seems we owe our lives to you, young miss. We would have been killed like nesting ducks if it had not been for your warning. How did you know about this attack?"

Printha cast a side glance at Waldulf, refusing to meet his eyes. "I was out riding and encountered the outcast, Folz. He had heard the thieves planning this attack. So you really owe your life to him. I only delivered his message."

Charles looked at her sternly. "You were not to ride by yourself."

"Yes, sire, but there was no one to go with me." She looked at Matthew. "It was as if the God of the Christians that you've talked about must have been guiding me. Even on the ride here, there seemed to be an unseen hand telling me which way to take—a most unusual experience."

A warm sensation flowed through Matthew. He may not have found the heir to the Alabaster, but he'd been able to influence this young pagan.

"What must I do to repay you, my dear?" Charles insisted.

"Set Folz free from his penance," Printha said without hesitation. "In spite of what he's done, he has surely suffered enough. I do not like to see anyone in bondage."

"It was the church that condemned him to be an outcast, but I will use my powers of persuasion to secure his release."

Charles was as good as his word, and as soon as they returned to his headquarters, the king sent Matthew to the bishop of Erfurt to intercede in behalf of Folz. Upon Matthew's return, he was ushered into Charles's chambers, where Hildegard was playing with their four children.

"My mission has been successful," Matthew said, handing Charles a document. "The bishop has granted pardon to Folz for his service in saving the life of the king. The sealed message explains that."

"That's great news. It's been a burden to me to know that a man who was instrumental in saving my life should be wandering around this kingdom in shackles. Send for Printha and Waldulf."

Printha was working at the loom when she received the summons. When she learned that Matthew had returned, she rushed into the king's quarters. Waldulf was there before her.

The king beamed on the two youths. "You will be pleased to learn that Folz has been pardoned, and I'm giving the two of you the honor of telling him so. Take some clean garments for the man and bring him to me."

Waldulf and Printha rushed to the stables, and in a short time they were traveling as rapidly as the terrain would permit toward Nehouse. As they neared the village site, a small flock of quail scattered at their rapid approach, and their horses reared and snorted at the sudden flurry beneath their feet.

"Pull back on the straps," Waldulf called as the two horses broke into a run. His mount took the lead, and looking back, he noticed that Printha was swaying back and forth in the saddle. "Hold on!" he called.

Waldulf soon brought his horse under control, and fell back to Printha's side. He pulled on the bridle, forcing her horse to a walk.

"Whew! What a fright!" she said, her blue eyes bright with excitement.

"At least we reached our destination sooner," Waldulf said as they approached the deserted village.

"Folz! Folz?" Printha called over and over as she slipped from the horse's back. She walked around the clearing and into the adjacent forest with Waldulf, but they didn't hear the clank of chains. Folz did not answer their calls.

"That's strange—he is always hanging around this area," Waldulf said. "And of all days for him to be gone when we have good news for him."

They returned in disappointment to report to Charles. When they couldn't find Folz on a second trip into the forest, Charles decided on more action. "Something must have happened to the man. He's at the mercy of the elements and wild beasts. We will search for him."

"I've heard, sire, that he's built himself a hut of twigs and branches around a cave opening. Perhaps he's there," a noble volunteered.

"Then take a contingent of men and find him."

Waldulf rode with the searchers, but Printha was commanded to stay at home. Two days later they brought in Folz's beaten and lacerated body. He'd been unconscious when they found him in his hut. The soldiers had removed the chains from his shrunken body, but Folz was still filthy when he was delivered into Matthew's care. Matthew worked with Folz two days before he regained consciousness.

"What happened to you, man?" Matthew asked. "Who attacked you?"

"The renegades. They must have learned that I'd sent warning to the king," Folz said quietly.

"Your warning reached him in time. None of his party was harmed."

"But many of the renegades were, and I paid the penalty for that."

After a week, Folz could be lifted to a sitting position, and Printha and Waldulf were his first visitors.

"We have good news for you," Printha said. "We came to tell you several days ago and we couldn't find you." Folz smiled encouragingly at her. "The bishop has pardoned you. Because your warning saved the king, you will no longer be an outcast."

Folz turned to Matthew. "I never thought the day would come. I had prayed for death, hoping that my debt was paid and that I could join my departed loved ones. Do you think my pardon is complete?"

"The bishop thinks so, and it's his decision that matters."

When Folz was able to walk into Charles's presence, the king said to him. "King Charles pays his debts. Because you have saved my life, you will from henceforth be part of my court. I appoint you as the count of the stable at this palace. If you will swear loyalty to me, you may be associated with me as long as you desire."

Folz was still weak from his injuries, but he tottered toward the king and knelt in front of him. Tears streamed down the man's face as he said, "I offer the king my loyalty and my life."

Then Charles turned to Printha. "I will also pay my debt to the Saxon girl, who has been my hostage for over three years. You will no longer be a prisoner in this court. You are free to return to your home. I will appoint a guard to return you to the borders of Saxony."

A tumult of emotions erupted in Printha's heart. She wanted to see her mother, but she turned toward Waldulf, who regarded her with tortured eyes. She would miss him.

Waldulf addressed the king, "May I be a part of the guard that escorts Printha to Saxony?"

"Your wish is granted."

Two days later, Printha came into the great hall carrying the few possessions she'd accumulated during her stay in Frankish Gaul, many of them the rich garments she had been given by Drago, who had also stated his intention to travel with the host that would take her to Saxony.

The king and queen waited to bid Printha good-bye. Little Pepin hobbled toward her, his awkward movements reminding her of a monkey's gait. She hugged the boy and held him in her arms as she paused before King Charles and Hildegard, each of them holding a son. Setting Pepin down gently, she took Hrotrud from her nurse's arm and kissed her.

"I thank you for your kind treatment of me. Much of the time I didn't feel like a prisoner," Printha said to the royal family.

"You have become dear to us, child," Hildegard said, "but we cannot repay your loyalty by keeping you from your own people. May God go with you as you leave us."

King Charles took her hand. "I pray the day comes when there is peace between the Saxons and the Franks. Perhaps you can be our representative among your own people."

Printha nodded agreement, but she remained silent as she turned toward the door. She couldn't understand her reaction. *Why should I feel sadness? These people are my enemies and have kept me imprisoned for years. I should hate them, but I don't.*

She stopped before Matthew, who reached out his hand to her. "We will miss you, Printha. I trust that you will continue your education with the books I've given you, and I'd also encourage you to think upon the Christian teachings I've imparted."

"Is the Christian God to be found in Saxony?" Printha asked.

"His Spirit is everywhere. You will find Him if you search for Him with all your heart."

Waldulf waited to help her mount a sleek black horse, a gift from the king. He rode by her side, the journey toward the Rhine passing much too quickly. Printha's sad leavetaking of the king's household was hardly painful when compared to her desolation at parting from Waldulf. She wondered how she would have survived those first months of captivity without his understanding. It was good to have him beside her as she started home, but the hour finally came for separation.

"Do you think we'll ever see one another again, Waldulf?" she asked sadly.

His face was as downcast as Printha's. "It's unthinkable that we will not. I would have taken you to visit my parents, but this all happened so quickly. I had assumed that the king might use you in a hostage exchange someday, but I hadn't expected your release to come so soon."

"I will miss you, Waldulf."

"Perhaps I can come to your village to see you."

She threw up her hands in dismay. "You must not, my friend. Franks are not welcome there, and Widukind moves often. We would not be easy to find. I fear this is good-bye."

"I will never forget you, Printha." Looking around, he saw that no one was in view for the moment. He leaned from the saddle and planted a kiss on her willing lips.

11

Frankish Gaul, 777

Matthew held his pen aloft after he wrote the date "777." The beginning of a new year, and he could not believe that it had been more than eight years since he'd left Constantinople, but as he looked again at the message he had just received, he recognized the passage of time.

> I regret to inform you, Master Matthew, that my father, Basil, has died. He was proud of his long years in service to the house of Trento, and his dying wish was that God might grant a speedy end to your mission and your return to this city.
>
> I have been appointed as steward over your affairs by the lawyers who hold the Trento wealth in trust for the next owner. If that appointment does not please you, please notify me and the lawyers by return message.
>
> I have other news for you also. In the closing days of the reign of Constantine V, he made another attack upon monks who opposed him. The monastery where you took your vows was leveled. The abbot as well as some other monks were killed. Leo IV, who rules in his father's stead, seems more tolerant, but this is encouraging the iconoclasts to further protests, so the religious situation in Byzantium is tense.

One other unhappy note. The servant Sophia wishes me
to convey the message that the boy, Alex, died in a rash of
dysentery sweeping through the city. Please be advised that
we made every effort to save the boy's life.

Respectfully yours,
Cyril, son of Basil

So the son of Charles and Desiderata is dead, Matthew
thought. *It is a sad ending to a marriage that was a mistake
from the beginning.* A few times during the years of fighting
between the Franks and the Lombards, Matthew had been
tempted to tell Charles about this son, but now he was glad that
he had not. *My efforts to remove the child from harm's way were
in vain,* Matthew reflected. *If not for that, I would have kept
Sophia here in Gaul with me.*

The letter had put Matthew in a melancholy mood, and he
lamented the fact that he had accepted his father's mission.
*What have I accomplished during all the wandering I have
done?* He had the Alabaster but not its owner. Now that his
abbot was dead, he was free of the command to bring the Alabaster to him, but it pained Matthew to hear of the destruction
of the monastery. In his moments of anguish and despair, he
had thought of the cloister as his home, a place where he could
finally go to seek peace for his troubled heart. Now it, too,
was gone.

The last two years had been wearisome in Charles's service
and more than once he'd been tempted to take the Alabaster and
return home, but he withdrew from his garments a message that
had caused him to delay his return to Constantinople; indeed,
he doubted that he would ever return. He had been betrayed by
the one he loved beyond all others and by another whom he had
called friend. The letter had been written by Sophia in 775, but
it hadn't caught up with him until a year ago.

My dear Matthew,

There comes a time when all of us must face reality. I have finally accepted the fact that there is no future for us. I don't believe you will ever be able to renounce your ties to the church, and I cannot go on hoping that you will.

Like most women, I want a home and children of my own. Gerona and I have married. Although I will always hold you as my first love in my heart, I have a fondness for Gerona, who loves me dearly. Basil gave me a position in your house, and Gerona has gone back to work in the silk industry. As man and wife, we are presenting Alex to the world as our own, although it grieves me to see this royal child deprived of his rights. Should you be desirous of hearing more about him, you may address me at the house of Trento.

Please forgive me for any anguish this letter brings, but even if we had married, you would have felt guilty every time you took me to bed. By marrying another, I have removed temptation from you. Believe me, it is better this way.

Sophia

After the shock of that letter, Matthew even had lost interest in finding the owner of the Alabaster and had spent his time in the company of Charles, who during the past two years had waged offensive wars in Saxony.

In spite of his words to Printha that he hoped to live in peace with the Saxons, Charles had started plans for another Saxon campaign as soon as the Lombards were subdued in 774. The next year, he had launched an offensive against the Saxons, stating his determination to convert them to Christianity. Missionaries marched with the armed host, attempting conversion by force. For two years, Charles had engaged in sporadic fighting with the Saxons, and the Saxons retaliated by attacking Frankish settlements and churches.

Their counterblows increased Charles's determination, and his armies moved deeper into the enemy's territory to burn and kill, the overall plan being to forge a massive invasion to build block houses and erect churches within them. The Franks dislocated many Saxons and massacred hundreds more. As a result, when the Franks rounded up sullen hostages and starving villagers to listen to priests stammering their Christian message, no conversions were forthcoming.

"What else can I do?" Charles thundered to his advisors when it was evident that another winter was approaching and he was no nearer a conquest of Saxony then he had been years ago. One by one, he scanned the faces of his advisors, questioning, "What else can I do?" and their replies were framed to soothe the king.

"Our men are good fighters and your strategy is well planned, but the Saxons are an elusive foe. Take Widukind for example," one priest commented. "His name is whispered among the border folk, but I've yet to find anyone who has seen him. He's the mastermind of the Saxon world. If we could defeat him, we could bring the others into subjection, but we'd have to catch him first."

"And what of the mystery surrounding this masked rider?" a count said. "For the past year we've heard of him, and Franks living along the border have seen him."

"Maybe the rider is Widukind himself," another noble suggested.

"That's possible," the count replied. "And consider the rumor that whenever the masked rider passes by, a death occurs."

"It's only a scheme on the part of the Saxons to intimidate our host."

"It seems to have worked," Charles said wryly. "You are silent, Matthew. Why, in your judgment, haven't we brought the Saxons to their knees?"

Matthew knew his opinion would not please the king, so he had remained silent. He still hesitated even after Charles directed the question at him. "Perhaps God is not pleased at the tactics of the Franks. Could it be that He is not blessing your actions because of the senseless slaughter and destruction inflicted upon the Saxon peasants?"

Charles stood up in a huff and pranced around the room. His hand rested on the sword at his side, and Matthew thought, *Perhaps I may be leaving Frankish lands after all. That is, if my life is spared.* His despair over what he considered the betrayal of Gerona and Sophia was so great that he didn't care if he lived or died.

"Have you intentionally insulted the king of the Franks?" Charles shouted.

"That was not my intention, Your Excellency, but you asked for my opinion."

Charles swung toward the two priests in the room. "Is this your opinion also?" he thundered.

The priests stammered instant denials.

Charles looked at Matthew again. "The Scriptures mention many holy wars. And what about the offensives of Constantine the Great, who established the church with his sword?"

Matthew had frequently studied Lucius Trento's account of the rise of Constantine, and he remembered Lucius's oft-stated despair that the first Christian emperor had extended the church by conquering his enemies and forcing his faith upon them.

"I doubt that was the way God intended for His church to be rooted. And the wars among the ancient Hebrews were for a special purpose. We are living under the day of God's grace now."

"I do not understand that statement," Charles said, calming down.

"I don't understand God's grace myself. I simply accept it."

It was obvious that Charles's anger had abated and he took his seat again. "Waldulf!" he called.

"Yes, sire," Waldulf said as he stood. Matthew looked fondly at the boy, who had become like a son to him in the past several years. Denied the companionship of his own father, Waldulf often turned to Matthew for counseling. He was the most handsome youth Matthew had ever seen, and his intelligence was keen. Waldulf was the only bright spot in Matthew's life.

"I want to talk to Father Sturm. It is your task to find him and escort him to this chamber. We will cease this discussion until you return."

It was a week before Waldulf returned with the priest. The hardship of his life had aged Sturm, and his shoulders sagged as he stood before Charles and listened to the king's problem.

"As I have told you in the past, I feel it is my destiny to spread Christianity among the Saxons, but in spite of all my efforts, they continue to spurn the message." Waving his hand to encompass the roomful of counselors, he continued, "We have not agreed upon the cause of that, and I would like your advice and your blessing."

Sturm leaned heavily on his cane, and he peered at the king from under shaggy brows. "You have called me from my sanctuary to ask me this?" the old man said angrily. "My answer is still the same as I told you years ago. The Saxons are a warrior race and attacking them is not the way to convert them to Christianity. In order to reform the Saxons' nature, the Franks must also change. Put away your weapons, share food with them instead of destroying their provisions, and leave them at liberty."

A scowl covered Charles's face. "I've repeatedly offered them peace."

"But only after you've punished them with iron weapons."

Though he was stunned by the aged priest's words, Charles could not be angry with him. "I do not agree with you, Father Sturm, but in appreciation of your many years of service, I am adding several acres of lands to your holdings at the monastery."

"I thank you, sire, but that does not alter my opinion of your many wars."

Charles spent the next several days in seclusion, but when he again called his council together, he had made momentous decisions that could affect the future of all nations of the West.

"I have been swayed by the opinions of those who have criticized my dealings with the Saxons," Charles stated. "I have decided to try the ways of peace. I will circulate this declaration throughout Saxony." He held up a parchment and read:

> Charles, king of the Franks, to the Saxons:
> I desire peace to reign between our peoples. I thereby call upon the Saxons to assemble in freedom to receive baptism into the Christian church and to take an oath of loyalty to me. Although I will become overlord of the Saxons, they will be allowed to keep their own laws and customs. Next summer, I will build a town at the headwaters of the Lippe River. It is there I expect you to assemble.

Matthew nodded agreement when Charles looked his way, and he gathered from this overture that the king had forgiven him.

"My clerks will make copies of this declaration to be distributed throughout Saxony. I want volunteers to serve as my emissaries in this task. You will travel in groups of two for safety, but even then you may be in danger."

Waldulf and Matthew exchanged glances and immediately lifted their hands. "We will travel as a team, sire."

As they left the council chamber, Waldulf came to Matthew's side. "In spite of the danger, Matthew, I look forward to this opportunity. If God is good, perhaps we will be able to see Printha again. I think of her often."

"To see Printha means that we will have to find Widukind since she's his daughter. I expect that chieftain is too elusive to be found by the Franks," Matthew stated.

"Nevertheless, I intend to look for her. I'm sure there have been great changes in her since our separation."

The edicts, printed both in the Saxon and the Frankish dialects, were ready in two weeks. The emissaries were commanded to make a speedy foray into Saxony.

❀   ❀   ❀

A month later Waldulf and Matthew returned to the royal headquarters, and they were the first of the emissaries to return. In reporting to King Charles, Matthew said, "We feel that the mission was unsuccessful, for we did not meet any Saxons face-to-face to deliver your message. When we came upon villages, we found that the people had fled. Although we felt that eyes were peering at us in the forest, we saw very few Saxons."

"The messages, man, what did you do with them?" Charles demanded.

"We finally started fastening them to tree trunks. We believe that the Saxons did receive them because when we circled back to see what had happened to the ones we'd left, some of them had been taken away."

"Then perhaps your work was not in vain after all," Charles sighed.

Leaving Charles to mull over the information they had brought, Matthew and Waldulf sought their rooms so they might refresh themselves after the strenuous journey. They had spent every night lying on the ground with little opportunity to bathe.

As Waldulf soaked in the tub of hot water brought to him, he dwelt on his disappointment in not seeing Printha. Widukind was as elusive as a flea, and the few Saxons they had talked with had been evasive about him, though they admitted he ruled the forest folk. Waldulf had seen the Saxon masked rider at a distance—a lithe form clothed in black that seemed almost a part of the beast he rode.

In a few days, the other emissaries returned with similar results, but Charles went ahead with his plans to build a town in Saxony. Charles summoned his host to meet him near the headwaters of the Lippe River by the first of May. The king requested the company of Father Sturm on the expedition to be on hand to preach the Gospel to the pagans, but Sturm replied in a terse message: "When the Saxons start arriving, then send for me."

So confident was Charles of his success that he planned to have his family travel with the host. With four small children and another on the way, Hildegard needed help, but Charles did not pay a great deal of attention to household matters. Matthew, who had been advising the queen on her poor health, suggested that Hildegard needed some help to effect this move. Charles assigned Waldulf and Matthew to that task.

"Thanks, Matthew," Waldulf said grumpily. "Just what I needed—playing nursemaid to these children."

"Would you have preferred to be responsible for baggage and provisions? This isn't a military expedition, my son, and you won't be covering yourself with military glory. That is, unless the Saxons attack."

Hrotrud, Charles's youngest child, was over two years old, and it was a constant problem to keep her away from the wheels of the cart. She was unhappy riding with her mother, but her legs were too short to do much walking, so Matthew ended up carrying her in his arms most of the time as he flanked the queen's cortege. The young hunchback, Pepin, who spent more time with his grandmother at Purm than with his father, rode on the cart with Hildegard. Pepin's sunny nature as a baby had submerged into a moody disposition, which Matthew attributed to Charles's continued neglect of his firstborn now that he had other sons.

The site Charles had chosen for his town was a watered plain at a junction of wilderness roads. The surrounding forests provided adequate hunting and a good source of logs for building. The river and its tributaries offered bathing facilities.

Upon their arrival, Charles sent a priest to bring a container of water from the river, and pouring the water on the ground, the king christened the town site Paderborn.

"The first building to be erected will be a church," the king said, and he directed two of his servants to cut four trees and outline the spot for the church. Within a month, the church was completed and close to forty other buildings were under construction, but no Saxons had appeared. The Franks scanned the forest area daily to see if any of the enemy would take advantage of Charles's offer. It was obvious that the king was becoming more and more vexed because the Saxons didn't respond to his overture of peace.

One morning Matthew awakened in his hut at the insistent call of Waldulf. "Matthew! Matthew! The Saxons are coming."

Matthew threw a robe over his shoulders and hurried outside. Waldulf pointed toward the forest, and Matthew saw about twenty peasants grouped near the woods. They looked fearful, and Matthew said, "Go alert the king if you have not done so already."

Joy overspread Charles's face when he came out of his quarters. "Do you think they come seeking peace?"

"That would be my assumption, sire," Matthew said. "They do not seem warlike."

"But how are we going to find out? Blast Sturm! Why didn't he come here as I requested? We don't have anyone to communicate with them."

"I might try, sire," Waldulf said. "I learned some of the Saxon language from Printha."

Charles beamed at him. "Then by all means, do so."

Waldulf walked slowly toward the Saxons, his right hand uplifted. He carried no weapon, and a smile spread across his face. Matthew's heart swelled in love for the boy, and he wished, as he had often done so, that the heir to the Alabaster might be the caliber of Waldulf. *Or if matters had turned out differently with Sophia, I might have had a son as precious as Waldulf.* Matthew shook his head to deny his longings and walked beside the king, keeping several steps behind Waldulf. They were close enough to hear Waldulf's voice when he spoke, although they could not discern his words.

"The king of the Franks welcomes you to Paderborn. Do you come in peace?" Waldulf spoke haltingly, trying to remember the words he'd learned from Printha.

The Saxons looked surprised that this Frank could address them in their own tongue, but one man stepped forward. "We are tired of war. We have heard of the king's edict, and we are ready to submit if he truly means what he says."

"I will let him speak for himself, and I will translate his words."

"You speak our tongue well, young Frank," the Saxon commented. "Where did you learn it?"

"From a Saxon hostage, a girl named Printha. Do you know her? We were friends, but I've had no word from her since she returned to her homeland."

The Saxon turned to look at his companions and several of them whispered and tittered, but he raised his hand for silence. "No, we do not know her," he said, but Waldulf didn't believe him.

By now, most of the Franks had awakened and assembled in a silent group before Charles's home. The appearance of so many people alarmed the Saxons, and they drifted toward the forest.

"Wait!" Waldulf cried. He motioned for the king to come forward, and Charles strode to his side.

"These Saxons have come to make peace, but they want your assurance of what their fate will be."

"They must accept baptism into the Christian church and take an oath of loyalty to me. Though I will become their overlord and will expect an annual tribute, I will be lenient in my demands. They can still follow their customs and make their own laws, as long as they are not contrary to the Christian faith."

While Waldulf repeated in Saxon what Charles had said, Matthew despaired at this method of evangelism. *Without a knowledge of the true nature of God's plan of salvation, how can these Saxons become Christians?* Father Sturm had told Matthew that the Saxons saw their gods as guides and protectors, much more human than the Christian God. Matthew believed the Saxons would try to accept another god without disturbing the old Germanic pantheon. Obviously, Charles's proposal would make conversion easy for the Saxons, but without regular preaching and teaching, their Christianity would be superficial, lacking power to change their way of life.

The Saxon man turned to his small band. After a short discussion, the leader bowed before Charles. With an exultant shout Charles lifted him to his feet.

"Ask him if other Saxons are going to submit," the king instructed Waldulf.

When Waldulf put the question to the Saxon, he nodded, and Waldulf translated his words to Charles. "If these few are treated well, others will come."

"Bring them forward. They will be fed. And you, Waldulf, take a contingent of men and bring Sturm to me. He said he would come when the Saxons came. Tell him I also want him to consecrate our new church building while he is here."

Within an hour, Waldulf and three other Franks left Paderborn and directed their mounts toward Fulda. Waldulf reasoned that their journey would be swift because the weather was good, assuming of course that Sturm was at the monastery when they arrived there. Waldulf's hopes of a quick trip were dashed before the afternoon was over when a thunderstorm drenched them. He was also concerned because he thought that they were being followed. Since they'd stopped for a break, he had heard the sound of hoofbeats, sometimes flanking them, sometimes behind them. *Could it be echoes of the approaching storm?* His companions had not seemed to have noticed anything, so Waldulf kept silent, not wanting to alarm them and embarrass himself if there was no danger. After all, these men were his seniors by many years. Surely with their experience, they would have detected danger should there be any.

They were still far from the monastery by nightfall, and they took refuge in an abandoned hut. Waldulf drew the last watch, and he left his bedroll reluctantly. Although they had left Saxony when they'd crossed the river, he was still uneasy. Loud peals of thunder rumbled across the heavens, and streaks of lightning periodically pierced the darkness. Wind buffeted the trees, and as the mighty branches swayed back and forth, Waldulf saw many weird shapes—as if witches were dancing across the field. He jumped to attention when one flash of lightning revealed a horseman at the edge of the woods staring intently toward their camp. This was not his imagination—someone was stalking the Franks.

Trying to stay in the shadows, he moved toward the hut to alert his companions, but a mighty wind blast swept the area, lightning cracked nearby, and a limb swirled from a tree to knock the strange rider from his horse. Forgetting his need for caution, Waldulf ran toward the man who'd been thrown to the ground.

The lightning had ceased for the time being, and without light, Waldulf groped his way toward the fallen horseman. He was helped in his search by the snorting of the horse when he approached. Dropping to his knees, he patted his hands over the ground until he made contact with the body. Waldulf's fingers examined the form and found that the rider's heartbeat was steady, but his hands halted in midair. *It can't be!*

Another flash of lightning illuminated the area, and Waldulf's shock intensified. The figure on the ground was covered with a flowing black robe, and a black mask completely hid the face. Widukind's legendary masked rider lay on the ground in front of him, and the rider was a woman.

The figure began to stir, and Waldulf said, "Lie still. You may be hurt."

"Waldulf?" He recognized Printha's voice, and momentarily he wondered if he was dreaming. Forgetting about any possible injuries she might have, he pulled her upward into his arms.

"Printha? Is it really you? You're the masked rider everyone fears?"

"I've been stalking Charles's new town for weeks hoping to find you alone. I thought that you were one of the men who set out on a journey today, but I could never get into a position so I could tell if you were among the travelers."

Printha winced when Waldulf helped her to stand.

"Are you hurt? Did the tree limb hit you?" Waldulf asked with concern.

"No, I think not. The falling branch spooked my horse and he threw me off." She walked a few steps without his assistance. "I feel bruised, but there is no bad injury."

"But why are you dressed like this? Have you been doing the evil things that are credited to you by the Franks?"

"I have done nothing. My mother, Redith, has died, and Widukind takes me with him when he's on raids. For my protection, he has me dress this way. He says that I'm maturing quickly into a woman, and he thinks I'm safer with a disguise."

"I noticed a change in you myself," Waldulf said with a catch in his voice. "Your father may be right."

"I must go now, Waldulf, before the others awaken. How long will you be at the new town? Can we meet somewhere?"

"Charles is hoping that the Saxons will all come to swear loyalty to him. Can't you come into the town?"

In the darkness he sensed that she was shaking her head. "Widukind has no intention of surrendering. A few of the Saxons will come and Charles will think he has won a victory, but as soon as the Franks return to their homeland, the Saxons will follow Widukind. The Saxons and Franks will never be at peace."

"I refuse to believe that. I do not want to be your enemy."

"Yet you serve the king of the Franks, and I am Widukind's daughter!"

By the dawn's first rays, Waldulf was able to distinguish her face, and her bright blue eyes sparkled from behind the black mask.

"You must go now," he said. "I'm going to fetch Sturm to Paderborn, and I should return with him in a few days. A week from today, I will come northward from Paderborn into the forest. You watch and intercept me when you think it is safe."

He watched with admiration as she leapt to the back of the horse and faded silently into the forest.

❀   ❀   ❀

Fortunately for Waldulf's mission, Sturm was at the monastery when they arrived. He immediately agreed to travel with them, taking with him some of his brother monks. Although he balked at riding a horse, the Franks insisted that he do so. Waldulf was shocked at the man's appearance—his body had shrunken until he seemed only a ghost of the man he had once been. He walked with a shuffling gait, and his hands shook when he lifted them in blessing. In spite of the fact that he'd made most of his previous journeys on foot, Waldulf thought the priest accepted the loan of the horse with relief.

When they entered the town of Paderborn and Sturm saw the assembled Saxons, tears streamed from his faded eyes, and he slid from the horse's back onto his knees. For years he had been working and praying for the salvation of these people, and now his hopes were going to be realized.

For the next two days Sturm preached the Gospel to the Saxons. On the third day, assisted by the monks who had followed him from Fulda, Sturm invited the Saxons to assert their belief in Jesus by being baptized. For most of the day, the old priest stood waist deep in the Lippe River and immersed scores of Saxons, Hessians, Westfalians, and Eastfalians who had not only come to swear loyalty to Charles, but also to take their places under the Christian banner.

After the baptisms, Sturm held a service to consecrate the church, which was not nearly large enough for the assembled throng, so the service was held outside. Once the last prayer was offered, rejoicing spread among the assemblage. The dragon standard and the cross standard that had led the Franks to victory in Italy was paraded throughout the town and among the Saxon camps. Sturm's monks followed the host chanting psalms.

Robed in his leather hunting trousers and wolf skins, Charles mingled with his own people and drank many horns of wine and beer with the long-haired Saxon chieftains. Sturm's visage darkened when Charles joined in the Saxon chants of heroes who sought Wodin in the heaven-hall of Valhalla, but it was hard to be angry amidst such a day of rejoicing, so the old priest did not repudiate the king.

Only Matthew voiced a note of concern to Waldulf. "Widukind did not come."

"Do you think this will last?" Waldulf asked Matthew.

"I wonder. Although they seem sincere, I'm not sure the Saxons understand what they have promised."

"It's a serious vow they've taken—never to abandon King Charles and Christianity else they will lose liberty and heritage."

"But we will count our blessings. The action has succeeded in staving off a campaign against Saxony for the year 777. It's a rare occasion for Charles to have a season without a military expedition. I will take peace instead of war anytime."

12

SAXONY, 777

Waldulf rolled from one side to the other on the hard cot; it seemed he'd been awake for hours. His legs twitched, his scalp felt stretched tight enough to break, and he stifled more than one nervous cough. He hoped to be able to leave the room without awakening Matthew, for he hadn't told his friend about his encounter with Printha. He was unwilling to betray the secret that she was Widukind's masked rider, a fact that had disturbed his dreams and waking hours for days.

His movements finally disturbed Matthew, who sat up and said, "What ails you?"

"I can't sleep, but I didn't want to disturb you. Now that you're awake, I'll get up and leave. I'm going for an early morning ride. I may be gone all day."

Matthew threw back a bearskin and sat up to peer out the window. "It's awfully early," he said grumpily. "I can't even see the building next to ours."

As he groped in the darkness for his boots and riding garments, Waldulf sensed suspicion in Matthew's manner. Perhaps it was only his imagination, but Matthew was hard to fool. He rushed out of the building without further conversation. The king's cooks were already hard at work, and Waldulf begged a slab of meat and a loaf of bread from them before he mounted his horse and headed northward.

177

For more than an hour, Waldulf traveled through the pathless forest wondering how he would ever find the girl he sought. He drew up his horse sharply when a Saxon peasant woman stepped into his path. She was garbed in a long flowing mantle, and a brown hood covered her head. Her garments blended into the landscape. He stopped before her, and she pushed back the hood.

"Printha!" he said, and vaulted from the back of his horse.

She took his hand and pulled him into the shadows of the trees. "I know a place where we are not likely to be seen, but the way is rough, so lead your horse. I must blindfold you. I do not want you to know where we're going."

"Do you live nearby?"

"Any place in the forest is my home. As a daughter of Widukind, I've learned to live anywhere. He does not belong to a clan anymore—he is the spirit behind *all* of the Saxons, and as he's traveled from place to place, I've learned to do the same."

"Where is he now?" Waldulf asked eagerly.

"I do not know, and even if I did, I wouldn't tell you."

"Do you think I would betray you?"

"You cannot tell what you do not know. We are aware that Charles wishes Widukind to bow before him, but as long as the majority of the Saxon people recognize my father as leader, he will not submit to the Franks. When he loses the trust of his people, who knows?"

Waldulf stumbled through the forest with his hand on Printha's arm, and with the many turns they took, he lost all sense of direction. Printha didn't remove the blindfold until she led him into an area that was obviously her camp. A black horse was tethered near a grass-covered hut constructed of saplings, and he neighed a welcome to Waldulf's mount. A spring bubbled nearby, and birds twittered among the branches of the tall trees overhanging the area.

"This is a pleasant place. How long have you been here?" Waldulf inquired.

"Since the Franks arrived at the headwaters of the Lippe."

Although Waldulf didn't confront her with the fact, he suspected that this camp was not far from Paderborn, and that she was acting as a spy for Widukind. *Does she have a vantage point nearby where she can look down upon the Franks?* Waldulf wondered.

"You need not be so secretive with me," Waldulf said tersely, for it pained him to think that Printha did not trust him. "I will not betray you."

"I do not fear for myself," she said, settling down on a fallen log near the hut and pulling him beside her. "I do not think Charles would harm me even though I am a Saxon, but you are a Frank, and you would not hesitate to betray my father to Charles. I don't think any less of you for that. You should be loyal to your own people."

"Let's forget our people and talk about us. I've missed you so much, Printha, and I'm amazed at how you've changed. You're beautiful."

"Was I so bad before?" Printha teased.

"You were a child when you left. You're a woman now."

"I'm fourteen, and I keep remembering that Hildegard was younger than that when she married the king of the Franks."

"Are you thinking of marriage?" he asked, partly in hope, partly in fear

"I'm thinking of it as inevitable, perhaps, but I have no plans." She ran her hands over his massive shoulders. "You've changed much, too, Waldulf. Your muscles are as strong as iron, and I'll wager you're at least two heads taller than you were two years ago."

Waldulf's pulse quickened as her hands touched his body and his skin tingled. *What is happening to me?* he wondered. Before the afternoon was over, he knew. This girl, who had been his childhood playmate, was now the young woman he loved. Printha must have experienced similar longings, for when they parted, she drew his head down to hers and kissed him longingly.

"But you are a Frank and I'm Saxon," she said sadly, and her depression matched his own.

Although Waldulf didn't know how much longer Charles would stay at Paderborn, they made plans to meet in seven days in the same manner. Charles seemed to be in no hurry to leave his new city. He'd brought his family northward to be with him, and Waldulf figured they would be there the rest of the summer.

Waldulf continued to keep secret his meetings with Printha. Although normally Matthew might have noticed his young friend's periodic absences, he was so involved with King Charles that he didn't notice Waldulf's change of habits, for not only had the Saxons changed their religious practices, Charles himself was undergoing a spiritual transformation.

"I feel strongly my responsibility," the king confided to Matthew one day, "of being the leader of a large number of new Christians. The baptism of these heathen people has created a great change in me. I now have many different nations under my control, but we all have one thing in common, whether we are Franks, Lombards, or Saxons—we are all sheep of Christ's fold. Dare I confess to you, friend Matthew, that in time I dream of becoming the leader of one great Christian nation? Do you think that is possible?"

"Possible, but not probable," Matthew answered. "A far-flung nation such as yours, sire, is hard to control. Many of your own subjects are not yet loyal to you nor to our Christ. Though the king may not agree with me, the growth of the church is not supposed to take place by use of the sword. Jesus mentioned in several of His parables that His kingdom would grow slowly."

"You can't deny that by bringing the Saxons to their knees, we have brought many of them to the cross also."

"No, I cannot deny that, Your Excellency."

"So I will continue to dream, Matthew. When we were in Rome last year I prevailed upon Pope Hadrian to give me a copy of Augustine's *City of God*. Are you familiar with that work?"

"Yes, sire. I've studied it often."

"I have tried to read it, but my comprehension of its message is slight. I would like for you to read it to me and translate the meaning." He lowered his voice. "I find you more astute and learned than many of my bishops, and I will value your interpretation of Augustine's words."

"It will be my pleasure, sire, but the volume covers a vast number of subjects. You may need to choose the ones that interest you the most."

For several weeks, Matthew rose each morning at daybreak to visit the king so that they might discuss spiritual matters before the needs of the day pressed upon Charles.

"*City of God* was written in response to a historical need," Matthew explained at their first meeting. "The king may know that in 410, the Visigoth king entered Rome and pillaged the city. Those barbarians carried off large amounts of plunder, leaving behind a city of death. This invasion marked the end of the Roman Empire."

"And I understand that many Roman citizens blamed this event on Christianity because it had replaced paganism as the state religion during Constantine's time. Rumors spread that the pagan deities were offended and that the Visigoths had been the chastisement."

"That is true, and Augustine's answer was *City of God*. He started the book in 413, and it appeared in installments over the next thirteen years."

"But how does he deal with that accusation against Christianity?"

"He reminds his readers that Rome had suffered disasters long before the coming of Christianity and that internal decay had brought about the destruction of Rome. He said the destruction was an event that had been coming for a long time. He contended that nations will come and go, but that God's kingdom would prevail."

"Does Augustine set a time line for the advent of the city of God?"

"Not that I can interpret. The book sets forth a Christian phi-losophy of history, saying that time is like a tale of two cities: an earthly city inhabited by people who reject our Lord, and the city of God inhabited by God's people. Residents of these cities engage in a struggle between righteousness and wickedness. The Revelator said, 'Here we have no continuing city, but we're look-ing for one in the future.'"

"Does he say where the city of God is to be located?"

Matthew could tell very well the way Charles's mind was run-ning, and he said, "It isn't likely that Augustine contemplated a physical city of bricks and stone. The city of God is a spiritual city inhabited by people who have a personal relationship to God."

Charles rose to his feet and paced around the room, deep in contemplation. "So the city of God may not be concentrated in one area?"

"Augustine argued that if the teachings of the Gospel and faith in Christ entered the heart and mind of every inhabitant of a city, that state would prosper. And when the word of God spread thus to all the cities of the world, a Christian empire would have arrived. Augustine believed it was incumbent upon Christian rulers to make every effort to bring about this city."

"And when that happens, the end of the world will occur."

"I do not know, sire—that may be."

"Which may be in our lifetime, as has often been predicted by our religious leaders?"

A look of ecstasy shone from Charles's eyes, and Matthew knew that Charles envisioned himself as ruler of the city of God. Matthew refrained from saying so, but he knew that even if any *earthly* individual ruled over such a city, Charles was not spiri-tually worthy to be a candidate. Therefore, at their next meeting, Matthew introduced a new subject by reading Augustine's de-scription of the basis of Christianity.

"'God's Son, assuming humanity without destroying His di-vinity, established and founded this faith, that there might be a way for man to man's God through God's man.'"

Charles stared at him uncomprehendingly, and Matthew explained, "He's saying that the only way for man to find his way to God is through Jesus Christ, who assumed the role of mankind and died on the cross to make clear the way for man to find God."

"I'm of the opinion that each man provides his own salvation through his deeds."

Matthew shook his head. "The Scriptures do not teach that, nor did Augustine. He believed that anyone who tried to save himself in any way other than by God's grace would accomplish nothing except to perish in His anger."

"The best of men could be mistaken once in a while," Charles said, still unconvinced about the nature of God's grace.

In the midst of their discussions, a tragedy struck the king and his family when a daughter, named for her mother, died as a two-month-old infant. For days, Charles mourned this child, and his thoughts of establishing the city of God on earth were forgotten in his sorrow, though he still sought spiritual counsel from his priests and from Matthew.

"Does God have no concern, or does He even exist at all? Is Christianity a myth?" Charles demanded.

Although some of the other priests in the room mumbled, "Heresy! Heresy!" Matthew smothered a smile. *How can this man who dares to doubt the existence of God envision himself as leader of the city of God?*

"May I read to you what Augustine had to say on that point," Matthew said, and some of the priests looked at him in disdain. Their knowledge of classical literature was slight.

"'Our God is everywhere present, wholly everywhere, not confined to any place. He can be present unperceived, and be absent without moving; when He exposes us to adversities, it is either to prove our perfections or correct our imperfections; and in return for our patient endurance of the sufferings of time, He reserves for us an everlasting reward.'"

"My faith is small at this time," the king answered ponderously.

"Then may I remind you of some Scriptures. Perhaps the king would remember the example of Job, who lost everything except his trust in God. And the brother of our Lord wrote in his epistle that if we would draw near to God, He would draw near to us. As for God's ever-abiding presence, John, the beloved disciple, said that we can know that He lives in us by the Holy Spirit that has been given to us."

"But why should a child be taken? Why does God cause us pain when we strive to serve Him?"

"We have much to learn about the human body and what is necessary for good health. Childbirth is a delicate process, and we are all barbarians when it comes to understanding the care of infants."

Matthew sensed the tension in the room, for none of these men knew of the five years he had spent in study and contemplation in the monastery. Though he knew they considered him inadequate to explain the Scriptures, he continued. He didn't want to miss this opportunity to focus Charles's mind on God's plan for human beings to be saved through faith in the death and resurrection of the Lord Jesus. He may have lost interest in finding the holder of the Alabaster, but Matthew was still dedicated to promoting the Trento creed.

"God has not promised, nor did Augustine teach, that Christians will live pain-free lives. Other mortals around us suffer. Are we any better than our Lord, who suffered all things for us?"

Matthew believed he had made some impact upon the king's spiritual depth, for Charles soon put away his mourning. Leaving his family at Paderborn, he sallied forth among his own Franks and those whom he had subjugated. Matthew went with him, and upon his return he reported to Waldulf, "His attitude has changed toward his subjects. They've achieved a new respect for him. He didn't neglect those of lowly birth, sleeping in their lofts as readily as he frequented the homes of his barons. He left gifts at many churches and roadside shrines, and hundreds of people freely swore loyalty to him."

"You are happy about this?" Waldulf inquired.

"It seems to me that King Charles is on the way to becoming the great ruler he aspires to be. In spite of his human frailties, he does have worthwhile goals. He wants to extend the frontiers of Christianity, maintain internal order, spread the faith among the heathen, and rule and protect the church. I believe he will eventually accomplish that."

During Charles's absence, Waldulf had visited Printha many times. Sometimes she appeared in her black garb, and they rode along the forest paths in areas so dense that Waldulf could never have found his way. Printha seemed to have an unerring sense of direction, however, and she always returned to their starting point.

Once when they spent the day at Printha's hut, Waldulf voiced what had been on his mind for many weeks. "We will no doubt go back to Gaul for the winter. Will you go with us?"

Shocked, Printha stared at him. "As a prisoner?"

"As my wife."

"But I'm a Saxon," Printha protested when she finally found her voice.

Waldulf pulled her into his arms. "What does that matter? I love you, and these visits with you this summer have been wonderful. I can't think about being separated from you again."

"Your parents would not wish you to marry me."

"You are looking for excuses. Don't you love me?"

Fiercely, Printha's arms encircled his neck, and she pulled his face down to hers. When she released him, he laughed. "Is that the only answer I get?"

Nestling provocatively in his arms, her lips curved into a slight smile. "Of course I love you, Waldulf, but I can't see any future for us. You serve Charles and I'm the daughter of Widukind. They're sworn enemies."

"But Charles is seeking to change that. He's made overtures to Widukind, but he won't come to the assemblage at Paderborn."

"Come to Paderborn to swear loyalty to Charles and to forsake the religion of the old gods?" Printha protested angrily. "Of course he wouldn't come! If Charles wants peace, let him return to Gaul with his hosts. As long as no Frank sets foot north of the Rhine River, there will be no problem."

Waldulf drew away from her. "I had no idea you felt so strongly about this matter."

Printha swiped tears from her eyes. "I want to be loyal to my people, yet I find myself loving you and even having a fondness for Charles and his family. I'm the daughter of Widukind. I should hate all Franks."

"But you don't hate me," Waldulf said. "Marry me and go with me to Gaul."

Printha turned from him and shook her head, and Waldulf traveled back to Paderborn with a heavy heart.

Drago was busily engaged in hawking his wares when Waldulf returned to the town. The man had been in and out of the town all summer, but Waldulf hadn't seen much of him while King Charles was away. Drago imperiously called Waldulf to his side, and looking around cautiously, he said quietly, "You should know, young Frank, that there is much interest among your peers in your occasional absences from the town. So much interest in fact, that you have been spied upon."

"How dare anyone question my activities? I answer only to King Charles."

"These Franks seem to think the king might not be pleased with you." Drago shrugged his shoulders. "I've given you warning." A converted Saxon and his wife approached, and Drago, all smiles, turned to them. "May I interest you in a tapestry from China or a silver goblet made in Constantinople? No one can provide better wares than Drago."

Drago's persuasive voice followed Waldulf as he went thoughtfully on his way. *Had anyone actually seen me with Printha?* Except when they were at the hut, she always wore a disguise, so even if any Franks had seen her, they wouldn't recognize the Saxon girl who had once lived among them. Besides, the change in her was so great, he doubted if anyone would recognize Printha if they met her face-to-face. His blood raced when he considered the attractive changes the years had brought.

Although Waldulf walked nervously among the townspeople for a few days, no one confronted him, and with the advent of visitors from the south, the Franks had something new to think about. Three grandees from Spain came to seek the Frankish king's aid in ousting Muslim invaders from their homeland. Charles was receptive to their petition because he had already received complaints from Spanish Christians about the Muslim conquerors. To extend his influence into Spain fit with his idea of spreading Christendom worldwide.

The Spanish brought gifts that pleased Hildegard, but most of the Franks watched warily as the visitors, with haughty bearing, laid vases of incense, painted glass lamps, strings of pearls, and brocades before Charles and his queen.

Before they returned to their homeland, the Saracens made elaborate promises of how they would aid Charles should he engage the Muslim conquerors in battle. Charles did not give them a firm commitment, yet Matthew believed that the king would march into Spain—if he was first convinced that the Saxons were under his control.

In spite of the many conversions, uneasiness prevailed among the Frankish noblemen. Although Charles had established a rapport with some of the Saxons by his journeys among them, whenever the Franks traveled through the countryside, snipers picked at them. It was almost as if the Saxon renegades knew in advance where Charles would be traveling. When he complained about this to his council, one of the Franks said, "Has the king ever considered that he might have a spy on his staff?"

Charles was so startled that he stood to his feet. "Name him!" he shouted angrily.

The Frank turned and pointed to Waldulf. "I saw him talking to the Saxon masked rider last week."

"That can't be true!" Charles thundered.

"Ask him."

Waldulf felt as if the blood were draining from his body as Charles turned angry eyes upon him. His guilt must be evident. He was determined, however, that he would not betray Printha, for he suspected that she was the one providing the Saxons with details of Charles's movements. *Have I unwittingly passed along information?* he worried.

Since it seemed that the Frank had seen him only once, Waldulf said, "That is true. I talked with the Saxon masked rider last week, but I did not convey any secrets about the Franks or our king."

"Why didn't you capture this man and bring him to me?"

"I didn't consider it. I believed we were to be on friendly relations with the Saxons."

"That would not include the famed masked rider. I am disappointed in you, Waldulf, you have betrayed my trust! You will be banished from this court. Return to your father and tell him what you have done."

"Yes, Your Excellency." Anger flooded Waldulf's heart. After all the years he had served Charles, it would seem that the king could have granted him a second chance. He didn't dread going home, for he knew his mother would be delighted and his father would understand, but he hated to leave without Printha. He knew he couldn't go to her now—every move he made would be under suspicion, and her hiding place might be discovered. He lifted his spear in a deferential salute and strode from the room. Waldulf had most of his gear packed when Matthew joined him in their cabin.

"I can't believe this is happening," Matthew said wearily as he dropped into a chair.

"I should have expected it, I suppose. Drago told me that spies had been watching me, but I didn't expect to be banished from the court."

"Why not ask the king's forbearance? I believe he is already sorry for his judgment against you."

"Then *he* will have to make the overtures. I have done nothing to harm Charles nor any of the Franks. I will not ask forgiveness for something I haven't done. To be honest, I have missed being at the manor, and Charles can get others who are more willing to serve him."

As his anger faded, Waldulf realized he wasn't as dejected as might be expected. He speculated that if he were no longer connected with Charles's court, Printha might be willing to marry him. Living an isolated life on the manor would not call undue attention to Printha's nationality.

"There's more to this than you're telling," Matthew commented.

"Printha is Widukind's masked rider, but I will not betray her to Charles nor the rest of the Franks."

"I might have known. I've noticed a difference in you the past few months. And how is she?"

"Grown to womanhood. She's beautiful, and I love her. I want to take her as my wife, but she refuses because of her loyalty to the Saxons. Please do not tell anyone what I've told you."

"I will not tell. It's a relief to know that the girl is safe. I didn't like the way she was sent from Gaul, and I feared some harm had befallen her. But as this masked rider, she is probably in danger since the Franks are superstitious about her."

"I would like to meet her once more and tell her that I'm being forced to leave. If Drago knows, he might spread the word among the Saxons, and perhaps she will hear it." Waldulf also considered the possibility that if she was spying on the town, she would see his departure and meet him on the trail.

With this possibility in mind, Waldulf hurried to leave. He reached out his hand to Matthew. "You've been my friend and my mentor. I shall miss you. Please pay us a visit at the manor."

"I shall do that. Each year I think I must go back home."

"Since today seems to be the time for revealing secrets, tell me why you've delayed going. It's almost as if you dread going back to Constantinople."

"I will tell you part of it. When I lost the woman I loved, I went into a monastery, which has now been destroyed by the

Byzantine emperor. I cannot return to that haven. When I found my beloved and pondered if I could renounce the holy orders to marry her, she married another man. I feel they both betrayed me, and I've not wanted to return home and face them."

Waldulf embraced his friend. "We've both had our share of trouble, friend Matthew. Perhaps time will heal both our spirits."

Neither King Charles nor the queen put in an appearance, but Waldulf received many sad farewells from the friends he'd made at the Frankish court. His heart lifted somewhat at that sign of friendship. The royal children stood on the balcony overlooking the courtyard. The girls wept as they waved good-bye to him, and the boys looked solemn. Young Pepin, who was paying a rare visit to the court, looked on with tearful eyes. It was evident Waldulf would be missed here, and when he turned his back on Paderborn, he believed that he would never serve Charles again.

At each turn of the trail, Waldulf expected Printha to be waiting for him. When he finally entered Gaul, he was dejected. Printha had not appeared.

13

The day had been hot and sultry, and Waldulf sought the river behind the manor house for a quick swim before he prepared for the evening meal. The barley harvest had been abundant, and Waldulf enjoyed being a part of it. He still missed the camaraderie of court life, but many of those days he'd spent in idleness. He enjoyed the busy routine of the manor. After swimming the width of the river a couple of times, he lay on the ground to dry and drowsily contemplated his year of exile.

A noise upstream startled him to action, and he quickly wrapped his mantle around him. Bearing down on him from the north was a barge, and the advent of this strange craft brought cries from the workers who had seen it. By the time the barge pulled into the bank, most of the inhabitants of Willehad Manor had arrived at the site.

The barge, which contained a dozen beehives, was poled by two burly peasants. Waldulf shook his head when he saw the other occupant of the craft. *Can my mind believe what my eyes behold? Has Drago become a beekeeper?*

Waldulf's isolation at the manor had made him happy to see anyone who brought news of the Frankish court, and Drago always knew the latest court gossip. With a smile, he hurried down the riverbank and gave Drago a hand up the slick incline.

"Welcome, Drago. When did you add honey to your merchandise?"

"When I learned how much profit there is in it. Do you have any idea, young Frank, how much honey is consumed among the Franks and the Saxons? That is their only source of sweetening."

The manor's tenants crowded eagerly around Drago wanting to barter for his products. Waldulf said, "Save a container of your honey for my mother. I'm sure she'll purchase her share, for several of our bee swarms disappeared this year. When you've sold your wares, come to spend the night with us. Mother will have a room prepared for you."

Smiling, Waldulf left Drago and the tenants haggling over a price for the honey and informed his mother that they would have a guest. An hour later, Drago arrived at the house, and in a rare spirit of generosity, he refused payment for the jar of honey he presented to Adela. Waldulf showed the trader to a room on the second floor. Though he had been disheveled and dirty upon his arrival, Drago appeared for dinner dressed in rich silk garments that outshone those of his host. Waldulf wondered who he'd conned into selling him such luxurious garments, but in spite of his distrust of the man, Waldulf was glad to see him. He missed all of his companions from court and longed for news of them. He particularly yearned for news of Matthew since he had heard nothing of his friend since he had set out with Charles and his hosts for Spain.

Drago brought word that the Spanish campaign had been a failure. "The news had reached Aix-la-Chapelle when I came through there three days ago. King Charles received the greatest defeat of his career. Apparently he's heading home."

"I'm surprised that Charles will admit defeat," Count Willehad commented.

"Yes, but he's been away from this area for five months, and he had not counted on the campaign being so long. I do not have all of the details, but it seems that the Spanish lords who promised to do so much for Charles did not honor their commitment. Besides, trouble has erupted on another front now."

"We were not aware of that," Willehad said. "Isolated as we are, we're usually the last to hear the news. Have the Lombards caused more trouble?"

"No, it's the Saxons again."

Busily engaged with the chunk of roast boar on his plate, Waldulf had left the conversation to his elders, but at Drago's comment, he stiffened.

"Saxons?" That word always brought Printha to mind. "But I thought they had sworn loyalty to Charles!" he said.

"Charles did not consider Widukind, whom you remember, young Frank, did not present himself at Paderborn. Widukind urged the newly converted Saxons to wage war in Charles's absence. They've swept down the Rhine to the Moselle, pillaging and destroying along the way. They burned Karlsburg, sparing neither women nor children."

Drago drawled the words as if they brought him pleasure, which irritated Waldulf, making him wonder if Drago gave loyalty to any man. His appetite forgotten, Waldulf left the table to pace around the hall. "And here I am in exile not able to lift a hand against the enemy!"

"Perhaps Charles would recall you to his side if you reveal your interest in Widukind's masked rider," Drago said slyly. Waldulf ignored his words, wondering momentarily if the man knew Printha's identity. Drago had befriended her when she'd been a prisoner of Charles, but the trader was always uttering innuendoes in his efforts to obtain information, so it wasn't likely that he had unearthed Printha's secret.

"Do you know when Charles's court will return?" Waldulf inquired.

Drago had disclosed all of the information he knew, and the manor's residents would have to wait to learn about King Charles's Spanish campaign.

❋ ❋ ❋

Matthew was to arrive at Willehad Manor at the end of the harvest season. By that time, Waldulf was ready to ride out and discover what news he could of Charles and the host, and he greeted Matthew with a shout of joy.

Matthew embraced Waldulf when the youth hurried down the steps toward him.

"How I've missed you, Matthew!"

Matthew held him at arms' length. "I didn't think it was possible for you to grow any more handsome, but I see I was wrong. I believe that life in the country has been agreeable to you."

"Agreeable, yes, but somewhat lonely. I look forward to hearing an account of court life. Do come in. You shall have time to recover from your journey before I start pelting you with questions."

A servant conducted Matthew to a guest chamber, but he did not tarry long because he knew Waldulf was eager for news. Waldulf and his parents waited for him in the hall, and a small table was laid with honey cakes and wine.

"Now, Matthew, what about the Spanish campaign? Was it a great disaster as we've heard?" Waldulf asked eagerly.

"I did not go into Spain with Charles. He took his queen and her children as far as the royal villa of Chasseneuil, where we celebrated Easter. I was delegated to stay with the court, so I was not involved in the invasion of Spain. Charles and the first division of forces crossed the Garonne into Gascon country, and when the second division joined them, they pushed on into Spain with very little resistance until they arrived at Saragossa. Contrary to the reports the Spanish lords had made at Paderborn, the city would not surrender. Although the Franks employed siege machines, the city held out against them four months until most of the Franks' supplies were gone. When Charles received tidings of a full-scale Saxon rebellion, he abandoned the siege and hurried home."

"Although King Charles had nothing to show for his trouble," Willehad said, "I can't see that is a disaster such as the one that Drago indicated."

"But you haven't heard the end of the story yet! On his retreat, Charles ordered the walls to be torn down at Pamplona so he could count at least one victory, but a few hostages and the demolition of a hill town were of little consequence when compared to the massacre that followed." Matthew bowed his head, and the others watched in silence as he fought to gain his composure.

Matthew's lips still quivered when he continued. "The soldiers were happy to be coming home, and they rejoiced as they exited Spain through the mountain pass. Because of the long narrow passage, the troops were drawn out almost in single file, so there was little communication between the two ends of the column."

"That sounds dangerous in itself to have the host so divided," Waldulf commented.

"But considering the ruggedness of the terrain, there was no other choice. The Franks assigned to bring up the baggage train and to guard the rear of the host camped in the pass while Charles and the main army moved on to spend the night outside the mountains. Unknown to the Franks, a forest high above the pass hid a band of Christian Gascons, who waited until the main group was far in advance. Without warning, they attacked the baggage train and the rear guard. The rugged terrain and the heavy armor of the Franks made them an easy foe."

"Christians?" Waldulf said in disbelief. "But they were the very people Charles went to help!"

Matthew nodded. "Charles and the advance troops spent the night at the foot of the divide. The next morning, when the rear guard didn't arrive, the king rode back to check on them. None of them were alive. The Franks had been attacked in the narrowest part of the ravine where trees screened the slopes."

Adela's quiet weeping was the only sound in the room. Waldulf stood with bowed head and leaned against the fireplace. His eyes went often to his sword, Wildsong, which hung above his head. He had dedicated that sword to serve his king. Matthew's words were so vivid it was almost as if everyone present had lived through that terrible event.

"Heavy boulders had been pushed down on the wagons, which had been plundered. Naked Franks lay in the ravine, in clefts, and caverns. Their clothing, armor, and weapons had been stolen. All horses and oxen had been driven away except for those that were dead or wounded."

"But why didn't they sound a warning?" Waldulf inquired. "Charles should have been expecting an ambush in such a spot."

"If they gave a signal, none was heard. When Charles and his host reentered the pass, the foe had disappeared. Pursuit proved to be futile, for the few trails disappeared into hollows that seemed to lead nowhere. Charles had trouble accepting that his men were killed by the Christians he had come to free from the pagan Muslims. He has finally realized that the Christian empire he hopes to establish may be more difficult than he'd imagined."

Adela touched Waldulf on the shoulder. "Thank God you were not with the host this time, son, or else you would be lying in that horrible place."

It did seem strange to Waldulf that he had been banished from Charles's court in time to avoid the march into Spain. *Does God have some further plan for my life?*

"What effect has this had on the king?" Count Willehad questioned. "It will be hard on his pride, I think."

"In my opinion, it's made a man out of him. That may be strange to say about a man already thirty-seven years old, but it's true. He's taken full responsibility for the defeat. He realizes now that his hope for a united Christian army is nothing but a dream. He's still determined to pursue the founding of a Christian nation under his leadership, however. He has vowed to make amends for the Spanish disaster and the failure of the Saxons to keep their pledge. It's the first sign of greatness I've seen him display."

"He may be known as Charles the Great someday," Count Willehad speculated.

"If he continues in this way, that's possible."

"So there will be another Saxon campaign," Waldulf said.

"He's already launched one. We rested at Paris for several days, and then he took his host north."

"Then Drago's report about Saxon raids is true."

"Widukind emerged from hiding soon after Charles departed for Spain, and the whole countryside from Deutz to the Moselle was put to sword and fire. He spared neither buildings nor people. King Charles knows now it will be a constant struggle until Widukind is brought to his knees."

"And the host is already on the move?" Waldulf asked, with obvious longing in his voice.

"The king launched an immediate campaign with some fresh troops. This time instead of disappearing into the forest, the Saxons decided to make a stand on the Eder in Hesse. It was a terrible defeat for the Saxons, who finally withdrew in disgrace, but even Charles admits that it's only a minor victory in his plan for the complete subjugation of his enemies."

Waldulf could almost hear the shouts of the Franks as they charged the enemy's front, shrinking at the bloodcurdling war cry of the Saxons. Waldulf had heard that shrill cry a few times, and it always sent chills down his back. It was hard to define the sound, which combined the roar of a lion, the bestial howl of the wolf, and the demonic screams of a godless people. The whir of arrows as they sped toward their marks, and the moans of the wounded were as vivid to Waldulf as if he had charged with the offensive army.

"The advent of an early winter has halted Charles temporarily," Matthew continued. "Since it's too late in the season for further campaigning, Charles retired to Heristal for the winter. As soon as the family settled in, I took leave to visit you."

"How is Queen Hildegard and the family?" Waldulf asked.

"While the host was in Spain, Hildegard gave birth to twin sons, but one is quite sickly, and he may not live. The queen is weary of moving around so much, and her body is weakened by so much childbearing."

Waldulf could have listened to Matthew's news all evening, but his father, aware of the late hour, suggested, "Perhaps we should allow our guest to retire for the evening."

"I am weary from the journey," Matthew admitted, and shortly thereafter, he and the Willehads headed for bed.

❀　❀　❀

Several days later, when Waldulf and Matthew were alone, Matthew asked, "Have you heard from Printha?"

"Not a word. I've even dared to ride into Saxony a few times hoping to see her, but I've not encountered her. This renewed struggle between Charles and Widukind will only make life harder for her."

"Would you consent to come back to Charles if he should ask you?" Matthew inquired.

"Yes, I would, but I will not ask his pardon. After serving him for so many years, I can't forgive him for dismissing me so readily on the word of another."

"Would I be violating your trust if I should drop a hint in his ear about the identity of the Saxon you met?"

"I don't suppose it can hurt anything now. I've almost given up hope that I'll ever see Printha again."

"Perhaps it's just as well. The king has his eye on you for one of his daughters."

"But they're only children!" Waldulf protested anxiously.

"Still it's not unheard of for royal houses to betroth their sons and daughters in childhood. I must return to Constantinople someday, and I would like to see your future settled before I go. I've grown fond of you, Waldulf."

"Return to Constantinople? I don't think you'll ever leave Gaul," Waldulf said jokingly. "You talk of it, but I've never seen you packing your gear."

"I've told you some of the reasons why I haven't returned, but not all of them. I came here on a mission, never dreaming it would take so long. I've been in Frankish lands for eleven years, and I've lost sight of my purpose so often that I'm no nearer to accomplishing that mission than when I left home. I believe I shall never solve the puzzle that confronts me, and I'm about ready to admit defeat."

"I remember when you first came here, you hinted at some special reason for being in Gaul." Hoping to keep his friend a little longer, Waldulf said, "Have you asked my father to help you with your mission?"

"No one in Gaul knows my mission except Father Sturm. I'm looking for someone, and all of my leads have been false ones. I do intend to make one last effort. I will talk to your father tonight."

That night after the meal, Lady Willehad took up her sewing and Waldulf sprawled on the floor in front of the fireplace. The count and Matthew sat at the table.

"Have you ever wondered why I came to Gaul?" Matthew said to Willehad.

"Many times, but I did not inquire. I considered your reasons to be your own."

"I came looking for a man."

"An enemy?"

"No, to the contrary. For someone who will inherit a vast fortune if I can find him." Matthew smiled. "You will wonder even more at my persistence when I tell you that the trail leading me here is over four hundred years old."

"That sounds like an impossible mission," Willehad agreed.

"My family can trace its roots back to an ancestor who lived in the first century, and the link that has tied our family together is this." Matthew lifted the Alabaster from the pack he'd carried into the room.

"Why, that's the vase you found at Irminsul!" Waldulf exclaimed.

Count Willehad picked up the vase and looked at it closely. "It's an ornate piece."

"But the story that surrounds it is more important than the vase itself." And Matthew proceeded to relate Suetonius Trento's purchase of the vase and its passage from one generation of Trentos to the next. "The Trentos who had guardianship of the vase lived in Rome, and with the fall of the Roman Empire and the problems that entailed, we lost contact with the family."

"And what is the spiritual significance of this vase?" Willehad asked.

"The person who owns the Alabaster has the responsibility to preserve the family's Christian heritage by passing to succeeding generations the fact that Jesus Christ died on the cross and rose again on the third day. Because of His death and resurrection, the way to heaven is open to all people. It's the evidence of God's grace."

Willehad stared intently at Matthew and urged him to continue.

"Seventeen years ago I took the holy orders and became a monk. My father did not approve of my action, and since I took a vow of poverty, he willed his estate to the present holder of the Alabaster. I'm fulfilling his dying request to find that person and bring him to Constantinople along with the Alabaster. After I do that, I will return to a cloister, although the one where I took my vows has been destroyed by the Byzantine government."

"So you have found him?" Willehad asked, motioning to the vase.

"I've found the Alabaster, but not the owner. This vase surfaced when the Franks destroyed Irminsul. I'm assuming that it was stolen from Gaul in a Saxon raid."

"But perhaps the heir of the Alabaster is a Saxon. Had you considered that?"

"It could be anyone. I've eyed practically every male I've met in Frankish lands or Saxony as a possibility. I've even suspected that Drago might be the heir, for he has a wood carving of the vase, and he may have seen it."

"Have you discussed it with him?" Willehad inquired.

"No. To be honest, I would not be pleased to take him home to inherit my father's estate, and I fear I can't even trust the man to tell me the truth if I should ask. I must have some proof that the person is a Trento descendant. I was hoping you could help me. Perhaps you have known someone by the name of Trento or Conrad, another name connected with the last-known holder of this family relic."

"I don't believe so." Willehad turned to his wife, who had laid aside her sewing to listen to Matthew's tale. Eyes wide with wonder, Adela shook her head.

"If you don't know, it isn't likely that I would," she said quietly.

"Then since neither of my parents can help you, does this mean you'll leave Gaul, Matthew?"

"Probably. Charles is talking about another trip to Rome. When he goes, whether or not I've found the Alabaster holder, I believe I'll leave. My father set me an impossible task."

❋   ❋   ❋

Matthew left for Heristal the next day, and soon after Christmas, Waldulf received a communication requesting his presence at the court again. When he arrived, Charles did not mention Waldulf's dismissal nor beg his pardon, but his duties resumed as if he had never left. Still, he found that the court had changed considerably, and the greatest change was in the queen. She no longer gave any motherly attention to young Pepin, but spoke much of her own five children being tutored in the palace school. The queen's health was not as robust as previously, and she constantly nagged at Charles to stop moving so much. He had ceased trying to explain to her that one estate could not support his large retinue full time and that frequent moves were necessary. It was obvious that the royal couple were not as close as they had once been.

"It may be that the king's attention is being directed elsewhere," Drago confided to Waldulf on one of his visits to the royal headquarters. "He's got his eye on a high Rhineland beauty. He saw her last month when he was hunting in the Ardennes preserve. Reports are that she *did* make a pretty picture, racing on horseback through the forest with the wind blowing her golden hair."

"Is there anything you don't know, Drago?" Waldulf laughed.

"Very little," he answered slyly, making Waldulf wonder if Drago *did* have the information Matthew desired.

❊   ❊   ❊

Because of the Saxon threat, Charles didn't make the anticipated visit to Rome, and Matthew remained at his court. For the next two years Charles searched throughout Saxony for Widukind. Always at the king's side, Waldulf was also on the lookout for Printha. Charles restored the frontier, but he never encountered a Saxon army. Unarmed villagers gave themselves up to accept baptism, but as soon as Charles passed on, their promises were forgotten.

Charles roamed far northward into the wilderness, pillaging into an area where no civilized army had gone before. Most of the Franks disliked the campaign, although Waldulf was intrigued at being in the land of the midnight sun. There was no news of Widukind until they returned to the Rhine. While Charles had searched the eastern border, the wily Saxon had roused opposition in the west. With Charles's homecoming, Widukind disappeared again. Depressed by his unsuccessful efforts to subjugate the Saxons, Charles made known his intention to visit

Rome for the Easter season. Matthew and Waldulf were requested to accompany the king.

"And I suppose you will leave for Byzantium at last?" Waldulf
asked with a smile.

"I may do just that," Matthew retorted, failing to see any humor in his situation.

14

ITALY, 781

King Charles started the journey to Rome before winter set in, taking with him the queen and her six surviving children. The entourage passed through the Alps and spent Christmas in Pavia. At Parma, on the journey southward, Charles met a forty-six-year-old English scholar, Alcuin, who was returning from Rome where he had secured the ceremonial pallium for his superior, Archbishop Eanbald of York. The king's long-range goal was to improve the culture and education of his people, and he hoped to do that by luring great scholars to his court. Recognizing in Alcuin a superior mind, Charles persuaded the man to return to Gaul after he completed his mission for the archbishop. Charles tarried in Lombardy to make some political changes, but he pushed on eagerly in order to reach Rome by Easter.

The king's anticipation was no greater than Waldulf's, who had lived in a state of constant surprise since leaving Gaul. His first sight of the Alps had left him speechless for several hours. Late in the Lenten season, when the red-brown roofs of Rome and the pine canopies of its hills came into view, Waldulf turned toward Matthew with a wide grin.

"The Holy City!" Matthew was delighted to share Waldulf's first impression of the imperial city, remembering what an important day it was when he himself had first arrived in Rome.

Before seeking out Pope Hadrian, Charles led his entourage toward the site of ancient Rome. The scattered remains of the forums of Trajan and Julius Caesar left no doubt of the glory that once was Rome.

"That's the Colosseum," Matthew said, pointing toward the four-storied stone structure with arched entries at three levels.

"The place where the gladiators fought to the death with wild beasts and other men?" Waldulf asked. "I would have liked to see that. Do they still have such contests?"

"Not since the fifth century. When I first came to Rome, my Roman cousin took me on several tours, and he knew the history of the city. He told me that when the Colosseum was dedicated in the year 80, nine thousand wild animals were killed during the one hundred days of celebration. During the reign of Constantine the Great, the slaughter lessened somewhat but didn't stop completely until the fifth century. A monk named Telemachus entered the arena one day and begged the people to stop the horrible practices, and he was stoned to death for his efforts. However, his martyrdom caused such a stir that the bloody shows ended."

"Not *all* shows surely?"

"Many celebrations still occur here today, I understand, but more civilized ones."

Charles stopped at the Arch of Constantine and looked it over carefully. Matthew wondered if Charles envisioned a day when such a monument would be raised in his honor as the "second Constantine." The king asked Matthew to read the inscription to him. "My Latin is faulty sometimes," he explained.

Matthew rode closer so that he could make out the letters, which had grown faint through the ages. "To the Emperor Caesar Flavius Constantine Maximus, the Senate and the people of Rome dedicate this notable arch in honor of his triumphs, because inspired by divinity and greatness of mind, he freed the republic by just wars from tyranny and from factions."

The words obviously impressed the king, for he said, "I would be such a man, Matthew."

"If God wills it, Your Excellency."

Waldulf's enthusiasm waned somewhat as they saw increased evidence of destruction by the barbarians. "Even the ruins of the city have a certain beauty about them," he said as they rode along the street leading to the old capitol area where victorious Roman emperors had once marched before their legions and captives.

"Yes, but it's still a pity that so many objects of antiquity were destroyed," Matthew commented.

"Why, Matthew? Why did God allow the destruction?"

"Too much internal corruption. The downfall of Rome had been coming for a long time."

When they turned toward the Holy See where Pope Hadrian awaited them, Waldulf noted that the normally self-assured Charles approached the pope in humility. "The king hardly seems like himself," he commented.

"He hasn't been to Rome for seven years," Matthew noted. "When Charles comes to Italy, he compares Gaul to the antiquity of the Italians, and he's cowed by the difference. That's the reason he was so interested in the Englishman Alcuin that we met in Parma. He wants to endow the Franks with more culture, and himself, too. Here in the midst of the great achievements of the ancient Romans, he's overly sensitive to his need for the finer things of life."

"Why did he choose to come to Rome at this time?"

"For many reasons. He needed a break from the Saxon problem, and the situation was so bad in Lombardy that he needed to make changes and overtures there. For a long time, he and Hadrian have also been carrying on a dispute by letters. Many years ago, Pope Stephen II bestowed upon Charles the title "Patrician of the Romans." Thus he considers himself the protector and temporal master of the Romans, and as such he believes that he should rule the dissevered portions of the peninsula, but the pope believes the supreme power should be in papal hands. Charles likes to come here occasionally to show that he's still in control, but I doubt that he'll antagonize the pope this time, for he hopes to have Hadrian anoint his sons as kings on Easter Day."

"So nothing will be settled about who has supreme authority here?"

"Probably not now nor for a long time."

❀ ❀ ❀

Charles commanded his retinue to observe the day before Easter in fasting and meditation, so the Franks entered the portico of Saint Peter's in a worshipful mood. The church had been started by Constantine the Great in 325 to celebrate his acceptance of Christianity. It was a rectangular building similar to a Roman meeting hall. Four rows of columns extended almost the length of the church dividing it into a nave with two aisles on each side. Statues of saints and angels guarded the crypt where Saint Peter was buried. Advancing between the purple hangings of the nave pillars, the royal entourage stepped up into the triumphal arch, where a thousand candles glowed. Charles led his assemblage to a position before the altar, which blazed with lights.

Matthew heard the intake of Waldulf's breath, and he smiled. Saint Peter's was quite a sight for this youth whose knowledge of church architecture was limited to the few log parish churches he'd known and to an occasional visit to the churches at Erfurt and Cologne.

The sound of singing filled the sanctuary with music, signaling the beginning of the processional. A server entered holding high a jeweled cross. Flanking the server, two priests carried lighted candles. Another man followed swinging a lighted censer. The choir and other servers dressed in albs preceded Pope Hadrian, who was followed by a deacon and subdeacon, both in adorned gold tunicles and dalmatics. Candlelight flickered over the golden threads interwoven in the white robe that Hadrian wore.

The pope motioned for the other participants to take up their places in the sanctuary, then he advanced into the nave and sprinkled the congregation with holy water. The choir sang, "I beheld water issuing out from the right side of the temple, alleluia."

The monks chanted the words of the Revelator, "He pointed me to a pure river, the water of life, shining transparent as diamonds, coming out of the throne of God and of the Lamb, Jesus Christ."

Waldulf had trouble following the chanting of the monks and the words of the pope, but occasionally Matthew would whisper an interpretation of the liturgy. As Hadrian moved among them dispensing holy water, Matthew explained, "This ceremony reminds the faithful that they've been purified from their sins by the waters of baptism."

Hadrian returned to the chancel, took off his large, capelike vestment, and replaced it with a sleeveless outer garment over the alb. He prostrated himself before the altar while the choir sang the opening anthem, "I have risen and I am still with you, alleluia." The deacon and subdeacon censed the altar while the choir continued to sing. The pope chanted a prayer, and the subdeacon read the Scripture lesson from the writings of the apostle John, "On the first day of the week, the woman Mary Magdalene came to the tomb before daybreak, and she saw the stone had been removed from the tomb."

While Matthew knelt listening to the words of the first Easter story, he thought of Suetonius Trento, who had been in Jerusalem on that first Easter morning. He imagined the other Mary going to the garden with an alabaster vase to anoint Jesus' body but finding instead an empty tomb. Tears came to his eyes. He had been given the awesome task of finding the heir to that Alabaster, and he'd failed to carry out his mission. Long-departed Trentos seemed to point fingers of accusation at him, while Trentos yet to be born begged to hear the Words of Life that could be carried to them by those who preserved the truth of the

Alabaster: "I am the resurrection and the life. No one can come to My Father unless he believes on Me." Matthew knew then that he could not return to Byzantium to find solace and peace in a monastery. He must continue in Frankish lands until he found the Alabaster's heir.

The choir sang another anthem while the deacon knelt to receive the pope's blessing. He then carried the Gospel book in procession to the north side of the sanctuary facing the people. The heavy leaves of the book were held open by two servers while the choir chanted the Nicene Creed. Quietly, Matthew said the words with them. "We believe in one God, the Father Almighty, maker of all things, both visible and invisible; and in one Lord, Jesus Christ, the Son of God . . ."

Matthew paused, thinking of the adoption of this creed during the age of Constantine the Great. No doubt the first Christian emperor had died secure in his belief that he had settled once and for all the matter of the divinity of the Christ, but the matter had periodically emerged since that time. Even now, if the rumors out of Spain were to be credited, it would be necessary once again for true Christians to defend the divinity of Jesus. No, Matthew could not leave Gaul—King Charles might need his help.

Matthew focused on the service again and noted that the deacon and subdeacon were preparing the elements for consecration, placing wafers of the Eucharist on metal plates and mixing wine and water in the chalice, both of which were deposited on the center of the altar. The pope turned to the congregation and said, "Pray, brethren, that my sacrifice and yours may be acceptable to God the almighty Father."

The choir singing ceased, and the congregation knelt silently until the chalice was elevated and the consecration complete. With his back to the congregation, Pope Hadrian recited the canon of the mass and the prayer of consecration. Handbells were rung each of the three times he blessed the bread and the cup. The congregation moved forward a few at a time and knelt around the altar to receive Holy Communion while the choir chanted an anthem proper to the feast, "Christ our passover is sacrificed for us, alleluia."

At the conclusion of the ritual, Hadrian addressed the congregation. "Behold a new and most Christian emperor has arisen." He motioned for Charles and his family to come forward while monks chanted, "Lord, save the king." A few of the servers murmured, "Amen," but the congregation as a whole looked on silently as Charles, flanked by his two younger sons, knelt before the pope.

A server stepped forward with two small crowns held on a pillow. Placing one of the crowns on young Carloman's head, Pope Hadrian said, "Upon this child I bestow the crown of the king of the Lombards, who from this day on will be known as Pepin."

Waldulf gasped, and Matthew nudged him slightly, although he was surprised himself. *Who would believe that Charles would set aside his firstborn in such an obvious manner?* Matthew lifted his head and looked toward Hildegard, who knelt several feet behind Charles and her sons. *Had Charles succumbed to her entreaties to favor her sons because of her poor health?*

The pope lifted the other crown from the pillow and placed it on the head of little Louis. "I crown this member of the Carolingian line as the king of Aquitaine."

That there was no crowning of Hildegard's oldest son, Charles, clearly indicated that the king intended for him to rule the whole territory of the Franks. As the recessional formed to leave the sanctuary, Matthew wondered if Hildegard's scheme might instead cause her grief. She would suffer the loss of her sons, for Charles would intend for the two children to live in the country over which they ruled with Frankish advisers and a regent. Waldulf didn't speak his mind until they were alone. "He disowned the hunchback, Pepin. I thought he was fond of the boy."

"The Franks expect their leaders to be strong of body, physically able to ride at the head of their armies. The hunchbacked son will never be able to do that. Perhaps Charles is only accepting the inevitable or, more likely, succumbing to pressure from the queen, who jealously guards her children's future," Matthew explained.

"But to take away his name! Surely you do not approve of this treatment?"

"It doesn't matter what I approve. It is doubtful that his first-born will ever marry, and Charles is seeking to perpetuate the name of his father. Probably in this instance he's thinking more of his father than his son."

"Printha was fond of Pepin. This would upset her," Waldulf noted.

When he mentioned Printha's name, a brooding look crossed Waldulf's face, one that Matthew was noting more and more often. He laid his hand on Waldulf's shoulders.

"Friend, don't you think it's time to put Printha out of your mind? You haven't seen nor heard from her for almost five years."

Waldulf shook his head stubbornly. "I loved her. I still do."

"You should marry."

"You haven't." That comment stopped further persuasion from Matthew. *Since I had been willing to take holy orders when I lost the woman I loved, who am I to advise Waldulf?*

As they continued toward their quarters, Matthew stopped abruptly, for on the other side of the street stood an official of the Constantinople court. There was no mistaking the clean-shaven countenance, the brocade robes richly adorned with rubies and diamonds, and the symbol of the Byzantium royal house on his cloak. The man's face seemed familiar, and Matthew searched his mind for the official's identity. The thirteen-year lapse since he had departed the Byzantine Empire had left him with a faulty memory. Nonetheless, the man was someone from home, and Matthew wanted to speak to him.

Experiencing a sudden twinge of homesickness, Matthew walked across the street without explanation to Waldulf. The Byzantine looked up at his approach and recognition lit his eyes.

"Brother Matthew! I had wondered if our paths would cross again."

"You have the advantage of me," Matthew said. "I can't remember your name."

The man bowed slightly. "We met on only one occasion—the day Irene was crowned empress of Byzantium. I was the one who admitted you to the palace grounds for the ceremony."

Of course, the eunuch Elisha!

The two men clasped hands, and Matthew turned toward his companion. "This is my friend Waldulf. Elisha is an official in the court of Constantine the Greek."

"Although like all Byzantines, we think of ourselves as Romans," Elisha commented.

Waldulf stared silently, awed by the magnificence of the man's garments, which put even the pope's to shame.

"I'm in Rome with the treasurer and the chamberlain of the court of Constantine. We have come to see the king of the Franks, and it was our fortune to reach Rome during his visit."

Although he was overcome with curiosity about their business with Charles, Matthew only commented, "You are more fortunate than you know. A trip across the Alps is not pleasant. May I invite you to our quarters for a cup of wine?"

Once in the room, Elisha said, "You will wonder at our mission, and since the two officials are waiting upon King Charles at this time, you may as well have the facts. The empress has sent us to arrange a betrothal between Charles's daughter Hrotrud and the Byzantine emperor, Constantine VI, Irene's son."

Matthew stared at Elisha. Waldulf sucked in his breath. "It's unheard of—an emperor wanting to marry a Frank. Do you think King Charles will agree to it, Matthew?"

"Constantine is a fine young man—the surviving heir of the ancient Caesars," Elisha said haughtily. "I doubt Charles will turn down such an opportunity."

Charles had spent most of his time with the pope since their arrival in Rome, and he had not held any meeting with his counselors, but the next morning he sent for them. One glance at the king assured Matthew that he approved the proposed marriage alliance.

"Great news, Matthew! Empress Irene of Constantinople has sent her officials to arrange a betrothal between her son and my daughter."

"I can see that the king is pleased," Matthew stated.

"To think that my grandchild might one day be emperor of the Roman Empire of the East! Of course it pleases me! It's a great honor proving that the Franks are not as uncultured as we once were."

"I take it that you intend to agree to the betrothal?" Matthew inquired.

"That's the reason I sent for you. You're from Constantinople— do you know of any reason why I shouldn't?"

They were interrupted when Pope Hadrain entered the room.

Charles moved forward to kiss the pope's hand. "You've honored me, Holy Father. May I offer you some refreshment?"

"I do not need refreshment—only the assurance that the rumor I've heard is untrue. Are you negotiating a royal marriage with Byzantium?" the pope demanded.

Charles dropped his head like a naughty child, but he soon rallied and faced the pope. "I've been approached by the empress's representative. I'm considering the marriage."

"Those people are our enemies. They constantly try to involve themselves in our political affairs, and the royal family has been responsible for the destruction of many monasteries."

"They are not my enemies—indeed, I think the Byzantines have much to teach us. My people have a lot to learn."

"I do not approve of the match. This will only give the Byzantines an excuse to meddle in western affairs," the pope said firmly.

"But have you thought it might also give us an opportunity to influence the Byzantium court?" Charles asked slyly.

The pope exited without further word, and Matthew thought of Charles's last comment. From what he'd heard about the empress, Matthew doubted there would be much opportunity for Charles to meddle in Byzantine affairs.

Hildegard had eased silently into the room during this exchange, and after the angry pope left, she said to her husband, "Must you take all of my children away from me? You're leaving Pepin in Lombardy, and Louis is going back to Aquitaine. Don't tell me you're sending Hrotrud away, too?"

He patted her arm, registering affection that Matthew hadn't seen between them for many months. "This is a betrothal, not a marriage; it will be many years before she will leave us."

"I do not want her marrying a foreigner," Hildegard said firmly.

In spite of his wife's protests and the pope's disapproval, Charles signed the betrothal agreement to align his family with the fabulous Byzantine court. To prepare the Frankish girl for introduction into Byzantine life, Elisha was assigned to Charles's court. "My task will be to teach Hrotrud the speech and writing of the Greeks and the customs of the court at Constantinople," the eunuch said to Matthew. "I do not look forward to it. The child is still quite young, and she doesn't appear to have a great thirst for learning."

Matthew laughed. "No, she doesn't, but her father does, and he wants all of his children educated."

"I will not like living at a barbaric court, but I've had orders from my empress," Elisha sighed.

Now that he had decided to return to Gaul and complete his father's mission, Matthew was pleased he would have Elisha's company. Elisha's presence would make Matthew feel less like an exile.

Charles's exit from Rome the next day had all the appearance of a celebration. Music played and banners flew. Charles was in high mood, for by his side rode Paul, the deacon whom he had persuaded to become an educator at the Frankish court. Following him was Elisha, ready to instruct his daughter in Greek culture. He also looked forward to the coming of Alcuin to his court. The king was determined that his country would equal Byzantium culture by the time his daughter married into the eastern empire. Perhaps under his family the old Roman Empire could be reunited. The trip to Rome had been highly pleasing to the king of the Franks.

15

FRANKISH GAUL, SAXONY, 782

Throughout the winter of 782, Charles contemplated the assembling of his host at Mayfield. Although he often asked advice of his counselors, the final decision was always the king's, and his plans for the summer surprised Matthew.

"I'm planning for a military campaign, but when I go into Saxony, I'm going to hold out an olive branch to the Saxons to give them one more chance to submit," he told his assembled commanders.

By the beginning of summer, enough supplies had been gathered for a military campaign, and again Waldulf rode at the head of the troops from his father's county. Charles's army crossed the Rhine at Cologne into Saxony and moved to the source of the Lippe River, where they pitched camp at Suntel. Instead of encountering hostile Saxons, village chieftains approached the Franks to pledge submission.

"Will this last any longer than their previous vows have?" Waldulf said to Matthew as he watched the Saxons bow before King Charles.

"I doubt it, but if it postpones war for a time, then it will be worthwhile, I suppose."

After the chieftains agreed to sit in council with Charles to negotiate rules for the Saxons' behavior, they pledged hostages as a guarantee. When the twelve hostages were brought before Charles, Waldulf grabbed Matthew's arm. "Look! The tallest woman on the left. Could it be? . . ."

Matthew's eyes swept over the group. The woman Waldulf indicated stood with bowed head, her back to them. *Could it be Printha?* Matthew hadn't seen her since she had left Charles's court as a young woman, and this person had the bearing of maturity.

Charles accepted the hostages as a pledge of good faith on the part of the Saxons, and he stalked before them like a general reviewing his troops. He stopped before the woman they'd been observing and stooped down to peer at her face.

"Is it Printha?" the king said wonderingly, and she threw back her hood. There was no mistaking that flaxen hair flowing over her shoulders, and Waldulf grabbed Matthew's arm for support. Charles placed his hand on her head. "We have missed you. I will assign you to become the companion of my daughter Hrotrud."

While the king discussed the disposition of the other hostages with his chamberlain, Printha swept the assembled Franks with a quick glance until her gaze lighted on Waldulf, and he lifted his hand in greeting. Her white teeth flashed in a brief smile before the chamberlain led them away. The hostages would be sent on the morrow to Charles's palace at Heristal, where his family was in residence. Waldulf sent a message to Printha to meet him by the river after sundown.

The river was sluggish at this point, and Waldulf skipped small stones across its surface, impatiently wondering if Printha would be able to come. Since Charles knew that she was Widukind's masked rider, he might have her closely guarded this time.

The night had deepened. Insects droned monotonously in the trees. Wisps of fog swirled around him, and he seemed isolated in a world of his own. The dank smell of fish and sodden sand stung his nostrils. Time stood still. His whole future hinged on this meeting with Printha.

As the hours passed, his depression increased, and he had almost given up when he felt a tap on his shoulder. He turned quickly. Printha stood behind him. A faint glow from the camp's fires enabled him to see her form but not her features. He reached for her, his hands exploring the contour of her face, the softness of her hair. He tilted her chin upward and his head descended slowly to hers. His touch was gentle at first, but then he pulled her closer, his lips seeking hers in a hungry, consuming kiss.

Printha drew back and looked at him wonderingly. A reckless and tantalizing excitement overwhelmed her. Her body blazed with warmth. She submitted her lips to his again, but this time his touch was more gentle, and he said in a husky voice, "I thought I'd lost you forever. I've even gone so far as to search for you in Saxony, but there was no trace of you. Please don't leave me again."

"If I were a Frank I would never leave you, but I have a loyalty to my people. I cannot desert them." Her hands caressed his shoulders and back, and she tugged at the hair on his neck, causing his muscles to tense. "But I wanted to see you again, and so I agreed to become a hostage."

"I'm looking forward to the day when there will be peace between the Franks and Saxons. Would that make a difference in your feelings for me?"

"No, not in my feelings for you because they are strong already, but it would make a difference in whether I could stay with you permanently."

"I feared you were dead or might have married another."

"A husband has been chosen for me, but I have not agreed."

Waldulf's arms tightened around her. "Who is it?"

"Abbio is a Saxon. That is all you need to know."

"But you don't love him?" Waldulf probed hopefully.

"I love only you, but Widukind wishes to have grandchildren. He would not want them to be Franks, although he does like you."

"How could he like me? I've never seen him."

"I've told him about your kindness to me. He likes that."

"Can't you persuade your father to make an alliance with Charles?"

"No, nor would I even if I could. Saxons and Franks will never mix, although I wish it were otherwise."

She stretched upward and kissed him on the lips. "I must go. Folz was put in charge of taking us into Gaul, and he trusted me to return after I saw you. It was good to see him again. I'm so glad that he's prospered in the king's service."

"He and I have often talked about you, my love." He stooped for one more kiss. "Perhaps the king will not stay here long, and I can soon join you in Heristal."

"I will await your arrival impatiently."

"Are you sorry to be leaving your homeland?"

"Not as much as I should be, and that troubles my mind. I should hate Charles for all he's done to the Saxons, yet I enjoyed his company in the past. I should dread these days with the Franks, yet I do not. Why is that, Waldulf?"

"I'd like to hope that it's because you want to be near me."

"Doubtless you are right."

Waldulf's heart and hands lifted in exultation as he watched her figure fade into the dusk, and he wondered how he could break down her resolve. He couldn't imagine spending his life without Printha.

Waldulf's impatience to be with Printha heightened during the next two months while Charles dealt with the Saxon leaders. He tried to be reconciled to the delay for he thought that the decisions being made would eventually bring peace between Saxons and Franks.

After taking their solemn oaths of loyalty, several Saxon chieftains were appointed as counts by Charles after they agreed to a series of regulations. The Saxons were required to give up many of their pagan religious practices, thus bringing them farther into the Christian fold. The Saxons could no longer engage in human sacrifice nor burn their dead on funeral pyres. They were to pay their tithes to the church and its clergy. Christian holy days were to be observed. With some surprise, Waldulf read the actions that would incur the death penalty: Robbing or burning churches, eating meat during Lent without a priest's permission, killing a church official, avoiding baptism, or plotting against the king's official.

"Death seems a stiff penalty for those offenses," Waldulf remarked to Matthew. "I'm surprised the Saxons agreed to them."

"Agreeing to them is not the same as obeying them. And a man has to be caught before he's punished."

"Then you think that these promises will not bind the Saxons any more than those taken at Paderborn?"

"I have no way of knowing."

At the conclusion of the conference, Charles beamed confidently upon his counselors and the assembled Saxon chieftains. "We have accomplished a great work at this assembly. I foresee the day when the Franks and all the Saxons will live as brothers. We have made a great beginning, and I urge you Saxon brothers to encourage your leader Widukind to surrender himself and abide under the rules we have made."

"Hail the king, Charles the Great," the Franks shouted, but the Saxon chieftains remained silent.

"I am gratified that our hosts didn't have to engage in fighting this year," Charles continued, smiling at the assembly like a benevolent father, "but rather that we have employed our time in the making of peace. We will leave tomorrow for my residence beyond the Rhine. I'm looking forward to a few years of peace."

Matthew rode beside the king the next morning, and Charles again congratulated himself on his accomplishment at Suntel.

Matthew agreed that the two months there did seem productive, yet as he'd commented to Waldulf at the dedication of Paderborn, he said, "Widukind was still not there, and he is the unknown factor in any negotiations with the Saxons."

Anger marked Charles's voice when he answered curtly, "He's losing his power—most of the Saxons are loyal to us."

Clearly, the king was not in a mood for disagreement, so Matthew said no more. For his own personal good, Matthew hoped that peace would reign in Saxony, for he was now convinced that the secret to the Alabaster heir must lie in that land. He had followed every possible lead in Gaul to no avail. He'd confided his mission to dozens of people, so much so that the knowledge had become widespread. Because he had omitted any mention of the huge estate awaiting that person, he hadn't been besieged with erroneous fortune-seekers.

Matthew's misgivings turned out to be well founded, for Charles had not been long in residence at Heristal before the peace was shattered by a messenger from Paderborn.

"I bring bad news, sire."

"Not the Saxons again," Charles moaned.

"No, trouble on a new front. A group of Wends are raiding, looting, and burning villages of the Saxons who have sworn loyalty to us."

Charles stood up to survey a wall map, and traced with his hand the boundaries of the land lying between the Elbe and the Saale Rivers.

"Is this the region under attack?" Charles inquired.

"That's my opinion, sire."

Angrily denouncing his enemies, the king immediately dispatched messages to three of his counts to take their armies into the area and punish the invaders. "I do not believe it's necessary to call out the full host. Surely these trusted commanders can dispatch the heathen without my help. Queen Hildegard is not well, and I do not want to leave her at this time."

Although the king expressed confidence in the abilities of his subordinates to put down the rebellion, he assigned a group of messengers to the battlefield to keep him posted on their progress. Within two weeks, news began arriving from the Frankish armies. The first communique from Count Palatine Worad was not encouraging.

> King Charles,
>
> We encountered difficulties upon our arrival in Saxony. A soon as the Franks crossed the Rhine into Saxon lands, Widukind came out of hiding and convinced his countrymen to repudiate the agreements made at Suntel. The Saxons are again in rebellion, pillaging loyal villages and putting Christians to the sword.
>
> In light of this situation, we have abandoned our campaigns against the Wends and are moving to subdue the Saxons.

Matthew had never seen Charles so angry as when he received this news. He bolted out of his chair, drew his sword, and brought it down sharply on the table. His normally high-pitched voice resembled the scream of an injured animal more than a human sound. "What! Do I hear correctly—that my commanders in the field have chosen to disregard the orders of their king and to take matters of defense into their own hands? Let them deal with the Wends. I'll handle the Saxons! They will submit or I'll kill every last Saxon in the country."

Fear for Printha showed on Waldulf's face as he whispered to Matthew. "What of the hostages? They were given as a guarantee for peace. Will Charles kill them?"

"He's angry enough to do so. We must think of some way to save Printha should this occur."

"All she needs is a horse and some provisions. Once she's away from this area no one could catch her in the forest. Probably all we have to do is warn her and she will escape."

Charles called for a scribe, and he thundered out a message.

"Send word to those three commanders to confine their efforts to fighting the Wends. Tell them that I want an immediate report of the damage done by the Saxons. Send a return message by courier without delay. Also, the counts who did not send soldiers to Mayfield should be notified that I may require their services within a few weeks."

Waldulf trembled for fear that he would be sent to notify the counts. He must be on hand to protect Printha. When he was not chosen, he went immediately to plot with Folz. As count of the stable, the former outcast would be able to provide Printha with a means of escape.

Without hesitation, Folz agreed to help. "I owe Printha my life. If it's in my power to prevent it, the king will not slay her."

Before Charles's emissary could have reached the area where the Frankish army was encamped, a courier arrived with another message from Count Worad. Charles handed the message to Matthew and asked him to read it aloud. "I can't bring myself to read more bad news—I can't hope that this message is good."

> As fortune would have it, soon after we arrived in Saxony, we were joined by your kinsman Count Theodoric, who had gathered an army as soon as he heard of the Saxon defection. He suggested that we spy out the strength of the enemy and then choose a suitable place where our men could challenge them. We have done so and plan to attack the Saxons tomorrow.

If the count had expected a commendation because of his strategy, he would have been surprised. Charles's response to this message was so loud that it disturbed the dogs lying around the room, and they added their startled yelps to his angry tirade. "Not only do I have three of my appointees taking matters into their own hands, but my own kinsman is attacking the enemy without my permission. Who's king of the Franks, anyway? Is there a plot underway to dethrone me?"

Before the day was over, another Frank, disheveled and dirty, rushed into the room.

"A tragedy, sire, a tragedy." He paused to get his breath, and as he seemed on the verge of collapsing, Charles ordered, "Give the man some ale to revive him."

The messenger gulped down the liquid, choking over it, but he caught his breath and swiped at his mouth with a dirty hand.

"The Frankish host under command of the royal emissaries did not follow the advice of Count Theodoric and they launched an attack without his assistance. They planned a hit-and-run assault, each soldier pushing his horse to the limit, but the Saxons had learned of the attack and lay in wait for our men. Most of the Franks were cut down, including two of your royal envoys, four counts, twenty nobles, and most of the common soldiers, who preferred to perish under the hands of the heathen rather than to live in disgrace because of this defeat. The few who were left fled into Count Theodoric's camp, and he dispatched me to bring you the word."

"I will exact vengeance for this!" Charles thundered. "For every Frankish soldier killed, I'll take the life of a dozen Saxons."

Matthew caught Waldulf's eye and flashed a message to him. Waldulf eased out of the room.

The messenger continued, "The Saxons were led by Widukind, who is calling for the overthrow of Frankish rule, the destruction of the missionaries and their churches, and a return to the old gods. His followers have marched through the district between the mouths of the Elbe and the Weser Rivers, burning churches, cruelly punishing Christian converts, driving out Frankish counts, killing any priests or bishops who did not flee, and setting up the old idols again."

"I've heard enough. Bring in the Saxon hostages," Charles said in an ominous voice. "We'll begin with them."

Matthew waited tensely until the bound Saxons filed into the council room. *Had Waldulf's warning come in time?* He breathed easier when he noted Printha was not in the group. If Charles noticed her absence, he said nothing. Actually, Printha had become so much a part of the king's household that Charles may have forgotten that she was a prisoner.

"Behead them," he ordered two bodyguards who stood by his side, and Matthew watched in stunned horror as one after another, the heads of the prisoners were severed. The blood of the martyred Saxons sprayed over the assemblage and the council hall.

This is no Christian act. Have the pagan ways of Charles's ancestors reasserted themselves in this man who considers himself God's representative on earth? Matthew wondered. He rushed out of the hall to wash his blood-spattered face and arms, and he detained Waldulf, who was on the point of entering the building. In the distance he heard the rapid sound of hoofbeats, and Waldulf whispered, "She's gone, but what's happening here?"

"Don't go in there. It's too horrible to contemplate. Thank God that you warned Printha. I may have taken a sword to Charles myself if Printha had been slain."

"You wouldn't have had to," Waldulf said darkly.

"I only hope you and Folz aren't punished for helping her." Whether through forgetfulness or deliberateness, the king didn't mention Printha. He focused all of his energies on seeking vengeance from his longtime enemies.

Charles showed no remorse for his destruction of the hostages, and his anger did not abate in the next week while he waited for his hosts to assemble. Though it was late in the season, Charles made a lightning foray into Saxony. Widukind's army, perhaps contented with the booty they had taken from the Franks who fell in the Suntel or frightened by Charles's invincibility, melted away. When Drago came into camp to display some wares he had gathered during a long absence, he reported the news that Widukind had gone north to Denmark.

With their leader gone, the Saxons who remained behind fearfully faced Charles. He compelled them to surrender all who had participated in the rebellion, and in a matter of a few days, forty-five hundred men were turned over to him as prisoners. Mercilessly, the king gave the savage command for all of them to be beheaded.

His counselors pleaded with him to desist from such slaughter. "Give them a hearing—some of these people may be innocent of rebelling."

"The Saxons have broken their oaths and destroyed many of our countrymen. They deserve the death penalty. Kill them!"

Waldulf had seen death in battle, and he had pledged his fidelity to the king, but his loyalty wavered on that day as he was commanded to stand at attention and watch the bloody slaughter. By late afternoon, the area was drenched with blood, and piles of heads and headless corpses were stacked around the camp. The stench of fresh blood was so loathsome that more than one brave Frank collapsed in a faint during the carnage.

The screams of Saxons and the horror in their eyes were so imprinted on his mind that Matthew wondered if he would ever be able to sleep again. As the day progressed, hundreds of waiting vultures hovered over the camp, so numerous they blotted out the sunlight.

Matthew and Waldulf sagged to the ground when the last prisoner was killed. "There is no excuse for this," Matthew said. "What a pity that a ruler who has subdued whole kingdoms couldn't overcome his own brutal rage."

"And it will only enrage the Saxons further. Why did I stand aside and watch the slaughter?" Waldulf bemoaned. "Why didn't I intervene? I'll never forgive myself nor forget what I've seen here today."

The rapid beat of a horse's hooves heralded the arrival of a rider, and Matthew lifted his head to locate the newcomer. Garbed in a long, black robe, a rider appeared on the horizon. Waldulf and Matthew leapt to their feet when they recognized Printha. She rode swiftly along a ledge, and when she was directly above the camp, she turned the horse toward the edge and urged the beast forward. For a moment the horse was suspended in midair. Her two friends stood breathless until the horse landed on all fours and Printha prodded him toward the assembled camp. Flaxen hair flowed out behind her, and her fierce Saxon yell froze Matthew's blood. She scattered the Franks before her until she was in the midst of the slaughter. She scanned the carnage, and her blue eyes blazed when she halted in front of Charles.

"Are you proud of yourself? The great and mighty Charles killing bound prisoners of war. The Saxons are known far and wide for their supposed cruelty and their worship of idols, but not even Widukind would perpetrate such a massacre. And your Christian God—is He pleased with your day's work? If He is, then I want none of Him!"

Her stormy glance fell on Waldulf. "And you stood by and watched it! I'm disappointed—no disgusted—with you, Waldulf. Never again will I call you my friend."

Slipping a hand down into her boot, she pulled out a dagger, and Waldulf sensed her intent. "No, Printha!" he warned. "Don't do it!"

He had spoken too late, for the dagger left her hand in a mighty thrust, and Waldulf jumped in front of the king whose life he had pledged to protect. The dagger Printha had meant for Charles sunk deeply into Waldulf's chest.

Horror spread across Printha's face, and Matthew thought she would fall from the saddle, but she looked quickly at the Franks who approached her menacingly and urged her horse into a gallop. Again the fierce Saxon war cry resounded over the camp as she took the incline at a gallop and disappeared into the forest.

Matthew ran to Waldulf. He pulled out the dagger and blood gushed from the wound. In a few minutes Matthew was as blood-spattered as the executioners had been. With deft fingers, he probed the wound. "Bring my kit," he gasped. "We must tend to him or he won't live an hour."

"Printha?" Waldulf whispered. "Did she escape?"

"Yes," Matthew assured him, and Waldulf's body went limp under his hands.

16

Waldulf lounged indolently on the bench in the garden of the manor house. He was immobile except when he lifted a hand to discourage the bees that buzzed around his head as they searched for nectar among the blooming flowers and fruit trees. Count Willehad watched his son from a window on the second story of the house. It had been over a year since Waldulf had been wounded, and yet the boy today was only a shadow of his former self. Adela joined her husband.

"Will he ever recover?" she whispered.

"Matthew assured me on his last visit that the wound was healed, and that Waldulf should be recovering. He hinted Waldulf's mind is the problem now. I'm sorry he ever heard of that Saxon girl. If only there was some way to stir his interest. I've hinted that he should go hawking, but he's even lost interest in that."

Adela twitched her hands nervously. "I know something that might arouse his interest in life, but I'm not sure it's worth the cost to us. However, I've carried this burden so long that I must share it with you, although I fear you will hate me for my deceit."

Willehad looked at her curiously. Adela was usually the calmest of women. *What has caused her distress?* he wondered. "Let's sit down, my dear." He led her into their bedchamber.

"Close the door, Willehad. I don't want the servants to hear."

Even after they were settled side by side on a lounge, Adela hesitated. "Waldulf is not our son!" she finally whispered.

Willehad couldn't speak for many minutes as he stared at his wife, who had hidden her face in her hands. He opened his mouth to speak, but no words would come. *Surely I haven't heard correctly!* "*Our* son or *my* son?" he finally gasped, his face a shade lighter than it had been.

Adela uncovered her face and grabbed his hands. "Oh, no, no, husband, I haven't been unfaithful to you, though I have been living a lie for twenty-four years. I love Waldulf as if he were my own, but I did not give birth to the boy."

"But how could this be? Why deceive me?" Willehad's mind was a confused jumble.

"I feared you might not accept him if you knew he wasn't yours."

"Start at the beginning and tell me everything," he commanded, and his stern voice calmed Adela.

"You will remember that at the time of Waldulf's birth you were away from home for most of the year. During that time, I visited my sister for several months. One night, someone left a baby boy on the steps of the monastery near her home. Since a famine was ravishing the countryside, it was believed that the mother could no longer feed herself and her child and that she brought him to the monastery hoping the monks could save his life."

"And that child is Waldulf?"

Adela nodded slowly. "The monks had no idea what to do with the baby, and they asked my sister to care for him. She had a large brood of her own and could hardly afford to take on another mouth to feed, so she asked me if I would adopt the boy. I had so much wanted to provide you with a son that I agreed immediately. Since I'd gone on the visit without any of our servants, when I returned home with a baby, everyone assumed that I'd borne him. My pride kept me from telling the truth."

"I can understand that you might not want to confide in others, but why not me? Why didn't you *tell me?*" Willehad said with sadness in his voice.

"I feared that you would put me away for a woman who could produce an heir for you, and I thought that Waldulf would be my insurance against that."

"Foolish woman. You are more important to me than an heir. Did you think I blamed you? Perhaps the fault was mine."

"Can you ever forgive me—not only for being so foolish as to doubt your love for me, but also for deceiving you?"

"At the moment, I do not feel kindly toward you, but I daresay I will get over it. My immediate concern is our son. I'm assuming that you believe telling Waldulf about his doubtful heritage will restore him to his former self. It's my opinion that such knowledge will only plunge him into further depression."

"But there's more, husband." She left the room and soon returned with a sheepskin, from which she unwrapped a brittle piece of parchment.

"There were two objects in the basket with the child when they found him. This note and an alabaster vase. The monk who had entrusted me with the boy brought me this note several years ago. It's written in Latin. He said the vase had been stolen."

"That isn't surprising, considering the thieves who often visit the monasteries in the guise of honest men," Willehad said. With shaking hands, he opened the parchment and read aloud, "My husband owned this vase, and upon his death, it became my son's. I do not know why it is important, but for some reason it is." The name Ursula Trento was printed at the bottom of the page, with an "X" beside it.

Surprise crossed Willehad's face as the truth dawned upon him. "So Waldulf is the one Matthew has been searching for."

"It would appear so."

"Why didn't you reveal this information when Matthew questioned us?"

"Do you want Waldulf to leave here and go to Constantinople?"

Willehad looked stunned, as if this possibility had not occurred to him.

"No," he said slowly. "No, I would not want that."

"Nor would I—that is the reason I kept this secret. If he were to leave, we would never see him again. I still don't want him to go away, but if the knowledge were to bring him out of his depression, I suppose I could bear it. Should we tell him and Matthew?"

Willehad shook his head slowly. "No. Not yet, at least. I must get used to the idea myself."

❀ ❀ ❀

Several months had passed since Matthew had been to Willehad Manor, and he urged his tired horse to greater speed. *Will I find Waldulf improved?* The year since the massacre had been long for Matthew, and more than once he had considered returning home, but he couldn't give up hope that someday he would find the man he sought. Besides, he had become so involved with King Charles and the Franks that his monastic vows seldom entered his mind. The Franks had become his people. Life had been somewhat erratic at the king's court, for Charles had determined that he would prevail over the Saxons. He had not left Saxony for the year since resistance had increased after the massacre. Charles knew that if he left the country, he would lose the tenuous foothold he maintained.

Even the Franks were losing spirit, believing that the invisible Widukind prevailed over their forces with a wizard's power. While the Franks were daunted by Widukind's invincibility, legends of Charles's prowess circulated among the Saxons. They believed the story of how the king's horse had balked at a flooded river, and Charles had swum the river and pulled the horse after him. Such feats appealed to a warrior race who had to respect a leader to submit to him.

During the winter months in Saxony without a foe to engage,

Charles continued his interest in education. The coming of Alcuin, the English teacher Charles had met in Italy, made a profound change in the Frankish court, and Charles was Alcuin's major pupil. Charles had a good memory, and he thought that through diligence he might gain the knowledge he coveted. He kept a writing tablet under his pillow, and in his wakeful hours of the night, he practiced writing his letters.

Since Alcuin refused to speak the Germanic dialect of the Rhinelands, he insisted that his pupils learn Latin and Greek, and he enlisted Matthew's help in this instruction. Alcuin had brought his disciples from England to teach the younger boys grammar, dialects, and rhetoric, while he instructed in algebra, music, medicine, and astronomy. Matthew had also aided Alcuin's limited experience with medicine by contributing his knowledge of herbs and potions. Elisha, the Byzantine eunuch, taught Greek culture to the other children as well as to Hrotrud. The eunuch supplied the students with many moments of humor as they watched him prostrate himself on the floor when he entered Hrotrud's presence.

Textbooks were scarce. Alcuin wrote out simple grammar and mass books, and throughout the kingdom skilled monks worked to make copies of these volumes and other books that Alcuin borrowed from his old library at York. Most of the students learned by listening to lectures and retaining that knowledge in their minds.

Since illustrations were a chief source of learning and the instructors found it difficult to teach without them, pictures were painted on church walls to educate the public. Matthew considered that most of these paintings presented a warped view of Christianity, for they depicted devils with forked tails persecuting sinners in the flames of hell. In contrast, Christians were herded by benevolent angels toward a heaven beyond the clouds. Sinners were naked; the redeemed wore clothing. When a few good pictures were available, the king arranged for artists to copy them or for wood carvers along the Rhine to copy the religious scenes upon wooden doors and ivory plaques. Drago was even able to sell his wooden carving of the Alabaster to the king for a high price.

The king was Alcuin's most zealous pupil because he had an insatiable curiosity. He wondered about the behavior of the stars, and Alcuin explained how the skies had been lifted above the flat area of the earth by God the Creator. He told the king that the heavens consisted of the first zone of air, then water, and then fire. He admitted that the moon was a mystery, as were the signs of the zodiac, and that beyond the farthest stars was the abode of the Creator God.

As Charles's knowledge of Greek increased, he took delight in reading the writings of Paul the apostle. The king identified with Paul because he, too, was a sinner of noble birth. He could recognize his own subjects in the words of Paul—their superstitions, exploration of unknown gods, and their love of women.

It was a sorrow to Charles that the queen wouldn't take part in the instruction, for she couldn't say even a simple sentence in Latin and had no desire to. With the frequent childbirths and the care of her large family, Hildegard had no time for education, but Charles couldn't understand that. Nor would he acknowledge Hildegard's poor health, although Matthew often suggested to him that the queen was not well.

Matthew had hoped that Charles's new interest in learning would distract him from his intention to destroy the Saxons, but in the summer of 783, the Frankish king pledged himself in a death struggle with the elusive Widukind. This expedition was postponed when Hildegard died after giving birth to a child in April. When Queen Mother Bertrada also died sixty days later, Charles retired from the battlefield to mourn the deaths of his loved ones and to do penitence for his sins.

Taking advantage of this mourning period, Matthew traveled to Willehad Manor to see Waldulf. When he arrived at the manor, Matthew compared his former visits to the languid greeting he received this time from Waldulf. Even Willehad and his wife seemed less enthusiastic in their welcome than at former times, but Matthew attributed this to worry over their son.

"I'm happy to see you, Matthew," Waldulf said when they were alone. "I sometimes think I'm losing my mind."

"You know what the problem is—you'll have to overcome it."

"I can't forget her. And it isn't only that she inflicted the wound that almost took my life, because I know the dagger was intended for Charles. It was the way she looked at me as if she hated me. How could love change to hate so quickly?"

"I don't think it did change. She was shocked at what Charles had done to her people, and at that moment she hated all Franks. I'm sure she's had her moment of remorse, too."

Waldulf sat upright. "You sound as if you have seen her."

"No, I have not seen her, but I have had a message from her. That's the reason I'm here. The message came through Drago. You know how he goes anywhere, seemingly without opposition. Though he's very secretive about his activities, I assumed he'd been in Saxony and had seen her."

"The message—is it for me or you?" Waldulf asked, with more interest than he had shown since the accident.

"For you. She had assumed that you had died, until she learned from Drago of your recovery. She asks your forgiveness and begs you to put her out of your mind. Since her attack upon the king, she knew she could never come to Frankish lands again . . ." Matthew paused because he knew his next words would hurt Waldulf. "Though she will always love you, she bowed to pressure from Widukind and married Abbio."

Waldulf stared at Matthew as if he hadn't heard correctly. He tottered to his feet, and Matthew reached out a hand to steady him. Waldulf walked as though he were in a daze and disappeared in the direction of the stables. Matthew started to follow, but in a few minutes, Waldulf appeared on horseback with a hooded falcon on his arm.

Willehad rushed to Matthew's side and clasped his hand. "Oh, friend Matthew, I can't thank you enough. You must have brought good news to stir my son from his lethargy. He's going to be all right now."

Maybe, but Matthew wasn't so sure.

❀   ❀   ❀

Within a few months, Charles put aside his mourning and married a noblewoman—Lady Fastrada, daughter of Rudolf, count of Franconia. With his new wife and his family, Charles spent the Christmas season at Heristal, where he remained through Easter of 784. When he sent out a call for troops to join him for the summer's campaign, Waldulf returned to the king's court.

Now that Printha was lost to him forever, Waldulf knew he had to make a life of some kind. Matthew, who knew firsthand the torture of a lost love, agonized over Waldulf's sorrow. Though he never mentioned her name, Matthew knew that his young friend still loved Printha and that his thoughts were never far from her. In his pity for Waldulf, Matthew lived again his loss of Sophia.

Through the next two years, Waldulf joined Charles in his assault upon the Saxons, and he fought as well as ever, but Matthew saw him cringe when tales of the heroic deeds of Widukind and his son-in-law, Abbio, were sung by the forest folk. The hold of Widukind over his people was broken at last when Charles gained the victory in a fierce hand-to-hand battle late in 785, and Widukind finally agreed to submit to the Franks if hostages were provided to secure his safe conduct among the Frankish hosts. Exulting, Charles called for the spring assembly at rebuilt Paderborn with plans to entertain the conquered Saxons.

Count Willehad and Waldulf rode at the head of their county's host, and Waldulf said, "Father, I've always wished that we could share the command. You'll never know how I trembled when I set out without you on my first campaign. That seems so long ago."

"Your mother is not happy that both of us are going this time, but I desire to attend one more assembly before I die, Waldulf. I do not expect to be around much longer."

Waldulf started to protest, but he desisted, for it was apparent that Willehad's health had deteriorated in the past year. He was not the same parent he had been. Where once he had been merry and energetic, he more and more left the supervision of the manor to his bailiff. Willehad seemed content to sit at home with Adela, who also was aging. The merrymaking at Paderborn with old friends seemed to revive Willehad for the time being, and he joyfully shared a horn of ale with his former comrades. But in spite of the feasting and drinking, tension gripped the Frankish host. Their collective thoughts seemed to hover over the assembly. *Will Widukind come? The man has become a legend. Are legends really flesh and blood?*

When the news circulated that the armed guard was arriving with Widukind and Abbio, the Franks gathered in the yard. Waldulf hesitated. *If Printha's husband and father come to submit to the Franks, does it not follow that Printha will come also?* He wanted to see her, but he dreaded to do so now that she was another man's wife.

Matthew and Waldulf stood together on a balcony and watched the procession emerge from the forest. A score of Charles's most trusted emissaries flanked the two men and a woman while another group of men protected them from the rear.

"It's Printha all right," Waldulf said. "I'd know that proud figure anywhere."

"The man on her right must be Abbio. But what's Drago doing with them? And where is Widukind?"

They looked at each other with sudden comprehension, and Matthew voiced what should have been apparent for years. "Drago is Widukind! How could we have been so blind? No wonder the Saxons knew everything the Franks were doing, when Widukind spent so much time at Charles's court."

"Look at the king's face. He can't believe it, either."

"Now I understand why he befriended Printha when she was a prisoner of the Franks."

The three Saxons stood before Charles now, and Drago bowed slightly. "I shall deceive you no more, King Charles."

"Are you Widukind?" Charles spluttered in a voice higher than usual.

Drago nodded his head. "I have lost the desire to fight. I've had an interesting and varied life. All I want to do now is to live at peace. I will not cause you any more trouble, nor will my family."

"You are ready to forsake the pagan gods and be baptized as Christians?" Charles asked, still incredulous.

Widukind nodded.

"Let the baptism be done at once."

The three Saxons laid aside their cloaks and followed the king and a priest he designated down to the banks of the Lippe River. Most of the Franks silently moved behind them to witness this historic moment. Matthew and Waldulf stayed on the balcony. Printha was led into the water first, and after she was immersed, Waldulf wept into his hands.

"I can't stand it, Matthew. You don't know what it's like when the woman you love is wed to another."

Matthew placed a hand on Waldulf's shaking shoulders. "Yes, I do, my friend. It's the worst agony I've ever experienced, but neither of us can do anything about the past. Let's rejoice in the present, anyway. The conversion of Widukind will make great changes in Charles's reign. Let's join the others in the council room."

Widukind had been a relentless enemy, but Charles easily put the past behind him. His clean-shaven face glowed with happiness, and he stroked his graying mustache as he watched the three Saxons take their first communion. He presented them with silver goblets and lengths of silken cloth.

Charles's counselors crowded around Widukind and his family, but Waldulf stayed hidden from Printha's view. When Matthew greeted her, she said, "Does Waldulf hate me?"

"No, he loves you still. He has not married."

"I didn't think I'd ever see the day that Widukind would surrender. If I had only waited." Her lips trembled and tears glistened in her eyes.

"But about your conversion, Printha. Are you doing this only because your husband and father agreed to? Or do you really believe in the God I serve?" Matthew inquired earnestly.

"I have not forgotten the instruction I learned from you and the priests at Charles's court, and I do trust my future to the God of the Franks, though I have much to learn."

"The most important thing for you to acknowledge is that your salvation comes through acceptance and faith in the death, burial, and resurrection of Christ. Do you believe that, Printha?"

"Yes, I do." Matthew squeezed her hand, content with her answer.

❀　❀　❀

Charles had requested all of his counselors and troop commanders to be present for the feast that evening, so Waldulf had no choice but to attend. He chose a small table behind a pillar, hoping to escape Printha's searching gaze. When all appetites were sated, Widukind asked Charles's permission to speak.

"Since it's my understanding that the Christian God expects confession of the penitent's sins, I have many sins to confess, and one wrong that I must right. While I have the reputation of hating all Franks, there is one that I love more than anyone on this earth." He paused and Matthew was surprised to see tears in the man's eyes. Drago had always been the most changeable person he knew, but he'd never before noted compassion in the man's character.

"I do not want to say what I must because it will cause a rift between me and the person I love." He pulled Printha upward to stand beside him.

"Printha does not know this—in fact, no living soul does—but she is not my daughter. She is a Frankish child, stolen from the village of Nehouse when she was a young child, too young for her to remember. Her father is Folz, the king's constable. I did not know the identity of her father until the priest Sturm told me a few years ago."

The blood drained from Printha's face, and she slipped from Widukind's grasp into her chair. Abbio laid a comforting hand on her shoulder, and Matthew noted her withdrawal from him. Widukind related how they had captured a few people the day the Saxons had burned Nehouse and that her mother had died to save Printha. Matthew couldn't suppress the anger that swelled in his heart. *This man has ruined Waldulf's life. And as for Father Sturm, why didn't he tell what he knew?*

Widukind lifted Printha's face until her eyes met his. "Do you hate me, Printha?"

She lifted her face and gazed at him in despair. "How could I hate you? You've been all that a father could be, but why didn't you tell me? You knew I wouldn't marry Waldulf because I thought he was a Frank and I was a Saxon. Why did you force me into a marriage with Abbio?"

"Selfishness. I hated the Franks, and I had no desire to lose you to them. I thought you would be happy as long as you didn't know, but I've seen sorrow consume you since you knew that Waldulf lived. I will not hold you any longer."

"But it's too late now," she whispered. All eyes were on them, and no sounds were heard except their voices and the rapid breathing of Franks stunned by the drama unfolding before them.

Widukind pulled her upward again and embraced her. Patting her hair, he said, "No, it is not too late. I think you would have been happy if you could have borne children, but how could any of us know that a battle wound soon after your betrothal would render Abbio impotent and prevent the marriage from being consummated? If it is your wish, I will ask Abbio to release you from your marriage, though you are free to stay with our people if you so desire."

Waldulf's throat tightened until he thought he would choke.

He half rose from the bench, but reason overcame his desire. The decision must be Printha's. He must not interfere.

Printha turned questioning eyes upon Abbio, a handsome man whose eyes now mirrored a living death. His love for Printha was obvious. "Oh, Abbio, I won't leave you. The accident was not your fault."

"It will not be your decision," Abbio said. "I am leaving you. On the morrow, I'm heading into the forest, and you will not see me again. I'm no longer a man. I will be a vagabond. I want you to follow where your heart leads." Without looking back, Abbio made his way through the surrounding group of soldiers and servants and disappeared into the night.

Printha looked at Widukind. She twisted her hands nervously, sniffed audibly, and opened her mouth to speak, but no words came. She scanned the crowded room, and her eyes locked with Waldulf's. He had risen to his feet and leaned against a pillar for support. Shaking like a leaf in a north wind, he held out a hand toward her. She hesitated only long enough to kiss Widukind before she rushed to him.

The Franks cheered loudly and pounded their drinking cups on the wooden tables. Willehad rapped on the table for silence, and he stood. "This seems to be the day for confessions. I have my own to make. Like Widukind, I do not want to make this news known, but I have no choice. Many of you know that our friend Matthew has sojourned among us for many years looking for a man who is connected to an alabaster vase. That man is the heir to a large fortune in Constantinople."

A weakness spread over Matthew's body. *Have I finally come to the end of the search? What does Willehad know? Not Widukind,* he prayed silently. He looked upon the count with anxious eyes.

"With great surprise, I learned two years ago that Waldulf is not my son, but rather an abandoned infant whom my wife passed as our son. I have the proof at our manor that Waldulf is the Trento for whom Matthew has searched. Waldulf has today gotten the desire of his heart since Printha has been returned to him. I cannot withhold his other good fortune. Matthew, Waldulf is the person you have sought these many years."

Weakness flowed over Matthew, and he moved as one in a trance. *God has at last vindicated my years of searching! I have kept my father's trust.* Matthew stood before the young couple. "More than once since I've known you, Waldulf, I've wished someone such as you were the heir of the Alabaster, but I had no idea it could be so. A vast fortune and a sacred heritage awaits you in my homeland. Will you go with me to claim it?"

Waldulf couldn't explain the feeling of destiny that flooded his soul. *What is the duty of the guardian of the Alabaster?* He heard again Matthew's explanation to Willehad. "The person who owns the Alabaster has the responsibility to preserve the family's Christian heritage by passing to succeeding generations the fact that Jesus Christ died on the cross and rose again on the third day. Because of His death and resurrection, the way to heaven is open to all people. It's the evidence of God's grace." *Has God really honored me, Waldulf, with this responsibility?*

In a few short sentences, Matthew explained the story of the Alabaster to Printha. Waldulf looked inquiringly at her, and when she nodded, he placed an arm around Matthew's shoulder.

"We accept the family heritage. We will go with you to Constantinople."

17

W aldulf awakened long before dawn on his wedding day, a wedding he anticipated with mixed emotions. Nothing could dim his joy that Printha would finally become his wife, but during the long hours of the night when he could not sleep, he admitted to himself that he dreaded this necessary move to Constantinople now that he was heir of the Alabaster. For several years, his only ambition had been to settle down at Willehad Manor with Printha by his side, and the idea of relocating to a foreign city was more than he could countenance.

Did I make a mistake when I accepted Matthew's proposition so rapidly? Waldulf took a long look at his room, where he would never be alone again, drew a deep breath, slipped quietly downstairs, and walked quickly to the barnyard. A heavy haze surrounded him as he guided his favorite horse from the stable and headed down the valley toward his customary hawking place. The falcon he had chosen was not the pet of his boyhood, but one that he had never used for hunting. The bird clutching his wrist felt comfortable, and as the horse raced over the uneven trail, Waldulf welcomed the strong breeze that blew his hair and eased the turmoil of his mind.

Reining in at the peak of a hill, he prepared the falcon for flight. As the bird fidgeted on his perch, eager for the hunt,

245

Waldulf thought, *The falcon is excited and impatient for this experience because he's doing what he was born to do.* That revelation hit Waldulf's mind like a thunderbolt. *Of course! What have I been born to do?* The answer was quite simple when he considered the circumstances. He was heir to the Alabaster. That was his destiny, and he shouldn't question it again. Just like the falcon, he should be eager and impatient to begin his new life rather than fretting because his comfortable life on the manor was coming to an end.

Although he returned to the manor with his mind strangely at peace, Waldulf still could not forget the obligation he owed his parents. Printha saw him coming, and she met him in the stable yard. He kissed her eagerly, but his concern must have been apparent, for she placed her hand on his cheek.

"What troubles you, Waldulf?"

He put an arm around her as they approached the manor house. "I'm fretting about my family. Will I ever see them again? And I still consider them my parents, even though I now know that my natural parents died in that famine long ago. They've made my life rich, given me everything. Am I ungrateful to go off and leave them now?"

"Does it make it any easier for you to know that I had the same difficult decision to make? I love Widukind as much as you love your father. Regardless of his war exploits, he was always good to me. It's a sorrow to me that he will live out his days as an outcast without anyone to care for him, while I'll be living in luxury in Constantinople. Don't you know that I've had many moments of self-doubt?"

"Forgive me, Printha. I'm so happy to have you by my side that I hadn't considered how you might feel."

"It's all right, Waldulf, for I want to be wherever you are. It's only normal for you to feel some doubts about this move, but your father knew very well that he might lose you when he revealed your true identity. If he wasn't willing to give you up, he wouldn't have told you. Talk to your parents about it."

Waldulf left Printha to have her breakfast alone while he sought out his parents. Walking down the long hall where he had once romped with abandon, his hand trembled as he knocked on the door to his parents' room. At his father's call, he opened the door, and the scene that confronted him was one he would remember forever. Count Willehad sat with his left arm around a weeping Adela, and their right hands were clasped tightly. *They look old and forsaken.*

"My loved ones," Waldulf whispered, and he knelt in front of them, his revelation of an hour ago forgotten. "I do not like to see you sad. Say the word, and I will not leave you. I can carry on the heritage of the Alabaster here in Gaul. It isn't necessary for me to go to Constantinople to do that. I don't need a large fortune, for I've never coveted riches. Perhaps I was hasty in my decision."

Adela continued to weep quietly, but she patted Waldulf on the shoulder and nodded for Willehad to speak, which he did with difficulty.

"We do not want to be selfish, my son. You've given us thirty years of happiness. Why should we deny you this opportunity? Perhaps when you reach Byzantium, you will decide that you do not like it there and will want to return, but the decision must be yours."

Now it was Waldulf who wept when Adela said softly, "I knew the moment I laid eyes upon you, Waldulf, that God had destined you for great things. I am sorry to see you go, but I consider myself like Hannah in the Bible who nurtured Samuel and then presented him to God. Even Jochebed, who risked her own life to protect Moses from his enemies, had to release her son when God called him into divine service."

"But you will need someone to carry on the work of the manor when you are no longer able."

"As you know," Willehad said, "the ownership of the manor is at the whim of the king. It is not a hereditary right. It's possible that upon my death, you might be appointed the count, especially since you're in the good graces of King Charles, but he will not always be king, and you could find yourself without any inheritance at all. In my opinion, it's the will of God that you go to Constantinople, and you should not question it."

Waldulf continued to offer arguments why he should not leave them, but, one by one, they allayed his concerns. With their full assurance that he had made the right decision, he returned to Printha knowing his parents were willing to make this sacrifice because they loved him.

Since their marriage would not follow the customary ritual where the families of the bride and groom presented dowries or marriage portions at the church door before the betrothal ceremony, the abbot from the nearby monastery came to the manor and performed a simple service that made Printha and Waldulf man and wife. Two days later, they left Willehad Manor in Matthew's company for their journey to Constantinople. Their first stop was to be King Charles's estate at Attingy where they expected to bid farewell to Charles and his family, but a surprise awaited them.

All smiles, Charles said, "We will not have to say good-bye so soon if you will agree to travel with the royal entourage into Italy." Facing Matthew, the king said, "In fact, I have one last favor to ask of you."

Matthew and Waldulf exchanged glances, but Matthew said, "At your service, sire, as always."

"We have received a message that emissaries from the Byzantine court have arrived in Rome seeking Princess Hrotrud. Empress Irene considers it time to consummate the marriage that we agreed upon several years ago between Constantine VI and my daughter. Hrotrud is eager to go, but it will be easier for me to send her away if she could travel with your party. Will you delay your journey to coincide with the one that takes my daughter away from me?"

Matthew glanced toward Printha, and she smiled in delight. "It would be a pleasure to chaperone Princess Hrotrud," she said.

"You will remember, King Charles, that she is a favorite of mine from the days I spent at the king's court."

"Then it is agreed. We will leave two days hence. It may not be a good time to cross the Alps, but pressing matters await me in Italy. Pope Hadrian is much concerned about several problems that need my attention. I cannot delay, for after I spend Easter in Rome, I must be back here to prevent further rebellion in my provinces. It is not easy to rule over such a large kingdom, friend Matthew."

❋   ❋   ❋

No one was happier to be on the way to Rome than Elisha and the other Byzantine envoys who had been preparing Hrotrud to become the wife of their young ruler. Weather favored the royal party, and they arrived safely and speedily in Rome. Matthew left the king's party when they became the guests of the pope and took Waldulf and Printha to stay with his Roman relatives.

Learning that the duke of Benevento, who had never sworn loyalty to the Frankish king, was warring against Naples, King Charles went off immediately to inquire into the trouble. Much disturbed, Elisha came to the Trento home and sought an audience with Matthew and Waldulf.

"I have arranged with the emissaries of the empress for your party to travel on the royal ship when we return to Constantinople."

"Then my homecoming will be more lavish than my leave-taking almost twenty years ago," Matthew said with a laugh. "We appreciate having you intercede on our behalf."

Elisha had always been a quiet man, but Waldulf quickly noticed that his friend seemed unhappy, and he said, "Is something bothering you, Elisha?"

"Yes. As soon as we arrived in Rome, King Charles rushed away without even receiving the emissaries from Constantinople.

They were very angry when they learned that he was gone. The captain of the royal ship is eager to start the return journey before sailing conditions worsen. The emissaries are preparing to follow him and discuss marriage settlements, for there is no telling when King Charles might return."

"Printha has a woman's intuition that we lack," Waldulf said, "and she's been saying for weeks that the king's enthusiasm for this wedding has waned. Frankly, she thinks he's going to back out of the betrothal. If so, that would explain his leaving Rome before he talked with the Byzantines."

Elisha shook his head with concern. "That confirms my own suspicions. And my head will probably roll if I return to Constantinople without a bride. Emperor Constantine is seventeen years old and should be wed."

❋   ❋   ❋

Within a week, the emissaries returned to Rome, highly indignant that Charles had repudiated the betrothal, a fact that Elisha speedily reported to the Trento household.

"What reason could he give except that he doesn't want his daughter to marry?" Matthew asked, surprised at Charles's action, athough Printha had predicted it.

"He said that he'd heard a rumor that a Byzantine army is on its way to attack his empire," Elisha reported.

"Is that true?" Waldulf asked.

"Not that I've heard." Elisha shook his head in frustration. "I can't imagine the turmoil this will cause in Constantinople. The empress will accuse me of failing to complete my mission, although all I was supposed to do was to train the girl in Greek culture. Not only will I suffer, but the empress is not one to be crossed, and the revenge she will perpetrate against the West is hard to imagine. We will know soon enough, for the ship sails tomorrow. Will that give you sufficient time for preparation?"

"We are ready and waiting. I'm eager to return home and see

Waldulf installed as heir to the house of Trento. Then I will resume my monastic life to meditate on what life has done to me." Matthew didn't add that one reason for his eagerness was to see Sophia again, but he wondered how he would like being in the same household with her when she was married to another.

When Printha went to say good-bye to Hrotrud, she found the girl in a rage. "He will never let me marry!" she exclaimed. "Perhaps my stepmother is right—she accused Father of having an unnatural affection for his daughters. I credited her remarks to jealousy, but now I wonder."

"Then you are disappointed?"

"Why wouldn't I be? Elisha has spent years teaching me what my lot would be as empress of Byzantium, impressing upon me what an exalted position I would hold. I thought it was in my grasp, and now it's gone. Instead of a golden palace, I'll return to stone and log palaces with dirt floors. Of course I'm disappointed!"

Placing her arm around Hrotrud's rigid shoulders, Printha said, "Indeed, I'm disappointed, too. I had looked forward to your company on the voyage and also to be able to count one friend in that foreign city. It won't be easy for me, Hrotrud, to go from a lifetime of freedom in the forests of Saxony to the fabled city of Constantinople. I am sure to be lonely, but I love Waldulf and I want to be with him."

❋　❋　❋

Their approach to Constantinople came at midday, and the convoy had an unobstructed view of the snow-covered Thracian Mountains to the west and hills dotted with vineyards to the east. The skyline was marked by high walls, towers, and mighty palaces with glittering roofs. The city was bounded by the sea on three sides, and ships in the harbor carried the flags of the world's nations. Because their ship exhibited the imperial colors, they were given preferential treatment for landing, and the empress's envoys were immediately conducted to land vehicles for their journey to the palace.

Before parting from the royal emissaries, Matthew said quietly to Elisha, "Please send a message to the house of Trento as soon as possible about the reception you receive from the empress. I am concerned for your welfare."

Since no one at the house of Trento knew of their arrival, Matthew hired transportation to take them to their destination. Waldulf and Printha stared out the carriage windows as they passed from the harbor area along streets where tall buildings were set among lovely vales and gardens.

When they reached his home, a tightness in his throat kept Matthew from speaking for a moment. He stepped from the carriage and gazed with fondness at the two-storied wooden structure. The numerous latticed windows spreading across the front of the house looked inviting, and doves cooed contentedly from the eaves of the red tile roof. When Waldulf and Printha stood beside him, he pointed with pride to the house. "My former home, and now yours. It was built by my grandfather. I hope you will be happy here."

Printha gripped Waldulf's arm. "It's a beautiful house, Matthew. I will feel much more at home here than I would have in some of the huge, gilded dwellings we passed."

Matthew dismissed the carriage and walked to the door, which was opened by Sophia. Though he had expected to see her, the encounter was unnerving. *Will this woman never age? Will she always be the radiant beauty I first loved?*

Sophia found her tongue first. "What a surprise, Matthew! Excuse, me *Master* Matthew."

He reached for her hands. "Never 'master' to you, Sophia." Her hands felt warm and soft to his touch, and her beaming gray eyes held him spellbound. Sophia became aware of the staring couple with Matthew, and she said, "Won't you come in, Matthew, and introduce me to your companions?"

Matthew shook his head to rid himself of the tumult this

woman always provoked in him, and he fleetingly wondered as he often had before why God had given him this burden to bear. He turned toward Waldulf, who stared at Sophia and at him with incredulous eyes. *He knows!* Matthew thought, remembering that once when he had been comforting Waldulf over his loss of Printha, he had told him that his only love was married to another. *I must get a grip on my emotions or the situation could become unpleasant and embarrassing.*

"Yes, Sophia, I've found the heir to the Alabaster. You may remember seeing Waldulf around King Charles's court when you attended his former wife Desiderata of Lombardy. Waldulf's wife is Printha of Saxony. We must do our best to make them welcome."

Sophia ushered them into a house that was neat and glowing with cleanliness, and Matthew knew that the house had been thus ready for his return since the day he had departed from Constantinople. The group walked down the hall to a large room overlooking the spacious garden.

"I will bring you refreshments in a short while," Sophia said.

Printha clapped her hands when she saw the shaded garden with the gray marble fountain cascading from basin to basin. Most of the trees, some of which had been mere shrubs when Matthew had left for his journey to Europe, were huge now and towered over the stone wall that surrounded the garden.

"I will like it here, Matthew. I can always retreat to that restful spot and under those giant trees transport my mind to the Saxony of my youth," Printha said.

When Sophia returned, a short, wiry man accompanied her. Although he looked familiar, Matthew was sure he had not seen him before.

"Welcome home, Master. I am Cyril, the son of Basil, who served both you and your father."

"It is my pleasure to meet you, Cyril, but I am no longer your master." Matthew introduced Waldulf and Printha to Cyril as his new master and mistress, and as they talked, Matthew went to Sophia's side while she placed plates of pastries, fruit, and a container of wine on the cabinet beneath the window. She was breathing heavily, and he realized she was not as indifferent to his presence as she would have him believe.

"Are you well, Sophia?" Matthew asked gently.

"Yes, and I am the mother of two children, both of whom are being educated as wards of the house of Trento at a local school. Cyril had no objection when I counted their education as a part of my salary. Matthew, because of my children, I beg you to forget that we have known each other in the past."

Her words fell like cold water on Matthew's heart, but he knew she was right. "I will return to a monastery soon, Sophia, and respect your wishes. And Gerona?" The words were as bitter as gall in his mouth.

"He is well and still employed at the Trento silk factory. He has not asked questions about my past, nor have I told him anything."

When Printha and Waldulf were taken to a room, Matthew walked about his home. It would be his no longer, but he had no regrets. Waldulf was as dear to him as any son could have been, and he would leave as soon as possible. To live under the same roof with Sophia and her family would not be a pleasant experience.

After the evening meal, Cyril conducted Waldulf and Matthew into the office while Printha rested in her bedroom. Cyril pointed out all of the account books that had been faithfully kept for the past twenty years, first by his father, Basil, and then by him.

"You may examine these at your leisure, but I believe you will find that the house of Trento has profited under our stewardship."

"I never had any doubt of that," Matthew assured him. "I'm reminded of our Lord's parables of the talents. You are obviously like the ten- and five-talent stewards who eagerly awaited their Lord's return." Matthew pushed aside the books. "I will study these at a later time, and with your help, introduce Waldulf to his new duties. For now, I am eager for you to apprise us of the political and economic situation of Byzantium. Except for your occasional letters, we have little knowledge of what has happened since I left here."

"You left on your quest in 768, I believe, so you were aware of the conflict at that time between Emperor Constantine V and the monks, who were the chief defenders of the images. Constantine waged war on them, and by his death in 775, there was hardly a monk left in this city. More than once my father thanked God that you were not here."

"What happened to the monks?"

Cyril threw up his hands. "The emperor ordered brutal executions. Monasteries were secularized, and the religious were driven out, imprisoned, or exiled."

"Did conditions improve under Leo IV when his father died?" Matthew questioned, while Waldulf listened intently to the conversation. The intrigues of the Byzantium court and the fight against image worshipers were new to him, but Cyril's words troubled his mind. *How can an insignificant Frank ever become master of this establishment?* He was nonetheless committed to this new role, and he concentrated on Cyril's words.

"Emperor Leo did relax some of the penalties against those found with images, perhaps because of Empress Irene's influence, as she herself is sympathetic to image worshipers. When the emperor discovered some images in the empress's apartments one day, his anger was violent. Although she declared the images were not hers, she lost the power to influence her husband. Fortunately for her and for the image worshipers, Leo died about six months later. As regent for her son, the empress restored orthodox worship in Byzantium, and some of the monasteries that were not demolished have reopened, but yours was destroyed, as I notified you."

"Does that mean that you need not return?" Waldulf asked hopefully, wondering how he could do without Matthew's help in this colossal undertaking before him.

With an understanding smile, Matthew said, "My vows were given to God not to a particular monastery. I can enter another, but I will stay until I am sure you can do without me. Do not be anxious. You will soon be ready to take over here."

Cyril shook his head glumly. "The young master may need quite a lot of help. There is always intrigue at court, and right now there is a power struggle between Empress Irene and her son. She doesn't want to relinquish rule to Constantine, who is ready to assume command. I look for a conflict between Irene's followers and those who favor the emperor. Businessmen in this city may have to take sides, and it will be important to align with the winner."

"Who knows whom that might be?" Matthew wondered, and when Cyril was silent, Matthew continued, "Now that King Charles has refused to send his daughter to wed the young emperor, perhaps the empress will be so angry at the West that she will expend all of her energies to punish Charles. That might give you time, Waldulf, to settle in before the city is rocked with more controversy."

"Perhaps," Cyril reluctantly agreed, "but the empress is a person who bides her time and plans her strategy well, although she doesn't always win."

Waldulf laughed shortly. "My head is beginning to ache with all of this information, and I can't sort it out in my mind. Is it too late to go back to Gaul?"

Matthew laid his hand on the younger man's shoulder. "Don't fret, Waldulf. You don't have to learn everything today, but I have no fear that you will soon be in command of your position. Remember, you have assumed a divine task. God will be leading you all the way." He nodded to Cyril. "Go ahead and tell us the rest. Waldulf probably won't sleep tonight anyway."

The gentle flow of the garden fountain and the soft chirping of birds as they sought their nests could be heard through the open window, and in spite of the tense political situation being discussed, Waldulf's peace of mind returned.

"After Leo IV died, the empress changed the personnel of the palace and courted the church hierarchy until she had many influential bishops supporting her," Cyril continued. "Last year she thought she had enough support to restore images to our worship, and, certain of victory, she called a council to meet here in the city. Unfortunately she had not considered the opposition of certain bishops and regiments of the imperial guard who were faithful to the memory of Constantine V. The soldiers stormed the meeting and threatened those assembled with death if they didn't disband. No punishment was inflicted upon the empress, and she became more determined than ever to exercise absolute rule with her own hands."

"It seems that the young emperor made a mistake when he didn't banish her from the city," Matthew noted.

"I agree, especially since her followers consider her a martyr. By bribery, she won over many of her former opponents and sent the army away on an expedition to fight the Arabs. In their absence, she arrested the families of the soldiers in the field and had their property seized. She has tighter control now than she did a year ago."

After Cyril left them alone, Matthew said, "It does seem that we've come back to Constantinople at a difficult time, Waldulf. I had forgotten how this city thrives on conspiracy. After you've been here awhile, the schemes of the Frankish king will seem tame to you."

"The political controversy doesn't concern me as much as the bickering of the church officials. To fight for years over whether or not to have images in our churches can't be the real purpose of Christianity," Waldulf stated solemnly.

"I can see that you are a worthy heir for the Alabaster, for you recognize the message that Trentos have been expounding for centuries. God is not pleased with internal or external fighting by His followers, but the church is still in its infancy and experiencing growing pains. It may take many centuries of struggle before Christians see the true role of the church in the world. In the meantime, it will be your duty to pass on the meaning of the resurrection of Christ to Trento heirs."

Matthew went upstairs and returned with the Alabaster, which he placed in a prominent niche on the office wall. "It will be there to remind you of your spiritual beliefs," he said to Waldulf.

❀   ❀   ❀

For the next few days, while Sophia introduced Printha to her position as mistress of the household, Matthew and Waldulf spent hours in the office going over the records of the Trento holdings. Since Waldulf had learned Greek from Elisha at the Frankish court, he was soon able to use the language in a practical way, and Matthew was well pleased with Waldulf's prompt and intelligent grasp of the family enterprise. They had just returned from a tour of the Trento silk industry when a visitor was announced.

Matthew found Elisha waiting in the main hall. "Come in," Matthew said, and he guided Elisha and Waldulf into the room where Printha sat. "You have not been punished, then?"

"No, the empress has other things on her mind. I believe she was planning to break the betrothal herself, for if the Council at Nicaea, which she is planning later on this year, goes as planned, the worship of images will again be a part of the church ritual here. That decision will please Pope Hadrian and serve to alleviate much of the discord between the eastern and western empires. The empress was using the Frankish king only as a pawn to keep the pope in line. She actually expressed relief that the marriage was off, hinting that Charles has become too powerful. She wouldn't want her son to have a vigorous father-in-law to intervene when trouble erupts between Empress Irene and her son."

"Then she intends to cause trouble?"

"So her counselors believe. Constantine wants to assume control of the empire, and his mother wants to rule—which brings me to the reason for my visit. While the empress is relieved that the betrothal has been broken, Constantine is crushed. He's determined that wedding plans will continue. He wants Waldulf and Printha to visit him so that he can talk to them about the young girl. Matthew, you are to bring them at midafternoon tomorrow."

Printha shrieked her protest. "Oh, no, Elisha! I'm not ready for that. Neither of us can speak his language well. Why can't you tell him what he wants to know?"

"The emperor knows that I am his mother's emissary and feels that I might not tell him the truth. He wants to be assured that King Charles ended the betrothal instead of his mother." He bestowed a piercing look upon the Frankish couple. "You do not have a choice. You will find that Byzantium citizens do not enjoy the freedom that you knew as Franks. If you want to reside in this city, take my advice and obey the emperor's summons."

Printha looked quickly at Matthew, and he nodded. "Elisha is right. You will have to go, and I will be with you if you need an interpreter."

❊   ❊   ❊

Although Printha wore one of the finest silk robes available in Constantinople, she still looked apprehensive as they entered the Trento carriage for the drive to the sacred palace. Weariness marked her eyes as well as Waldulf's, indicating that neither of the Franks had slept well. To take their minds off of the interview with the emperor, Matthew directed the driver to travel first to the Church of Saint Sophia with its lavishly decorated balconies and beautifully carved pillars. As they viewed the splendor of Constantinople's magnificent buildings, Printha and Waldulf appeared to forget momentarily what awaited them at the end of the journey.

They drove first through the busiest part of the city on the

Mese, a long avenue that started at Emperor Square in front of the Church of Saint Sophia and continued to the city walls. Under its colonnades, they saw the workbenches of the goldsmiths who were manufacturing gold boxes, jewelry, and intricate enamel pieces. Matthew pointed out the long tables of the money changers who swapped coins from all over the world.

When they came to the bazaar, Matthew halted the carriage and guided his young friends through the narrow streets of the tinsmiths and coppersmiths, passing by stalls containing household items, and then to the area where sheep, pigs, cattle, and horses were offered for sale. A profusion of languages filled the area as shoppers bargained for the items of their choice. Sensing that the time for their appointment with the emperor was near, Matthew drew Waldulf and Printha away from the exciting area, which surpassed any fair that Waldulf had attended in Frankish lands.

"It's intimidating for me, a girl from the Saxon woods, to have an audience with one of the three most powerful people in the world," Printha said anxiously as they resumed their journey.

With a smile, Matthew said, "I assume that you are counting King Charles and Pope Hadrian as the other two powerful people, but you should add a fourth—the empress Irene."

"I'd forgotten her."

"A very bad mistake to make in Constantinople—never forget about the empress and her power."

What they had seen on their drive through the city had not prepared the two Franks for the splendor of the sacred palace. They passed from the noise of the streets into the quiet peacefulness of flower gardens and fountains flowing with sparkling water. Inside the buildings were magnificent doors of silver and ivory, curtains of purple hung on rods of silver, and gold-embroidered tapestries featuring fantastic hunting scenes. Huge golden lamps swung from exalted domes, and the furniture was encrusted with mother of pearl, gold, and ivory.

"The palace covers twenty-five or thirty acres," Matthew

explained as they were conducted by two of the emperor's guards through a portal supported by four columns of marble. "I have been here only one time so I do not know the extent of the palace, but it's reported that there are five hundred gold mosaic halls, all connected with the other. There are many chapels, and one of them—the Holy Chapel—is constructed of silver."

"Can you imagine the cost of human life to build all of this?" Waldulf mused.

"When gold and silver became plentiful in Constantinople, human life became cheap, which is another reason I do not believe God is pleased with our interpretation of the work of His church. He would prefer more humane uses of our resources, I'm sure."

Entering the throne room on mosaic floors magnificently displaying an eagle, Matthew, Printha, and Waldulf felt their eyes immediately drawn to the emperor on the glittering dais. Matthew prostrated himself before the ruler, and Printha and Waldulf awkwardly did likewise. Even as he did this obeisance, Waldulf remembered a childhood teaching, "Reverence belongs to God alone." *How far we've come from the teaching of the Scriptures. Indeed, I have a huge task if I am to spread the message of the Alabaster,* Waldulf reflected.

When the soldiers helped her to her feet, Printha took a closer look at the emperor. Seated as he was and swathed in a purple, gold-embroidered robe decorated with pearls, she couldn't determine his size, but she judged him to be of medium build, because the imperial crown encrusted with rubies and sapphires appeared to weigh heavily on his head. Deep-crimson boots peeped from beneath his robe. Matthew stood in the background, so only Waldulf and Printha approached the royal throne. Printha was glad to have Waldulf's steady hand under her arm, for her palms were wet and her legs trembled.

"I understand that you were a friend to Princess Hrotrud," the emperor said to Printha, and she was surprised that she could easily understand his speech. Elisha had been a good teacher.

"Yes, I served as her companion for a few years."

"Tell me about her."

"Please excuse me, Your Excellency, if I do not communicate well in your language," Printha said slowly.

He nodded.

"Hrotrud is a pleasant girl, a comely youth, and she has received the best education available to a girl in Frankish lands."

Constantine's gaze shifted to Waldulf. "Why didn't she come to be my bride?"

"We do not know," Waldulf answered. "She had traveled with us to Rome and the date had been set for departure when King Charles refused to allow her to accompany us." Not wanting to mention that the king had supposedly heard of Byzantium interference in western affairs, he added, "She is very young, and King Charles may have wanted to keep her with him longer."

Eyes brightening, Constantine said, "Then you think it's possible to resume negotiations."

"Oh, I didn't mean that. Once the king has made up his mind, he doesn't change it," Waldulf explained.

"But I intend to try." The emperor gestured to one of the many servants around the huge room. "Please ask my mother to wait upon me."

Printha tugged at her robe. Although she was dressed in one of the Trento's finest fabrics, she feared the woman would be able to see beneath her present finery to the roughly woven woolen garments that she had worn all of her life.

Matthew moved closer. "Don't fret," he whispered in the Frankish tongue, which the emperor couldn't understand. "I doubt she will come."

Matthew was wrong, for soon a majestic woman floated into the room, flanked by six attendants. Matthew remembered well this woman he had seen on the day of her wedding to Emperor Leo IV, and in spite of the years that had passed, she was still beautiful. An exotic perfume heralded her approach, and she swept by the visitors without a glance in their direction.

Printha was dazzled by her splendid robe of deep purple embroidered in gold. Glittering jewels adorned her hands and ears, and she wore a diadem of precious stones and pearls. The garments of her ladies-in-waiting more than equaled the robe that Printha wore.

Constantine introduced his visitors to the empress, and she gazed coldly at them without speaking. Matthew quietly translated Constantine's rapid Greek as he said to his mother, "These visitors from Frankish lands have brought me news of my beloved. I will not take King Charles's repudiation as final. I intend to contact the Franks again about this alliance."

"I do not discuss matters of the state before strangers. Don't presume to summon me into your presence again. If you want to discuss the matter, come to my apartments *alone!*" the empress snapped.

Constantine looked like a whipped dog after Empress Irene turned on her heel and left the room with her attendants behind her, and he coughed apologetically. "The empress was not pleased with your presence nor my conduct. I will ask you to excuse me."

As they were escorted out to the street once again, Matthew, Printha, and Waldulf were silent. Waldulf rubbed the back of his neck as if he could feel the pain of an axe blow. "Were we lucky not to be made prisoners?" he asked.

"I don't know that we were in much danger, for the empress obviously knew that we had been summoned to this meeting. What did you think of her?" Matthew asked Printha.

Shuddering, Printha said, "She's evil! I've never seen colder eyes. I felt as if I was in the clutches of a viper."

"Exactly the same opinion I had of her when I saw her crowned in 768. She's a woman driven by ambition, one who will accomplish her wishes by fair means or foul."

"Do you think she will be swayed by Constantine's wishes?" Waldulf asked.

"Not unless it suits her purposes to be so!" Matthew replied.

❀   ❀   ❀

Matthew was right. During September and October, a council of 365 bishops met in Nicaea to discuss the use of holy images. The council decreed that statues or pictures could be displayed in churches, and that they should be given salutation and honor, but not the degree of worship belonging to God.

Though the ruling would no doubt be rejected by King Charles, when Pope Hadrian defended this the Second Council of Nicaea, the eastern empire and the pope were on agreeable terms again. Empress Irene didn't need Charles's cooperation any longer, so, disregarding Constantine's own wishes, she sent envoys throughout the kingdom to find a wife for her son. In November 788, Constantine was married to a wife of his mother's choosing.

Still not completely subservient to his mother, the young emperor joined in a plot against Prime Minister Stauracius, who was the empress's tool. When the conspiracy was discovered, Irene retaliated brutally by having Constantine beaten with rods and kept under arrest. Other conspirators were tortured, exiled, or cast into prison.

Not willing to leave Waldulf, who was still inexperienced in Byzantium political intrigues, Matthew again delayed returning to holy orders. His decision was made somewhat easier when Gerona and Sophia moved their family into another house, with Sophia coming to the Trento household on a daily basis. The nearness of her presence was still agony to Matthew. He avoided her whenever possible, and he honored her request to refrain from referring to their past love, but no pledge could prevent Sophia from occupying his thoughts.

18

Frankish Gaul, 792–794

Hrotrud had been writing a letter for several days, and the unaccustomed activity caused her to lay aside her pen often. She marveled that so many things had happened since that day in 787 when King Charles had canceled her plans to go to Constantinople.

Dear Waldulf and Printha,

It was a pleasure to receive your letter and to know that you have settled into life in Constantinople and that you have avoided involvement in the political situation. What a horrid woman Empress Irene must be, but I'm thankful for the soldiers who were loyal enough to Constantine to restore him to favor. I'm still disappointed that I couldn't marry him, but I shudder to think what my life would have been with a mother-in-law like Empress Irene. Perhaps my father was right after all, but I haven't completely forgiven him for breaking that betrothal.

To think that it has been more than five years since we've seen you! I enjoyed hearing about the antics of your two sons and know that you're proud to have someone to carry on the family heritage. It's generous of Constantine VI to include you and Waldulf in so many court activities. The city of Constantinople must truly be a fabulous place.

The king was pleased to have news from his old friend Matthew and to know that he had again entered a monastery. I can hardly perceive him as a monk when I think of the years he lived among us garbed in the elegant robes of Byzantium.

Conditions here in Gaul are not good. My father puzzles me. Several months ago, he started negotiations to wed my brother Charles to a daughter of Offa, king of Mercia, but when it became obvious the marriage would be conditional upon securing a Frankish princess for Offa's son, Father angrily broke off negotiations. It seems to me that he wants none of his daughters to wed.

I became angry, too, and told him that if he didn't allow me to marry, I was going to become a nun. He laughed at my suggestions, but it wasn't an idle threat. I've already talked about it to my aunt Giesla, who is in a nunnery. However, I've cast my fancy upon Rorico, count of Maine, and he seems to favor me. I will see how that turns out before I make a drastic move.

Even as sheltered as we are, I'm aware that all is not well in the kingdom, for the king has lost touch with his people. He doesn't go out among them as he once did, and the populace doesn't like my stepmother, Fastrada. She has a cruel streak, and she vents it often on Frankish subjects—even to members of our household. She is especially spiteful to Pepin the Hunchback, who has left the seclusion of the monastery to spend more time at court than he has for several years. I hate to call him by such a dreadful name, but we must differentiate between him and our fourth brother, who was also given the name of our grandfather.

Except for Pepin, our household is composed mostly of females now. All of my full brothers have kingdoms to rule in distant lands. Fastrada has borne two daughters, and with my sisters, we make up a lively household. My

sister Bertha is enamored with Angilbert, the chaplain, and
he is constantly among our family circle.

Hrotrud laid aside her writing materials, deciding to finish
the letter tomorrow in time to have it dispatched with her father's
couriers to Rome. She put on a silk robe, bound her golden hair
with a purple ribbon, and hung a gold chain around her neck.
Then she joined her family in the courtyard for the evening, the
time when King Charles wanted all of his family around him.

This palace at Ratisbon was more commodious than the rude
dwellings Charles had lived in at first. The family's quarters
were separated from the main reception hall where the king conducted matters of government, received his ambassadors, and
acted as judge between his people. Each of the girls had her
own room, made comfortable by embroidered wall tapestries,
imported from the eastern empire, and latticed windows, which
let in the evening breezes. The dirt floors of the past had been
replaced with tiles brought from Italy. Although she didn't like
the king's present wife, Hrotrud gave Fastrada credit for the
improvement in their lifestyle.

When Hrotrud entered the courtyard nearest the family's quarters, King Charles was already stretched out on a comfortable
bench. A smile wreathed his face, for this was his favorite time of
the day. His work was done, and robed in comfortable silk brocade garments, he looked with fondness upon his family. Bertha,
with Angilbert close by, looked beautiful in a flowing blue garment secured by a gilt girdle, with an ermine cape over her
shoulders. Hrotrud noticed her sister's diadem and realized that
she had forgotten to wear hers. Perhaps the king wouldn't notice.

"Come, my child," King Charles greeted her. "Favor us with
a song." He motioned to a harp near his bench.

Hrotrud didn't like to perform in public, but from past experience she knew her father wouldn't stop asking until she had
sung. She drew the harp toward her, strummed it, and in a soft
voice presented her father's favorite evensong.

Before the ending of the day,
   Creator of the world, we pray
That with Thy wonted favor Thou
   Wouldst be our Guard and Keeper now.

From all ill dreams defend our eyes,
   From nightly fears and fantasies;
Tread underfoot our ghastly foe,
   That no pollution we may know.

O Father, that we ask be done,
   Through Jesus Christ, Thine only Son;
Who, with the Holy Ghost and Thee,
   Doth live and reign eternally. Amen.

Her duty performed, Hrotrud arose and walked over to where Pepin the Hunchback sat in the shadows. It had been this way as long as she remembered—he always seemed to be on the outside of the family circle looking in. His eyes lit up with the attention she gave him, and her compassion stirred for this brother with the fair, intelligent face and twisted body.

"Don't sit back in the shadows, brother. Come and join us."

He started to rise, but at that moment, Queen Fastrada swept into the courtyard, her shimmering golden hair streaming down her back. She was followed by silk-robed and bejeweled retainers, one of whom carried a silk pillow for her to sit on. Pepin spat derisively and a look of hatred spread over his face. He resumed his seat on the bench.

"Don't be so bitter, Pepin," Hrotrud said gently. "She is unkind to us girls, too. It's only from our father that she hides her evil side, so he doesn't know the extent of her cruelty."

He tossed a stone from one hand to the other. "It would take so little to bring her down."

Hrotrud gasped. In spite of his deformity, she knew that Pepin was strong. "Don't even think of it, brother. She has spies all around us, and if she were gone, there would soon be another to take her place. You know our father would never be long without a wife."

"It angers me when I think that he murdered my mother because she plotted his death, while this one can have his subjects killed and gets by with it. She's been responsible for more deaths than my mother ever was."

Pepin's attitude alarmed her, and Hrotrud wandered back to her father's side, but she was alert to what was going on. She observed when a man entered the courtyard and beckoned to Pepin, an event that occurred almost every night. *What is Pepin up to?* she wondered. If one of her other brothers was at court, she might discuss it with him, but she wouldn't betray Pepin to her father.

❀   ❀   ❀

The hunchback had never been so flattered. For the past few months since he had returned to his father's household, Pepin had made many new friends. Often he dined at the home of Count Wala, a young kinsman of the king. The discontent of the count's advisors found lodging in his mind.

"You have been mistreated by the king," Wala said one day. "His firstborn should succeed him, yet you've been overlooked. You're a man now, and his other sons are mere children—too young to be entrusted with leadership."

"But the king's advisors have put forth the word that I'm of illegitimate birth," Pepin said angrily.

"Which is not true! Your grandmother, Bertrada, has always insisted that the marriage was legal. Only your enemies, those who do not want you to rule, are speaking such words." Although Pepin often reasoned that Wala might be using him for his own purposes, against his better judgment, he listened to what the man had to say.

As the weeks passed, Hrotrud continued to watch Pepin's

stealthy behavior, and once she was convinced that he was involved in some secretive situation, she finally approached him. "What are you doing, Pepin?"

At his look of consternation, she insisted, "I must know what is going on. Where do you go every evening?"

"To visit our kinsman Wala. That isn't a crime," he asserted belligerently.

"Wala! You know that he is no friend of our father."

"But he's *my* friend, and he believes that I've been treated unfairly."

"No one can dispute that, but I beg of you, don't become involved in any of Wala's plots. You would be a pawn in his hands."

Although Pepin resented Hrotrud's interference, he was uneasy in his mind about what Wala might be planning. He was stunned when Wala finally revealed his plan. "It is time that you become ruler of the Franks. We intend to apprehend the king when he goes for morning prayers at Saint Peter's."

"But his life?" Pepin protested. "You won't do him any harm?"

"Of course not. We'll send him to a monastery—just as he has exiled many other people. He has ruled almost twenty-five years, which is long enough. He needs a rest."

Although he had tried to hate his father, Pepin had not been completely successful. He reasoned that if he was on hand, his father was certain to be spared. On the day of the planned takeover, Wala refused to let Pepin go along. He left a guard behind to ensure that Pepin didn't do anything to thwart their plans. Pepin began to fear that he had been misled about the nature of that day's activities.

❈   ❈   ❈

King Charles was never a heavy sleeper, and he awakened readily at the soft knock on his chamber door. At his summons, a servant entered the room, lighting his way with a candle.

"There's a man at the palace door, sire, who demands that he must see you."

Since he never turned away anyone with a problem, day or night, Charles commanded that the man be brought into his presence. Lighting a candle, he wrapped a robe around him. When a breathless, shaking man was ushered into the room, Charles thrust a cup of wine into his hands.

"Who are you?" Charles demanded, while his servants hovered around himself.

The man choked on the wine he had gulped. Coughing, he said, "I am Fardulf, a poor deacon at Saint Peter's."

Taking note of the man's ragged, bloody mantle, Charles said, "Have you been attacked?"

"Somewhat, my Lord, but it is you who are to be the victim of an attack. Armed men sneaked into the church before daybreak. I learned that they intend to slay you when you come in for early prayer. I hid when I heard them enter, but I was discovered, and they extracted my promise that I would not leave the church. God forgive me that I've broken that oath, but I had to warn you about these conspirators."

"Who are they?" Charles demanded, as his servants helped him don his outer garments. He also strapped on his sword.

"I recognized only Wala, the king's kinsman, but I heard them mention the name of your son Pepin."

"Pepin is in Lombardy," the king stated.

"Not your firstborn, the one called the hunchback."

Charles halted his battle preparations. *Not the hunchback!* If all others turned from him, he would still not have expected his firstborn to plot against him. For now, the king pushed aside any filial thoughts. He dealt with intrigue as it came.

"You will be rewarded for this day's work, Fardulf. Remain here so that my enemies will not know that you have warned me."

By daybreak, Saint Peter's was surrounded with dependable Franks, and the conspirators were soon captured. When one of the prisoners was forced to reveal their plans, King Charles was astonished at the extent of their scheme. They had intended to slay the king and his younger sons and bring forward Pepin the Hunchback to rule. Wala intended to be Pepin's chief advisor, seeing himself as the power behind the throne.

It took weeks to round up all those involved in the plot, but when they finally believed most of the rebels had been apprehended, an assembly of Charles's lords tried the conspirators at Ratisbon. They condemned the majority to death, although a few were exiled. Charles himself handled the punishment of Pepin, not willing to turn his own son over to the assembly.

The hunchback had been put under house arrest as soon as his part in the plot was known, and the king met with Pepin privately. "My son, I would not have thought this of you," Charles said, and as he looked at the scared, penitent young man, his thoughts recalled his joy at the birth of this son, the one he had cherished above all others for a long time.

"I was duped, my Father. I didn't anticipate the extent of the conspiracy. I have not had an easy life. Perhaps that is why I was susceptible to the slick words of our kinsman."

"I'm convinced of that—otherwise, I would not save your life. I cannot, however, overlook your disloyalty, so you will be beaten and committed to the monastery at Saint Gall. I pray that God will grant you mercy and forgive your sins. Perhaps in the future, I may pardon you and restore you to my presence."

❀ ❀ ❀

After his close call with death, King Charles began to assess his past accomplishments and the extended role he was to perform in the future. He relied heavily upon his friend Alcuin for advice when he met with the priests who made up his spiritual council.

"I've passed my fifty-first year, reigned as king of the Franks for twenty-five years, outlived two wives, and overcome conspiracy, defection, and defeat. To the lands inherited from my father, I've added Saxony, much of Italy, and a portion of Spain. I've tasted enough adventure for any man, and I've not set out on a military expedition for more than two years."

"The king of the Franks should be strong enough now to keep the peace without warring," Alcuin said.

"Peace is not always good. I believe it's my duty to defend the church of Christ everywhere not only from invasion of pagans, but also to strengthen it spiritually by our devotion to the true faith. I want to devote the rest of my life, which may not be long, to establishing the religious and cultural life of the Franks."

"You've already moved in that direction," Alcuin said, "when you founded the palace academy, which has promoted outstanding scholarship. And you've strengthened the church in Gaul. What more can you hope to achieve?"

"To establish the city of God Augustine talked about," King Charles said in a ringing voice. "I talked to Matthew of Constantinople about that years ago, but I've not persevered in my goal. Augustine believed that city could be founded upon earth, and I would set myself at the head of such a city."

"That would be a great responsibility," Alcuin stated gravely.

"But with God's help I will do it." He looked from Alcuin to the other priests who were seated around the table. "I've set many goals that I will need your help in implementing before the city of God can become a reality. Please copy down my requests."

The priests reached for parchment and waited in silence while Charles anticipated the spiritual needs of his kingdom.

"I want choirs in every great church. The choirs are to sing words that glorify the Lord. Have older men copy the Gospels so that we may spread the Word of God to every part of the kingdom. I want the Word preached that the unrepentant will be cast into the flames of hell but that the Christian will live forever with our Savior in heaven."

"But, sire," one priest protested, "many of the parish priests are unlearned. They do not have that knowledge of the Scriptures."

"Then our first task is to teach the clerics so they may be proper examples. And if they cannot preach the message, have pictures painted on the walls of churches so that all eyes may see what damnation awaits them if they fail to repent."

Charles did not ask his priests to do what he wouldn't do himself, so whenever he walked along the streets or rode through the countryside, he spread a message: "Repent of your sins and believe on the Savior. A person is not saved by works alone, although they are necessary, but a person must believe in the work already done by our Savior when He died on the cross to save us from our sins."

Later, when Charles was referred to as another Constantine the Great, he thought seriously upon that title. In June 794, he called an assembly at Frankfurt to discuss disturbing news that was filtering into Gaul from the outside world. Alcuin met with Charles and a large group of clergy, who surrounded him in semicircular ranks.

The council began with the public reading of a letter from the Spanish hierarchy supporting the belief of Felix, bishop of Urgel, who challenged the concept of the Trinity, maintaining that Jesus the man had been no more than the adopted Son of God.

The Frankish council soundly condemned this latest heresy, with Charles stating that Jesus had shared the divinity of the Father, using as his proof that it was impossible for an ordinary man to bring salvation to all humankind. Although the heresy was squelched in Gaul, it continued to spread throughout other sections of Europe, and Charles realized that he had not heard the end of the matter.

When Charles learned that Pope Hadrian had approved the Second Council of Nicaea's decision to restore the images to churches, he was convinced that he was now the sole defender of the church.

19

CONSTANTINOPLE, FRANKISH GAUL, 797–800

S he's been planning this disaster for six years," Waldulf
stormed to Printha when he returned from the marketplace
with the latest news that could end in no way except with the
downfall of Constantine VI.

"Calm yourself," Printha said, as she called a servant to take
their two sons to the nursery. The boys were old enough now to
understand when there was a crisis, and she didn't want them
unduly disturbed. "What has happened?"

"The monastery of Sakkudion in Bithynia has been destroyed.
Supposedly Emperor Constantine went to Prusa on a holiday to
take the waters, but we all know it was to placate the monks
who have been the chief accusers in his adulterous marriage."

"Apparently his overtures didn't work," Printha said as she
knelt beside Waldulf and removed his sandals. She placed a cup
of wine in his hand and sat at his side.

"No, it's said that one monk insulted him to his face. The
inhabitants of the monastery have been dispersed. Some were
beaten, imprisoned, and exiled."

Printha's hand went to her throat. "Matthew! Do you think
he's in danger?"

"I don't suppose this will be widespread, but I do wish he
hadn't returned to monastic life. To be an ordinary citizen in

275

Constantinople is dangerous enough, but taking a definite stand on any religious matter is risky."

Waldulf paused while he recalled Matthew's hasty departure for the monastery seven years ago. It was obvious to Waldulf that Sophia was the woman Matthew had loved for years, and when her husband, Gerona, had died, Waldulf had hoped that Matthew would wed her at last. To the contrary, Gerona's death had hastened Matthew's return to holy orders.

Printha tugged at the sleeve of his robe. "How is Constantine's action going to affect us?"

"Perhaps not at all, but it will ruin the public support that Constantine has enjoyed. He already has enemies in the army because he had one of their favorite generals blinded and imprisoned. He will have few friends left now."

"So this gives the empress the advantage she's waited for."

"Yes. I saw Elisha today, and he said the empress Irene has been preparing her defenses during Constantine's absence. She has brought Constantine's wife to the sacred palace for the birth of their child, knowing that will be an incentive to bring Constantine back into her clutches."

Printha picked up the garment she had been mending when Waldulf returned. "I wonder how Elisha can put up with the woman. He's a compassionate person."

"He's also loyal. He took an oath of loyalty to her years ago, and he cannot forget that. Besides, if he forsakes her, his death is certain."

"Elisha is getting too old for intrigue."

Waldulf nodded in agreement. "I believe that Constantine would have become a great ruler if only he hadn't restored his mother's title of empress in 791 after she rebelled against him."

"He isn't perfect, either. I can't quite forgive his unkindness to his wife when he put her away to marry Theodota, one of his mother's ladies-in-waiting."

"That didn't matter much to the populace as a whole because many people sympathized with him when he had to marry the young Armenian girl his mother forced upon him rather than Princess Hrotrud. They were willing to forgive him for having mistresses, but the adulterous marriage was more than the orthodox Christians would tolerate."

Absentmindedly, Waldulf ran his fingers through Printha's long hair. "His downfall is even worse when one considers that he had the qualities to become a good ruler. He has intelligence, and while his mother was in exile, he picked up the reins of government efficiently. He's a brave, capable soldier. His religious dogma is beyond dispute, so up until now the church has sanctioned his rule, and he's popular with the lower classes. He was destined to be as great as the first Constantine."

"If only he could have had a different mother." Now that she had children of her own, Printha often wondered how any mother could be so unfeeling toward her offspring as Irene was. "I told you the first time I saw the woman that she was evil, and I haven't seen anything yet to change my mind."

Waldulf put his hand over her lips. "Even the walls have ears."

Their sons could be heard in the hallway, and soon a soft tap sounded at the door. Waldulf smiled and said, "Come in," and the two boys rushed to his side. Angelo, the firstborn, had the physical characteristics of his mother, having a small build and a winsome face. Galen, on the other hand, didn't look like either of his parents, so they reasoned he must be a throwback to some ancestor that they had never known. With an arm around both of the boys, Waldulf turned to Printha. "Why don't you take the boys and go back to Gaul for a visit?"

"Good try," she said with a laugh. "You needn't think I will leave you here alone. We've been fortunate so far. Surely, we won't be directly involved in this newest intrigue."

Waldulf shook his head. "I wish Matthew were here to advise me. I miss his counsel so much, but I won't bother him at his retreat. He wanted to put worldly things behind him, and I must not intrude." He walked to the wall niche where the Alabaster stood and picked it up. Never a day passed that he didn't think of the meaning of this relic. Sometimes the memory of the Alabaster's message was all that kept him going, but what should he do now? He hoped the Alabaster could give him an answer.

Seeing the struggle on his face, Printha said, "Why don't all four of us go home for awhile? Cyril can handle our affairs."

"I cannot do that. Just like Elisha, I must remain loyal to the emperor I've sworn to serve. It pains me to see the man destroying himself, but I cannot leave."

❀ ❀ ❀

After the destruction of the Bithynian monastery, when Constantine learned that Theodota had borne his son in the sacred palace, he rushed home only to find that the empress had solidified her power by winning most of the palace guards to her side. Before his mother could carry out any plot against him, he hastened to fight the Arabs in order to establish his crumbling position. Within two months, Waldulf's worst fears were confirmed, and Constantine returned home in disgrace.

"He didn't even encounter the enemy," Waldulf reported to Printha. "He accomplished nothing, and the populace turned away when the returning army marched down the streets."

"This is all Irene's doing, too," Printha said, "if I'm to believe the current talk among the servants. To discredit her son, she sent an envoy with a false message leading Constantine in the opposite direction from where the Arabs were attacking Byzantine borders. By the time Constantine learned that he had been tricked, the Arabs had dispersed."

A week later, during the night hours, Elisha was admitted to the house of Trento. His face was morose, and Waldulf knew the eunuch had a sad message.

"The emperor has been blinded upon his mother's orders and imprisoned in a local residence where his wife can join him," Elisha reported.

Offering Elisha a glass of wine and some sweet cakes, Waldulf said, "The sad part of it is that very few Byzantines will even mourn him."

"That's true, for the religious community believes that he's being divinely punished because of his adulterous marriage and the way he treated the monks at Bithynia."

"Have you come to warn me, Elisha? Are those of us who supported Constantine in danger?"

"I don't know, but I wanted you to be prepared. Now that she is in complete control, the empress may be more lenient to those who opposed her. Although I've been in her service for many years, I've never been able to foretell her actions. Just be on your guard."

The next day when a message came from the sacred palace for Waldulf's immediate appearance, Printha threw her arms around him. "Don't go, my loved one. I can't bear to part with you. Can't we escape to Gaul and forsake all of this?"

"But what about the Alabaster?" Waldulf protested.

"We can carry on the heritage of the Trento family in Gaul as well as we can here. Please, Waldulf, let's leave."

A sharp knocking on the door interrupted them, and when Waldulf opened it, two members of the palace guard stepped inside. One of them said, "We have come to escort you to the sacred palace. At once."

Waldulf kissed Printha. "Be brave. God will protect us."

To say he wasn't afraid would have been a lie, but for Printha's sake, he walked down the street ahead of the two guards, his head high, his back straight. If she watched him until he was out of sight, as he knew she would, he didn't want her to note his apprehension. He doubted he would ever see his family again.

Expecting to be thrown immediately into prison or loaded on a wagon and exiled to a far country, Waldulf was surprised to be escorted directly to the throne room. The empress sat on the golden throne, splendid in glittering robes of purple and gold. *She's showing her age,* Waldulf thought, *although she is still beautiful.* He bowed before her. Her first words brought him further surprise.

"I understand that you were once a member of the court of King Charles of the Franks."

"That's right, empress. He is being called Charlemagne by his subjects now."

"What is the meaning of that word?"

"The name Charlemagne is a corruption of the Latin *Carolus Magnus,* that is, Charles the Great."

"It is my wish that you return to the Franks on a mission for me. You may take your wife and children, but while you are gone, your wealth and property will be held in trust by the Byzantine government. If you do not successfully accomplish my mission, you will not be allowed to return, and your property will be confiscated."

Waldulf would have preferred to know the nature of the mission before he agreed, but he realized that the empress wasn't offering him a choice.

"What is the mission you're entrusting to me?" Waldulf inquired obediently.

"It is my desire to unite the two Roman Empires into one nation as it was in the time of Constantine the Great. I'm sending Michael Ganglianos of Phrygia and Theophilus, a priest of Blachernae, to arrange for a marriage between King Charles and me. I want you to accompany them as guide and interpreter."

In spite of himself, Waldulf caught his breath sharply and stared at the woman.

"You find it so preposterous that the Byzantine empress would stoop to marry that man whose uncouth ways have often been recounted in my presence?" she demanded.

Waldulf shook his head. "That was not the reason for my amazement. The rough ways of Charlemagne have been overemphasized. Since I've known him, the king has made an effort to improve his mind and his manner of living. But to my knowledge, the king of the Franks *has* a wife. He married his fifth bride, Liutgard, two years ago."

With a cruel smile, the empress said, "That should be no

deterrent to another marriage. There are ways to get rid of an unwanted partner."

As soon as the empress said those words, a chill ran down Waldulf's spine and he feared what might await him in Frankish lands.

❀ ❀ ❀

Charlemagne and his court were at Aix-la-Chapelle when Waldulf and Printha finally reached them after a six-month journey. When last they had been at Aix-la-Chapelle, the palace had been nothing more than a well-constructed house, with auxiliary quarters of mud or wood, surrounded with stables and granaries. The courtyard had been enclosed with a stone portal. Now it appeared that Charlemagne was enlarging his residence.

As they approached the group of buildings, Printha said, "You will remember that Princess Hrotrud had written that her father was determined to make this residence into a palace worthy of an imperial residence. He has apparently started on the project."

"Yes, if I recall, she said the plans called for four groups of buildings to be constructed in a great square resembling a Roman camp. She indicated that there would be a bathing area of several pools where the old Roman baths had previously been."

"All of it looks very drab after the gilded buildings of Constantinople, but no doubt it will take many years to accomplish all Charlemagne has planned. At least our old friend is improving his domain. I'll be happy to see all of them, but I wish we could have come without the fear of disaster that hangs over our heads."

Waldulf sighed resignedly. "In spite of the circumstances, I am not unhappy that we were sent on this expedition. Although I haven't admitted it, there have been times when I've longed for my homeland. If this mission fails, and I'm sure that it will, I would not find it burdensome to be permanently exiled from Byzantium. What about you?"

"No, I could easily spend the rest of my days in quietness at Willehad Manor, but I don't believe that will be our lot. As holder of the Alabaster, you were called to Byzantium, and the God we serve is greater than Empress Irene. I believe we will eventually return there. Actually, we didn't even leave the pomp and ceremony behind when we traveled." She motioned to the retinue that followed them.

The empress had provided for their passage on one of Byzantium's swiftest ships, and once on the continent, they were served with equipage brought from the sacred palace. Colorful striped tents and soft-cushioned pillows sheltered them at night, and the gaudy garments of the ten members of the palace guard that accompanied them brightened the landscape as they journeyed westward.

"Now that we're in Frankish lands, I'm not much concerned about our bodyguard. I remember a fiery Saxon female who had the skill to disappear into the forest when her enemies pursued her. Once in her old haunts, I believe she could deliver her family from the giants," Waldulf said, smiling.

Printha eyed him pertly. "Perhaps I could at that."

Charlemagne had gathered his family and counselors into the large reception room to receive the envoys from Constantinople. The room was decorated with paintings representing ancient Frankish heroes. The king didn't recognize his visitors until Waldulf addressed him in the local language.

"Greetings, King Charlemagne. It has been a long time since I left your court."

Charlemagne, grown more robust over the years, peered closely at the man before him, as if his eyes weren't as keen as they had been in his youthful hunting days when, from his running horse, he could spot a stag from a great distance.

"Is it really you, Waldulf?"

He strode forward to clasp Waldulf in his strong arms. Then he turned to Printha. "And your lovely wife!" Charlemagne leaned forward to kiss her forehead. "The years have been good to both of you."

Waldulf indicated his children. "My sons, sire—Angelo and Galen."

The boys fell to their knees and prostrated themselves before Charlemagne. Waldulf laughed as he recalled the boys to their feet. "The influence of Constantinople, sire," he explained.

"We are glad you have returned." The king looked around at all the grand equipage belonging to the Byzantine government. "You have done well for yourself, Waldulf."

"None of this belongs to me, King Charlemagne. I am here only as a guide for emissaries from Empress Irene of Constantinople to the Frankish court. She is responsible for this escort." He indicated Ganglianos and Theophilus. "These men have a message for you that they should discharge without delay." To the two Greeks, he said, "King Charlemagne is conversant in your language."

"Speak then," the king said.

Ganglianos stepped forward. "First, I will present the gifts that the empress has sent you." Two servants bowed before the king and laid a golden vase, several bolts of tapestry, and a jeweled crown at Charlemagne's feet. Then Theophilus drew a parchment from the bag he carried and read:

> Greetings from the Empress Irene to Charlemagne, king of the Franks. I have punished my son, Constantine, for his crimes, and I am now the sole ruler of the eastern empire. I desire the friendship of the Frankish king.

Ganglianos bowed, and Waldulf noted amusement on the face of the Franks, who weren't used to such ceremony. "The empress has delegated me to ask you, King Charlemagne, if you would be interested in aligning your western kingdom to the eastern empire by a marriage between yourself and the empress."

Waldulf knew that it took a lot to surprise the Frankish king, but astonishment flitted across his face, and he eased gingerly to the throne, as if his legs could support him no longer. He was silent for several minutes, but Waldulf had the impression that he was not displeased with the offer.

"But I have a wife," Charlemagne said, motioning to the young woman seated to his left, surrounded by his daughters.

"Yes, sire," Waldulf said. "My wife had learned that information in a letter from Princess Hrotrud, and I apprised the empress of that fact. She still insisted that the offer be made."

Charlemagne returned his attention to the Byzantium envoys. "This is not a decision to be taken lightly. I will need several days to consider my answer to the empress. In the meantime, you will be welcome guests at my court." The king called to his servants, "Show our visitors to their quarters. Give them the best we have."

As the Byzantines were conducted from his presence, Charlemagne turned again to Waldulf. "We have news occasionally of the political situation in Constantinople, but we did not know of these latest developments. What kind of woman would depose her own son?" he asked, bewildered.

"A very ambitious one, sire."

"But what of her future? Is it possible for a woman to be the sole ruler of this last throne of the Caesars?"

"She has much power, and she rules like a man. She is an ambitious woman," Waldulf repeated.

"How much time do you have among us?"

"There was no time set for our return to Constantinople except that we were to depart when we had a positive answer from the Frankish king." Waldulf refrained from telling Charlemagne what a personal loss he would sustain if the king rejected the empress's offer. He wouldn't use their friendship to influence the king's decision.

"I will have to think long upon this matter. I'll admit that joining the two empires would go long toward fulfilling my dream of establishing Augustine's city of God, and therefore it entices me. Please prepare a letter to your empress thanking her for the offer and telling her that I will give my decision within a few months. Now, I must not delay any longer in sending you to Count Willehad. His eyes will brighten to see you again, as well as these two boys. He still considers you his son."

"As will I always consider him my father. I am eager to see both my parents again."

"You may have the opportunity to spend the winter at Willehad Manor, for by the time I make my decision, weather conditions will prevent a voyage across the Alps."

"I will welcome that, sire, but perhaps you could entertain the Byzantium envoys while I am there. Willehad Manor does not have room for so many visitors."

After a night's rest, Waldulf sought out Ganglianos and Theophilus and explained that King Charlemagne wanted time to deliberate about his answer. He told them they would be obliged to winter in Gaul. This was displeasing to the two Greeks, but since the empress had said they must await Charlemagne's answer, they had no choice. While Waldulf found a private place to compose the letter to Empress Irene, Printha visited with Princess Hrotrud.

"My wedding will be in the spring," Hrotrud said. "You must not leave before then. I am so happy that father has agreed to my marriage to the count of Maine. You will like him." In a quieter tone, she asked, "But what of this marriage between my father and the empress? Do you approve?"

"I wouldn't want my worst enemy to marry Empress Irene. She's an evil woman. But we had no choice except to come on this mission. Now that she has complete rule, our lives were threatened. If Charlemagne refuses her offer, I doubt that we will ever return to Byzantium."

"Will you miss that?" Hrotrud inquired.

"I do not like the danger and intrigue of the imperial court, but there is much to be said for the luxury there. I've grown accustomed to it, and it's spoiled me for rustic living. Do you think your father would consider wedding the empress?"

"I doubt it. He is very fond of Liutgard. In fact, he probably loves her more than he has any of his other wives, but my father is not always easy to understand. The empress may be ambitious, but so is my father."

"I doubt either of them would trust the other to the extent of sharing their power. In the end, it will come to naught, I suspect," Printha said, wondering what effect Charlemagne's answer would have on their future.

❋   ❋   ❋

More than eleven years had passed since Waldulf had left his home, and upon his return, he was not displeased with the state of affairs. Surprisingly, Count Willehad had regained some of his vigor and strength, although Adela was stooped, wrinkled, and gray. Their joy at seeing Waldulf and his family was overwhelming. Although he was uneasy about the outcome of the struggle between Empress Irene and Charlemagne, Waldulf settled down to spend the winter with his parents, who never seemed to tire of the rowdy Angelo and Galen as they romped and played away the winter days.

In early spring of 799, Charlemagne summoned Waldulf to his court at Aix-la-Chapelle. Upon his arrival, the Greek envoys and Waldulf met with the king in his council room. He did not keep them waiting long for his decision.

"Although I look favorably upon a union of the western and eastern Empires, I am not ready to make a definite decision at this time. Therefore, I would bid you, Ganglianos and Theophilus, to return to your empress, thanking her for the offer and begging her to give me a few more months to deliberate. I will send several Frankish envoys with you so that they may discuss terms of this alliance. You, Waldulf, I will retain in my service until the empress and I come to terms."

Anger consumed Waldulf, but he held his peace. *Have I become a pawn in the hands of these two rulers? Do I have a life to call my own?*

Before he returned to Willehad Manor to remove his family to the king's palace, he had a word with Hrotrud, who said quietly, "Liutgard is very ill, wasting away. I believe he doesn't want to close the door on the Byzantium offer until he knows whether Liutgard will survive. I know you must be frustrated with the delay, but I will be married in a few weeks to the count of Maine, and I'm pleased that you will be present for that."

Throughout the remainder of 799 and into 800, Waldulf and Printha remained with Charlemagne, journeying with him and once again involving themselves in the life of the Frankish court. When Queen Liutgard died, they shared the king's grief, which must have been genuine, for although he soon surrounded himself with mistresses, he made no move to acquire another queen.

The months passed, and no word was received from Empress Irene concerning any further alliance between the two empires. The Frankish envoys did not return, a fact that gave Charlemagne concern. Waldulf was convinced that if the empress had not taken their lives, she had imprisoned them. His own future looked bleak, but there was never any boredom at the Frankish court, for Charlemagne was often involved in affairs in Rome, defending a new pope, Leo III, against dissident factions in the imperial city. Encouraged by his religious advisors, and especially Alcuin, the king took more seriously his role as defender of the church. Once he showed Waldulf a letter he had received from Alcuin in which the cleric had written, "The providence of the Lord has made you ruler of the Christian people—you, exalted in power and wisdom above the seat of Saint Peter and the secular power of the second Rome in Constantinople. Do you not see how the fate of the churches of Christ depends upon you alone? Upon you it falls to avenge crime, to guide wanderers, to comfort mourners, to raise up the good."

"This is a high accolade Alcuin has paid you, sire," Waldulf said, "but I have no way of knowing the truth of his words. I am not learned in matters of the church."

"Nor am I. How I wish to speak to my old friend Matthew again. He could always advise me to the right way."

Believing that Alcuin's opinion was worthy, Charlemagne called a council in August to once and for all refute the Spanish heresy that denied the divinity of Jesus. The council met in the great hall at Aix-la-Chapelle where Charlemagne sat in royal splendor wearing an embroidered cloak, girdled with his jeweled sword, crowned with a jeweled diadem. In the presence of his lords, secular and ecclesiastical, he listened for six days to the debate between Felix of Urgel, who maintained that Jesus was only the adopted Son of God, and Alcuin of Tours, who argued that the Scriptures upheld the Trinity of God—Father, Son, and Holy Spirit. Charlemagne rejected the arguments of Felix and banished the Spanish bishop to a monastery. He was pleased that he, like Constantine the Great, had a role in upholding the divinity of Christ Jesus.

With the situation in Rome still turbulent between Pope Leo III and his enemies, Charlemagne made elaborate plans to journey there. Once again Waldulf and Printha found themselves on the road to Rome. By late November, they arrived in the vicinity of Rome and were met by the pope and loyal Roman leaders, who conducted the Frankish king and his entourage into the Eternal City.

While Printha and their sons stayed in the same house with Princess Hrotrud and her attendants, Waldulf followed Charlemagne throughout Rome as he investigated the difficulties confronting the city and the church of Rome. After several weeks of investigation, the charges against Pope Leo were dropped. When Waldulf was able to return to Printha, he said, "This has been a momentous day for Charlemagne, for he's long wanted to have the church subservient to him, and it probably will be now since Pope Leo owes his exoneration to the king."

"He's a long way from establishing the city of God he talks about, isn't he?" Printha inquired.

"In my opinion, yes. There is still too much evil and sin in the world to justify the founding of Augustine's city."

"It does seem that Charlemagne has reached the peak of his reign," Printha said.

"Undoubtedly, and it's difficult for me to comprehend that the rough, uncouth Charles that I knew when I was a boy could have reached the position of power he holds today. He's the defender of the church and the judge of the pope. He has a large area of Europe under his control, and he's on friendly relations with Muslims in Spain and rulers in the Far East."

"But what about us, Waldulf? I would like a permanent home—someplace we can raise our family. Will Charlemagne keep us with him forever?"

"I have no answer now, but I intend to speak with the king as soon as possible. He has requested that all of his court worship with him at Saint Peter's on Christmas Day, and I don't know the future beyond that."

❋　❋　❋

On Christmas Day, the bells in the tower of the four-hundred-year-old church summoned Christians to worship. Charlemagne's entourage passed between the purple hangings of the nave pillars into the sanctuary lit by a thousand candles. The king was dressed in the garments of a Roman patrician—a tunic, chlamys, and light slippers.

Waldulf and his family paused at the back of the church while the clergy of Saint Peter's and dignitaries of all nations preceeded Charlemagne down the aisle as he moved forward to join his family at the altar. His servants carried the king's gifts—a silver table and a plate and chalice of gold, the weight of the king in precious metal. The echo of the bell in the tower ceased as Charlemagne knelt to pray above the crypt of Saint Peter.

When the king rose from prayer, Pope Leo stepped forward and placed a bejeweled crown on his head. The assembled Romans shouted in chorus, "To Charles, Augustus, crowned by God, great and peace-giving Roman Emperor—long life and victory!"

Waldulf was so startled that at first he could not speak, but he turned to Printha and whispered, "Emperor? Who would have thought we would live to see this day?"

Charlemagne's face was passive as he strode silently to the courtyard after the service, and it was impossible for Waldulf to guess what his thoughts were. *Was Leo's action a surprise to him or had he pressured the pope toward this move?* Waldulf doubted that he would ever know.

Although it would seem the day had already held enough excitement, when Charlemagne exited the courtyard of Saint Peter's, a small group of men awaited him.

"Printha," Waldulf said eagerly, "those are the Franks who went to Constantinople!"

Charlemagne recognized them at once, and he shouted his joy. "I had feared you were dead. Welcome home."

One of the Franks stepped forward. "Our mission has been completed, sire. The empress of Byzantium sent us home with the message that she was no longer interested in an alliance with the empire of the West."

"Nor would I contract an alliance with her now, not after the events of this day. But, tell me, how were you treated?"

"We were prisoners to the extent that we could not leave. Otherwise, we were treated as royal visitors," one of the Franks explained.

Still chatting with his envoys, Charlemagne continued toward his residence, but one of the returning Franks came to Waldulf and handed him a missive.

"When it was known that we would return to Gaul, the steward of the house of Trento begged us to carry this letter to you. I am thankful I could discharge this duty for you."

Smiling his thanks, Waldulf clasped the letter gratefully. "At last, we have some word from our home. More than two years have elapsed since we left there."

When they were in the privacy of their own apartments, Waldulf broke the seal of the letter and settled down on a bench with his family around him to read Cyril's words.

Dear Master,

Elisha has sent me word that the Frankish envoys, who have been in our country for over a year, are returning home without having contracted a marriage agreement between Empress Irene and Charlemagne. What a foolish idea in the first place! While the eunuch still serves the empress, he felt he should not contact you directly, but he realizes that you might fear to return to Constantinople when this alliance was not arranged. He urges you to return and take up your role in the city, as he feels the empress will do you no harm.

For a year or more, we were under constant surveillance by the empress's representatives, and they took most of the profit that the Trento business made, but your fortune is still intact. I felt lucky that I was able to remain in the house and retain enough servants to keep the property in order. I, too, would urge you to return home.

As for the political situation—at first, the empress was hailed as a savior by our people. She was most generous with the monks and continued to build new monasteries. She reformed taxation and financial administration, but she could never tolerate anyone trying to usurp her power. When her brothers-in-law conspired against her, she prevailed over them and had them exiled.

Empress Irene is old and her health is failing. The throne will be vacant upon her death, for Constantine VI is spending the rest of his sightless days in a monastery. Already her court favorites are vying for control. It's disgusting to see how the worn-out woman still clings to the throne, but her power is not as great as it once was, and I predict by the time of your return, she will be ousted. It is time for you to take up your duties here.

Waldulf and Printha did not speak for several minutes, then Waldulf read the letter again, more slowly this time.

"Will we go?" Printha whispered.

"I hesitate because of possible harm to you and the boys, but I do feel that I owe it to my ancestors to return. Fortunately, we brought the Alabaster along with us, but the rest of my heritage is in Constantinople. If you are not afraid, we will go."

"I want to go. I'm happy that we've had this sojourn in the West, but I have no qualms about leaving now. The responsibility of the Alabaster lies heavily upon me, too."

"I've often wondered which of our boys should receive the Alabaster after I'm gone. It will not be an easy decision. God has given me a great responsibility, but He will give me strength to carry it out." He hugged Angelo and Galen, kissed Printha, and stood up.

"Where are you going?" Printha asked.

"To the docks to book passage to Constantinople. My heritage is calling me home."

EPILOGUE

CONSTANTINOPLE, 801

Matthew didn't often have visitors at the cloister, and as he moved on stiff knees toward the receiving room of the rebuilt monastery, he recalled that day thirty-three years ago when he had been summoned to hear the news of his father's death and had been given the commission to find the Alabaster. He thanked God again for the successful completion of that mission.

Waldulf had fulfilled his highest hopes as the heir of the Alabaster. He was industrious and had increased the prosperity of the Trentos in spite of the political and religious controversies that had rocked the Byzantine Empire during the past few years. He and Printha had taken seriously their responsibility to perpetuate the heritage started by Suetonius Trento in the first century by training their two sons in the grace of God.

Matthew was not surprised that his visitor was Waldulf, for he knew the Trentos were returning from an extended visit to Gaul. Waldulf rushed forward and embraced Matthew and kissed him on both cheeks.

"We have missed you, Matthew. How good to see you looking so fit."

"When did you return from your journey?"

"Only yesterday."

"Thank you for coming to see me immediately. How are Printha and the boys?"

"They are all right, though I believe that Printha was a bit sad to return to Constantinople. Her upbringing did not prepare her for the life of this city, and she misses the forestland. Now that tensions have eased somewhat, I hope to buy a home outside the city."

"And how did you find your parents?"

"Well-advanced in age but happy that they had lived to see me again and especially to see their grandchildren."

"What of King Charles and his family?"

"Hrotrud has finally forgiven her father for breaking her engagement with Constantine VI, especially after we told her of the bickering between the young emperor and his mother, Irene."

"I would have hated to see her treated as the empress treated Constantine's first wife. How is Charles?"

"Physically, he is as robust as ever, but all isn't well for the king of the Franks. He has been involved in a spiritual controversy over the deity of Jesus with some bishops from Spain."

"A situation similar to what Constantine faced in the fourth century, I believe."

"The matter has been resolved to King Charles's satisfaction, but he continues to have rebellions among the Saxons, Bavarians, and his other conquered people. And then Pepin the Hunchback joined in a conspiracy to oust his father and take control. That revolt was soon squelched, but it saddened Charles. As he grows older, he's content to sit in his palaces, and he's losing contact with his people."

"His queen is still Fastrada?" Matthew inquired.

"No, after she died several years ago, he remarried once again, and that wife is also dead. The king has taken many mistresses since then."

"It's difficult for me to reconcile the king's mistresses and his warfare with the fact that he's a sincere Christian. Unfortunately, in our day people have strayed far from the teachings of Jesus. How can they believe in true Christianity when the king sets such an example? He believes that what he has done for the church is sufficient proof of his piety. Although I tried to teach the Frankish king that he needed to follow the way of personal repentance, the message went unheeded."

"The pope seems convinced of the king's piety. As we started our homeward journey, we traveled with the king and his family to Rome. In a special service on Christmas Day, Pope Leo acclaimed Charles as another Constantine, and the Romans proclaimed him as emperor."

Matthew smiled. "So he has at last achieved his highest goal—to be the Holy Roman Emperor ruling over a Christian empire."

"And he's more qualified to rule now than before. He is building a large palace at Aix-la-Chapelle, modeled on palaces of the East. The Franks are becoming more cultured as Charles makes education available to many of his subjects. More and more, people are calling him Charlemagne—Charles the Great."

"I wonder how Empress Irene likes having someone else acclaimed emperor?" Matthew speculated.

"Cyril says that she has lost interest in the empire of the West, thinking she doesn't need Charlemagne's help now."

"But how much longer can she rule? She must be aging like the rest of us."

"She has a large following, but there are plots against her. She will not be empress much longer."

"It's strange that I was on hand when both Charles and Irene were invested with their kingdoms, and that I lived to see them rise to the height of their power. My life has run full circle."

Waldulf moved closer to Matthew and took his hand. "Perhaps more than you know, friend. I come now to the main reason for my visit. We learned upon our return that our beloved Sophia has died."

Matthew's heart faltered a beat. "When did this happen?"

"Six months ago."

"But how could she have died and I did not feel it in my heart? My love for her is so deep that I should have known."

With compassion evident in his voice, Waldulf said, "But Sophia is still living *somewhere,* waiting for you to join her. Perhaps that is the reason you were not aware that she had departed this life. Your affections changed long ago from a physical to a spiritual love."

Matthew rose and pulled his habit around him—it had suddenly become colder in the room. "Please leave me now, Waldulf. I must be alone in my sorrow. Take my greetings to Printha and the boys."

He shuffled down the long hall toward his cell thinking of the past. He had all he had ever wanted in life except Sophia. When Gerona had died, he once again asked Sophia to marry him, but she had refused.

"It is too late for us to reclaim our youthful love, Matthew," Sophia had said. "Your spiritual convictions are too strong. You would worry about forsaking your vows, and I do not want to be the source of discontent to you. I will not marry you."

When he had gotten over his disappointment, Matthew had conceded that she was right, and he had enthroned her in his heart. Her dark, curly hair, which had never grayed in his memory, was vivid to him. He overlooked her wrinkles, remembering only the smooth olive complexion that he once had caressed. Her luminous gray eyes and voice had not changed with the years.

Matthew stretched out on the hard cot, his mind strangely at rest. He had fulfilled all the obligations he owed his family, and he vowed to have no more communication with the outside world. The cloister would be his refuge until that time when he went to join those Trento ancestors who for centuries had upheld the truth represented by the Alabaster. *And will Sophia be waiting for me too?* He smiled, knowing that she would be, and that they would be together throughout eternity.

PONTIUS PILATE
A Novel
Now in trade paperback!

PAUL L. MAIER

Follow Pontius Pilate, Roman governor of Judea, as he rises from the political intrigues of imperial Rome and survives the treacherous plots of Herod Antipas. Behind him stands Procula, a wife who fires his ambition for political advancement; before him stands the bewildering clash of Jewish leaders, national extremists, and religious zealots.

"A tremendous story. . . . In drama, romance, color, scope, and depth, this novel is comparable to *Ben Hur*, *The Silver Chalice*, and *The Robe*." —*The Christian Herald*

"Unique in biblical novels . . . raises the genre of the historical novel to a plateau it has rarely reached." —*The Chicago Daily News*

"We commend this book as an exciting supplement to the New Testament itself." —*Moody Magazine*

PAUL L. MAIER is professor of Ancient History at Western Michigan University and an award-winning author whose expertise in first-century studies and extensive travels in the Middle East and Asia Minor provide historical authenticity and compelling drama to his writing. His other writings include the ECPA Gold Medallion Award-winning volume *Josephus: The Essential Writings; The Flames of Rome* (a companion to *Pontius Pilate*); and the 1994 best-selling novel, *A Skeleton in God's Closet*.

0-8254-3296-0   paperback   384 pp.

THE FLAMES OF ROME
A Novel
Now in trade paperback!

PAUL L. MAIER

In the years preceding and following the Great Fire of Rome in A.D. 64, the splendor, sensuality, and pagan excesses of Roman society are illuminated against the explosive struggle between the established power of Rome and the life-changing faith of Christianity.

Based upon the experiences of the family of Flavius Sabinus, the actual mayor of Rome under Nero, this work recounts their own history as crucial converts to Christianity.

"A soul-shaking novel of the time when society was at its worst and Christians were at their best!" —*The Christian Herald*

"Impressive . . . illuminates a crucial time and place in world history." —*Publisher's Weekly*

"Flames sizzles [and] doesn't fiddle with the truth." —*The Detroit News*

PAUL L. MAIER is professor of Ancient History at Western Michigan University and an award-winning author whose expertise in first-century studies and extensive travels in the Middle East and Asia Minor provide historical authenticity and compelling drama to his writing. His other writings include the ECPA Gold Medallion Award-winning volume *Josephus: The Essential Writings; The Flames of Rome* (a companion to *Pontius Pilate*); and the 1994 best-selling novel, *A Skeleton in God's Closet.*

0-8254-3297-9   paperback   458 pp.

THE HEART OF A STRANGER
A Novel

KATHY HAWKINS

King David's reign and the greatest battle of the Old Testament provide the setting for this captivating story of political intrigue and romantic love.

Jonathan, one of David's thirty "mighty men of valor," returns from war with Ailea, the beautiful, spirited daughter of the defeated Aramean commander. Her own inner battle between love and mistrust is equally matched by her struggles with the cultural and religious life of the Jewish people. The battle for her heart is waged not only by Jonathan, the perspective bridegroom, but by Adonai, the God of Israel, as well.

KATHY HAWKINS is a graduate of Southeastern Bible College and holds an M.A. in Biblical Studies from Dallas Theological Seminary. She and her husband—Christian broadcaster and author Don Hawkins—frequently speak at Bible conferences and seminars across the U.S.

0-8254-2867-x   paperback   304 pp.

MARTYR OF THE CATACOMBS:
A TALE OF ANCIENT ROME

ANONYMOUS

This classic fictional account of the early church in the city of Rome describes the historical persecution of the early Christians, consigned to live out their lives in the burial caves underneath the city.

Discover the legacy of faith these faithful believers bequeathed to following generations!

0-8254-2143-8   paperback   144 pp.